Bridgewater Aeternum

Bridgewater Aeternum

Sometimes to move forward, you must first go back.

Bernard J. O'Kelly

Copyright Bernard J. O'Kelly

First published in Ireland (Bridgewater) in 2024 by the author

All rights reserved; no part of this publication may be reproduced or transmitted by any means, electronic, mechanical, photocopying or otherwise, without the prior permission of the publisher

ISBN 979-8-339-77232-3

Contents

Chapter 1
Chapter 2 - Almost 4 years ago
Chapter 3 - Almost 3 years ago
Chapter 4 - Almost 2 years ago
Chapter 5 - Almost 1 year ago
Chapter 6
Chapter 7 - College
Chapter 8
Chapter 9
Chapter 10
Chapter 11
Chapter 12
Chapter 13
Chapter 14
Chapter 15
Chapter 16
Chapter 17
Chapter 18
Chapter 19
Chapter 20
Chapter 21
Chapter 22
Chapter 23
Chapter 24
Chapter 25

Acknowledgement

To the places that gave me the space to work on this book, and there were many. To my brother and sister who lent me their eyes and wisdom, and some old friends who weren't shy about being honest. Lastly, to my parents who helped make this possible, I'll be forever grateful.

To who we were then, and who we are now...

Garry,

A Read between Illness & fatherly chores!

Hope you enjoy it,

Your friend

Chapter 1

Chippings fell away like scree as the handle whomped off the old, fortified wall and sent an echo into the dusky May evening. It was followed by a racket that only those who had survived a year of educational internment could create. The hostess thumbed the scotched steel and glowered after them.

'Did you like it, guys – did you?' Dot capered from one person to the next like a hyperactive canine.

'A little too much,' Finn groaned, rubbing his stomach through his package-vacation white and green linen shirt. 'Why did it have to be all-you-can-eat?'

'Even though they put spikes through my food it was alright.' Simon said, feeling a little hollow and underfed, something that rarely happened.

Dot was put out by Simon's lack of enthusiasm. She had combed the town in search of a place that would not just fill their hunger, but also broaden their cultural horizons. It wasn't as if Bridgewater was the culinary capital of Europe and Dot was sure she had seen Simon up at the buffet table more than once. 'It's not Kebab World, dummy, that's how they serve kebabs over there.'

'And we got to play swords!' quipped Leo, having to think smart to avoid a simulated clothesline from Simon.

'Yeah, and you nearly stabbed me in the eye, Leo!' Two hours of being trapped like a snared hare between the wrestling brothers had broken Finn's spirit and almost, but not quite, his appetite.

'I didn't know Turkish people ate bread?'

Rock, the elder statesman of the year, looked over at Louis who had to jink around a shopping trolley that had been dumped on its side. 'What did you think they ate?' he asked.

'I don't know,' Louis replied, 'beans or something.'

'Where to next, Dot?' Mia said, one of the few to have eaten the food of Turkey in the manner it was meant to be eaten.

Dot was almost winded by the enquiry. Organising the restaurant had been one thing, but being responsible for choosing the bar as well was really asking a lot. 'Did I have to organise the bar, too?'

'Let's get shots-' Billie squealed, who was now in the throes of a post drinks bloom, '-and go somewhere with cute guys!'

'Shots? Mia, the reigning class president, replied, 'That's a bit lowbrow isn't-'

'Bobs!' Billie continued, anticipating the possible *what if*, 'they've got guys there!'

Rock ran his hand under the side of his peaked caip - the one Simon said made him look like he drove taxicabs (or 'tacksicabz' with his speech impediment). The hair that had yet to disappear felt fuller. Must be just the Turkish raki playing tricks on him, he assumed, reverse alopecia for middle-aged men wasn't a thing, unfortunately. 'You still after the D, Billie?'

Billie licked her finger and crouched down to expunge a barely perceptible blemish on the fabric of her shoe. 'Been a bit of a dry patch lately, Rock,' she replied in earnest.

'Louis will help you out. He'd get up on anything.' Rock helpfully suggested.

'Don't think I'd be able for Billie,' Louis replied, nipping in between bodies, and burrowing back into the clique's core.

It had been a while since Billie was made to feel like a woman in the truest sense, and despite the kinks in his sexuality, the more the night went on the more of a lure Louis was becoming. 'Me is woman,' she vociferated upon straightening, 'hear me roar!'

They all laughed when Finn said that Louis was more interested in the 'almost-dead' variety of mate as they warbled under the Norman archway that led to the main square. Streetlights had taken up the baton from daylight and somewhere music was seeping from a speaker. The town was surprisingly quiet, nearly too quiet for a balmy Bridgewater evening, but this went completely unnoticed by the mob as they made their way to Bob's bar and the merrymaking afters.

*

'Oi,' said a sinewy figure, elbowing someone else behind a line of trees that the streetlights dared not go, 'would you look who it is.'

The guy bit down on the end of his cig butt so he wouldn't cry out. 'You sure that's him?' he replied, grittily.

'I'd know that stupid hat anywhere.' If it was possible to feel cortisol spilling through the floodgates, then the geezer that Finn called 'Loudmouth' was feeling it right then.

'You got Etna?'

He tapped his pocket three times, ritual for when he knew she might be making an appearance. Loudmouth had had knives before, but not like this one. This one would slide into a person as easily as crack cocaine slid into his bloodstream when he could afford to get some, which wasn't often enough for his liking. 'Right here,' he replied.

The throbbing from the bunt was wearing off. 'Can't remember the last time she was out,' his friend said, as a final blink of orange illuminated his jaundiced skin as he inhaled.

Loudmouth answered as if he was keeping a mental log. 'New Year's.'

'Oh, yeah,' the other guy croaked, recalling how the fella had looked like one of those toys that you wound up by pulling the string and which shoots all over the place, 'not sure *where* he thought he was going!'

Loudmouth ignored the guffawing. He also tried to ignore his friend's breath; it was nothing short of foul. 'Going to have a go at that little butterscotch bitch after I do your man,' he said, trailing a girl whose insolence had put him off on a day that changed everything. It sounded like ball bearings around a tumble dryer when he added; 'be the last time she gives me daggers.'

The responding cackle was almost as unpleasant. 'Wouldn't mind getting that tourist dope, too.'

'You're going to help me out this time?' Loudmouth snapped, glaring at his supposed best friend, who had been about as much help as a case of haemorrhoids the last time.

His reply came out small and mouse-like. 'Course I am, spa gave me that stupid spiel, remember – then he called me a bean sprout?'

'I don't remember because if *you* remember I was on the ground at the time!'

'Said I'm sorry alright,' his friend replied, knowing that this time he'd have to step up if things went south. 'What do you want to do?'

Loudmouth hocked thick phlegm from the bowels of his throat and painted the stem of a sapling pale yellow. 'Let's follow them,' he said.

*

Finn's shoulders convulsed gently on the barstool. 'Still can't get over Dot falling down those stairs,' he said.

'That's what happens when you spike a hookah,' Rock replied casually, sipping his honey whiskey.

'The waiter was in such a tizzy checking to see she hadn't broken anything that he didn't even apologise for dropping that tray of hummus on the Eskimos.' He chuckled again. 'Bet they weren't expecting that while in full flight – so to speak.'

Rock grimaced at the gooey image and even gooier whispered sweet nothings. 'You had to remind me of the Eskimos, didn't you?' He had never been one for extreme shows of affection in public, even if it was amorous noses and not mouths. 'Thought it was funnier you pinned in the corner between Leo and Simon.'

Finn caught a glimpse of Dot escaping out to the beer garden with something cupped in her hand and he assumed it was something that would soon have half the place looking like pink elephants. 'I considered jumping out the window.'

'Not sure it would open that wide,' Rock teased him in return. 'Mia swapped seats with Louis – think she might have forced him actually.'

Finn mourned the fact he hadn't thought of it first. 'Leo wouldn't stop complaining about his fingers. Tried telling him to use a bread stick because the sauce was hot.'

'Well, I'd a great time with Red.' The surface of Rock's whiskey became choppy as he started to laugh. 'He asked the waitress for some bacon and cabbage. She didn't know what to make of him.'

Finn thought back to when he first met Red, and how Red had refused to engage with the roll call because he feared that if he confirmed his name he would have 'changed' and become an instantaneous dork. 'Was he being serious?'

'As serious as the look of disappointment on his face when she said they didn't do bacon and cabbage! Got to eat most of Billie's food as well because she didn't like it.'

They watched as Billie threw shapes on a deserted dance floor. 'Guess the empty stomach is the reason for that?' Finn suggested.

'Yep.' Rock replied, easing off his stool, 'just going for a whiz.'

Not far from where Billie was dispatching a lone tango, Hugh (who had spurned the implorations of his barber - who was also Turkish - to let him take a pair of clippers to his face) and Sophia were slapping each other in a kind of animalistic, pre-mating ritual; at least that's what Hugh hoped it was because Sophia was his dream girl and a girl he'd dreamt of at least seven times since she'd flowed into the room as the inaugural class had been in progress.

'Who's winning?' Finn called over the elbow of the dogleg-shaped bar.

'I am,' Sophia replied, the swelling on Hugh's hands kindling something deep inside her, 'look at his hands, they're all red and puffy!'

'That's because Sophia's a cheat.' Hugh protested by vigorously throwing his arm out like a disgruntled football fan, 'She keeps - AAGGHH!' he yelled.

Sophia had taken advantage of Hugh's mithering by connecting perfectly with the tender nerves on the outside of his hand. She followed this up with a clean smack to his head. Unlike Hugh, who was generally a pacifist, Sophia tended to become a little sassy – warlike, even – when she did shots.

'Yes!' she cried, throwing back another one like a loyal servant of Odin.

Hugh rubbed his hand against his head with such ferocity that friction burn could now be added to his wodge of insults. 'Don't think I want to play this game anymore,' he said.

On the way back from his first grudging emptying of liquor, Rock spotted four girls nursing prosecco with their pinkies stuck out like the Queen. 'Hey, girls.' Any semblance of personal space was suitably ignored as he scooched in between them and a six-foot berserker replica who acted as gatekeeper to the bar. 'Just like to give you my friend's card,' he said, handing each of them a business card with an illustration on it.

The chattering went quiet as they regarded the card with something bordering on surly suspicion. 'Is this him?' stammered one of them with a disgust she failed to disguise.

Rock had seamlessly grafted a picture of Finn's face onto Donald Trump's body in another of his 'leisure projects'. He didn't know if it was a real image of Trump or if it had been digitally doctored but that didn't matter. 'It is, yeah.' When Rock stood tall he and the fiberglass warrior were at eye level. 'We're over at the bar if you fancy chatting. Just go easy, alright? He's a bit sensitive about it.'

Red vaulted up onto the corner stool as Rock was heaving himself back onto his seat. 'Alright, me buckos?' Red said.

'Are you responsible for that?' They noticed Fredrik sitting alone and in the middle of a separate section. There was nothing inherently odd about this, as Rock thought Fredrik was an oddball who belonged in an underground lab somewhere.

'Fred fancied something quirky,' Red replied to Rock, 'so I got us titty twisters.'

'How many has he had?' If Finn knew Fredrik like he thought he knew Fredrik, it wouldn't be many.

'That's his third,' Red said, clutching his own luminescent beverage. 'He leaves it behind when he goes to the pisser so maybe someone bunged in a popper when he wasn't looking?'

Feeling the weight of curious attention, Fredrik looked up to see Rock, Red and Finn staring at him.

'No,' Finn admitted, 'two's his limit. Last time he drank three he got us thrown out of a club in Silver Strand for pulling down his tracksuit bottoms and doing Riverdance on a table.'

A girl appeared in front of Finn and threw her arms around him. Two others smiled sympathetically in the background, while another loitered behind the protective wall of her friends. 'I just wanted to come over and tell you, that - you know - size isn't everything.'

The bear hug had pinned his arms across the girl's chest. 'Oh...thanks? he replied awkwardly.'

Rock snorted and the hug suddenly made sense.

'Will you stop giving those to every girl you see!' Finn snared the one Rock was holding as the royal attendants hastened away, one of them moving faster than the rest. 'Better off with bloody Fredrik as a wingman.'

Fredrik looked around and caught his blurry reflection in an antique mirror on the far wall. 'What am I doing over here?' he asked, eyes bloodshot, as if trying to figure out how he had come to be in such unfamiliar surrounds.

'Got you a hug, didn't it?' Rock said, wagging another heavy-duty card he'd taken from his wallet.

Red tugged on the shaggier-than-ever ginger cone that billowed out from his jawline as if ruminating over the unsolved mysteries of life. 'Is it really that small, Finn?'

'For the love of God, Red, it's a fake!' he snapped.

Rock was now heartily laughing at what he considered his most precocious endeavour of the past year. 'The likeness is freakish,' he said, holding up what could have been a nude playing card close to Finn's face, 'I can see why people might be confused.'

Finn ignored him. The last time he'd been out collecting his hot and spicy noodles from Mister Chow, a customer had approached and asked if he was the guy on the card after Rock had scattered them in every available space. He changed the subject. 'Anyway, what's the plans for the summer?'

'What are you girls yapping on about?' Hugh said, meandering over and wrapping his arms around them as if they were in a halftime huddle.

'First of all,' Rock replied, 'I'm getting this godforsaken leg fixed.' He sized it up like it were somehow foreign and not a part of him. 'Then I'm going to Greece, maybe drive around and do a photo story. And after that, I'm going to sit on the beach till there's a perfect impression of my arse in the sand.'

'That poor beach.' Hugh shook his head wanly. 'I'm–'

'We know what you're doing,' Finn cut in, having lost count of the number of times he'd been told about the summer of 'many holidays', 'haven't stopped going on about it since mid-term.'

Hugh was sliding his elbows in opposite directions while pulling a duck-like pout, 'Yeah, but I added another holiday last night. This time next week I'll be drinking cocktails on a beach and–'

'Watch you don't fall into Rock's sandy hole.' Red said, indecorously thrashing at his cocktail with his swizzle stick.

Hugh winced as if the thought alone could ruin his holiday. 'I won't be going near that beach, be staying away from Greece full stop.'

Talk of beaches put Finn in a time warp back to sun, seashells, and sinners. 'You guys remember the day we went out to the coast?' Even though it had mutated into a malformed tale of two cities, Finn still thought it was a day that could have duelled for bragging rights with any other.

'The day Rock declared war on the junkies,' Hugh replied whimsically, his hand deadened from extended axons and alcohol.

Red was pulling the miniature umbrella up and down, protecting tiny townspeople from the rain. 'Day he became famous.'

'All thanks to my photo!' Ashley piped up, as she and Mia, who both looked as if their heads had been wedged under the hand dryers in the bathroom, came over and joined them.

'Takes something for me to admit this,' Rock replied, 'but absolutely, best photo of the year.'

Though the photo, and not necessarily the act of how the photo was taken, got the most attention – and the biggest cheer at the end-of-year exhibition – Ashley always preferred being commended for demonstrating valour in the face of evil, rather than for taking a photograph. 'Thought he could scare me?' she groused, ruffling her luscious caramel hair as if trying to dislodge a battalion of nits, 'won't try that again.'

Finn had seen Loudmouth's reaction to Ashley's small act of defiance. It was transient, almost imperceptible, a ripple in the fabric of that which up until then had known itself and was sure of its place in the grand order of things. He raised his glass aloft, 'Then let's drink to that,' he said, and declared in medieval fashion: 'To the best damn class in the college.'

'Wait for me,' Fredrik slid out of his chair like it was made of hardened jelly, 'I want to toast something.'

The sound of clinking glass strangled the sound of the music.

'The best damn class in the college!' they shouted.

*

'What's keeping them so long?' Loudmouth's friend blew warm air into his hands and rubbed them together like a scout guide attempting to start a campfire. 'We could be hanging out by the river instead of waiting on some traveller-looking dude and a limousine driver. Dying for a cider.'

Loudmouth took no notice of the protestations that drummed in his ear. 'They must be having a piss-up.'

'Were Ireland playing today or something?' His chum's breath dispersed outwards like a toxin, 'because it's not Christmas, that's one thing for sure!'

'No shit, thick brain.' came the barbed response.

All he was doing was making a point. 'What are you going to do to him?'

'I'll let Etna decide.' Loudmouth never really knew how things were going to go down, preferred it instead to be a beautiful blend of instinct and opportunity which he could look back on and marvel over. 'She normally knows what to do.'

'Yeah, she does!' Sensing that the time was drawing near, his friend picked up an old beer bottle from the ground. He was the resourceful type, never one for premeditation. The last time it had been a stolen camera that he couldn't operate (the whore he took it from had engraved him with a stamp that was more talon and less fingernail, but he had the last laugh when he heard a crunch as she hit the curb).

'Don't touch the tourist till I gut that bald fishy, you hear me?' Rock was the primary target; Finn was just collateral.

The glass bottle was cold but was solid in his hand. 'Got it,' he replied.

Loudmouth slid Etna from his belt line on seeing the first of the group converge outside Bob's. Running his finger along the blade, and revelling in its unremorseful sharpness, he glanced at his friend. 'Let's get them.'

Chapter 2

Almost 4 years ago...

Dong shuffled from foot to foot like he had no control over what his legs were doing. 'You want to play for ten thousand?' he repeated, making sure he had heard correctly.

'That's right, I want to play the best player here for ten thousand pesos.' Little did Finn know, as he flashed around the colourful notes like some demented gringo, that amounts of money like that not only attracted the attentions of pool-table predators, but street ones too.

The little Filipino's moustache twitched so much that it broke into dance. 'Ok, you wait a minute,' Dong said and then scurried off like he was on a treasure hunt. He came hurrying back in case the tourist saw sense and changed his mind. 'You play him.'

A man of about mid-fifties, possibly a little older, was stood easily at the far end of the table. Finn noticed that he looked remarkably calm, but he couldn't tell if this serenity was down to ingrained confidence or if he'd just had one too many San Miguel, the national pride of the Philippines.

When Finn had to borrow a cue from another player because he didn't have his own, the Filipino's eyes narrowed to slits. Finn was sure he saw an impish grin appear before it disappeared just as quickly. Dong smelled foreigner blood. And foreigner blood always meant a bigger commission. 'You want to play for fifteen thousand?'

Finn chalked his loaner with the house chalk. 'I think I'm doing a good enough job of hustling myself, wouldn't you say?' he replied.

Dong gave a small grunt and began explaining the rules. They chose to play 9-ball – or, rather, Finn's opponents chose to play 9-ball – no doubt because it worked in their favour. But that was alright, he wasn't looking for favours. He was looking for the ungarnished truth, and if that meant getting whitewashed by this placid-old Buddhist, forcing Finn to play only the occasional game of Killers in the pub, then that was alright too. If he was serious about joining the circuit, he had to know if his earlier talent was still there, or if it had atrophied with age like his memory for names.

Finn used his t-shirt to dab the sweat from over his eyes. Both sleeves were now wet. The boxy air conditioning unit huffed and puffed like a defeated wolf and didn't have the breath to make much of a difference. Dong set the balls carefully into a diamond shape, with the yellow 9 in the centre, and then rested the cue ball against the bottom rail. He took a coin from his pocket. 'What you want?'

Shadowy faces squinted from the dimness as word had spread that a strange white guy had challenged the best player in the club for a large sum of money. Photos of famous players looked down on them through a haze of cheap tobacco and the funk of stale beer entwined with sizzling pig head and chicken liver, combination of choice for ravenous players.

Dong's thumb sprung forward, and he sneered when it landed on tails, handing Finn the advantage in a race to eleven. His opponent made no reaction, remaining stoic all the while. Finn thought there was something suspect about someone so inscrutable.

'You break.' Dong said, before withdrawing a safe distance away.

Taking up the white ball, Finn placed it six inches from the cushion. He was keenly aware of the crowd that was bumping and grinding around him. Leaning over, a drop of sweat stung his eye as he broke off, potting the 7 in the bottom corner. Rubbing the cue on his polyester shirt, he measured up his next shot. It was an easy one as the 1-ball was sitting over the middle pocket. Despite the sting on his skin as he pushed the cue forward, his tracking was good and the white came to rest just below the 2-ball, leaving an angle to get back up the table.

Two hours later, Finn unscrewed his cue and, somewhat dazed, handed it back to the wrong person. As it turned out the unflappable Buddhist had been a shark, and in that hall, he was the Great White. Finn had been beaten so soundly that after potting the first three balls (the fourth a pot he never would have missed as a teenager), he didn't pot another ball until the fifth game and by then his confidence had drained away like blood from a bite wound. He lost eleven-two, and had he not set up the hustle himself, he might quietly have slunk out the back and sought solace in the nearest girlie bar.

It wasn't so much the humiliating loss (and sniggers from idle watchers who he couldn't see) that made up Finn's mind about being a pool player, but what he would have to sacrifice to do so. Like prisoners in the nearby City Jail, the players didn't exactly spend much time on the outside. Relationships, like fresh air, would suffer; current ones would fall away and new ones - except for those made with fellow table rats - would be almost impossible. He'd spend his days chomping fried food from plastic plates and using the services of ladies of the night, while memories of what sunshine felt like would fade like his vision beneath a layer of smoky murk.

He stepped out into the alleyway, the heavy door slotting with a chunk behind him. It was approaching midnight and the streets groaned under the weight of late-night traffic. The sounds of voices and the drone of bass from bars dotted along the strip blurred into one, making the city a muddle of noise. He started towards the lights ahead, and as he neared the first bar, Finn felt sure it was humid enough for a storm.

*\ *\ *\ *

Rock munched on a chicken roll and watched the drizzle frolic in the headlights. The bread was hard, having wilted in the artificial heat as he'd raced across England to make it on time for the ferry to France. The cost of any new fare would have been docked from his paycheck, which Rock thought was very unfair – and possibly illegal – so lunch was cast aside when he realised he was running late.

He had made it to the port three minutes before the gates opened and he was being ushered up the ramp. Again, his lunch had to be paused – though, technically lunch was hours ago – and he threw the unappetising stub of a roll back onto the passenger seat.

'When am I going to get a *fucking* break?' he growled. 'All I want is to eat my fucking lunch, is that *too* much to ask?!'

After butting the truck in front of him (and causing the usher guy to emit a small yelp), Rock tossed the remains in the bin and quietly made his way upstairs to the bar. England was far bigger a place when you were steering a rig across it, and he needed a stiff drink after what felt like a month's driving. 'Double whiskey, straight up, please,' he said to the barman.

The barman held a glass up to the light. 'I'm sorry, sir, the bar isn't open yet.'

Rock glared at him. 'Then why are you standing behind it?'

'The bar will be open once we've left port, sir, and are a few miles out to sea,' he replied robotically, without taking his eyes from the contemplation spot. 'Would you like a mineral instead?'

'No, I don't want a fuc...no, I'm fine. I'll just wait till the bar opens – when we've left the port...when we're out at sea.'

He continued to pretend to be the busiest person on the boat.

'Very well, sir.'

Rock dropped back into one of the recliners and stretched out his rangy legs. 'Very well, sir,' he was muttering, 'who am I, the fecking king?' Four brats were sprinting up and down and whizzing past where Rock was mooching (a face-full of frozen precipitation meant he couldn't even admire the wake from the ferry as it sliced through the water; the one thing that always relaxed him), their exuberant screams drilling into his head like a woodpecker with a chip on its shoulder.

'You can't catch me! You can't catch me! You can't catch me!' one of them squealed back to his friends.

'Oh yes we can!' came high-pitched responses.

Rock was being nudged to the edge of his wits. 'I'm going to catch *all* you little bastards and throw you *all* overboard and then do a jig while you're drowning.'

A woman sitting behind him scowled and bore a hole through the back of Rock's head as his thumbs made swirling shapes on his temples.

'*Attention, the bar is now open on the main deck, thank you.*' The intercom announced before going quiet.

Whiskey whirled around in the glass and the sound of ice colliding with the sides was soothing. Rock hated ferries. They were loud and impersonal things and the kids always acted as if they'd done lines of speed, while their doting parents got ramped on wine. He felt old. He had been driving trucks for almost twenty-five years and Rock felt every second of those years like he was wearing them. All that time on the road, all those nights spent in the cab on that slip of material that tried to pass itself off as a mattress. All those times he'd woken up with an aching back and all the times he'd had to put up with snotty-nosed little runts who never failed to make his head ache.

He took another sip, the heat making him feel just a little bit better. Why was he continuing to do a job he hated? He used to like it when he was younger, sure, but now he dreaded pulling out of the yard at midnight or midday and heading to God knows where. It was like a relationship that had soured; both parties resented the other, but both were too afraid to admit it was over.

* * * *

Finn felt as if two fly-catcher strips had been lowered over his eyes as he continued to serial-click websites. A ring of meltwater from his iced coffee stained the wooden table, but a refreshing breeze blew in through the marbled lobby from the private beach at the back of the hotel. Sighing, he looked out at the tuk-tuks that were zipping along the narrow road, flinging dust and pebbles high into the air.

Finn knew he had to get out of the Philippines, it was becoming a bad habit. If he didn't leave soon, chances were good he'd become a Rum-and-coke-drinking womanizer who'd grow fat and die long before his time, probably from a massive coronary, or from swimming on a stomach stuffed with belly pork and bargain booze. He glanced down and noticed the writing on his t-shirt radiating outwards like a vast, slow-moving glacier; the signs were already starting to appear.

But for some reason, Finn was finding it impossible to figure out his next move. He was ready to leave and continue on with his eastern safari, but to where? The whole of Asia unfurled before him like a wall map and all he needed to do was plug it with a hypothetical arrow. He still had half the winnings so going home wasn't an option (before he'd left there was a feeling that the walls were closing in. Finn didn't know what this meant but he did know he wanted no part of it). The bet had been a moment of inspired madness, his first ever trifecta, and Finn had hugged at least four different people – including the guy that everyone stood well away from because he never showered – when the third and final horse, who happened to be the nag of the field, crossed the line ahead of a fast-finishing fourth, turning a throwaway two-euro coin into fistfuls of travelling euros.

Finn had left the shop sporting wads of fifties (the occasional hundred interspersed among them), held together with elastic bands, and rolled up like small but powerful 'rapture' grenades. He felt like a drug dealer after a score and put the grenades in his coat pocket. Then he changed his mind and crammed them into his inside pocket for safer keeping. He remembered being woozy walking home, convinced he looked like someone concealing a large amount of money, and bracing himself for the impending ambush.

And in the vein of a drug dealer, Finn stashed it all away in the safest place he could think of, his underpants drawer; admittedly, he wasn't the coolest of dealers. He then bought a few toys he didn't need, including an obscenely expensive bicycle that he hardly ever cycled, but which came inclusive of an air horn, and a pair of waterproof hiking boots, which would have been better suited being dustproof as they still hadn't seen the light of day.

Finn watched as bands of colour quilled and lapped over each other at the bottom of the old-style monitor. The owner of the establishment – who spent his time playing solitaire on a disc-like coaster with pegs and holes – probably thought Finn was some online connoisseur of everything vulgar. But who needed that in the Philippines? The place was already like some twisted version of a catholic brothel. He looked to Singapore, then to China and Vietnam, even as far as Kathmandu, but nothing was coming together.

Ignoring any doubts, and to end his three-day state of catatonia, Finn booked a flight to Bangkok. As much as he loved the country, the allure of its dark side was irresistible. People went to places like Tibet and India to find redemption and cleanse their souls by living with monks. They went to the Philippines for different reasons, and despite the weighty godly presence, this wasn't the place to be saved. No absolution was to be found here.

He would leave the Philippines before any surviving morals were peeled from him like the clothes of a cheap Filipina hooker, and to protect whatever chance he had left of living a noble or virtuous life. From Bangkok, he would make his way north to Chiang Mai, where he'd find a job - teaching the youth of Thailand, perhaps - and live a simpler, more wholesome existence. Perhaps he'd meet someone, maybe even stay there; anything could happen, Finn thought, as he clicked the 'Fly Away' button.

That's when the migraine started.

* * * *

The drizzle had turned into an unrelenting deluge as Rock made his way back along the A26 from Calais. He was tired and hungry, and the chicken roll was a distant memory – like the claggy remains of a bad dream.

It was after five when he got finished unloading the cargo and it was already coal-shed dark. Rock detested the wintertime with a passion normally reserved for those who abused animals. It was depressing and dour and dismal, and all those other horrible 'd' words, and it always made him want to dive for cover under his duvet, especially now as the thought of being torn away from his blanket to drive a truck filled him with an inner malaise. He thought about the road home, the wipers smearing the windscreen, and the feverish, sleep-inducing heat as he tried to keep it from fogging up. If he turned around now, he'd only end up falling asleep at the wheel and killing someone. He thought about those kids on the boat and imagined ploughing head-on into their Renault Scenic; it wasn't entirely unwelcome.

Rock made an executive decision: He would stay in Reims. And he wasn't going to spend another night in that cab-coffin either, he was going to check into a hotel, a real swanky one, and get a king-sized room with a king-sized bed. Then he was going to go to the restaurant and enjoy whatever meal came with the most courses. And after that, he was going to deplete the bar of its whiskey reserves, and what's more, he was going to do it all on the company's dime.

'Always sleep in the cab – and never spend more than €5 on lunch!' that parasite Mr. McCormick had told the drivers after rounding them up for an impromptu telling off one Monday. Well, Rock figured, Mr. McCormick was going to choke on his tuna and artichoke sandwich when he looked at the expense statement next month, and then he chuckled vengefully.

As if dictating a memo to a secretary; 'this will do just fine,' he said, before throwing the truck in neutral and setting it down outside a hotel that was palatial enough to cause Mr. McCormick severe retching.

The next morning, Rock woke slightly hungover but feeling far more refreshed for having slept in a bed with an actual mattress, and on pillows that weren't made from his clothes. He showered and went to the dining room, where he allowed himself two cups of coffee with his breakfast, one before his eggs and one after. This was the one time he was in no hurry to get home, and if there was another drop waiting to be done, well, they could just get someone else to do it, couldn't they?

The drive back was almost pleasant. The weather had perked up, traffic was light, and Rock managed to avoid a three-car mash-up by minutes which would have caused a tailback so long he'd have missed the boat for sure. He stopped in a lay-by and ate his lunch – which was fresh for a change – while the melodious trickling of an unseen stream aided his digestion.

The seas across the Strait of Dover were calm and the ferry even passed the acid test; no screaming children going native and making him have visions of genocide. Rock thought he could get used to this, but he knew it was a one-off, a joyous fluke. Most of his long-distance trips were the complete opposite, a batter of leaden eyes blinded by undipped headlights, cold, plastic food, ignorant French border officials, haste – and stress.

He could deal with everything except for the stress. That was the killer. When he was younger the stress was enjoyable, and he thrived on the challenge of delivering on time (that he was better than all the other drivers was just frosting). As the years wore on, instead of spurring him on to be the best, all it did now was drain his energy and make him want to hijack the ferry and crash it bow-first into the Isle of Man.

The sun was setting as Rock rolled into a little town just north of London. Many of the shops were boarded up and footfall was low despite the fine evening: London had swallowed the town's population and with it the town itself, he supposed. The truck lurched forward as Rock eased down a gear passing an electronics store, which, if he could make out the curls and loops of the calligraphy correctly, was called 'Electric Treasures'. Since he was in need of a new toaster after his last one blew up from overuse (Rock would often go through a loaf of bread in a single sitting), and as he was in no rush to get back for an ear-bollocking, he decided to pull over beside a tapering wall that was putting a short squeeze on any available sidewalk.

The shop was dimly lit, and the smell of dampness filled his nostrils. A floorboard creaked as Rock ducked beneath a splintered beam that was partially impeding the way of taller people. 'Hellooo?' he coughed up to the salesperson, who was busily tucking into a pie.

Crumbs fell onto his newspaper as he waved a distrait hand in Rock's direction. 'Bollocks,' he cursed, sweeping a forearm across the page.

Most of the stuff looked old and uninteresting, while some of it needed the skills of a technological surgeon to restore it to life. Rock picked up an old transistor radio, but before he could examine it, the strap broke and it plonked back down onto the shelf, throwing up a little cloudlet of dust. He coughed again and saw that the salesman was too engrossed in what he was reading to notice the misdemeanour.

Despite its bygone charm, Rock speculated how long more the shop could survive in a modern world. He was just about to leave when he stopped in front of a cabinet in the middle of the floor. The glass was scratched and dainty cobwebs - probably there since the first German blitzkrieg - sprouted from the corners. Some centrepiece, he mused. But what stopped Rock from leaving was what was inside the cabinet; it was a camera, a humdinger of a white collar - the type he had always wanted to own. It was also the type that didn't need a faulty miniature spotlight in order to stand out. It was a camera that should have been out in the wilderness, or down some side alley in a romantically hectic foreign country, or behind enemy lines, and not locked away in a cabinet that a family of spiders called home. What's more, it looked in surprisingly good nick.

Something inside Rock stirred, like something that had been asleep for a long time was now suddenly awakening. He felt an overriding urge to buy it as if his future happiness somehow depended on it. Though it was second-hand, Rock knew that cameras held their value well and that this wondrous thing would still be outside of what he could afford. Whatever it was that had woken up was now taking a big, yawning stretch. It couldn't hurt to ask, he figured.

'How much is the camera?'

The salesman was now halfway through his pie and his cheek was stained with brown sauce. He took only the briefest glance before returning to the back page of the red top. 'Seventy-five pounds.' His beloved Chelsea were having a mixed time of things with the reappointment of the manager, with some pundits questioning the decision. But Jose was blue through and through and would lead them back to the summit where they belonged, he had decided.

There were two cameras in the cabinet. Below the one he was coveting was a regular point-and-shoot. The paintwork was scuffed and there was a small scar on the lens which would have resulted in every photo having permanent birthmarks. Rock considered the price. The salesman must have thought he was asking about the compact, though at that price he wouldn't be getting rid of it anytime soon.

'And for the Canon?'

'I told you already, mate,' he replied impatiently, keeping his head buried between the pages, 'seventy-five quid.'

Rock wondered how this gombeen got any customers at all. But more important than that, this camera was worth far more than seventy-five pounds - ordinarily it was, anyway. There had to be something wrong with it. Maybe it only took black and whites, or maybe it didn't even switch on.

Rock flounced out of the shop like he'd won top prize in a raffle. After checking it did indeed work (the salesman - whose name was Dave - had trudged over like he was being forced to attend his own funeral when Rock asked if he could inspect the camera), he quickly took out his wallet from his back pocket. A moment of panic set in - like the panic you feel when you realise your fly is undone and you happen to have a hole in your boxers - that he mightn't have enough cash. He did, by four pounds.

When the camera was in his vice-like grip, Rock asked why he had sold it so cheap. Dave replied that all he wanted to do was get rid of the stock and close down the 'stupid' shop so he could spend more time watching the football. Then he went back to reading about the media overreaction to Chelsea's managerial dilemma, leaving Rock in no doubt whatsoever that the conversation was over.

* * * *

It was as if Finn's brain was being inflated by two Oompa-Loompas jumping up and down on a foot pump, and that soon it was going to burst through his skull and pebbledash the wall. When Shakira had left that morning (he nicknamed her this after hearing her sing, thinking he was listening to *the* Shakira) Finn had felt fine, and he wondered between the almost constant waves of pain if she was some sort of high priestess who had put a hex on him.

He groped for the packet of pills that was somewhere amongst a stack of empty water bottles on the nightstand. The woman in the little apothecary had shown real concern when he had kept his eyes closed during the transaction, flinching as he opened them to accept the pills which, currently, were having little if no effect. His flight to Bangkok was in a few hours but Finn knew the odds of him being on it were lengthening all the time. He let out a low groan and pressed his fists against either side of his head. Maybe his inability to resist the seductive charms of the Philippines was finally catching up to him.

Pinching six tablets from their foiled catacombs, he gargled them down and settled back into bed. He considered going to the hospital, but Finn thought in his delirium that he might get even sicker by going there as he imagined cockroaches chasing mice between the cracks in the walls. Maybe if he waited an hour or two the medication would kick in and he could grab a taxi to the airport to begin his new life, a life that would most certainly include copious amounts of sunshine, a fulfilling mentoring job, and a beautiful Thai wife who would worship his every move.

Sometime later the owner of the hotel beat on the thin plank of wood that acted as a barrier between Finn's room and the outside world (and which sent a laser beam straight through the places where he had knuckled earlier). He was holding the water that Finn had requested after his one-man odyssey to the street chemist.

'Finn?' the hotelier gasped.

What he saw was an appearance so different from the one that kept him company as he won game after game of solitaire that he had to scramble to catch and re-catch the bottles. Finn's hair was trying its best to get away from his head and his skin had lost all trace of the 'tourist tan' he had acquired in the preceding weeks. The owner had seen it before, youngsters looking at all sorts on their computers and moving farther from grace and closer to the other fella. 'Too much porn, I think.'

For Finn, it was the look of bewilderment recoiling back at him, and not so much the unceasing pain, that made up his mind about going to hospital. He didn't care if it was a crumbling shack in the middle of a rice paddy that used bamboo shoots as needles and bags of anthrax as drips, he was going. 'Get me a taxi, would you?' he said, as the owner shook his head with genuine compassion.

When Finn finally extricated himself from the cramped tuk-tuk – which clearly had been designed for Asian body types – night had fallen, and as he teetered through the sliding doors of the hospital, using the wall and pillars and door frames to guide him, the thrum of his plane to Bangkok flashed by overhead.

Chapter 3

Almost 3 years ago...

Despite the small drops of rain that had begun to fall, Rock was in fine fettle, and he smiled as Athena nudged playfully against his arm.

'Good girl,' he said, giving the dog a quick pet and a couple of pats on her rear. 'What do you think, nice?'

His Honda had spent the autumn and winter hibernating and gathering dust in the shed, but it now gleamed from hours of dutiful polishing. Along with touching it up with some satin finish, Rock also rehoused a couple of Zebra Jumpers who were squatting in the crevices of the engine block. For him, restoring the bike's lustrous brilliance was almost as satisfying as driving it; almost.

This was Rock's second bike. The first was a birthday present he'd gotten from his fiancée Suzy. Rock thought she had lost it when she dragged him outside in his Y-fronts the morning of his 40th. He spotted the red and black easy rider wrapped in a big bow on the driveway at the same moment he realised there would be no birthday romp. He had never been interested in bikes, and up until that day had never even sat on one. He was a trucker, a petrol head, and drove things with four wheels, things that kept him dry; and if it wasn't trucks then it was cars.

He had owned a few beauties over the years, including an original Metro specially imported from England. Rock remembered installing a makeshift cup holder (and believed he was the first in Ireland to have one), which had been designed mainly for beer cans.

After his first jaunt on the bike - when Suzy had gripped him so tightly that Rock felt as if he were being hugged by a small yet powerful panda - he was completely hooked. The freedom was like a drug, and unlike something with doors and a roof, he had felt intimately connected with his surroundings. Rock's new obsession led him to upgrade to something with an extra few horses and the Honda was a perfect fit; powerful, sexy as hell, and comfortable enough for long journeys without needing to stop every twenty miles because pins and needles were goring his nether regions. Suzy teased that if it wasn't for the bald head and complete lack of facial hair, he could have been a Hells Angel in all his leathers.

Athena - the Rottweiler Rock adored and who was the embodiment of the term 'man's best friend' - could sense as he stroked her coat that Rock was lost in the glimmery sheen of the bodywork. They spent much of their time together and Suzy thought their relationship was so good because they were so similar; strong and stubborn, but with a bad temper when things didn't go their way.

Things were okay in Rock's world. That was about as flattering as he could be about them. He yearned to be back in Greece, in his slice of undiscovered, un-vacationist paradise, where his bungalow overlooking the Aegean Sea was waiting for him, baying for him to return and live in it. Greece was his *real* home, and every day that went by that he wasn't there felt like he was losing time. Since leaving school at fifteen, Rock had worked like a carthorse and he was annoyed - pissed off, more like - that he was leading a life that was heaped upon him rather than the one he thirsted after.

But he needed money, and a continuous flow of it at that. Wages in Greece bordered on third-worldish, so he had to find a way of forging his own trail without having to rely on the pittance of a nine-to-five. But the only things he could think of were a job as a topless barman (he didn't think his stomach was washboard enough for that), or getting in on the lucrative olive market, though that was risky, the mafia had apparently got it cornered and he liked his kneecaps just fine, thank you very much. There was also the small matter of having no olive trees, no fields to grow the olives, and nobody to pick the olives when they grew.

Then he thought about the internet, where every blockhead since Adam seemed to be coining it. When that eluded him too, he thought that maybe he could use photography to sustain him – but who'd want to buy his photos, he was hardly National Geographic material. Still, he had a decent job that he could just about stomach and which paid the bills if little else.

On his arrival back from France some months previous, Rock had lumbered into Mr. McCormick's office and made it clear that he wanted to be repositioned in the company.

'Why?' Mr. McCormick had asked. 'Apart from being uncharacteristically late back, you're one of our better drivers.'

He had ignored the jibe. 'Do you want a small child's death on your conscience?'

'Now come on, Rock, aren't you being a little dramatic?' Mr. McCormick replied, letting out a short throaty scoff.

Rock felt like leaping over the table and punching him in his button nose. 'I almost made mincemeat of a woman pushing a pram in Holyhead. I don't *think* it will happen, if I keep driving, I *know* it will happen...even have fucking nightmares about it happening!'

Mr. McCormick could tell Rock was serious. He had that look that suggested if he didn't give him what he wanted, Rock might start snapping at his ankles. 'Alright, I'll put you behind a desk,' he said with a haughtiness that suggested he was doing Rock the favour of all favours, 'we're going to need a new logistics guy when we expand. But don't think you're getting a pay raise!'

'Thought never crossed my mind.' Rock had replied, exiting the office.

Despite having to sacrifice on luxuries, he and Suzy were managing to squirrel a bit away in the hope that eventually their Grecian dream would become a reality. As he was thinking about foregoing their weekly date to the steakhouse (he'd eaten the house filet so many times he was now seriously considering changing dish) so they could jump ship even sooner, Athena's searching whine drew Rock from his daydream. He patted her head and rose on numb legs from the ground. Maybe he'd go for another bike ride tomorrow, he thought, hobbling back towards the house, Athena by his side. After all, the weather was supposed to be dry and fine.

* * * *

Rock jimmied the zipper to the very top. The sun was out but it had turned cold, and the odd drop of rain fell from a stray cloud. It wasn't quite the day he hoped for, but he was in the mood for a cruise and when he felt like that nothing and no one - except for maybe Thor himself - would get in his way.

'And what do you think you're doing?' he enquired, as Suzy swung her leg over the front of the bike with the same level of agility she had when she was a gymnast in her younger years. Rock leaned back so she could straddle him.

'Oh, you know,' she said, wrapping her arms around his neck so that he was firmly immobilized, 'just wanted to send you off with a nice thought.'

Rock's voice was tinged with ardour. 'It won't be just nice thoughts you'll be sending me off with.'

'Is that such a bad thing?' she replied playfully, knowing that it drove him crazy.

'It is when you're wearing seven layers that would take about an hour to get off!'

She was looking into his eyes the way you would a deep wishing well. 'You'll just have to think about me lying on the bed instead and wearing very few layers.'

'Don't do that,' he said.

Suzy was enjoying the hold she had over him. For a guy who was normally so self-assured, this was the one way she always wore the trousers. 'Is someone a little hot and bothered under all those leathers?'

Rock lowered his head so she wouldn't see the lack of conviction. 'No.'

A small smile crept across his face: he couldn't hide anything from her. Rock was too transparent, and Suzy knew him far too well to be deceived by mere words. She leaned in close and kissed him lightly. As she went to break away, he grabbed her face with both hands and pulled her towards him, kissing her like the throttle had been jerked back. When they parted, he could tell by the heaviness of her breathing that Suzy wasn't the only one with the Midas touch, and he was pleased by the subtle shift in power.

'Now get off me and let me hit the road.'

Rock slapped her hard across the ass as Suzy was climbing down off his hog, cementing a rare victory. He winked before pulling on his helmet, and then without delay drove off leaving her floundering in the driveway. The smile returned to his face. He was sure she'd make him pay for that one.

She watched Rock drive out through the gates, weak-kneed and rubbing the irritation and repression from her bum when a sudden gust of wind rose up and swept past and through her. Goosebumps stood to attention below the layer of wool, and a chill spiked the back of her neck. Suzy grasped both sides of her cardigan and a microscopic tear formed in the material as she pulled them tightly around herself. The roar of Rock's engine caused her to look back once more before she shut the porch door and the cold out behind her.

* * * *

A golden shaft of light pierced the gap in the curtains and bounced off the mirror and into his face. Finn turned over and glanced at his watch: 11:34, he'd slept in again. No matter how often he resolved to get up rather than sleep his days away, his promises to himself were always broken with such drowsy apathy. He set his watch back down.

It was exactly a year to the day since Finn had fled the Philippines. The migraine lasted for four days and had dowsed any spark of adventure left in him. The hospital had been amazingly modern – so modern that he'd been the only patient, and he guessed it was because the locals couldn't afford to be treated there.

After receiving the usual jab of fluid (which he didn't feel as he'd been trying hard not to vomit on the orderly), they sent him away loaded up with painkillers strong enough to take the edge off a broken arm, and a promise that the pain would dissipate by morning. Finn thought about going back and questioning the doctor about his 'educated' guess but had instead spent the following days supine with a cold towel draped across his head and a 'Do Not Disturb' sign on the door.

When Shakira came by uninvited, the sound of her knuckles rapping against the door had sent him scrambling beneath two bloated pillows and two decorative ones that Finn didn't have the energy to push to the floor. After she stopped whooping his name (he remembered her sounding a lot less gravelly when she sang) and left him alone in his misery, Finn stopped stressing about where to go and booked a one-way ticket home.

Nothing much had changed since then. He slept, ate, and slept some more. His life was on autopilot, but the autopilot was malfunctioning and had no idea where it was going. It was like the thing that made him...him...had been gouged out and taken to a safe location to be stored. He thought back to the shifty doctor who had shooed him away that night. Had he extracted some vital marrow and Finn in his grainy state hadn't realised it?

He watched as two midges chased each other, sporadically face-planting a ceiling he knew all too well. He had plans - hazy, imprecise plans, but plans, nonetheless. He tried to think what he could do differently this day that would bring an ounce of happiness, a tiny reprieve from the darkness. But like most days the only thing that came to mind was fleeing the country and running from what he was feeling. Then he would remember that the bank was still after him for unpaid debt, and he'd settle back into his familiar groove of noxious thinking and lethargy.

Anyway, Finn knew how he'd feel if he left his bed. In fact, lately, he was feeling precious little at all. He had become numb to the extent that he was even impervious to the cold on his skin. What was the point in getting up if you couldn't feel anything? Finn found himself wishing that something would happen to prove he was still here, still cognizant. He didn't care what it was: pounced on by skinheads, thrown in jail for smashing up the bookmakers, mauled by a pack of homicidal meerkats at the zoo - at least if he felt pain, terror, it would prove he was still alive.

Finn looked as bad as he felt. His weight had skyrocketed, and he was ashamed to show his face in the midst of a right-thinking, right-feeling society. He retreated further into himself until the only clothes that fit were tracksuits and baggy sweaters; clothing of choice for the excessively weighted, and his chin sagged so much it looked as if it was wearing its own beanie. It was hard to keep fit on his schedule, he bitterly thought.

He held up his watch again. It read 12:12. Since he could think of nothing to get up for - and only a fool would believe this day would be any different from the others - he closed his eyes. The last thing Finn remembered was wondering how his eyelids could feel so heavy after sleeping for so long.

* * * *

In spite of the cold being made worse by the speed he was going, Rock felt alive. There was nothing quite like the open road, he thought, as a blur of green interlaced with strands of black and white passed by as cows grazed happily in the fields. Rock's last ride had been a dreary New Year's Day outing when he and Suzy had been buffeted by easterlies, and after the recent storms, which weirdly were making landfall every Friday like they were on the clock, Rock was itching to get out; so much so that even Suzy wished for the rain to stop just so she could get a break from his incessant grumbling.

He ate through the miles, going deeper and deeper into the countryside, the static of biking inactivity blown off with every corner he took. Rock regressed to the happier times of last summer and he began to make mental plans for the next few years. If he kept putting in as much overtime as he could, then Greece might be within reach by the time fifty came along. He imagined heading up to the lake with Athena, both moving effortlessly in the sun's heat. He'd go for a cooling dip in the waters by the mountain and Athena would do the same. Then he'd take some photos, even if he and Suzy were the only ones who'd see them.

Rock had decided that photography would stay a hobby. If he was honest with himself, it would probably never pay, and he just couldn't afford to take that type of risk. Maybe in his next life, he could come back as one of those lucky sons-of-bitches who got paid to travel the world taking snaps of what they saw. Rock knew he was good enough, but circumstances just hadn't fallen into place. And he was somewhat resentful about that.

He increased his speed and tore confidently along the sleepy roads. New Zealand was a place that Rock longed to capture, and he prickled thinking about all that raw beauty – he'd do a photo story for sure, though he didn't think there was a scrapbook big enough for it all. He'd start by going north from Auckland to the very tiptop: Ninety Mile Beach. Was it really ninety miles? Not a Sunday afternoon type of walk if it was, he reckoned. He'd tour *Lord of the Rings* country; just him, his camera, and his trusty hip flask, and then he'd weave his way down to the bottom of the South Island, stopping at every point of interest and conceding that it may take quite a while.

As he was thinking about different perspectives he could use on Frodo's house, a car edged out into the road ahead. In the past few minutes, the clouds had knitted together and, like a grey blanket, had thrown a gloom over everything below them. Rock hadn't noticed the world dimming. He also hadn't noticed the nose of the car peeping out like the snout of a curious beaver either.

The motorist, obviously used to the road being deserted, had assumed nothing was coming when a cursory glance hadn't registered a tractor or something more substantial. Rock emerged from his reverie like he was coming out of a pool wearing goggles. He'd seen the mole-coloured car too late, which effectively took swerving out of the equation. He pulled the brakes with all the hope and might he could muster, but instead of the **ABS** kicking in to at least slow him, the motorcycle locked and Rock was pitched forward like a fastball from a seasoned hand.

The car brushed the staggered white line when Rock and the Honda – which had flipped sideways and was twisting violently, yet oddly pleasingly to the eye – reached it. The bike thumped the rear like a welt to the kidneys, tearing out the tail lamp, and changing its trajectory, casting it high into the air. Rock slid under the back bumper after a deft somersault that defied his age, narrowly missing having his head taken off. As he neared the apex of the bend, the Honda came down with all its bulk just below his knee joint. An atrocious wail was muffled by his helmet, and they came to rest a couple of feet apart on a grassy verge, fragments of wing mirror peppering down around them.

Still in first gear, the car goggled to a halt. The woman's disbelieving face stared out through the windscreen at a hide-clad biker who was sitting bolt upright. She watched him, unable to move. He unstrapped his helmet and placed it on the slickened grass, scratched, but still in one piece. He sat there for a while. He looked as if he were trying to figure out what just happened. He didn't appear to be in pain, just confused. Her temporary paralysis subsided, and she decided to get out and check on him.

Ignoring any possible damage to her car, she hesitantly paced to where Rock was sitting up straight as if risen from the dead. 'Are you alright?' she asked, acutely aware of her role in things.

He appeared not to hear, or perhaps he was ignoring her. Rock looked down at his leg like it was jostling for attention. He noticed that his tibia was jutting out at an improbable angle and caught his breath at the sight of it; though bizarrely he felt no pain, must have been in shock, he figured. As Rock started to become aware of his surroundings, he saw a woman standing there, thin lines of black mascara streaking down both of her cheeks.

'Are you alright?' she said, sobbing.

He considered the question for a moment. 'Do I look alright to you?'

'I'm...really sorry,' she replied, falling over her words, 'I have some aspirin in the glove compartment–'

Rock's mounting anger gave way to a dejected acceptance, and he ignored the annoying snivelling, wishing she'd just get back in her car and piss off. He pulled out his phone, which somehow had been spared in the carnage, and the woman watched incredulously as he began talking to someone.

'Hey Christine, Rock. Just letting you know I won't be coming into work tomorrow – in fact, mightn't be in for quite some time.' There was a pause as Christine responded. 'Yeah, some silly bitch pulled out in front of me. Now my leg is all fucked-up.'

The woman could only stare dumbly as Rock hung up after describing to Christine, the company secretary, what had happened. He started tapping the screen again and the distraught woman took a few steps backward.

'I'd like to report an accident. No, I was involved in it...I'm trying to tell you if you'd listen. I'm the one who's hurt. Yes, that's right.' Rock glanced up. 'Where exactly am I?'

The woman still hadn't closed her mouth, and it was hard to know if this was because of guilt, shock, or watching Rock orchestrate events with the same level of ease he would were he in the office.

'I...I–'

'Hang on,' Rock said into the receiver. 'Missus, I don't have time for this, I'd like to get seen to sometime today. Now, where are we?'

'We're, eh, on the road – I mean...we're in Clogh, about eighteen kilometres outside Carlow,' she finally managed to coax out.

Rock brought the phone down after relaying his location. The emergency dispatcher told him to hang tight, that an ambulance would be out to him in less than thirty minutes. He told her not to worry, he wasn't going anywhere. He took a few deep breaths, once again making as if the woman wasn't there. The situation had gotten too much for her and her arms were held like pokers by her side. Noticing her distress, Rock told her to go back along the road and flag down the ambulance when it got there. She was of no further use.

* * * *

The volume bar went as low as it could, but every time Finn saw the screen light up it was like being subjected to the Chinese torture of *death by a thousand cuts*. It was the fifteen-year anniversary of a memorable summer he'd spent in San Diego and many of the friends he'd made, many of who he hadn't seen since, were coming together to mark the occasion. Some were even coming from towns as far away as the end of the country and that he was consciously choosing to miss it – if it even was a choice – made him brim with regret and, strangely enough, guilt, like his future self, who wasn't this same sorry excuse for a human, was furious that he was missing out on this night.

But what would he say if he did go? 'Gee, guys, you're all looking so great...me? Well, I've been working up at the North Pole for the past few winters, which is why I'm so pale – you know they only get eleven minutes of sunshine a day, right? Unfortunately, I also contracted a rare permafrost disease that targets the brain, which is why it's operating at the speed of glue.'

No, he didn't think so. It didn't matter how much he wanted to go, he couldn't. He'd been like this for so long now that he was fearful of being around others. The outside world had grown claws and was ready to slash and devour its weak, of which he was one.

His phone continued to skid and make repulsive buzzing noises on the table. Could people not leave him alone? He couldn't go. He snatched up the phone and fired it into a stale knoll of unwashed garb (his 'smelly Everest' as he had dubbed it) on the floor. Finn slithered onto the bed and tugged the blanket up over his ears.

He quavered with the simmering fervour of his emotions as the clothes pile whirred like it was trying to give him a message.

'I'm not going! I just can't!' A damp imprint of his face was embossed on the bedsheet, and the memory foam distorted the sound of his pleas. 'Can people not just leave me the hell alone!?'

Chapter 4

Almost 2 years ago...

Red and black motorbikes flanked Rock's computer like custodians guarding his desk. He picked one up. As much as he loved the models, they always made him hanker to be out on the road and as far away from the office as he could get - the coast of California, maybe.

Rock had been given the undertaking of trying to find ways of combating the spiralling fuel levies delivered by the newest gluttonous government. Of course, the easiest way to achieve this was by tightening truck routes and making sure that no excess mileage was being done.

'*I don't care if it adds time to the journey. If Benny has to sit in traffic a little longer, then tough chumps, that's what he gets paid for!*'

Rock had never liked his boss. Now that he shared a building with him, that liking had descended into something that could get him sent down until he was ready to hold out his cap for his old-man money and book a one-way to Greece.

'*Yes, Mein Führer,*' Rock had replied.

It took a while for him to adapt to the rigours of office life. It had felt alien and claustrophobic, and he didn't care for the way the room remained perfectly level, made him feel fidgety. Still, he managed to find a way of knocking sixteen miles off the route (there could have been more too, but there was no way he was going to be responsible for making Benny's piles even worse), which had the effect of making his normally crotchety boss smile – even if it was an uncanny impression of the one that always materialised with the squat after a bad tuna sandwich.

Rock knew the roads of England and France nearly as well as he knew the roads of his own country. He even knew the back ones, often getting him out of a bind and allowing him to get to the terminal on time. This meant avoiding having to spend the day in Holyhead waiting on the next ship: God how he hated Holyhead! If there was such a place as limbo – like how he was taught in school – where unwholesome people had to go and wait around for a hundred years to repent their sins before catching a lift upstairs, then this place was surely it.

Christine came into the room as he was daydreaming about blue skies, sandy beaches, and revered lyrics. 'Excuse me, Rock?'

Rock temporarily lost control of the red bike, teleporting him swiftly back to when his own bike had gone rogue. 'Jesus, Christine, you took the heart out of me!' The flashbacks were becoming less but there were times – like when he was holding a motorbike by its skinny handlebar – they still struck with all their jarring vividness.

'I did knock.' Christine said.

'It's fine. I was a million miles away – actually,' he chuckled, 'it was more like eight thousand.'

'What do you mean?'

His hand went out in a straight line, portraying the unhampered locomotion of his rented chopper. 'I was just dreaming about cruisin' the roads of Cali'.'

'Sorry, what?' she replied blankly.

Rock thought Christine had definitely sacrificed brain power in return for her looks. 'Nothing, don't mind me.'

Christine nodded in a professional manner, which made her look even less like she knew what was going on. 'Mr. McCormick would like to see you.'

'Tell him I'll be there in a minute.'

'But he asked you to come now?'

'Oh, did he?' Rock replaced the bike into its fixture. 'In that case, I'll get my bony butt in gear and skip into his office like Mary Poppins, shall I?'

Christine stared at him. She never knew if he was being serious or not. 'Okay, I'll tell him that.'

Rock threw his eyes to the sky. 'Hope you keep your looks,' he muttered, following her out into the common area.

Mr. McCormick was hovering a green nozzle over a potted cactus when Rock entered the room. A long, and much too powerful, surge of water almost knocked the plant off the filing cabinet.

'You wanted to see me, boss?'

'Yes, Rock, come in - take a seat,' he replied, motioning to the chair opposite, and repositioning the cactus a safe distance from the edge. 'How are you keeping, how's the leg?'

Something was wrong. Mr. McCormick was never this friendly. Rock doubted he was even this friendly to his family. He was often friendly with Christine but that was for altogether different reasons.

'Apart from some pain, not too bad, I suppose,' he said.

'Good...I mean apart from the pain, that is.' Mr. McCormick used his fingers to smooth down either side of his spindly moustache. 'There's no easy way to say this, we're overstaffed...we're going to have to let you go.'

When Mr. McCormick continued to hold his gaze, Rock knew it wasn't one of his puerile gags. 'You're having me on?'

His moustache became even thinner as his mouth stretched into a frown. 'I'm sorry.'

'But I was only moved in here?' Rock uttered. He wondered if this was a reprisal for staying in the master suite in Reims.

'I know. But listen, there's a job on the trucks that we've set aside *especially* for you.' Mr. McCormick pointed at Rock as if he'd just been selected from an audience to take part in a televised game show.

Rock shook his head slowly. He didn't exactly love working in the office, but it was better than driving and at least he – 'Hang on,' he said, a lightbulb going on somewhere in the cerebral vicinity. 'You know I can't drive long distances because of these shagging poles.'

Mr. McCormick shuffled uneasily in his seat when Rock lifted a leg that was more artificial than real.

'You're pushing me out? You don't want a cripple limping around the office!'

He was now wriggling like a fish with a hook caught in its mouth. 'I'm not sure what you're insinuating, but I can assure you it's nothing like that.'

'You know what, McCormick, you're nothing but a sleazy weasel who deserves to get run over by a truck. Preferably mine!'

'I realise you're upset, Rock, but any more of that and I'll have to take the driving job off the table.'

'Are you deaf?' Rock retorted, rising from his chair, 'Or have you been banging that tart out there too long and now you're fucking stupid as well?'

'Now look here –'

'You can take your driving job and you can stick it up your tailpipe – that's if Christine hasn't already beaten me to it!'

Christine thought strongly about challenging Rock over his comments but soon acquiesced when she saw his expression as he stormed out. She thought he looked like one of those psycho employees who end up coming back and murdering the entire office after they're laid off, and she was sure she'd be first if she said anything.

Rock had no intention of working a month's notice, or even till the end of the day for that matter. He scooped up his belongings, which consisted of a framed photo of him and Suzy in the Balearics, a laptop (which technically was the company's, but which was his now), the lunchbox he brought in every day so he could save on food expenses, and his two models - McCormick could have his job, but it would be over his dead corpse that he'd get his bikes, too!

'That prick,' Rock spat, squeezing the laptop into his rucksack, 'I should put him through the paper shredder. See how full of himself he is then.'

He contemplated redecorating the room in his inimitable style but decided not to in case McCormick withheld his final pay packet. A few replaceable bits of furniture didn't warrant losing money that was rightfully his, and which he'd need now more than ever. Mr. McCormick didn't expect to see Rock's burgundy-coloured face and was startled when it poked through his still-agape door.

'I expect to receive the next six month's pay in full!' the face shouted at him, 'call it compensation for firing a cripple.'

Mr. McCormick started to protest. 'I wasn't firing you because you're a cripp-'

'Tell it to your tart!' Rock kicked open the front door with his bad leg and barged out of the building for the last time.

****

The water seemed to explode as it crashed into the boulders jutting out from the torrent, and Finn imagined his head doing the same were he to jump. It would be quick, most probably painless, and would immediately free him from the demons that had taken up occupancy of his mind – the sort of occupants that didn't care if they got their security deposit back or not.

Finn's world had shrunk down to a four-square-mile shoebox that held him as securely as a padded room in a bin of loons. His was an amorphous dungeon, cordoned off by some subliminal force, and he was free to roam only within its confines. He rarely went outside, nervous by even the thought of doing so. His waistline continued to expand while his world continued to close in. The only way Finn could tell he had a penis now was by looking into a full-length mirror; soon, he'd have to hitch his stomach up like he was presenting it for inspection at a cattle mart.

Below him, gnashing pockets of whitewater continued swamping the weary rocks. Everything he needed – including these tempestuous waterfalls – was within those four miles, and memories of times he'd been outside of them began to fade into the bleakness of his thoughts. Finn couldn't tear himself away and he hated himself for it. He had sunk into his narrow cell until he became part of it, merging like a gnarled case of Stockholm syndrome. Was it his fault he was stuck on this never-ending carousel, or was some malevolent energy toying with him and taking perverse pleasure in watching him squirm and flail?

If I step off, maybe I'll go to one of those childhood farms that pets go to when they go missing, he thought, thinking about when over-protective parents lied to their children about Rover's sudden and ill-fated departure.

At least there, there would be no invisible barriers and he would be free to roam wherever he chose. The clean-up wouldn't be a hassle either; the river would take care of the blood and brains, while the fish would nibble his remains until he never existed. It would be like he had never jumped at all.

Finn glanced over at the right-angled wall that was surrounding a sewage pipe, clearly constructed on purpose to conceal the remains that were being belched into the river. '**LIFE ENDS**' was sprayed in the colours of a rainbow, and after it, as if acting as a full stop, was a heart impaled by a blackened cylinder of steel.

'Even the graffiti wants me to jump,' he sighed, as a billow of water vapour drifted up and out, taunting him from the nothingness.

Finn felt a compulsion to take action, any action once it involved putting one foot in front of the other. It was like a benevolent energy was fighting back against the badness, trying to help him by prodding him ever closer to the metaphorical cliff edge; defying him to take a leap of faith. But his legs were like anchors and were stopping him from taking that one measly step – and even if he *were* able, what that step should be or what part of the cliff he was meant to leap from was a mystery.

He was forever pouring over maps and exploring travel sites for somewhere he could go that would give him the sense of inner peace he pined for. It was a fruitless exercise, even if he did find the right place, he had no way of making it a reality. So, the perennially packed rucksack was left on the floor to be the base for his Everest.

'It doesn't matter where you are,' the psychologist with the full mandatory beard had snapped when Finn shared why he thought he felt the way he did, 'location is irrelevant.' Finn had only agreed to see him to placate his grandmother's worries and already he was urging on the creep of the minute hand.

Tell that to the people in Afghanistan, he had replied in his mind, watching as the curt shrink scribbled out a prescription not even half an hour into their session.

'No, what matters here are drugs. Your serotonin levels are low, so we'll need to give them a boost.'

Finn's resistance to working - or being a 'puppet on a string', as he referred to it - would always hold him back, and possibly even result in his eventual demise. It wasn't that he was lazy, he just wanted to care about what he did. He saw so many people living a lie and doing things they hated, slowly dying inside. But at the age of thirty-three shouldn't he at least have an idea of what he'd like to be doing? Finn wondered if he would ever find this, or if he was simply one of those unfortunates who were destined to wander through life like a rudderless vessel bobbing on the current and becoming increasingly bitter the closer to the end they came.

'I could end it right now,' He pictured his other self disappearing into the translucent cloud of vapour, 'spare myself a very lackadaisical and agonising downfall.'

Wasn't it your responsibility to change your life when it wasn't working? Finn couldn't tell if killing yourself qualified as changing it, but either way, just like in life, he couldn't take that final, salient step. Maybe it was hope that kept him from ending it rather than fear, a feeling that things would eventually turn around.

But he couldn't see any hope - no light at the end of the hypothetical tunnel, no nothing. Maybe it *was* fear, maybe he *was* a coward. After all, was it not his fault that he'd been consigned to this state of perpetual miserableness? Maybe emotional bottom-feeding gave him a source of identity, something to blame besides himself. Maybe he *would* be better off dead, free up some valuable space for someone who *would* use their time on this earth.

But Finn knew somewhere deep down that this wasn't the case. He mightn't exactly know what he was supposed to do - or even who he was supposed to be - but he knew that this phantom at the controls was not that person. There was a need, a constant gnawing, a voice coming from within telling him - pleading with him - to drop everything, open the front door, and go.

Finn had gotten very good at gagging this voice, keeping it pinned beneath swathes of cotton wool. He had convinced himself that things would eventually improve if he just stuck them out and stayed the course. But they never did. And as time pushed slowly yet ruthlessly forward, that voice began to grow louder. It became more and more difficult to ignore and, at times, was so distinctive, that Finn thought somebody was talking to him - though he kept this to himself in case the shrink handed him a complimentary pass to a bona fide *this-padding-is-the-real-deal* kind of room.

He wasn't sure why (he had a feeling that the 'voice' might have been involved), but lately, he'd been thinking about a place he used to go when he was young; a place that had always held wonder - magic even. It was a place that had given him some of his best memories, including his first blue movie, which had been discarded amongst the sand dunes, and his first kiss, which had not been anything like how it was in the movie. Although he didn't know the reason for thinking about this place, he felt it must have some meaning, some importance.

Then he saw a news report on TV about how the city of Bridgewater was becoming the new poster child for start-ups, that if you had an idea, a mere seed, you'd be supported so you could nurture it and bring it out into the world. Startling a bird that was perched on a rock and causing it to fly away, Finn suddenly exclaimed: 'I could be the start-up!' It was like hitting the note of a guitar on the sweet spot, the twang and reverberation of something that felt just right. 'If a business can be started from scratch,' he teased out, watching the rapids' endless onslaught, 'then why not a person?'

That was it, he realised, rather than throwing himself off the bridge, he would return to the city he hadn't seen since boyhood, and rather than starting up an enterprise to gain financial abundance, he'd start up himself to gain an abundance of purpose. Finn wasn't sure if what worked for something that was essentially inanimate could work for something living, and not many would ever accuse him of having a business bone in his body, but it had to be worth a try. He backed away from the banal blue railing that kept people from falling or jumping in. If things didn't work out with the new 'product', the raging waters, and timeless grey behemoths capable of ending it all, would still be here.

'*Oh, to be a fish for a day–*' Finn paused for a second before sending a box of pills as far downstream as he could manage, '*-or however long these tablets last,*' he sang gently, departing for home along the shoebox perimeter, always with a foot just inside.

* * * *

Rock was propped up in his hospital bed fussing over a packet of grapes that seemed to be fused shut. The doctor had said he needed nutritious food to aid his recovery; a cupcake and a few grapes should just about cover all the bases, he thought, showing off a full set of gnashers.

'Stupid bag,' he murmured.

Tensing every muscle from his core to his chest, the bag ripped apart and the tray inside flew like it was shot from a fruit cannon. The grapes unfurled across the linoleum floor like chubby marbles, finding their way under everything that was raised even slightly off the ground.

'Shit!'

He stared at the grapes, mulling over how clean the floor would be, and whether he would catch **MRSA** if he ate them. A nurse entered the room and stopped abruptly.

'Having a hard time with the grapes again, Rock?'

'Every time!' he replied, 'why can't they make easy-to-open packets – or packets with a flaming zip?!' Rock was frustrated at having been beaten by a tray of fruit again. 'Would you hand me that cupcake over there?'

She cocked her head while taking in the sea of mixed grapes. 'Not exactly the healthiest of foods?' she said accusingly.

'Trudy, this is my third operation.' He sounded exasperated. 'I don't think food is going to magically bind my leg bone to the pole they've shoved in, do you?'

She handed him the last cupcake from the wheelie table. 'I guess not,' she conceded.

Dark specks littered the frigid white sheets as he took a large bite. 'Now why can't everything be this easy?' he asked.

Trudy smiled at the chocolate veneer coating his teeth and then began plucking up the runaways. Rock had been given a private room this time where he could sulk in peace. Normally he had to sulk in a room where other people were also sulking. Since his accident last year, he had been in and out of hospital like he was entering and exiting through a revolving door.

Rock thought back to when the ambulance had arrived – over an hour and a half after he rang for help – and it had taken two police officers and two paramedics to bundle him into the back. One of the cops had a dollop of mayonnaise bubbling at the side of his mouth and had stood on Rock's hand as they were moving him. Rock roared that he was a 'fucking eejit!' and the policeman spent the next two minutes grovelling for forgiveness. The only trace of blood from the incident came from Rock's hand and at the time had irked him even more than his shattered leg.

When the reams of leather had been pared off using industrial-strength scissors in the emergency room, the doctor, without warning, snapped the leg back into a position less likely to elicit dry-heaving. Rock had blacked out instantly and spent the next fourteen days in the hospital – four for his leg, and ten for the subsequent infection that had set in.

'When am I getting out of this kip?' he said, coming back to the present moment.

'Shouldn't be too long now, Rock,' she called from the other side of the room.

Trudy bent over to retrieve the final transient grape, which had nestled naughtily in the corner. She was an attractive woman, all that running around after patients keeping her toned and trim. Rock tried hard not to stare but it was difficult to control his wandering thoughts when he had nothing better to do. 'Yeah, well, better not be,' he replied distractedly.

'What's the game plan for when you get out?' She was leaning so far forward that Rock thought her scrubs were going to vanish like tissue paper up the hose of a Hoover.

He guessed that Trudy wouldn't want to hear how he was going to take out his pent-up frustrations when he got home. As his thoughts migrated to less inflammatory subjects, he realised that he didn't know what he was going to do. He suddenly felt light-headed, as if the fairy cake had been doused in brandy without his knowing. What *was* he going to do? His plan of blitz-working for a few years and then retiring to Greece had shattered at the same moment as his tibia. Lifting his head, he looked at her solemnly:

'I don't know,' he said.

* * * *

Finn slumped to the floor, but he was laughing hard at the same time. After hearing raised voices on the street outside (which were quarrelling about the rightful ownership of a cheeseburger), he had leapt to the end of the single bed to see who would go home with a meat squeegee in their tummy.

'Idiot,' he said, still chuckling from underneath the sumptuous beige curtain that had come crashing down on top of him after the momentum of his zestful leap had carried him straight off.

Finn had forsaken the lure of the bridge (temporarily, at least) and followed through on his hunch to return to the place he used to come as a child. He had felt queasy before setting off, bringing back up his tea and buttery toast before he'd even gotten his grandmother's car into first. Here was someone who had charged into a pool hall in a dodgy neighbourhood of Manilla, demanding a big-money pool game, and now the idea of taking a trip to somewhere he knew – but which was outside the boundary fence – reduced him to a quivering clump of cells.

He spent the night in a cheap hotel near the river, and apart from seeing a homeless man pummel a public toilet because it refused to let him in, the night was largely uneventful. Despite a few nightcaps in an equally cheap bar, his sleep had been fractured. He kept waking in a flap not knowing where he was and the lamp by his bedside spent more time lit than not.

As he rubbed the sleep from his eyes the next morning, Finn noticed a sign for Silver Strand. Disjointed wisps of a forgotten time came drifting back to him. He remembered that place; the amusement rides, the excitement, the chaste happiness of youth and, for a reason he couldn't comprehend, a killer swan. When the arrow appeared, he bludgeoned his way across two lanes of traffic against the backdrop of indignant honking. It had taken him long enough to cross the picket line in his strike against cognizance, he'd stay outside one more night.

Silver Strand was located ten miles from Bridgewater and was a classic seaside town. Because of this, it had been one of the worst hit areas in the country during the crash, the cold fist of economics reaching down and pulling out the town's guts with one sickening wrench. Windows were boarded shut, businesses closed, and people were forced onto distending welfare lines. It all happened overnight. Worst of all, the tourists stopped coming.

But through either hard work or kismet, things were beginning to turn around. Windows were being liberated from their wooden captors, shutters were thrown up, and the mood now matched the cheerful walls as they were given colourful licks of paint. The opening of a new coffee shop on the promenade was a risky move, but a move that mirrored the emerging optimism of the town. It was faint, and one that couldn't yet be voiced aloud, but it was an optimism that had been missing for the past eight years.

It was unseasonably warm for February and Finn strolled the prom in short sleeves. Any lingering alcohol had been mopped up with a hearty, fat-laden breakfast - the best hangover cure known to man - and despite a lump crowning on his head from being bopped by a curtain railing, there had been no permanent damage from last night's acrobatics.

Though winter had only just exited stage left, plenty of people were out walking, and a kite surfer was fighting a losing battle a short distance away, the breeze puffing in patches and far too lightly to propel him through the waves. The coffee shop was doing a brisk trade, and signs of a resurgence were apparent by the amount of wagging tails and wagging bottoms as people bent over to clean up their dog's poop.

Finn felt surprisingly good, almost like he weighed less. He knew this was impossible, particularly after that second helping of black pudding (maybe the gravitational forces were less here, he buoyantly thought). The positive energy was like a dragon's breath down his throat, and he lazed about with no need or desire to be anywhere else. He walked up through the old part of town, exploring its ancient lanes and back streets and playing 'gotcha' on a checkerboard of light.

Silver Strand was built on an impossibly steep hill – the steepest in the country, locals would brag – and every year brave cyclists would converge upon the town and test their mettle in a sprint to the top. Finn was gasping for air on reaching the spot where the tape was normally drawn; actually, he was gasping for air well before that and had to stop twice on the way up with a stitch in his side.

The salt air infused him with a sense of euphoria as the thudding of his heart subsided. The sky was wide open and chased a promenade that ran parallel to a crystal-studded sea. A narrow spit of sand continued on long after the prom had ended, eventually colliding with towering dunes four kilometres away. Finn could see tiny blips rounding the vast structures and inching their way back. He didn't remember this as a child, but back then all Finn cared about was funfair rides and candy floss; not much had changed there, he thought, smirking.

Something felt right about the place, like he could live here - even belong here. Finn had always gone far afield to find his place in the world but rarely had he looked on his own doorstep. But could he drop everything (and by 'everything' what he meant was his neurosis and his hiking boots) and move here just like that? Finn could have sworn he heard an affirmative coming from somewhere, but when he looked around the only person he could see was a postman hurdling a small gate and a line of a whistle note wafting after him.

He'd need money, of course, which he didn't have; years of gambling cleaning him out, and ever since that big win that took him to the Philippines, he'd been firing blanks like someone in critical need of a smoothie made from every herb and spice of the forest. Finn had made the rookie mistake of returning to the scene of the crime after his trip, and like any other witless offender, had practically hog-tied himself to the bookies alter to be sacrificed.

Still, he wouldn't need much to make the move; a month's rent, same again for a deposit, and with enough left over to stock up on instant noodles until he found work. What he would need though was courage. And there wasn't much of that left in the pantry.

* * * *

When he made it back to the car (thinking it would be much more fun to have a bike race *down* the hill), Finn had driven home with the intention it would only be temporary, vowing that he'd return to Silver Strand. He wasn't exactly sure what he was looking for, but the idea of moving there clung to him like wet paper and he owed it to himself - and his lucidity - to at least explore the idea.

Searching the rentals that night - or, rental, rather, as the town had only one available room - Finn had called the number and with prattling anguish confirmed that he would take it. He was amazed at how easy it was. It was like the room had been waiting for him to get his act together all along.

'She'd be breakin' her bollox laughing, she would,' Jake said, his accent sometimes difficult for Finn to follow, 'I'd end up looking a right palooka!'

Clenching his glass in both hands, Finn let out a deep sigh, but instead of it being a way to expel the fiendish demons that were trapped within, it was a sigh of contentment. 'We all get laughed at Jake,' he replied to his new housemate after talk had turned to girls when Jake confessed that he would be terrified to approach one. 'You're eighteen, hardly expected to be Casanova.'

'Who's Cosanava?'

'Casanova?' Finn wondered why he had waited so long, and waiting for what he didn't know. He had begun to think that it would take a tragedy to nudge him onto the right track, but in the end, it was a brusque and clamorous voice that was coming from inside his head. 'Ah, just someone who used to be quite good with the ladies.'

'Oh.' Jake said, unmoved. 'Has a doll ever laughed at you?'

'A what?'

'A doll – you know, a woman.' Jake was from the country and had the configuration of a boxer who spent his teenage years punching people in the mouth. He had come to stay in Silver Strand to learn about equine breeding, but despite the industry he was hoping to enter, Jake had none of the grace of a horse.

Finn found his choice of words amusing. 'Are you kidding?' he replied, 'of course they have.'

'I'd hate to be rejected like that.' Jake kept his voice low in case any of the surrounding strangers overheard and assumed it had once happened to him.

'Rejection isn't so bad.' Finn swilled a mouthful of Guinness, his go-to libation whenever he was happy or sad. 'It's probably our own fault anyway.'

'What do you mean?' His reply came out almost hostile.

Though the sun had given way to stars, the evening was warm and pleasant, and the sounds of the band spilled out into the beer garden whenever someone wanted to escape the heat inside.

'Think about it for a second. A guy sees a super-hot-looking chick and says to himself, *I want me some of that*, and then he storms over, half-cocked, and takes her completely by surprise.'

Jake nodded reluctantly, still unsure of what point Finn was trying to make.

'He doesn't suss out if she likes him back or not,' he was obliged to go on, 'doesn't even give her any warning – you know, a glance, smile – that type of thing. He charges over–' Finn mimicked the laborious movements of someone wearing size fifteen clodhoppers, '–interrupts her while she's talking to her friends –

cardinal sin, by the way – and now he's scared her off by coming across like a bumbling desperado. So, unless you got some serious game, or you look like an Italian underwear model, forget about it.'

'Okay,' Jake replied, now with a keener understanding of the point Finn was making, 'you're saying that if I want to bag me a nice doll, I should give her the eye.'

He thought for a moment. 'Well...you're on the right path, I guess.'

'See if she shows any interest first?'

'Now you have it!' Finn replied, 'Build up a rapport with the girl – I mean, doll – and you'll be knocked back far less.' He looked past Jake's pumped biceps which were almost entirely blocking his view. 'See those two over there?'

The door opened and another insider was ejected from the furnace. 'Them two dolls?' Jake had turned around and made it completely obvious they were talking about them.

'We don't know them, do we?' Jake shook his head. 'We're going to go over and see how we do.'

'What about the advance-warning-system thingy?' Jake said, but Finn was already getting farther away and didn't hear the question.

He watched as Finn interrupted their conversation (wasn't that a really bad thing to do?) and seconds later all three of them were laughing together. Feeling self-conscious standing on his own he hurried to join them.

'Ladies, this is Jake.' Finn said, gripped by the confidence that came from being in a place where you weren't known and were free to be anyone you wanted, 'my handsome and only slightly younger friend.'

'Eh, hi...there.' Nervousness oozed from every one of his pores.

'Hi Jake,' the girls, both of whom were mid-thirties, slim and sister-like (though Ciara would later confide in Finn that they hadn't spoken in years because 'that bitch had off with my fella' and were anything but sisters), replied smiling.

After Jake had reached the stage where direct eye contact and conversation were both possible, the lights flickered on and off warning punters that it was time for last orders before glasses were strategically placed over taps.

'You guys want to come clubbing?' Ciara said, having decided just that second that the grudge with her 'sister' had been held long enough.

Finn knew Jake's apprenticeship didn't start for another few days. 'You need to be up in the morning, Jake?'

'Tomorrow, no?' Jake was about to remind Finn they had just been talking about it only for him to pre-empt the reply.

'Guess we're going clubbing then,' Finn said, and they swooped on the swinging doors like a well-drilled SWAT team.

The club was quiet. Silver Strand was a resort town, and tourists wouldn't start appearing till May. Still, there were plenty on the floor looking for love or lust, and before long Jake and Stephanie (who found Jake's inability to use his words flattering) were locked in a drunken embrace, hands frantically exploring each other's bodies as people danced awkwardly around them. Across the way and just out of sight, Finn ordered two drinks at the bar.

'It's not going to happen, you know.' He leaned in so he could hear Ciara above the music. 'If you want to be with someone you should stop talking to me and find another girl!'

'If only it was that simple!' Finn shouted. It wasn't just his absence from the realm of love that would stymie his chances, but also the location. Silver Strand was hardly Asia when it came to ease of coupling.

'I'm not into one-night stands anymore,' Ciara explained, stopping short of disclosing a chequered past.

Finn wouldn't turn down a snog if it was offered, but for now, he was content with baby steps; just engaging a member of the opposite sex was a feat. He wondered how she would feel about his spell of monk-like abstinence. Was that something girls liked now? It proved he wasn't a player, or maybe it proved he wasn't in the game at all, which was probably worse than screwing everything in a skirt.

'I'm not talking to you to sleep with you.' The bass made the floor hum and rumble and the soles of his feet tingle. 'I'm just happy chatting.'

'That's alright because it's not going to happen,' she stated defiantly, but whether it was to herself or him he couldn't tell.

In his peripheral vision, Finn saw Jake bounding over like a gazelle across the Serengeti. 'Have you got condoms?' he said, the gravity of the request causing the muscles in Jake's cheeks to twitch and contort.

Finn frowned and rubbed his ear. 'You must be one hell of a kisser.'

'Seriously, do you have any? She wants to come back to the house!'

'Yeah, I guessed that.' He sighed. Since he wasn't going to need them, the least Finn could do was help someone else have a good time.

Jake looked from Finn to his date and back again like he thought somebody was going to lug her off to their cave. 'Well?'

'If you go into my room there's a box in the bottom drawer.'

'Ah, budgie!' Jake exclaimed. He locked arms with Stephanie and then they made a beeline for the exit.

'Don't mess up my stuff!' Finn looked at Ciara and she chuckled when he said, 'the noblest of martyrs.'

The night wound to a close and the drunk-but-happy stragglers trickled out into the still night air. Ciara put her hand on Finn's arm. 'Are we going back to yours?'

Finn felt like the ground was shifting beneath him. He stared at her, confusion emerging through the din of alcohol. He had discovered in his time locked away that acute melancholy affected more than just your mood. 'I thought you said nothing was going to happen, that you're over one-night stands...that they're a thing of the past?'

'Nothing *is* going to happen. We're having a drink, that's all.'

Finn's memory of sex may have been tenuous at best, but he wasn't gullible, and thoughts cropped up unbidden of the possibility of more than just a drink. 'Right.' he replied.

Ciara's fingernails dug pits into his chest as he ran in bursts with her on his back. Finn was supercharged with energy and when he jumped the threshold like a young buck, Jake was nowhere to be seen. He presumed he and Stephanie had already found their way to the bedroom.

Finn let his rider off in the front room and went straight over to the drinks cabinet. 'What do we have here?' he said, the glass door clicking softly in the elegant way mahogany cabinets usually did.

Ciara's words came back at her as she toured the room, the only things absorbing her voice a large exotic plant in the corner and beside it a medicine ball. 'Where's the landlady?'

'Away in some fat camp,' He handed her a glass, 'she was complaining that bouncing on the ball was getting her nowhere.' Finn smiled a smile that felt lopsided. 'Cheers.'

'Cheers to you, too,' she replied.

Suddenly the silence was penetrated by actual penetration from directly above them. Jake's grunting was drowned out only by what sounded like a wrecking ball crashing against the wall. After a moment of hesitation, they both began laughing.

'Is that Stephanie's head?' Finn asked.

Once upon a time, Ciara had liked being the wrecking ball and a sordid yet immediate past came gushing back to her. 'Don't know,' she replied, 'could be?'

The atmosphere became charged with incommunicable expectancy, the moaning from above allaying any inhabitations the alcohol hadn't already stripped away. Ciara eased back into the couch and delicately placed her legs across Finn's lap. A lance of primal want sped across the synapses in his brain, galloping its way downwards like a great stallion, and he offered up a small prayer of thanks when his jeans began to solidify around him. Ciara let out a low moan as Finn's hand travelled slowly northwards to the hem of her dress, which had slid up when she had leaned back.

'Do you want to go to your room?' she whispered.

Finn glanced at the Grey Goose which, without ice or mixer, wasn't quite the indulgence it should have been. 'More than I want this.'

He skulled what he could and, using the arm of the couch for balance, Finn stood and held out his hand, which trembled like the rest of him. Ciara took it and he led her to the staircase. He swotted at the light switch like it was something to kill and after three attempts the lights finally went out.

Chapter 5
Almost 1 year ago...

Rock's hunched profile threw a half-moon over the keyboard and the office chair he'd spent a week's wage on was providing very little comfort. Since losing his job for being a 'physical retard', as he morosely put it, he had become increasingly sullen. Like an overzealous tactician, he spent his days trying to figure out ways of making money so he could get back to what he considered his real home.

He dreamt of lazing by the water's edge, heating his bones under the mulberry tree. He knew that if he could only make the internet pay, he'd be able to live happily in the sun for the rest of his days. It didn't even have to pay that well. Greece was cheap and Rock didn't want for much; basic food rations, enough to cover the running costs of his home and camper, and the odd bottle of whiskey every few days and he'd be as happy as a pig in muck. But finding a way to achieve this continually eluded him and made him feel like a failure. Was he not entitled to live where he wanted?

He snapped the laptop closed and stared out the window. The rain was coming down in fits and flurries, but the last shower had turned into a continuing downpour that didn't want to stop. 'Prickin' May,' he mumbled to himself, but loudly enough for Suzy to hear as she was passing by, 'wouldn't be like this in Greece.'

Athena nosed the door open and went straight over to Rock, forcing her head between his arm and elbow and resting it on his lap.

'Ah, Athena, leave it out!' Rock was in no mood to be bothered by either man or man's best friend.

'What's wrong, love?' Suzy asked, following Athena in as she shrank back from her master.

'We're still here,' he replied, watching the droplets of rain thump against the ground outside. There was a certain beauty to the regimented order of it, he had to admit. The ground had no choice but to accept the onslaught and he wished he could be more like that about his own situation. 'I can't figure out a way.'

Suzy felt Athena brush past as she retreated to the kitchen. 'A way for what?'

'A way to get out of this hole we call home and–'

'How's the search for a course going?' Suzy loved Greece as much as Rock, but she had accepted that unless a miracle fell into their laps they were staying put, and she wasn't going to give herself a heart attack obsessing about it. She wasn't normally the pragmatist in the relationship, but when it came to Greece, Rock was like one of those window-suckers that would stay on indefinitely until you pry them off.

He leaned back and rubbed his forehead like he was trying to erase squiggles from a magic marker. 'I don't know. There's so many.'

Since ending up in the one place he despised, and the place he swore he'd never end up – the unemployment line – Rock had started looking into the possibility of doing a photography course. If he could just hone his skills enough then maybe, and he knew it was a long shot, he could still have a future in it.

Suzy put her hands on his shoulders and began kneading the muscle. 'What about the college you mentioned the other day?'

'That one is a year, and it's full-time.'

'What's wrong with that?' she replied, attempting to disengage one of the taut bands, 'not as if you've much else going on.'

'Suzy,' Rock said, the tone of his voice conveying just how he felt, 'I'm forty-five. I didn't even know how to *spell* college until I saw the brochure – I used to spell it with an 'a' for Christ's sake.'

She couldn't help giggling but quickly gathered herself up. 'Did you ever think that maybe your accident happened for a reason?'

The muscle fibres rubbed against each other as he looked back at her sharply. 'You know I don't believe in that crap.'

'Let's just for one minute assume it might be real–'

'But it's not!' he snapped, facing forward again.

'I said assume,' Suzy replied softly, coming around the front of him and laying her hand on top of his. 'You love photography, don't you?'

Rock slashed at the mouse with his free hand, sending it scurrying backwards a few mousey inches. 'You know I do.'

'You should never have been out on the bike that day.' She knelt in front of him so that she was now looking up into his eyes. 'That was always the day you went to Wales in the truck.'

'I just *had* to change jobs, didn't I?'

'That doesn't matter, forget about that,' she said, 'you changed jobs because you weren't happy. You did the right thing.'

Rock's reply was acerbic. 'Tell that to my hip bone, the one they carved up to put in my leg.'

'Let's just *say* the accident and all the pain you've been through happened so you could finally have the chance to do what you love.'

'And I couldn't have done that without being on crutches for five months?' Rock felt like sending the mouse across the room.

She was gently rubbing his hand, the way Rock would Athena when they watched TV together at night. 'You can be pretty stubborn at times, love. Would you honestly have considered doing the course if you were still working?'

'Hmmm.' Rock knew full well he had already decided that photography would stay a hobby. 'Yeah, well...'

Suzy sensed his dogmatism beginning to wane. If she could just choose her words carefully, she might be able to help him. 'College has changed since our day. It isn't just for young people anymore –'

'You make us sound like we're artefacts in a museum,' he replied.

'– it's for everyone,' she continued, annunciating her words. 'It doesn't matter if you've never been before, now's your chance. You're just being fashionably late, that's all.'

Rock's mood began lifting like a morning mist. Why did she always sound so convincing? He still didn't believe in that 'fate' mumbo-jumbo, but he was starting to warm to Suzy's spatchcock logic. 'You know I hate being late,' he said, any earlier acidity gone from his voice.

'You're going to prove we're not ready to go on display yet.' She said with a firmness Rock wasn't used to hearing. 'Now, are you going to open that laptop and click 'apply', or am I going to have to do it for you?'

Rock looked back out the window. The dancing raindrops had begun to slow, and his shoulders had dropped a little after Suzy did what she always did and helped him to see things clearer. With only a few well-placed sentences his path was suddenly visible again, despite Greece being farther away than ever.

* * * *

Finn's leg was tangled up in Ava's duvet like a beetle in a Venus flytrap and he watched the crystals hanging above her chest of drawers glint as they caught the light from the lamp. It was a muggy night and his whole body was slick with sweat after having spent the last hour engaged in what could only be described as 'frenzied' exercise.

He had met Ava in a Bridgewater bar soon after Ciara had cracked open Pandora's Box. That night was a defibrillator to his libido and, like the crystals that oscillated gently, had reinvigorated him with a sparkly new sense of self-esteem. One unintentionally witty remark to her and the other 'hens' about the inadequate head on his drink and Finn had been guaranteed a summer romance.

'You want a reading?' The drawstring of a satin pouch slipped enticingly through her painted nails and made Finn want to recommence exercising.

Ava was an avid reader (she held that she was communicating, not reading) and was convinced that the angels spoke to her like she was hearing them through the walkie part of a walkie-talkie. When family and friends had problems – which they invariably did – they would come knocking at Ava's door at the strangest of hours seeking angelic counselling.

'Alright,' he replied, feeling the slightest bit apprehensive that he was going to hear the word, *bridge*, 'just don't tell me how I'm going to die. Prefer to keep that a surprise.'

As Ava shuffled, Finn's mind wandered, and he thought about his situation in Silver Strand. He had trawled the business community looking for a job; not that it took very long, it wasn't exactly a hub of commerce. If you didn't want to serve alcohol to ebullient tourists or sell them tickets for the big dipper where they could bring back up said alcohol, then there wasn't much in the way of work. Though he shouldn't have been, he was relieved. The thought of standing at a ticket booth every day telling people to 'keep your hands and arms in the carriage at all times', while a roller-coaster thundered past overhead wasn't exactly his idea of a compelling career.

Then things began to unravel when his landlady got back from her detox trip to Bali – looking completely the same as when she had left, was Finn's take on things. She approached him one day after he'd returned from watching a surfer get wiped out by driftwood and told him as he was sliding a pizza into the oven that she was raising his rent.

He wondered if she knew about the night of debauchery that had occurred in her house while she was in the process of going vegan. Had she noticed the missing bottle of vodka? Had Stephanie's head put a dent in the bedroom wall and that was the reason for the paranoia? When Finn stood strong and insisted that they'd already agreed on the rent, she told him he had a week to move out.

Why were his plans always imploding like popping candy in his mouth? Was it because he was so sure they would, or was this attitude only fostered because of chronic and habitual disappointment? After three paltry weeks – and because he'd been unknowingly judged for leading his landlady's sweet nephew astray – Finn was forced to leave the roomy backwater wilds and return to his pokey and insignificant holding pen in the Big Smoke.

'Your turn,' Ava said, handing him the stack of man-size cards. 'Don't tell me the question, just focus on it and the answers will come through.'

Despite the setback, Finn had finally taken the step he needed to take. Like a snake shedding its skin, he was ready to rise like a phoenix from the ashes of his lacklustre existence and soar like a raven toward something better.

But was he just hurting himself with these fanciful whimsies? He was often accused of being a dreamer and having spent the last few seconds pondering animal metaphors, Finn could see why people would think that. Should he just accept the life he'd been given and settle loathly into it like

a pre-teen donning a uniform for the first day of school? Or had people just lost the ability to dream under a hail of obligation?

Whatever the answer, Finn knew he couldn't fall back now, not after getting a taste of what life *could* be like. He didn't just want to change where he lived, he wanted to change everything that had become insipid and redundant. Finn wanted to strip the rotten flesh from the bones of his life and build something worth something; that counted for something. Anyway, had he not taken that original leap of faith, he wouldn't now be shuffling cards with angels on them across from a girl who looked like an angel herself about to be told his future. That she was wearing only a lace thong made him agree with himself that he'd made the right choice.

A card flew from the deck and nestled between Ava's legs as she comfortably held the lotus position. 'You just can't stay out of there, can you?' she said.

Finn traced his gaze from the stray card up to her stomach, the breast that was covered by tousled hair, her neck, and finally her eyes before a hungry smile emerged through the veil of unambiguous motives. 'Kind of hard to resist,' he replied.

'Now mister, behave, I don't think the angels would be pleased if we interrupted them for hanky-panky.'

'Not sure about them but I'd be quite pleased.'

Ava pulled the card out from between her thighs. 'We're going to use this one, sometimes a card wants to be heard. Pick one more.'

Before he was excommunicated from Silver Strand, Finn had seen an advert for a journalism and media course in the local paper. What caught his attention wasn't the marketing for erectile dysfunction treatment that was new to Ireland, it was the image for the ad. It was a picture of smiling students hosting a radio show. They looked so stimulated, so happy. Finn had always thought there was something quite spellbinding about the way your voice could be heard by thousands of people as they went about dusting the shelves or preparing supper. He pondered while reading the caption about 'jockeying your own show' if maybe he would be that happy too if he signed up. Or maybe, as usual, he was just kidding himself. Finn studied the cards and handed her a second.

Ava lay both cards face up on the bed. The artwork depicted archangels Gabriel and Raphael materialising in the sky, striking yet reassuring. Finn's fingertips played a soundless piano as he waited for Ava to tell him his future – or at least if all his obsessing had been worthwhile.

'Nervous?' she asked.

'No, why would I be nervous?' he answered nervously.

Finn believed in things like fate and in things you couldn't see – especially what others couldn't *see*, he always thought – which is why he criticised himself almost daily for stressing about things he had no control over. There were, however, a couple of potential snags that could scupper his plans; the spectre of money, for one, which seemed to troll his every step, and then there was the more abstruse of burdens: Was it the right thing to do? Finn was often paralysed by transcendental notions of right and wrong which served to transform him into one of the world's finest procrastinators.

'Oh, interesting,' Ava purred.

'What?'

She smiled at Finn's impulsiveness. 'You have the Angel of Money card, the one that flew out-'

Some angel, Finn thought.

'-combined with the Destiny card.'

'It's a good thing you already know I'm skint or those cards would seriously be dropping me in it.'

'Angels, not cards.' Ava leaned towards him, shifting the way her hair had settled. 'Whatever it is you have in mind you needn't worry about money. The means will arrive to support your plans.'

'Sounds promising,' he mouthed, having to force his attention back to what she was saying.

'And this thing you're thinking about, it *is* the right thing to do,' she said, as surely as if she were privy to the mystical workings of the cosmos. 'When all looks forlorn, a mistake will right things and a new course will be set.'

For someone like Finn, who was always going to be susceptible to this kind of numinous salve, this was like manna from heaven - or whatever sustenance came from the place that Ava was plugged into. The way she said these things filled him with a hope that seemed lucid and vexingly real.

She held up the Destiny card under a sentient smile. 'It also features heavily in your future.'

Most people yearned to match those six little numbers so they could buy the Ferrari they've always dreamed of owning, even if that 'dream' was only very recent; or the mansion on the hill with separate wings to keep away annoying family members; or the computer that's able to control everything in their lives at the touch of a button; or the Rolex that attracts members of the opposite sex like bees to honey, but not Finn. Finn didn't play the lottery. He knew that without a cause or a motivation – something to give shape to your life – then those *things* were exactly that and could never lead to long-term happiness. Could a bijou Rolex fill the void of being lost; could the Ferrari put its arm around you when you're sad if it wasn't a *Transformer*; or could a 400-inch 4K TV with pixels coming out the wazoo make up for the experiences you were missing out on because you weren't able to face the world? He had watched enough reruns to know the TV certainly couldn't, he couldn't speak for the other two, but he had his misgivings.

Finn had finally accepted that without change he would never discover that sense of purpose, that sense of self. It would be lost forever in the world of what-ifs, his life devoid of substance or fulfilment as he continued along on the gormless, zombie-walking path he'd been treading for so long. But if what he was being told – or, 'communicated', as Ava succinctly put it – was correct, then things were about to change in a very big way.

'Are you happy with the news?'

For a second, Finn thought Ava was channelling some otherworldly entity as a tint-like sunset seemed to surround her. 'It's not the worst news I've heard today,' he replied, grinning like a goof.

'Good, I'm glad.' Ava flicked her hair back, knowing full well the effect this small action would have. 'Now,' she said, 'how are you going to repay me?'

Finn's blood pressure spiked like the needle on a Richter scale after a modest quake. Ava was lying on her side, head resting on one hand, and nipple straining for consideration. She looked like a fallen seraph who had just discovered the delights of carnal pleasure. The cards, which were spread across the rumpled and unmade bed, were knocked to the ground as Finn crawled towards her, shrouded in a red haze.

* * * *

Rock fell against a boulder that had been put there by a river of ice and which had decided to hang around for an indeterminate amount of time. 'Bloody mountain,' he growled, seeing that there was still a long way to go. Athena stopped and looked back. 'It's okay, girl, mountain's just a bit god-damn high, is all.'

Grimacing, he rubbed his sore leg as if doing so would make it better. He hadn't even come to the steep part yet and already it felt like the rods (which Rock was convinced were inserted by a surgeon at the back end of a forty-hour shift) were rearranging themselves through new parts of his leg. He adjusted his camera. The straps were digging into his shoulder, and it felt like there was a kettlebell pulling on his neck.

He continued on, each step bringing fresh pain. Rock's first thoughts were defiant; he wasn't going to let a silly crash stand in the way of his getting these shots. They were the type pros dreamed about, and if he was going to walk the walk of a photographer, then he was determined to put in the hard yards, even if that meant having to hobble up the stairs for the next month just so he could have his alone time on the toilet.

As he inched agonisingly-slowly farther up the mountain, his resolve began to weaken. He thought about turning back, of sparing himself the humiliation of getting any higher and then being forced to abandon his mission. But he wouldn't. Rock knew one thing about himself, it would take an almost guarantee of death to stop him when he got the bit between his teeth, and even then, it wasn't guaranteed. Like the time he had brought in the company's biggest contract by driving twenty-four straight hours to the Spanish border on nothing more than coffee and Cheetos. The phrase *dog with a bone* could apply to Rock, only the dog would be a little insane – possibly with rabies – and the bone would be prehistoric in makeup – possibly from the limb of a T-Rex.

When he eventually made it to the top, Rock felt as if he'd scaled Mount Kilimanjaro. His face was bathed in sweat, and he no longer shivered from inadequate clothing. The sun had moved across the sky faster than he'd have liked, meaning he wouldn't make it back down till after dark.

After regaining his breath so he didn't feel like throwing up, Rock surveyed the scene. It looked like a scrapyard for replacement plane parts, and he was stunned by the sheer amount of debris strewn among the tufts of wispy grass. The fuselage had broken into two halves, each almost identical in length. The wings had snapped off and were nowhere to be seen – probably scattered with the rest of the rubble, he figured.

Nuzzling against the body of the aircraft was a solitary seat. Rock stared transfixed, wondering how the seat had come to be settled so snuggly against the outside.

'*Sit down, Rock, I'm pretty comfortable considering I fell from the sky, and you sure do look as if you could do with a rest with all that limping you've been doing,*' the sage-coloured cabin seat whispered to him.

Maybe there was still a shortage of oxygen getting to his brain and he was imagining things. The fog closed in on the mountaintop (on a clear day the gasworks in Bridgewater could be seen in the distance), settling around him and the wreckage, making him feel that not only was he the only person in the world who knew about the accident, but also the only person alive. Apart from Athena, of course, couldn't forget about her. If something happened and he should become marooned, Rock was confident that Athena would rescue him. She'd run back and raise the alarm or drag him down the mountain with his ankle clasped in her powerful jaws. Maybe he'd just get her to run down and raise the alarm.

The fog swaddled them in silence as if they were in a huge vacuum devoid of life. And that's exactly what it was on that lonely mountain, devoid of life. Rock suddenly felt vulnerable though he wouldn't have been able to say why. He stepped over shards of carbon fiber and titanium, careful not to add another injury to the list. The last thing he needed was to be skewered by a piece of metal and for gangrene to set in and for his leg to fall off – alright, that would be worst-case scenario, but there was no point in tempting fate, he thought.

Rock upped the ISO a notch so the images wouldn't soup. He photographed both halves of the fuselage, which had come to rest close to one another, and apart from charred grass there wasn't much between them. The scorched earth suggested at least one fire if not many smaller ones. He counted eight seats in total and guessed – with his limited knowledge of all things flying – that the plane was probably some sort of Cessna, something a well-off businessman or public personality might have owned.

A faint whine was coming from a little way off, but it wasn't a whine of pain or even fear. It sounded like something was bothering Athena and she was trying to figure it out.

'Alright, hold still. I'll follow your voice because you're obviously not going to lead me.'

Rock trod cautiously while focusing on the direction of Athena's whimpering. As he neared, he heard a low, guttural growl coming from just behind a rather large piece of wing; so that's where the wing had gotten to, he mused, peering around it. His foot jammed in the earth and, like a painting that had been shaken clean of its colour, his face briefly matched the complexion of his surrounds. Beneath the inquiring and excitable sniffing of Athena's nose was a woman's foot. Rock knew it belonged to a woman because it still wore a black heeled shoe, the type worn with a dress suit. What struck him most was that it was a slip-on, no strapping, nothing to bind the shoe to the foot; it was like neither wanted to be separated and were waiting to be reunited with the rest of the body.

Rock believed that very little was off limits when it came to the business of a camera and its glass. Though some thought certain subjects were taboo, Rock enjoyed capturing the brutal and unembellished outliers of life. He wanted to stir the emotions. It didn't matter what those emotions were; love, hate, sadness, hope – they were all the same once they were stirred, and on this occasion, he was merely documenting the more sombre side of it.

Some of his favourite photographs were those that skirted the bounds of morality and walked the fine line between ubiquitous acceptance and widespread antipathy. He knew that an image could be seen as immoral – odious even – by one generation, but then worshipped and hailed as a defining piece by the next.

One of these is of a young Vietnamese girl. She is running down the street, naked and terrified, napalm burning and scarring her skin, armed soldiers following closely behind; and in the background, thick black smoke rises from a village on fire. This photo could be seen as making light of a tortured girl's trauma, or an invasion of her privacy, or it could even be seen as 'dirty' because the girl is naked, but to Rock, she's a symbol of the horrific reality of war, and to turn away from her, would be to turn away from every victim affected by war. He believed photographs could alter perceptions. He also knew that the pain etched on this small girl's face was like a taser to the sensibilities and had the power to end a war – or potentially stop one from starting.

He brought the camera up and pictured everything. In one, the foot – a fusion of dried blood and mud – was sharp in focus and made a frightening contrast with the broken and bleary dirty-white fuselage. Ominous spurs of fog had settled between the two, generating an image that would work for even the most harrowing Stephen King thriller.

The fog finally began to clear as Athena and Rock made their way down the mountain. Athena walked quietly, matching her master's demeanour. The sun poked its head through gaps in the haze and the evening stretched out. The light accompanied them all the way home before quickly fading to night. Athena went to her water bowl and drank deeply, before carrying on straight past her food bowl. Rock watched as she neglected to do her usual body turns and instead flattened without parade onto the bed. She lay her head down on her doggie pillow and pooped out. He figured she was just tired from all the exertion. What he didn't realise is that Athena was fully aware of what had happened on that mountain. She had a keener sense of smell than he could ever hope, and the stench of not just death, but fear, had zapped her of her energy.

'How was it up there?' Suzy's voice was low and reverent.

'A mess, pieces of plane everywhere,' he replied, slouching in the chair at the head of the kitchen table.

She shook her head slowly and repeatedly. 'Was there any...you know, remains?'

'A lot of blood.' Rock's leg had to be kept almost completely straight. He'd be lucky if he didn't need to crutch it in for his consultation with the specialist. 'And a foot.'

'Jesus,' Suzy said in a whisper. She unwrapped Rock's camera from around his neck and helped him out of his coat. 'I'm glad I didn't go with you.'

'I'll show you the photos.'

She drew back from him. 'You didn't take photos of it?'

'Of course I did, almost killed myself crawling up that bastard mountain!' Rock felt suddenly tired, the physical and emotional slog of the day finally wearing him down.

'I think I'll pass on seeing those.' If there was one thing she didn't want to see, it was a photo of that, and was thankful to be able to change the subject. 'There's some dinner for you in the oven. You're lucky I didn't eat it all because it was beautiful, if I do say so myself.'

He smiled warmly at her. 'It always is when you make it.'

When his jaded eyes impelled her to continue to the best part, she sighed as if put out, 'steak and kidney, with a couple of surprises thrown in.'

As Rock broke through the puff pastry, the memory of what he'd seen earlier began to loosen its grip. Maybe it was because he was tired, or it might just have been that it was his favourite meal, but Suzy thought there was something more to his savouring every bite. She thought that maybe he was relieved it hadn't been him on that plane, and as bad as his leg was, at least he was still attached to it.

Whatever the reason, Rock would be in no hurry to share it.

*\ *\ *\ *

Finn felt like he was in a dentist's waiting room before having something very unpleasant shoved in his mouth. Seven seats had been lined up against the cream-coloured wall in preparation for the onslaught of prospective students. A pimply teenager sat across from him, and apart from the usual pleasantries, they sat in silence. The young man fumbled continuously until he was beckoned, and Finn was surprised that a squiggly line of pee didn't follow him as he disappeared into the room.

The corridor was peaceful now. It was that peculiar period when schools went into a sort of hiatus and seemed to lose their way, forgetting what their function was, and leaving only echoless nooks and crannies. The building was from an era long before Finn was born; a time when carpets ruled, and hardwood flooring was a thing of the future. Finn had already been to a modern-day college, with its wide impersonal hallways that kept you a wingspan away from other students, its bland tiled flooring, and its bare white walls that created a sterilised feel so palpable you could almost taste the bleach.

The young man came out and faltered like he'd gone a full round with the undisputed champ. There was a build-up of glittery perspiration on the sides of his forehead, and he made a hasty exit through the automatic double doors, the most modern feature of the building.

'Finn?'

Finn looked up at the sound of his name being called.

'Could you follow me, please?' said a blonde woman with dangly earrings and an agreeable smile.

He was led into a makeshift interview room, where the usual scotched and gum-laced stalwarts had been pushed up against the walls. To his surprise, a second interviewer was sitting at a desk in the centre of the room, also blonde. She had arrow-straight hair that stopped abruptly about a centimetre above her shoulders, as if scared to touch them. A solitary chair had been taken out of suspended animation and was set on the opposite side.

Finn shook their hands and then planted himself in the chair like he was germinating from it. He had been to enough interviews to know that he should have waited for an invite to be seated, but he had no time for such trivial power plays that meant nothing in the grand scheme of things.

After a brief spell getting to know each other, the woman with the fossilised hair folded her arms and leaned back, as if to say, *I really don't care what answers you give, they won't affect my life, but I will judge you on them, nevertheless.*

'What would you bring to the course if we granted you a place?' she asked, exaggerating the word *if.*

Finn scraped the stubble on the underside of his chin, wondering if this was a trick question that required more of a response than just: *Myself.* 'Well,' he said, 'I'd bring a bit of craic...a few laughs.'

There was no point in lying, Finn liked to laugh, or at least the former version of himself did. What's more, he liked to make others laugh, too. *The women are going to think I'm some sort of loutish troublemaker*, he thought. But that was only partly true.

'I'll also help people,' he continued. Why did he have to sit down before being asked? 'I'm sure most of the class will be younger than me so my experience might come in useful.'

'We like people to think for themselves,' came the snipped reply, 'if you help them too much, you're in essence doing their work for them.'

Finn held his tongue; cheeky comebacks wouldn't help him get a place. Maybe this was a test too, a test to see how he handled stupidity. That was often the biggest test of all, he mused, hoping they weren't somehow reading his mind - could professional interviewers do that type of thing these days? 'I'd be looking to give more general guidance rather than answers to an exam,' he said calmly, and only a small bit cheekily.

'I see.' She scribbled in her notepad and Finn wondered if that was good or bad.

The other blonde woman - who he guessed was playing good cop - sloped forward and smiled sympathetically. 'Why should we admit you onto the course?'

Finn's hand spread unconsciously over his recently shaved hair. He was stumped. His plans over the years hadn't amounted to much. If anything, they were mostly highfalutin plots and plays that would have made even the hardiest of dreamers blush. He loved to write but had no real interest in becoming a journalist. He would often take detoxes from the news because it was so draining, one shooting spree or deceitful politician tended to roll into the next shooting spree and deceitful politician. He knew he wasn't going to beg, but he also didn't want to concoct some ornate story about why he deserved a place in case it ended up being another dead end.

Finn decided to make the bold move of being completely honest. He'd air his dirty laundry and come clean, that way the onus would lie with them - how was that for an unexpected power play? Some might have said this was taking the easy way out, but what was wrong with speaking truth and letting the chips fall as they may, he thought?

'I'm not sure why I deserve a place. I love to write – at least in theory, haven't done much recently. I also don't know how interested I am in journalism; often turn off the news because it's so bleak. It's not even the first time I've been to college.' He looked from one to the other, reflecting on when sincerity would start becoming detrimental. 'Things haven't been going my way lately, so I thought I'd take a chance and move to Bridgewater, try something different.'

He felt good saying that. Finn considered telling them about his fantasy of jumping off a bridge but decided against being quite *so* honest.

'What I can promise,' he went on, enjoying what felt like a deep psychological cleansing, 'is that if you give me a place, I'll turn up every day and give it everything I have.'

The women gave a look to each other. Finn couldn't tell if it was a look of respect or ridicule.

'Thank you,' the good cop finally said, her sidekick remaining seated and scribbling yet more notes as she rose from her chair. 'That just about wraps it up.'

Though he was pleased with the way the interview had gone, his grandmother, who was his biggest fan, and the one person never to give up on him ('you're never too old to turn things around', she had told him many times), had branded him a ninny for his most lax approach, scolding that he'd ruined any chance of receiving an 'epistle in the post-box'. After finding out what an epistle was, Finn tried explaining that if he was upfront and still got offered a place, then for sure it was the right thing for him to do. Then again, he conceded, he could be a 'ninny' and his grandmother could be right. Finn left the college wondering if he would be one of those padding the carpeted halls of Bridgewater Tech come September.

Chapter 6

Rock stared at the envelope. He was swaying slightly from the effects of too much cider. It had been one of the nicest days of a not-so-good summer and he and Suzy had gone to a BBQ to celebrate the sun's decision to finally come out of hiding, if only for a day.

The label was handwritten and unfamiliar, but in the top left-hand corner was a blue and white logo. He recognised the logo from the last letter he had received inviting him for an interview. It was from Bridgewater Tech. And it was early. In fact, it was much earlier than he'd been led to believe. He was told when leaving the classroom that he'd receive notice of their decision in roughly two months. It had been two weeks. His swaying ceased, the letter having an acutely sobering effect.

He felt the interview had gone well; granted one of the interviewers was a complete cow, but he got on well with the other one (they were both blonde, he recalled). He had shown them some of his better prints, and they swooned over a photograph he'd taken of the Milky Way in the Dolomites when it looked like a billion twinkling bulbs were lighting up the night sky. Even cow-face had liked it.

The photos had helped to deflect attention away from his writing experience. Rock's area of expertise was the visual medium, not the verbal. The last time Rock had written something was in school when he had to write about what he thought of Hamlet; he remembered it not being much. Since then, his writings had been strictly limited to greeting cards – birthdays, weddings, and funerals, and more of the last than he'd have liked. It seemed like the black armour was making more and more appearances the older he got.

Suzy followed in after rounding up the doggie bag, which, annoyingly, was dispersed across many smaller bags. 'Some help you are.' Two baked potatoes in foil dropped on the ground as she shoved past where he'd taken up as an effigy of himself. 'Not even going to eat any of this,' she griped.

Rock looked at her. 'It's from the college, think it's an acceptance letter – or non-acceptance letter as the case may be.' The sobering effect of the letter hadn't quite reached his voice box and most of his words ended with a hiss.

'Well, what are you waiting for?'

His eyes were wide and expressive. 'What if they've said no?'

'What if they've said yes?' Suzy replied, setting the never-to-be-eaten potatoes on the dish drainer.

'I think that would be worse,' Rock joked, but he wasn't entirely sure it was a joke. When he continued to dither, Suzy lost her patience and demanded he open it.

He felt a thrill as he tore the envelope, accidentally ripping what was inside. Holding the mangled letter, Rock was a smorgasbord of conflicting emotions; if he was refused, he'd remain stuck in this limbo he'd been in ever since losing his job, but if he was accepted, he'd be entering a world he'd never been in before and never before thought he belonged.

'What does it say?' Suzy said.

'Not sure,' Rock replied, 'can't bring myself to read it.'

She held out her hand to accept the letter. 'Do you want me to do it?'

'Yeah, don't have my glasses on anyway,' he lied, trusting it at her with both hands as if it were ticking.

Suzy took her time reading the first few lines, and in that short space of time, which seemed to go on forever, Rock came to the conclusion that he did want to be accepted; fancy that, he thought. He'd need to buy a school bag – and a pencil case – a notion he found highly amusing. He might even get one of those *Minions* pencil cases he'd seen at the jumble sale last weekend. 'Come on, woman, you're killing me!' Images of *Minions* churned in his head, and he now yearned for that pencil case. 'What does it say?'

Suzy grinned like a Cheshire cat who'd just been presented with a bowl of full-fat, double-chocolate milk.

'You're kidding me?' Rock was overcome by a tumult of emotion he hadn't expected.

'Take a look,' she replied, offering him the letter.

But he knew she was telling the truth. As genial as Suzy was, she would never cod about things that could wound. Rock decided there and then that not only was he going to buy a *Minions* pencil case, but he was going to buy *Minions* everything; pencils, pens for taking notes, erasers for when he made mistakes with the pencils, correction fluid for when he made mistakes with the pens, ruler, pencil sharpener – everything that would fit.

Rock was going to college.

* * * *

'Do you believe in fate?' Finn asked, lifting the cup of tea Ava had made to his lips.

Dropping in a cube of sugar and stirring it around with pronounced delicacy, she replied, 'Angel-fate, sure. Why?'

'You remember that course I told you about?'

'Think I remember you mentioning it alright.' She said this in a manner that suggested he might have mentioned it quite a few times.

After his most recent dalliance with the 'messenger' temptress, Finn had slipped coming into his house and had whispered a quiet obscenity as he did a reel of the mashed potato. His knees had taken on that post-sex jelly sensation: actually, he thought, it was more like a post-apocalyptic-sex jelly sensation. He looked down to see an epistle lying face-up on the tarnished floor. It was addressed to him. Most of the letters Finn received were from the bank or the government, or solicitors of the bank or the government...basically no one good.

He was about to step over it, really in no mood to be dealing with such official matters, until that is he saw the logo at the top of the envelope. It was the emblem from the college in Bridgewater and his first debilitated thought was that it was an early rejection letter.

'Before I moved back here from Silver Strand,' he continued undeterred, 'you know, to spend the summer giving you the best sex of your life –'

'Is that what you call it?' Ava quipped.

'–times like these it's perfectly fine to lie,' he replied, granting her all the permission she needed to make her nose grow long. Finn never had any complaints in that department, though he wasn't so wet behind the ears to believe that 'paid-for' conquests would be totally forthright with their feedback.

'Where was I? Oh, yeah. I called into the college to pay the application fee, but it was busy, and I had to get home for my sister's engagement party.' Finn paused, remembering the ribs. The meat had been so tender that it fell from the bone completely unprovoked. 'The closing date was a couple of days later, so I figured I'd drop in when I came back. 'Anyway,' he went on, 'I catch the afternoon bus to Bridgewater two days later, not realising that the college might be closed – it was Easter after all, why would it be open late? When I got there the door was unlocked, but there was no one inside; no queue, but no staff either.'

Ava made a small slurp sound. 'What happened?'

Finn had torn open the letter with the kind of dexterity that was missing from his legs, anxious to know if the universe, God, or any other entity was finally going to give him a get-out-of-the-mire-free card. This course was the only way out of the cavernous hole he'd dug for himself over the past few years. He read with a sense of urgency, knowing that his life hung in the balance and could be tipped either way, towards a new start and salvation, or enduring sameness and certain oblivion.

'There was a sign at the reception saying that it was open till three.' he replied to Ava. 'I was a quarter of an hour late.'

'So, you missed the deadline?'

He cut a serious expression. 'I resigned myself to the fact that the course mustn't have been right, I would have made it otherwise.'

'You give fate a lot of credit,' she said, placing a cup whose handle was a pair of angel's wings back down.

'Tends to play a pretty big role in my experience.' Finn ran his finger around his gum line to glean what was always the tastiest part. 'Have you any more of those biscuits? Whatever they are they're delicious.'

Ava groaned before taking out four biscuits from a tin in her press. 'Mustn't have been what you wanted, otherwise-'

'Hang on, I'm not finished,' he said, taking a proffered biscuit and biting it in half. 'I walk to the front door to let myself out, but as I'm turning the handle a voice behind me asks if I need help.'

A crumb had stuck to the fine hairs at the corner of Ava's mouth, and she was now fully engrossed in the story. 'Who was it?' she asked.

Finn's jellied legs had now gone full wobble mode and he lowered the letter without bothering to read the rest after he'd seen the word *able*. In the dappled dawn light of his hallway, he began to smile. It was a tight smile, more relief than happiness and more gratitude than relief. He let out an audible sigh that was nearly loud enough to disturb his grandmother upstairs. This was his ticket. He'd finally made it to the front of the queue and was now ready to board the elevator to the top. Finn had been invisible to the world for over three years, an ethereal being, neither alive nor dead. He'd been forgotten about and left outside to shiver in a blizzard of neglect, waiting for someone to bring him in and thaw him out.

'The janitor,' he replied, 'saw me from the broom cupboard. Long story short, says if I make it to the bank and pay the fee before they close, he'll rise above his station and sign me up.' The 'admin costs' had nobbled Finn's selection for the big race that day, as the janitor's generosity had not come without preconditions.

The biscuit particle from her mouth dropped onto the cloth angels below. 'Well?' she said, drawing out the word.

It suddenly struck Finn that he had read the letter wrong, and that really it said they were *unable* to offer him a place. He had quickly resumed his deciphering of the epistle: *and we look forward to seeing you in September!* That was all he'd needed. He folded the letter and put it behind the radio - filling cabinet for all his grandmother's 'correspondences'.

'Well, you are now looking at a mature - but very young at heart - college student.'

'Oh, Finn.' Ava was beaming and giggling like she'd been the one who was going to college. 'I'm delighted for you!'

Finn eyed the marshmallow, which was pushing out through its shell like a hernia. 'Thanks,' he said, 'pretty stoked about it.'

'Does this mean no more of that good loving?'

''Fraid so.' He was just about to send the other half of the biscuit down his gullet when Ava grabbed his arm.

'Guess we better make the most of the time we have left so,' she replied, dragging him off to her celestial boudoir, and leaving a layer of pink gently see-sawing on the surface of his tea.

Finn was going back to college.

Chapter 7

College...

Rock singed a slowly moving Fiat, the driver moving even slower as he shook his fist to convey exactly how he felt about Rock's driving. He pulled across just in time to avoid clipping an on-coming car, but not before the motorist made the horn sing aloud.

'Can't you all see I'm late for college!?' he roared out the window.

It was 9:05 and he was already five minutes late. These doddering pensioners obviously had the wrong day and thought they were out for a Sunday drive. he cursed, accelerating towards the college. The lights changed and Rock slammed the brakes. The tyres of his motorhome screeched to a halt and the sound of something smashing came from somewhere behind him.

'Ohhh no,' he groaned, 'not my Spartan mug.' In the adjacent lane a box Fiat came to a stop.

'You were driving very fecklessly. Do you know that?'

Rock peered across at the passenger side window and saw nobody, the old man not sprightly enough to lean into view. 'Who said that?' He wondered if he was seeing one of those self-driving cars that were all over the news lately.

'I did!' The man extended his arm into Rock's line of sight and began shaking his fist.

He couldn't help laughing out loud. 'Ah, it's you me oul ham. Well, it's not my fault you drive like an old woman.'

The man's face was now the colour of the beetroot Rock had eaten the previous night. 'You cheeky young pup!' he blurted.

'I haven't been called young in many a moon,' Rock replied, howling, 'I'll even let you away with calling me a pup.' The lights went green. 'Nice chatting to you old timer, but I've got a class to get to!' He put his foot to the floor and the motorhome took off like an out-of-commission rocket shuddering towards space.

It was 9:09 when Rock skidded into a disabled parking spot right outside the college, stopping a camera snick from the bonnet of a red Mercedes. The parking was definitely one of the perks of being handicapped, he thought, jumping out. He ignored whatever had fallen during his morning rally of Bridgewater and glanced at his tracker watch.

'First day and I'm late. Not a good start, Rock.'

A car swerved as he ran across the road. His determination to get those plane photos had come back to haunt him, as he figured it might, and now even a gentle stroll in the countryside left him feeling like some little reprobate had gone to work on him with a hammer and chisel. Panting, and his leg balling from the sudden dash, Rock was ambushed by a matrix of doors when he got into the building. 'Shit!'

A girl decked out in black trousers and a chaste white top – which could only mean she was a budding beauty therapist – fixed him a curious look. Rock wondered what it would be like to follow her to class, him in a roomful of pristine females painted like a Papuan tribe, they'd get some shock, he chuckled, thinking of his pasty disposition and dislike of skincare products.

'Concentrate!' he chided himself, frantically rifling through his bag for the timetable everyone had been given at registration. 'Aha! Now where am I supposed to go?'

'Excuuuuuuse mee,' said a girl with almond eyes and chestnut hair, as she shimmied past where Rock had sunk to his hunkers trying to make sense of a chart that displayed the rooms for different subjects, and into the classroom to his left.

Rock mumbled something but didn't seem to notice her. The glossy sheet of paper told him he needed to go to classroom number two. Time ticked unsympathetically by, and his mind was a tardy jumble. Where was classroom two? His gaze fell on the listless blue carpet that ran to the room at the end, which Rock guessed was probably a storeroom of some sort. He couldn't see the numbers inscribed on each door as they were built into hollows. He looked to his left and there, highlighted like a gold numeral angel, was the number *2*.

Rock's breath momentarily caught in his windpipe. He was in college. He was going to walk through this door – door number two – and like some far-fetched fantasy film enter a completely different world for the next nine months. He didn't think he would feel this nervous, yet at the same time, he felt that surging tingle of the new and unknown – and the downright scary – that he hadn't felt since his early days of driving a truck.

'Well, didn't come this far.' Rock grabbed the knob and turned it while exhaling the air that had become trapped, and just like entering a fantasy world, a flood of splendiferous light burst forth and pulled him back into the room with it.

* * * *

Finn watched as a tall man wearing a black cap followed the girl into the room. He looked flustered and was sweating as if he'd run there, totally the opposite of the girl who had walked in calmly and without a hair out of place, and every male eye – and most female ones, too – watched as she cut between a gap in the tables so she wouldn't have to play duck, duck, goose and took a seat beside a coat rack that was all matter and no substance. If Finn wasn't mistaken, one pair of eyes was especially effusive, and a girl with tight red hair blushed when he caught her leering a little too intently.

During registration the week before, when new students had been given welcome packs and a speech by the principal about 'punctuality being the crux of success', the thought that he was in the wrong place had hit Finn like a lightning bolt and all his muscles went limp. How had he chosen so wrongly? All the signs pointed to Bridgewater and this course. He had glanced over his shoulder but all he could see from up the front were bodies and he didn't want the loss of face that would come from being the only one to have skulked off.

But his fears had been fleeting and he soon found himself relaxing into the bustle of the canteen afterwards.

'My friend did this course last year.' Hugh had hair that once would have told of affluence, and he scrolled on his double-handed phone like an artist making final touches to a canvas, seemingly able to devote equal attention to conversing, 'said the teacher's a wacko.'

Finn sipped on powdered coffee provided by the college. 'Wacko how?'

'Kinda just makes it up as she goes along,' he replied.

As Hugh continued to artfully manipulate, telling Finn and another woman, who was dropping in and out of waking dreams like she'd ingested a sleeping potion, how United were set to gain revenge on their most abhorred rivals for beating them last season (and he was so sure of it that he was going to wear a City kit for the entire summer if they didn't), a bald man clutching a foam cup hustled out of the canteen. At least he wasn't the only mature student in the place, Finn had thought, looking around at a sea of people barely old enough to turn their coffees Irish.

The teacher's legs swung as if to a beat and she gripped the edge of the table for support. She wore a cream blouse, dark blue jeans, and overlaying them, tanned boots that wouldn't have looked out of place at a rodeo. The tips of her mousy hair were tinged with copper, but beneath the curls and femininity, the rutted lines the concealer couldn't hide spoke of a fizzing and discernible toughness.

'This year will be what you make it,' she was saying, 'you're not in school anymore and I'm not going to be riding your asses telling you what to do.' A ripple of laughter broke out among some of the students. 'If you'd prefer to be getting dizzy on the zoomers out in Silver Strand or uptown in Bob's downing pints, then that's your business and I won't interfere. If you do decide to make the effort and come to class *most* of the time –' her wink was met by kiddish grins '– then I'll be right here to help you. If you have a problem, we'll solve it together, and if I see you have potential, then we'll damn sure bring it out together.

'But beware,' Sadie's legs were now moving to a slow ballad, 'if you have talent but are too scared or apathetic to bring it out, I will push you for everything you're worth until you're ready to stand atop this table here-' she drummed on it like a tribeswoman beating a drum '-proclaim your birth-right and take your place as king or queen of the class.'

Jittery laughter met Sadie's promise. There was something about her that made the class take what she was saying very seriously. What if you weren't ready to be pushed? Finn thought, with primitive yet refined angst. Being out of the 'box' was progress enough, but he'd crawl back into his hutch before showboating on a table like nobility with a mantle and sceptre.

'Okay, that might be a bit of an exaggeration,' she said, and they listened beguiled by her words, 'but I mean it. What's the point in investing your precious time if you're not going to get the most out of it? I guarantee that if you put in a bit of effort and a bit of yourself, then you might get something from the year you hadn't been expecting.'

Finn wondered if she meant more than just good grades or a perfect attendance record.

'But enough of my ranting.' Sadie lowered herself to the ground with such finesse it was like she came down on a wire. 'What we're going to do is start with a little get-to-know-you, journalism style – since this is a journalism course, sound fair?' Mesmerised heads nodded in global agreement. 'You're going to pair up, person next to you is fine; and guys, if you're not used to talking to girls, now's your chance.'

Rock smiled. He had never suffered from such shortcomings. Women were just men with no dipstick and gremlins in their heads, that's what he thought, and it hadn't failed him so far – though, he accepted, maybe if he'd been a little more wary, he mightn't have ended up in a marriage that almost killed him, to a wife who made him want to kill her.

Finn was paired with Hugh, whose Manchester United jersey was so long it could have doubled as a pair of shorts. Hugh was slim; although slim wasn't quite right, Finn figured a moderate gust of wind could have carried him away. He had a head of spongy, luxuriant hair, and purposely crafted sideburns that swept into his cheeks. His sculpted appearance was a great source of pride for Hugh but, in typical institutional fashion, would earn him the nickname, *Wolfman*.

The class responded with a collective 'yes' when Sadie asked if they all had a partner. 'Good, now what I want you to do is conduct an interview,' she said, moving sinuously like a cat, 'journalists must be able to communicate in a clear, calm and concise manner - the use of alliteration being completely optional, I might add - while collecting the relevant info.'

A male voice with a lisp spoke out from behind a triplet of female forms. 'Can we ask them anything?'

'I'm glad you asked that person-with-a-name-I-don't-know-yet-but-will-do-in-about-two-day's-time,' Sadie responded to the boy blocked out by styled locks and tresses. 'As it's the first day, you might want to avoid things that are too personal or embarrassing, so if you once tried to drown yourself so you could be saved by Mitch Buchannon - yes, I may have had a crush on David Hasselhoff in the nineties - or if you went to Thailand on holiday and brought back more than you'd bargained for, then you're probably better off not divulging those type of details.'

Finn looked around at the wide-eyed faces, doubting if any of the younger students had ever encountered this type of teacher before. He, too, was pleasantly surprised, as most of his past teachers had been reluctant to stray too far from the how-to-behave handbook.

'You have twenty minutes, so don those reporter hats and paint me a picture.'

Stilted conversation soon turned lively as they went about delving into the other's lives. It was awkward at first, everyone careful to ask safe, generic questions, conscious they might accidentally unearth some buried secret that would attract the attention of the boys in blue – or even the men in white. It was a gentle introduction to the world of journalism, and rather than standing up in a room full of strangers and talking about yourself like you were at an AA meeting, you instead got to read what you discovered about someone else, absolving the more timorous of that sickly pressure.

'Time's up!' Sadie boomed over the boisterous scavenging for details. 'Because it's fun to do things in the wrong order sometimes, we're going to start in the far corner and work anti-clockwise around the room. You,' she said, 'with the braids – love them by the way – and the boy with the navy top, you two can start.'

After a pause, Kennedy, the girl with the braided hair, began telling the class what she had discovered about the boy with the navy jumper. Kevin had recently moved from the suburbs of a destitute urban sprawl – where fireworks had twice been thrown through his window (and once onto his bed as he slept) in the last year – and he much preferred the smell of seaweed to that of smog and car fumes.

'He'd also like to go on a date with a girl, but he's too shy to ask one out.'

Kevin began stuttering like he'd swallowed a stalk of broccoli the wrong way. He had expressly asked for that sensitive information to be kept from the rest of the class. 'I thought that was off the record?' he inquired.

'Be careful when somebody asks you to keep something confidential,' Sadie said, 'if you get a name as someone who can't keep secrets, you'll be writing obituaries before you know it because the dead aren't bothered if you stay tight-lipped or not.'

'Sorry,' Kennedy replied. 'Kevin really has a beautiful girlfriend – in fact,' she continued, adding misinformation to loose lips, 'I'm his girlfriend.'

Kevin's fingertips patted the part of his cheek where Kennedy had planted a kiss, before sharing it wasn't the first time Kennedy had braided her hair; and not the first style either, the fishtail had apparently started off the trend. Her best friend in the world was sitting beside her, and although Blanche was more interested in writing poetry and stories about magicians, she had agreed to sign up after losing a best two out of three game of rock-paper-scissors.

Sophia, the girl who had sashayed in ahead of Rock, resulting in few people realising he'd walked in after her, was a keen photographer and had won last year's summer fair beauty pageant. First prize had been a free hairdo in *Cuts n All* – the salon where she'd gone to get her hair done for the pageant in the first place – and a voucher for the only store in town where a camera could be purchased (and where you could also replenish your home heating supply or browse the latest in cutting-edge frock fashion).

Leo was American – though he'd strongly dispute this as he had moved to Ireland as a toddler – and a wrestling fanatic. He loved nothing more than guzzling maple syrup straight from the bottle and his only regret was that it was so expensive in Ireland. Finn thought this could prove to be the sticking point in validating Leo's claims of Irishness.

'Do you want to tell us something about Barbara, Leo?' Sadie asked him after Leo had made Barbara finish with how he believed that Canada should re-join America for their own sake, and the sake of all the 'snow people' who lived in igloos up north.

Leo stood up. If he was going to make a speech, he was going to make sure everyone heard him. 'I found out that Barbara used to be an altar girl when she was a girl, and every weekend she helps to clean her local church - and' he added as if uncovering a juicy morsel of previously unrevealed knowledge, '- she also failed last year's course.'

Barbara went red as Leo's outstretched arm made her feel like she was on trial for larceny or tax evasion.

'But she didn't fail because she's dumb, she failed because a tick gave her a lion's disease and she missed the year because she was really sleepy.' Leo gave a silent murmur of satisfaction. 'Case closed.'

'I think you mean Lyme disease,' Sadie said, smiling ironically, 'but it's nice to see that journalistic spirit coming out already.'

Leo didn't care about exact names. He cared about cracking cases, which he had done. 'Yeah, that's what I meant.'

'I'm going to pass this time, guys,' Barbara said timidly, after what felt like being stripped of all her clothes and flogged in the town square, 'I promise!'

Then there was Daisy, the girl, who, as the famous song went, was turning Japanese. Cherry blossoms wound their way atop their stems around the front of her kimono like they were alive, and a pair of bunny ears adorned her head like a coney crown. Daisy was in love with all things Japan; the culture, music, fashion - the boys, too. Apart from Japan, she also liked to trace charcoal illustrations (normally of very light-skinned people) and read books (which were normally set in the Far East).

Hugh discovered - after Finn had told the class that Hugh would crouch in a corner licking peanut butter off a spoon whenever Man United lost a match, and that, if given the chance, he would travel to Mars on the stipulation he was allowed to bring a TV, spoon, and an unlimited amount of peanut butter - that Finn wasn't from Bridgewater, and that the apartment he rented was in the worst part of the city and didn't contain a television ('But how do you watch matches?' Hugh had baulked).

'He wants to be a writer, but he doesn't know what to write about. Why don't you try writing a story about someone who buys a TV and watches the football?' He suggested.

Rock was next in line as they worked backwards along the second of four rows that were cleaved into unequal hemispheres by a walkway that students would take when they had to present something to their peers. He was buddied up with a girl with sawtooth auburn hair, and more piercings in her face than he could count. They stared at each other like animals from different species, neither quite sure what they were looking at. Rock glanced at the girl's t-shirt (her name - apparently - was Spikester, and this, when Rock heard it, had made him flinch involuntarily), which boasted a massive skull with blood spurting out the top of it. Spikester was similarly unimpressed by Rock's plain blue t-shirt which had nothing on it, let alone a cool bloody skull.

'This girl's name is Spikester.' *She's messing with me for sure,* Rock thought, waiting for the sniggers of bemused students, but all that greeted him was a stifled laugh from Finn who thought for sure she was messing with him. Surprised, he carried on; 'and she's nineteen. Her favourite music is metal and deathcore: "Those metalcore breakdowns are the shit", and she'd love to follow Avenged Sevenfold on their world tour...whoever they are.' Images of Spikester on her back with the band standing over her came to mind, but he kept these to himself.

When he'd finished educating the class on Spikester and her quareness – had the world changed so much since he was young? Back then people were normal, they liked music with lyrics that could be understood, hair colour was predictable, and girls wore clothes that didn't involve brains and skulls – it was his turn to be in the limelight.

'His name is Rock and it's his first time in college. He's forty-five, almost forty-six,' Spikester said loudly, and letting it linger. Why would anyone come to college at his age, she wondered, shouldn't he have been preparing to go into a nursing home or something? 'He often takes in mistreated dogs until they can be re-homed because he has a big garden. He loves Rottweilers and his one will kill someone if he utters a certain word...*ripe*, probably.'

Jabbering ensued as this last detail was met with awe. Maybe he would bring his dog in and give them a demonstration; maybe he'd even tell them the one-word mantra so they could command the dog themselves. It really was a far-out thought.

'His first car was a Cortina, and he had to have pins put in his leg after crashing his motorbike – he has pics if anyone wants to see. Oh, yeah, he also wants to be a professional photographer when he grows up.'

No one had ever heard of a Cortina before, but by the time Spikester (who added the 'grows up' part herself) had finished talking, everyone was enrapt by this character seldom seen in academia.

And so, this continued. Finn thought it would make a great technique if you were a spy trawling for information, or if you wanted to find out more about someone you liked without them realising it - though his younger classmates would have told him that's what social media was for. Even Sadie, who had slipped back onto the table, got in on the act and offered up a little about herself.

'As a tot starting out my first job was reporting on the sport. I'd get all bundled up and trot off to the football games with my thermos. Probably would have been content to do that indefinitely,' she said fondly, 'but alas, it wasn't meant to be. One day the senior journo got sick - and this chick was never sick, hard ass if there ever was one -- and I was given the gig of interviewing a very contentious world leader who was about to authorise the unlawful invasion of another country.

'He had this most oppressive aura. Looking into his eyes was like looking into a tar pit. I was so nervous I could barely hold my pen still, not that it mattered as he'd dismissed me from the start on account of my being a woman.' There was contempt there that hadn't diminished with the years. 'This president also felt that his power was reason enough to make rapacious advances-'

'What's rapacious mean?' Leo quacked.

'Think it means "licentious",' Daisy replied, clearing the way for Sadie to continue on an unbroken keel, and leaving Leo none the wiser.

'-and this is something you'll need to be keyed in about, power and perversion are bedfellows and at times people might expect something in return for a scoop.'

An indistinct tap-tap-tapping was coming from the underside of one of the tables. 'I'd have kneed him in the shrimps.'

'You can't just knee the president in the shrimps, Ashley,' Mia scolded, smiling self-consciously at a roomful of people she wasn't on speaking terms with yet.

'Why not?' she lashed back, her leg settling down, 'he was using his power to be a creep.'

Mia shrugged. She had known Ashley long enough to know there was a good chance the president would have been writhing around in agony and wheezing out for his security team to come in and save him.

'I couldn't afford to lose that job.' When the unabashed groping had continued, Sadie decided that she would use the pen rather than the sword and her piece had gone viral long before the days when anything went viral. 'Instead, I wrote a slightly different composition than they expected, and the reason why I never covered another sports story.'

'Who was the president?' voiced a fresh-faced teenager, who was swivelling deftly on one chair leg.

'You'll have to use your snooping prowess if you want to know that.' Sadie replied, goading the draftee into utilizing what was a journalist's bread and butter.

'I'm going to find out,' he said, adamantly. 'What's your second name again?'

Sadie chuckled. 'Louis, isn't it?'

Louis grinned and his scraggy mop top threatened to smother all capacity of observation as thin strands fought their way like vines into his eye sockets.

'Finding that out is the easy part, Louis.'

Daisy couldn't stop a restlessness promulgating her entire body. She was imagining a man who wasn't Japanese regarding her expectantly and it struck her with a deep-seated repugnance. 'What do we do if someone wants something for a scoop?'

'Depends on who's asking.' Rock replied.

'Only you can decide what you would do in such a situation,' Sadie answered, 'but there are things that once you sell, you can never get back.'

'Like, what would we have to sell?' Leo was unaware that becoming a journalist would require him to sell his possessions.

Spikester twisted one of the piercings that cut through her chops till it twinged just enough. 'Probably your wrestling figurines.'

'The most important thing to know about the media,' Sadie made eye contact with everyone in the class, 'is that it's rotten. Don't believe a word you hear or read. It's all bullshit.'

By this stage, Leo was totally confounded, and he wasn't the only one. And if he'd known he might have to sell his wrestling figures just to make someone spill the beans, he never would have traded his Hogan bandana for that voice recorder.

'Every owner and every editor are run by an agenda,' she said. 'This can be a simple bias on their part, or it can be something far more sinister. We all know actions speak louder than words, but narratives speak louder than both.' Her seriousness gave way to a wry smile, 'but we'll get to that in due course. Until then, go home and get some rest, because tomorrow is the start of things to come.'

* * * *

Rock pulled the can away as pilsner toppled over the goblet and onto the counter. Grabbing a wet cloth, he swabbed it up: if Suzy didn't get home soon, he'd have to ring one of those helpline numbers just so he could tell *someone* how his day went.

Athena got up off the floor and pootled out to the hall door, a sure giveaway she was home.

'Hi, love.' Rock said, a mite less than breezily.

Suzy hauled a carrier bag up onto the kitchen table. 'Shops were manic. Then there was an accident on the way back and we had to be diverted around it.' She held a breath for a count of five to centre herself before fishing out a dozen free-range eggs. 'Dinner's going to be a little late.'

'Oh, right, that sucks...I mean about the accident.'

Suzy could sense him fretting from a good way into the fridge. 'How was college?' she asked into a jar of mayonnaise. 'God, it feels weird saying that.'

'I was late, can you believe it? - me, of all people!' Rock replied, dragging out a chair and slugging down more foam than liquid.

Extricating herself from between the cottage cheese and yesterday's leftovers, she said, 'Actually, I can't.' Suzy was about to add that whenever she kept him waiting he would throw a strop before he sailed on.

'The teacher gave me this look when I walked in. Now I'm going to be branded the late kid for the whole year!'

'Don't be silly,' she replied, 'of course you won't.'

'The others didn't seem to notice,' he said, 'too busy staring at one of the girls.'

Suzy rummaged through the groceries, looking for any more perishables. 'I hope you weren't staring?'

'Of course not, honey.' Rock wrapped his arms around her waist and pulled her towards him. 'You're the only girl for me.'

Holding a litre bottle of skimmed milk, she smiled down at his upturned face. He could be such a charmer sometimes.

'Though if you suddenly got really fat or lost your looks I might have to reconsider.'

Suzy passed the milk to her other hand and cuffed him across his head. 'Unless I'm six feet under, you're not allowed near another woman. And even then there's conditions.'

He carped like someone in great pain and buried his head in her stomach. 'Don't go near your friend Janey, I know, you've told me a thousand times.'

'You know she's got the clap?'

'Right she does,' Rock replied cynically, withdrawing from her belly button.

'Got it from one of those greasy Italians last summer.' Janey didn't have the clap, but Suzy didn't want Rock thinking about her till she was deep in the afterlife, then she doubted she'd care.

He groused dolefully before returning to the safety of her midriff. 'But she's the only one of your friends I let into the house!'

Suzy was pleased by her cunning. He could be so naïve at times. 'Apart from being a late Larry, how was today?'

'It was good.' Rock didn't think Janey had gotten with anyone in Italy. He'd be sure to bring it up next time she popped by for a spritzer just in case Suzy was playing him for a halfwit. 'Teacher's nice, class seem alright...although some of them are right kooks.'

'What do you mean by kooks?'

'You know young people these days,' he replied, 'illuminous hair, names they got off cereal boxes, rings through every part of their body - kooks. And mine is a schoolyard moniker because no one could knock me off the hill, so don't even go there!' he said when he saw that Suzy was about to challenge him about his name.

'You'll be one of them soon,' she teased, 'cool and carefree.'

Rock turned playful. 'You want to fool around with a college guy who can go without checking his phone for a full twenty minutes?'

She wove her arms around his neck. 'How long have you been waiting to say that?'

'For a while now,' he replied, chuffed to be able to say it. 'We could go to third base?'

'Do you even know what third base is?' She ran a finger lightly from the crown of his head down to his nose. She'd always been turned on by bald men. Janey could never understand why.

'Nope, no idea...but I think it might have something to do with boobs.'

He felt her clinch tighten perceptibly. 'What about dinner?'

'Who needs dinner when you have a hunky college guy,' Rock replied, and they left the room hand in hand as suds continued spuming and fizzling over the side of the glass.

Chapter 8

Finn passed the scrap of paper to Rock who was sitting one seat over. The lecture, which was about how to communicate effectively, had taken a turn down Boring Street. It was warm and the sun was blaring in through the windows, making paying attention - or staying awake - quite the chore. It had also come straight after Orwell's sermon about the origin of hats and how they stemmed from the ancient court system; or something like that, it was hard to tell with the college equivalent of bread dipped in coddle.

Rock unfolded the paper. It read:

I have your ruler, the Minions one. If you ever want to see it again you have till the end of class to come up with €3. If you don't pay, you'll have to walk all the way uptown to buy a new one!

He smiled and took up his pen.

You're bluffing. You wouldn't dare harm my ruler. I'll give you €1.50.

Finn read the reply.

Make it €2 - it's a long walk to the stationary shop.

Little went on in the classroom that escaped Ms. Humphreys' attention, just as it didn't now when she saw a note being pushed across Kevin's legion of books for a third time. During the very first lecture - after Sadie had made the class feel good about themselves and the year ahead - Ms. Humphreys had made everyone sit bone straight in their chairs after avowing that as a body-language expert, she knew all the tell-tale signs of when people were up to no good.

She would know, for example, if a student was texting even when there was a backpack and a jumper concealing the phone *and* if that particular student happened to be looking ahead, supposedly paying attention to what she was saying.

Ms. Humphreys was known to like nothing more than using her behavioural analysis skills to humiliate those not giving her class the respect it deserved. There was a rumour going around that after making a boy whose body shape meant his pants were more down than up cry last year, he had been so traumatised after wetting himself (which made his pants droop even further) that he'd never come back.

'Could the two mature students in the back row *please* stop passing notes?'

The class stirred from their affable daydreams and began to laugh when they realised the two oldest had been caught behaving in a way that didn't match their ages. Rock flushed. He wasn't used to being publicly told off by anyone of authority and he thrust the crumpled paper into the side chamber of his pack, the one normally reserved for his flask.

'Quiet!' Ms. Humphreys barked. 'Did you really think you could pull a fast one on me?'

Finn didn't know if they were meant to reply. 'Eh-'

'What was on the note?'

He flushed even brighter than Rock had under the weight of the classes' attentiveness. 'It was a ransom note.'

She looked around again only this time with the aim of whipping up a joint accord in denouncing absurdity. 'What was the ransom about?' she said.

'Rock's *Minions* ruler.'

Her exasperation was trained and punctured, like the headmistress of a boarding school after pulling someone up for playing truant. 'And why, pray tell, were you ransoming Rock's *Minions* ruler?'

'I thought it would be easy money,' he sheepishly answered, but when Finn heard the resumption of laughter he was spurred on by the classes' amusement. 'We were just practicing one of those old-fashioned methods of communication you were telling us about.'

The room went as quiet as her glacial stare. 'What was that?'

'Nothing,' he replied quickly, figuring it best to quit while he was ahead.

'It had better be,' Her eyes narrowed and became hard like lacquered teal, 'because if I ever catch you passing notes again, I'll–'

The church bell rang out as it did at the same time every day, and as fortune would have it, the call to prayer also coincided with the call to journalise, which meant a change of venue.

'Go, go, go,' Finn urged, as he and Rock scuttled out like quick-moving crabs, leaving Ms. Humphreys stuck behind a languid crowd.

* * * *

Having made a swift getaway from a huffing Ms. Humphreys, they nipped in ahead of a group of girls whose faces had been layered with spread-on tan, and they grabbed the last of the benches on the campus grounds.

'Tough luck, ladies,' Rock said. Oblivious to their death stares, they continued to the shelter just off the car park. The shelter was a godsend in the rain but cold in the shade and today the sun was out, just as it had been since the first day of college.

'Wonder what Ms. Humphreys would do if she caught us again?' Finn also wondered if Ms. Humphreys had been recruited from one of those clandestine military installations.

'Not sure I want to find out,' Rock replied.

The space was quickly filled as the others caught up with them, and just when Leo thought he'd secured the last bit of real estate, the leaning tower of student weight spouted him from the bench.

'Ha!' Simon commiserated, gawking down at a disorientated Leo, and using the ball of his foot to tip him over again.

Louis took a lengthy box from his bag and placed it in front of him. 'You guys want to play Bad Boy Cards?'

Louis was in his late teens and grew up in an area barely big enough to support the obligatory two-pubs-per-town rule. And, being from a small town, it wasn't always the most forward-thinking place and Louis's personality – which was a mashup of sleuth and purveyor of the untried – hadn't always been given the type of free reign it craved. He often felt so restricted living there, that games like these were his way of being able to express himself without being judged too heavily by the town's folk.

'What's Bad Boy Cards?'

Louis paused for a second. 'Well, Rock, the rules are simple,' he replied, doling out cards to everyone who'd taken weight off their legs, 'whoever has the funniest, most offensive set of cards wins.'

'Think I'll be good at this,' Rock said, and a good-natured slap almost sent Leo from the bench a second time.

Aggrieved that he'd been usurped by Sophia, beauty pageant princess with a dark side on the very last deal, Louis pressed forward after Kevin had made everyone aware of what time it was by playing Morse code on his watch face. 'Still think mine was better,' he muttered, stomping his way past Sadie.

Finn nudged Rock with his elbow. 'The Amish are a tough act to beat, Louis.'

'Nothing beats brown people!' he impugned.

'Come on in,' Sadie said, after feeling the rustle of air-in-motion on her skin, 'I won't ask why you're late – those cards can be surprisingly gratifying though, can't they?' Louis looked back to the others with a smile as wide as a circus clown. 'As I was just saying guys, you're going to split into three groups. Each group needs to come up with six questions, a question each basically.'

'What kind of questions should they be?'

'I was just getting to that, Leo,' Sadie replied with a whiff of impatience. 'I want you to think of questions that move the dial, questions that are difficult to answer because the answers aren't necessarily black and white. For example, if I were to ask, let's see…should a woman be responsible for using or supplying contraception if she decides to sleep with a man?'

'No way!' Mia protested, 'Why should the woman have to be responsible for that?'

'Kind of makes sense. You know how irresponsible guys can be,' Rock replied.

'Good, that's exactly what I'm looking for,' Sadie said, interjecting before a condom fight broke out, 'questions that divide opinion because of the moral dilemma they pose. The only thing I ask is that you are completely honest. You're naturally going to have conflicting viewpoints, but that's perfectly normal, doesn't mean you're right and the other person is wrong...so hold your judgements – *judge ye not*, and all that jazz.'

As they were mustering into their groups there came a knock at the door. On the heels of the principal loped in a rather serious student who looked as if he were caught under an interrogation lamp. Finn guessed it was probably the fright of being thrown into a class as it was ongoing, something that had once delayed his own schooling after he'd soiled his itchy and ill-fitting pants.

'This is the new student who will be joining you, Sadie.' The principal stated incisively. 'His name is Rodrick.'

'Fredrik.'

'You're most welcome, Fredrik,' Sadie said cheerfully, catching his utterance. 'Which group is short a person?'

'Think we are.'

'Perfect, jump in with Hugh's group over there.' The new student trooped wordlessly to the edge of the foreign group and flopped onto the spare seat.

The class began brainstorming, attempting to come up with meritorious parameter-pushers like Sadie had asked. Finn's group was still one short when Fredrik, who'd been mute ever since sitting down, finally spoke. 'Would you rather fuck a goat, and everyone believed you hadn't, or not fuck a goat and everyone believed you had?'

If introductions could win medals, then this guy, who Finn thought looked Mexican - albeit an unusually pale Mexican - took the gold. 'That's our last question,' Finn said, wiping the tears from his eyes. Maybe being under an interrogation lamp wasn't quite so accurate, he mused. 'Who's going to say it?'

'I'll do it.' Red offered before anyone else could reply.

Red had come by his nickname because of the fluffy red tussock germinating from his chin - and he was quite content with that because he hated his real name and still held it against his mother, who'd called him Ernesto after an unrequited love during the Psychedelic era. Like Rock, only two decades his junior, Red hadn't seen any further education after the age of fifteen. He found his place on ships, often spending weeks trawling the seas until enough fish had hurled themselves into his net. He liked being at sea, he was comfortable there, and until over-fishing had decimated fish stocks, the last place Red saw himself was in a stuffy college with stuffy rules. Red did whatever Red wanted whenever Red wanted and being trapped in a classroom made him considerably antsy.

When the issue of contraception came up again (with most agreeing that both parties should share responsibility, particularly as men often misplaced their wallets), Louis said the only time he had ever worn a condom was when he'd put one over his head and blown it up using his nose. Rock also suggested that if a marriage runs aground, traditional roles should be reversed, that men gain custody and women pay men maintenance so *they* could go on shopping sprees every month.

'It's probably good that women aren't presidents,' Dot piped up, answering her own question, but forgetting to voice aloud if women could do the same jobs just as well as their male counterparts.

'What do you mean?' enquired Mia.

'In fairness like,' Dot replied, head twitching slightly like she was fighting a nervous tic, 'we're a bit all over the place, aren't we?

'I mean we're always changing our minds,' she continued, 'not exactly the most decisive people in the world. Like, what if there was a war or something important and we kept changing our minds and everyone died...that'd be a balls.'

Finn thought that a swift return to the days of lynching was imminent as a taut pall emanated from the perfumed nucleus of the group.

'I'm not sure we're any worse than men when it comes to that?' Daisy said, lacking conviction.

'Were you asleep during the whole Little Mix girl-power revolution?' Ashley said, gobsmacked at such a slight against their gender – and by one of their own!

Rock and Finn smiled at each other, basking in the awkward, almost primordial quandary the girls found themselves. It was like Dot had held up a mirror and forced each of them to gaze into it.

'I believe we can,' Mia replied robustly, 'look at Merkel in Germany and your one in Argentina. They seem to be doing good jobs and there hasn't been a world war yet, not like when men are in power.'

Louis was jouncing backwards and forwards with two chair legs off the floor. 'You guys would be too busy gossiping about the ride of a minister sitting next to you in an oval office.'

'You mean *the* Oval Office?' Daisy said.

'Yeah, those round rooms where the politicians go and have tea and talk about stuff.'

Kevin blushed when Mia kneaded his arm and mouthed thanks after he said that he thought 'girls...females' were very competent.

'Only been two World Wars so far,' Finn said after Louis had clarified the inner workings of the establishment, 'and men have been in power forever.'

'Maybe if women were in charge there wouldn't have been any.' Mia retorted, smiling dismissively.

'Maybe there would have been three?' Finn was enjoying stoking the battle of the sexes' embers.

Dot projected her arm outwards like a tremulous superheroine, 'First equality,' she cried, 'then the world!'

'Shut up, Finn,' Mia said, berating her more mature classmate, while at the same time blanking Dot who wasn't doing womankind any good, 'I know you're only messing!'

He grinned and did as he was told. Mia was right, women were taking over. And if they were anything like Angela Merkel then he wanted to keep on their good side.

'My turn.' Ashley had decided to touch on the current hot potato that was hoarding the international presses. 'Would you take in a refugee who needed a place to live?' Her main reason for asking this was to lessen her feelings of self-reproach for not fostering a refugee because she didn't have the money – or ultimately, desire – to share a twenty-box of McNuggets with them, her favourite food.

'No way,' Rock said determinedly. 'They'd rob my cameras!'

'I have expensive trainers. What if he was the same size as me and he put them on and went walking around in the mud?' Hugh added, utterly concerned.

'If they were escaping the boogeyman and were genuinely in trouble then yeah, I'd consider it,' Finn said, as the answers came in a flurry.

'What do you mean the boo-' Leo tried asking who the 'boogeyman' was before his words were coated by a shrill avalanche.

'Yes!' Emily sounded like a pre-adolescent boy who had discovered that his magic wand could conjure more than just pee. 'I'd bring them home and love them!'

When the laughter eventually died down the topic changed to animals - in particular, pounds - and whether dogs should continue to be put down if they aren't claimed. Most were totally against the idea of killing - 'murdering', as Sophia insisted - innocent dogs who had done no harm to anyone.

'Anyone puts Athena down and they'll be following her up there.' Rock jabbed his pencil into the desk, chipping the nib away.

Leo regrouped and tried again. Emily might have been kind, but she sure was rude, too. 'Like, why would you put them down?'

Rock hoofed his pencil into his oversized yellow and blue parer. 'It's cheaper to do away with them than fee-'

'No!' The nebulous timbre of Emily's voice enfolded the anger in Rock's like fascia enfolding organs, 'I'd bring them home and love them!'

'Is there anything you wouldn't love?' Dot turned to Mia. 'She's cracked, that one.'

Emily was one of those who struggled to fit in with the harsh realities around them, especially in their formative years before fantasy could become something more tangible. She disappeared days later, never to be seen again, no doubt searching for that elusive white rabbit, or white refugee.

It was now the turn of the last group. But before they delivered their own white rabbit, Finn asked: 'Would you help a close friend or relative take their own life if they felt they couldn't go on?'

'Oh, good one,' Sadie quipped, appreciating the question's complexities, though unaware of its origins. 'Hugh, what would you do?'

Hugh puffed his cheeks. 'Don't think I'd be able to watch someone die in front of me and be the one responsible for it.'

'What if a Liverpool player asked you?' Gibby said, raking her scalp. Gibby was the one who Rock alluded to as having illuminous hair and the purple dye she was always applying came from a can and caused a 'hell's itch', as she put it.

'That's a different story,' Hugh replied candidly.

Spikester said she would but only if she could choose the manner of death; 'petrol and a match, quick and easy,' she maintained, much to the others' dismay.

'Remind me never to get with her.' Rock whispered over to Finn.

'Don't think there's much chance of that,' Finn whispered back.

Rock said there were some people he'd help even if they wanted to go on living. Few cared about the legal consequences – though Hugh did remind people that he was far too pretty for life behind bars – but rather the thought of seeing someone they love, and someone they didn't want to die, leaving them.

'How about you Simon,' Sadie was now moving fluidly between seats, 'what's your take on it?'

Simon looked away, unable to speak, save for some incoherent muttering.

Sadie's teacher antennae clucked to alert her that something was amiss. 'Are you alright, Simon?'

'Yeah...just, I've been through that before,' he replied, low enough that only Sadie and his group could hear.

'Leo, you're up next,' she said, swiftly taking the reins and trotting on.

It turned out that Simon's pen pal, in a letter he'd received from him when he was young, had jested about killing himself after losing his first crush to a 'bronzed boy' down the street. At least Simon had thought it was a joke, but when he never heard from Pablo again, he assumed that he'd gone ahead and trekked off into the desert (he wasn't sure how Spanish people took their own lives), and the memory of his death was still raw.

'Only if I could finish them off with a wrestling move – like a tombstone,' Leo said, perfectly serious. 'I've seen people die from that move!'

'Where did you see that, Leo, Imagination World?' Sophia asked sarcastically.

'No, just...places,' Leo replied, not expecting to be challenged. What was wrong with sprucing a story up a dink if it made it better?

Finn set out that he absolutely would help someone. It wasn't long ago that he himself had considered jumping and he remembered the option had given him morbid comfort; maybe just by knowing you had a way out could give you that comfort, he mulled. Now he shuddered at the thought.

'And Red, last but certainly not least,' Sadie blazed, relishing, as she always did, the peeling of onion layers and the emergence of candour and the often-suppressed veracity of feeling, 'the honour of the final conundrum.'

'Alright,' Red began, 'would you rather fuck a goat...'

'Ok, folks, that's us for the day.' Sadie heralded once they'd finished discussing the intricacies of Red's catch-22. Simon, after recovering from the recollection of his long-dead pen pal, said he'd prefer to 'make love' to the goat and had instantly regretted answering first. Billie, the class tomboy who valued cute shoes above all else, said she wouldn't fuck it but would enjoy telling the story of how she had, while Louis said he'd once seen a film involving such a thing; no one was much surprised.

'Remember,' Sadie said as they were packing away their stuff (and as Rock was making sure that no *Minion* was left behind), 'this is your safe year, a year to push the boundaries and see how far they budge. Don't be afraid to voice opinions. It doesn't matter if you're the only one in class with them, that's your entitlement. It doesn't even matter if they're wrong – if there is such a thing.'

Finn nodded intently like he was listening to a stranger giving him directions. He had really lucked out getting this teacher, though he could see some of the younger ones around him were perplexed by the idea that 'wrong' might not exist.

Sadie held up her pen like it was Excalibur's blade. 'So be brave with your speech and bold with your pen and you never know what you might discover about yourselves,' she said like she knew something the rest of the class didn't.

*　*　*　*

Finn arched his neck upwards as six planes played swords with their contrails across the sky. He had just come from the Department of Education, a domed erection that looked like the inflamed privates of a woman who'd let too many suitors through her door. The man he'd been dealing with was not one bit happy as he relayed how, despite not being entitled to an education grant, a clerical booboo had been made, and now that he'd physically relocated to Bridgewater, it couldn't be rescinded.

Finn presumed that some fed-up pencil-pusher rushing to leave the office on a Friday had used the wrong stamp, and he had grinned broadly against the glower of the civil servant. He could now afford to live with a roof over his head for the entire course and not just till the spooks came out at Halloween. And what better way to celebrate the bungling of a dozy bureaucrat – and the opportunity to include a daily helping of meat in his diet – than an early evening pint of Guinness?

'You look happy,' said the bargirl, throwing down a beer mat and setting his drink onto it.

'I'm celebrating,' he replied, Ava's prediction of a fortuitous 'mistake' not landing as Finn had been elsewhere when she'd said it.

'Oh? What's the celebration?'

Ingrained wrinkles manifested as he smiled and drew a line in the condensation on the glass. 'Things working out.'

'I love that feeling,' she replied, and then added an easy smile of her own, 'doesn't happen often mind.' Her voice peaked at the end, suggesting she'd already exonerated life of any further stork deliveries.

'Just keep expecting it all to fall apart,' he said.

'If it does, it does.' She waved her hand as if swatting away a wasp. 'You can always try something else, and then if that fails, come back here and I'll join you for a few of these.'

Finn resumed watching the aerial dogfights after she hastened back inside. He couldn't shake the feeling that this was all a dream; that he was going to wake up in the morning and be right back in his bed, the one that hugged him so tight it was impossible to leave. Why was everything turning out the way it was meant to, the way he wanted? *Maybe one of the pilots will make an error in judgement and I'll be decapitated by a hurtling propeller – or toilet seat lid,* he thought, tracing the white streamers above. *That would derail my fancy new life for sure.*

There was only one thing for it. He'd just need to listen out for any mid-air collisions from now on; wouldn't hurt to be careful when out walking, too – lots of cracked pavement slabs in Bridgewater, even tripped on one on his way to the meeting. 'Don't want to ruin a good thing before it starts,' Finn mumbled into the velvety lather of his drink, concluding that he'd have to be careful with everything. 'Might go to the furniture shop and relieve them of their bubble wrap, wrap myself in it just in case.'

Chapter 9

The sun continued its relentless assault as the bus pulled up to the college. It was just after nine, normally the time Hugh was running stop signs and lecturers were consoling each other about what room they were going to first. But this Monday was a little different, this Monday there were no classes.

Instead of being stuck inside learning about media law (and how best to legally rip someone to shreds without having all your money taken away for defamation), the class was going on a field trip, and that they'd be missing Orwell's snooze-fest made that Monday all the sweeter. Orwell was moulded from early generations of education-givers and had a habit of going so far off the syllabus reservation that most of the time students had little idea what he was talking about; or, for that matter, what subject he was teaching. The monotony was so overwhelming at times that students would stand up, mutter some unintelligible excuse, and groggily leave the room to keep their sanity intact.

Boarding first, and instinctively yomping down to the back seats, perhaps the type of rebellious personalities journalism tended to attract was the reason the bus was late setting off. Along with signing his name, Leo also jotted down the name of one, Nikola T. on the attendance sheet. It had taken much counting and brainwork for the accompanying chaperones to realise that Nikola was not part of the entourage and would not be travelling with them.

'Shocking behaviour that,' Rock quipped, as the chaperones sought their seats at the front after realising that they'd been had.

'Truly electrifying.' Louis agreed from the row behind, gently placing his hands on Rock's cranium to better assess its shape.

Having misjudged the seating arrangements, Harold, a student from the art class, found himself isolated and cornered like a buffalo that had become separated from its herd. Contrasting sharply with the almost Zen stillness of the more creatively-minded who sat silently up the front (*they* would have respect for the teachers and for the bus driver who had been entrusted to drive them safely to the coast), Finn watched as Harold pulled his rucksack and portfolio bag close against the raucousness, unsure if he liked hugging things or if he was just one of those people who wasn't quite the full block of cheddar.

The destination for the day was the beach and, by either divine luck or blessing, it was also a day when no cloud dared cross in front of the big ball of flames in the sky. The bus turned into an empty car park that overlooked a wide expanse of blue, shimmering in the sunshine, and remains of an old castle guarded the entrance to the bay like an antiquated defender. Rock said if they couldn't get some proper photos they should all be kicked off the course and their cameras seized by some form of photographic authority.

The coastline jutted out like wide smiles rising and falling, leaving curving beaches in its wake. Small hills of white stones cleared to sand before running into tiny wave breaks which were like ripples from the flickering of tadpoles in a pond.

'You guys on for a climb?' Rock nodded to what was ahead. 'Get some great shots from up there.'

The ocean had gorged its way through the cliff, leaving a proud stack standing in the water. Even though it looked like a difficult ascent, Rock had already made up his mind. If he could scale a mountain, then a sea stack would be a cakewalk.

Finn glanced up, the stack towering over them like a wild animal, dangerous and dramatic. 'I think we could get up there.'

'Count me out, too risky for my liking.' Simon stated. 'Anyway, I had three jambons before we left so I'm not really in the mood for climbing.'

Rock poked Simon's gut with his tripod. 'You certainly aren't, big boy.'

He moved his hand to the place where he'd been poked. 'I'm going on a diet, Rock, okay,' he replied indignantly, 'I've already bought loads of ingredients.'

'Say most of them are out of date at this stage.' Rock turned around and didn't see Simon clenching his fists. He couldn't remember the last time he'd been in a fight, but at that moment Simon would gladly have slapped that stupid cap – which made him look like a taxi-cab driver – right off Rock's head. 'Who else is up for a little treacherous climb?'

'I'll come,' Hugh said, running his hand through his Panthera-esque mane. 'I'm a good climber and I'm not carrying any extra weight like Simon.'

'Fuck's sake, lads.'

'Sorry, Simon, but you know what I mean,' Hugh replied.

Simon snorted and fished a bar of chocolate from his pocket. 'Whatever.'

When Gibby, who was concerned about her ability to hold on and massage the itch at the same time, and Mia opted out, Leo pointed to a boulder and said it would skewer his whole body were he to fall on it.

'You're not going then?' Rock queried.

'No, it would make me into a toffee apple!' he replied.

'Not going, lads,' Dot chittered, 'I'm on my period and I'm not wearing my rock-climbing tampons.'

Simon spluttered on the square of chocolate that he'd popped into his mouth.

'Oh, Dot,' Mia said, wincing at Dot's coarseness.

'I want to go too.' They all turned to Sophia. 'You guys aren't the only ones who want good photos, you know.'

The four of them trotted their way across the wet sand to the base of the cliffette, which looked even higher up close. But the vista from the top made the slick hustle across sheeny rocks worthwhile as an ice-rink calm sea skated its way out to the horizon. They took silhouettes of each other against a luminous sky before black and whites helped to create a sanguine sense of solitude.

'What are you lot doing up there?!' The art teacher's voice was distant but laced with anger. 'Come down here at once or there'll be trouble!'

Hugh deposited his hand-me-down palm shooter – which Rock said equated to a disposable – back into its pouch. 'Guess we better go before she turns green.'

'Should just put collars around our necks.' Finn grumbled.

'Come on guys,' Sophia called, skipping her way to the grassy edge, 'let's go and get some more shots!'

They had almost made it safely down when Finn slipped on one of the rocks which had been dampened by earlier waves when the tide had headed back towards the shore. He grabbed a handful of grass – the strong, wiry type common to the coast – and managed to right himself before he came to grief on the same rock.

'Did you enjoy your fall?' Hugh joshed, before immediately slipping. 'Agghhhh, shit, shit, shit!' he said, blowing out his cheeks and grasping his shin.

'Ouch,' Finn said, smirking. 'That looked kind of sore.'

Hugh rolled up his jeans to reveal what looked like a nick from a lightsaber. 'I'm bleeding, look.'

'Ah, that's nothing, Wolfie. Your body will have that healed in minutes.'

Hugh glanced up, ready to tell him where he could stick his *Wolfie,* but Finn was already climbing down off the last rock. 'Did you enjoy your fall?' he was saying, shaking his head, and chuckling at karma's instant redress.

From the beach, they traced their way along tiny boreens, roads where horses and carts once clip-clopped and where sprigs of green broke through and prospered along the asphalt meridian. A river, untroubled by time, guided them to a castle that was so old that Rock was forced to admit he hadn't been around when it was built. The surrounding valley rose gently and fell from the turrets back to the mouth of the bay, and an elevated position on the hillock meant that invaders from the east would have been seen hours before they arrived, allowing plenty of time to prepare for the siege, but also plenty of time to stew about what might be.

Below the ruins and not far from where a thicket of thorns was allowing graveyard residents an uninterrupted slumber, Rock corralled everyone for a group photo. Being the consummate professional, he had wirelessly synched his **DSLR** with his phone, meaning that his phone had now turned into his camera. At least that's what Finn concluded had happened, technology was like sorcery to him, and he was yet to figure out what 'tagging' somebody meant.

After a picnic lunch, they set off along the river on the two-mile walk for the bus. Yellow gorse bushes flared out across the path and ran up the banks making it impossible to see over them and made you feel entombed in the countryside. The sun at their backs, Billie took photos of long shadows that jived and whirled and recast themselves into animals and cowboys and famous actresses wearing cocktail dresses. It was so idyllic that Finn felt the only thing missing was an upbeat 60s tune playing in the background.

They wheeled past where Simon and Harold had found a small clearing for a breather. 'Look at them dancing like that just because they can see their shadows,' Harold grunted, snapping off a corner of chocolate from his 1kg block of rum raisin. 'I see mine all the time.'

Simon stuffed a handful of crisps into his mouth and they both belched at the same time. 'So immature.'

'Not a lot has changed since I was young,' said an old man who had collared Finn and one of the star pupils from the art class after they'd spotted a dragonfly sunbathing on a bird feeder, 'apart from a pathway and a few benches, that is.'

They both nodded, humouring the man who was leaning on a cane.

'The castle was ransacked by Cromwell and his merry men, you know,' he told them without much encouragement, 'what's more, it never would have fallen if her protectors weren't so desperate for a drink – and I'm not talking about the stuff you get out of there.' He pointed his cane at the river.

The girl was carrying a small pad and had sketched the dragonfly with more realism than Finn thought possible. 'They weren't allowed a drink?' she said.

'By decree of the lady of the house, they certainly weren't. And how they had mocked her when she ordered they be given milk when all they wanted was a drop of mead to ease their frayed nerves.'

Finn could only imagine the kind of thirst that defending a castle for a day would build.

'Obviously gave no thought to creatives in those days,' the star student replied glibly, flicking at the wing with her pencil a final couple of times.

The art teacher sent Harold across the laps of Mia and Billie on the bus as she fought to get past. 'What was that?' she asked.

'Yeah, that's why they're late back,' Rock replied, after Hugh noticed the empty space in front of him and enquired as to Finn's whereabouts, 'they've snuck off into the reeds. God only knows what they're getting up to.'

Billie shoved Harold out of her space. 'The dog!' The way Billie was feeling lately, she would gladly have gotten her shoes wet for a chance to sneak off into the reeds.

'But...' the teacher stammered, 'she has a boyfriend?'

Rock lumbered across into his seat. 'What can I tell you?' he said, 'Finn's quite the operator.'

'So desperate were they for mead,' the old man continued, 'and thinking that Cromwell would reward them handsomely for handing over the castle, the gunner raised the white flag and surrendered.'

'Did they get the mead?' Finn pressed, enthralled by the old man's story.

He pulled his flat cap down as if out of reverence. 'Possibly in the next life,' he replied, 'Cromwell set to butchering them and he hung the gunner for being a traitor. They left one person alive in which to bury the dead.'

Finn was still dwelling on what it would have been like to have been the only one left alive, having to bury all your family and friends (and if being slaughtered wouldn't have been kinder providence), and he was bemused by the commotion as cheers went up when they finally got on the bus. The teacher frowned at the girl; she had thought more of her. Finn looked at Rock who brought his hand to his mouth and pretended to kiss it. He grinned and took a bow, and the teacher pursed her lips and told him to hurry up and take his seat.

*

Harold was snoring with his cheek buried in Simon's shoulder as Bridgewater Tech loomed into range.

'I don't even care what it looks like,' Billie was saying to Mia, 'just want to see one again.'

Finn looked out the window as a factory that wasn't there last year flashed by. Their tagline was, *Crisps for a Modern Generation*, and Finn had already tried most of the new flavours, which promised to 'satisfy a contemporary palette'. He still preferred good old salt and vinegar, but that was probably because he wasn't modern anymore.

'I'm sure you'll meet someone soon.' Mia knew what it was like not to have anyone she could brag to about her achievements, and she felt an empathy that stopped just short of pity for Billie.

She pared back the rubber sealing that had come loose from around the window. 'What's your fella's like?'

'I'm not telling you that.' Mia replied.

'Go on - how big is it?' Billie pulled her thumb as far away from her index finger as she could, 'this big?'

Mia laughed and pushed Billie's hand away. 'No!'

'Lads,' Simon chirped from a few rows back, 'he's asleep on my shoulder here.'

'He's drooling on it too.' Rock reached into his case for his camera.

Simon was about to shake him off when Rock told him to keep still. 'It is a photography course after all,' he said and began taking photos of a diffusing wet patch that looked as if a newborn had regurgitated on him.

'Give him a little kiss, Simon,' Billie encouraged, and this time Simon shook him off like an over-grown bluebottle.

Harold drowsily used his sleeve to dry his mouth. 'What are you doing?'

'What do you mean what am I doing? You were asleep and–'

Simon saw the congealed pool of saliva on his t-shirt. 'Ugghh, look what you've done!' he wailed, horrified that his favourite t-shirt had become a spit bowl. 'There's even a chocolate stain – look!'

'I didn't mean it!' Harold rounded up his stuff and charged from his seat.

'Awhhhhh!' Simon's expression changed from disgust to agony as he leaned forward and clutched at his ankle, 'he stomped on me!'

Harold's considerable girth clanged against the seats on both sides of the coach, and he ricocheted forward like a pinball, bags threshing uncontrollably from his shoulders. Hugh's head got in the way of the first and Finn jinked away just in time from the other.

'Boorish miscreants!' Harold spat, before finally extricating himself after the pneumatic door had finished decompressing.

*

Finn didn't want the day to end. It had been perfect, the type of day that was so rare it had to be milked for everything it was worth when it did come along. Most of the class loitered on the path outside the college, seemingly uninterested in catching lifts or walking home. So, the troupe - or eight of them, at least - strolled uptown (the song could have been *Uptown Girl*, Finn thought, as a skateboarder bobbled by them on the cobbles). They bought coffee out of a dispenser from a local shop - which had bucked convention by employing only refugees - and sipped them on a huge tree that had been fashioned into an organic chaise longue in the centre of town.

Finn held his face up to the sun. *If only it could be like this all the time*, he was thinking. 'You doing that assignment tonight?'

'In this weather?' Rock replied dreamily, enjoying the feel of warmth on his skin, 'more chance of me letting Simon go down-'

The sound of raised voices distracted Rock from relaying that he'd rather let Simon pleasure him than do an assignment under such delightful atmospheric conditions. Three men were singing, but it wasn't the smooth, rhythmic singing of people who could hold a note, but the grating rasp of people who were either drunk or high - or both.

'*I'd love to make love to you...you little daisy doo*,' the loudest of the men crooned at an approaching strut, who was wearing as few clothes as the good weather allowed. 'Jasus!' he proclaimed, seeing how her pink booty shorts strained to keep everything in check. 'Look at the ass on you, girl?'

Rock took a slurp of hot coffee through the square opening that always seemed to encourage sploshes. 'Prick,' he muttered.

'Wasn't a bad effort to be fair.' Finn watched as she looked back briefly before quickening her catwalk stride. 'When's the last time you serenaded a girl?'

'When I was about fourteen,' Rock replied, remembering what might just have been the most cringe-worthy moment of his life. 'Didn't go well, she never talked to me again.'

'Should have done the same thing with your ex-wife.'

Rock was about to agree when the boss of the trio did a double take and caught him peering over, disrupting his cock-hardening surveillance of a backside which hot-pants tried but could not tame. 'What the fuck are you looking at?' he said.

Rock shrugged and looked away.

'Hey, I'm talking to *you*, Baldy!' the loudmouth shouted, pawing at his crotch. His two friends were now standing as firmly as they could manage by his side.

'Not looking at anything.' Rock called back. If there was one thing he abhorred, it was being called 'baldy'.

Hugh scrapped circles on the ground with his foot, and the girls bunched together. Finn sipped his coffee as the three began making their way over, annoyed that the perfect day was now tainted by uncertainty and fear.

After he put his caip back on, Rock handed his camera bags to Hugh. 'If anything happens mind these, they're expensive.' Hugh nodded, fumbling, trying to put them around his neck or his shoulder, he wasn't quite sure which. 'And remember to take photos,' Rock stressed to the others, their earlier serenity now a thing of the past.

Rock was always keen to capture events and people how they were. He eschewed anything staged or faked and would never lower himself to being dishonest to his trade, his great love. After his encapsulating stills of the plane crash, he became known as the *Master of Disaster*. If there was anything that needed to be caught for posterity – no matter how tragic or squeamish – he'd be there, camera in hand, lens cap hanging by a rope.

'Taking your bags off, Baldy?' Loudmouth's badgering became more threatening as he spoke. 'Fancy your chances, *do ya*?'

Finn knew things had gone too far, and that no amount of sweet talk would calm the situation. These guys were on something strong, and they weren't going to be appeased by words: They wanted blood.

One person, however, was showing no signs of nerves. With soft, strawberry-blonde hair falling gently over her shoulders, she might have looked dainty and delicate, but Ashley had moxie. She had that irrepressible mix of innocence and sass that could drive a man stir crazy, and rather than cowering, her hand went to her camera like a gunslinger reaching for his gun.

'This your posse of bitches?' Loudmouth said, assaulting Ashley with his deviant ogling. 'You mind if I have one?' but he was slightly unsettled when she didn't look away.

Daisy moved so close to Hugh and Sophia that they almost merged into a new entity, and she focused entirely on a patch of long dried-in street gum that would have taken a wire brush, some acid, and two hours to remove.

'I'm talking to you, ya *BALDY* cun–'

Before he could finish, Rock had risen to his feet, jumped on the born-again tree – praying his leg would take the exertion – and lunged at the ringleader. Rock believed that if it was inevitable you were going to be in a fight, you should always try and get in the first blow, no sense in waiting for a blooded nose.

The timing was perfect. Like two distended paddles, his hands landed on either side of Loudmouth's sternum and bunted him backwards. He let out an angry grunt, but any thoughts of regaining his composure were dashed when Rock landed a box squarely on his chin. The window of the lingerie shop wobbled, and Loudmouth would have fallen into a bin of last season's swimwear if it hadn't been reinforced.

His face darkened as if the sun was being eclipsed by a diurnal moon. Rock was standing over him, fist drawn back, ready to strike again. Loudmouth was a tortured mess of outrage and confusion as he lay in a heap on the ground. His friend, who was almost as shocked as he was, kicked into gear and ranged towards Rock, who had his back turned to him.

Alert to the move, Finn inserted himself between them. 'I wouldn't do that if I was you,' he warned.

The friend's upper lip was now retreating from his yellowing teeth. 'What are you going to do about it, *tourist*?'

Finn heard Hugh titter nervously behind him. For some reason – maybe it was the clothes he wore – Finn always gave the impression of someone who was on holiday. He could never understand why, he'd never even *worn* a Hawaiian shirt before, let alone owned one.

'First of all,' he replied, 'I'm not a tourist, I live here. Second of all, if you decide this is the way you want to play it, you're going to end up lying on the ground over there beside your buddy, probably hugging each other in some pathetic leave-us-alone-we're-not-actually-bad-people-we've-just-had-a-hard-life type of embrace; and let's face it, that would be embarrassing for everyone.'

Finn hoped that a touch of outlandishness could stop the situation from escalating into full-blown-out druggie warfare, and the ugly sneer remained on his face as Loudmouth's friend mulled over his choices.

'But if you want to boogie on down then I'm hot to trot - you beanstalk.'

The guy was unsteady, but he was charged like a battery and lusting after an attack. Finn had already decided that he'd take his legs if it came to that. But the eccentric patter had thrown just enough doubt into the friend's mind, and he couldn't quite bring himself to go through with it. Finn relaxed slightly. He looked around for the third member of the crew, but he'd slunk away after seeing his friend caroming off a knicker-shop window.

Despite Loudmouth being the one on the ground, it was Rock who was seething.

'Please don't hit me, I'm sorry!'

'You're a fucking idiot, coming over here acting like king dick when you have a tiny one!' Rock roared down into his face.

Loudmouth's hands were out in front of his chest like a wounded animal begging for mercy. 'I know. I'm sorry!'

Having capitulated so quickly, rather than making him eat his fist, Rock thought he'd abase him enough so he would think twice about intimidating anyone else in the future. 'What do you have?'

He whimpered. 'A tiny dick.'

'I can't hear you!' Rock's demand caused people to pause over their lattes outside the coffee shop across the square. 'What do you have?!'

'I have a tiny dick!' Loudmouth shouted, sobbing all the while, his hands now covering his face in shameful defeat.

Rock stepped back from the pitiful chunk of entrails which had arranged itself into a foetal position. He was still fuming but his heart rate had slowed some. 'That's exactly what you have.'

Finn moved away from the friend, keeping an eye on him all the while. Passers-by who had stopped to watch also moved on when they saw Loudmouth curled up and crying.

'Sorry it came to that, guys.' Rock took his bags from Hugh whose face had drained of colour. He had been in plenty of fights – and won most of them, Rock would proudly say – but he was struck by a tremor of guilt. He was supposed to be the mature one in a class full of youngsters and he couldn't shake the feeling of being partly to blame for drawing them into a situation that put them all in danger.

'Not much you could have done,' Finn replied, sensing his unease, which was echoed by the others.

Rock caught his furrowed brow lowering back at him from the window of a costume shop. 'Yeah, maybe...thanks for having my back by the way.'

'Pizza this Friday, always a good way to show your appreciation.'

The slightest hint of a smile tugged at his mouth. 'How does a deluxe combo and a milkshake sound?'

'Like you should get into fights more often.' Finn grinned like someone who was on a promise to the best kind of weekend start.

It was more like an urgent exploration than a question, afraid that an opportunity may have been lost forever. 'Did anyone take photos?'

'I did,' Ashley beamed, 'think I got a couple of good ones, too.' Something told her she might just have got one that was better than 'good'.

Rock's wrinkled mush softened like pounded dough. 'Ashley, you little star you!' he said, putting his arm around her and squeezing tightly.

Still skittish from healthy doses of adrenaline, the eight of them floated back towards the college, each amped with the thought of being able to tell everyone they knew what had happened, and how Rock had given some loudmouth idiot - in Leo's words - the smackdown of all smackdowns.

Chapter 10

Twenty-one people had signed up for the journalism course and many of them were sitting under two old oak trees that were still in leaf. The trees had been there for decades, seemed no one knew exactly *how* long, and they towered high above their heads and threw shadows that curved and weaved in between them.

Louis was helping a worm to displace some dry earth. It hadn't rained in so long that even the insects were confused as to why the ground wasn't sodden. 'Where's Rockapoodle today?' he said.

Finn watched the worm disappear into an aperture so deep that a ferret could have hung a *Home Sweet Home* placard on the inside. 'The police called him in to head up a new crime force after hearing what went down yesterday.'

It was the day after the field trip. It was also the day after Rock had rocketed to stardom and would eventually go down in college folklore as 'that scary dude who bashed the junkies'.

'Is he leaving school?' Louis' hand came out of the hole when he couldn't feel the worm anymore.

'Nah,' Finn replied, the concern on Louis' face heart-warming, 'I'm sure they'll let him do both.'

After everybody had gone their separate ways the previous day, Ashley went to the city pharmacy to get some photos printed. Cathy Mac's had a small photography section with a printing hub and was the only place in town to run off digital photographs. Everyone used Cathy's, and if a student forgot to pre-order their prints, they'd be awarded big fat zeros when they couldn't submit their assignments on time. The first time this happened to Louis he tried pleading his case to Lena, the photography teacher, but his appeals had fallen on deaf ears because she overheard him telling Spikester that he didn't do the assignment because 'how could he take a photo of *postulation* when he didn't even know what the word meant?', and that the whole concept was 'as daft as a man with nipples'.

Aside from Harold, who was sitting alone in the canteen, Ashley had been the first into the college that morning. Her knuckles were white from clasping her backpack like she was protecting some far-reaching government dossier. She ranged up to the first of two main notice boards, the ones everyone walked by at some stage of the day and went about clearing a space. Ashley had told the cute guy in Cathy's that she wanted people to be able to see them from the beer garden in Bob's. The cost had stung, but he only charged her for one and she had given him an extra-long wave leaving the store. Removing a pouch from the bag, Ashley went about sticking four red-headed push pins through each corner of the overflowing photograph. She did this twice, and when she had finished it felt as if Rock was coming at you from every direction.

After being absent from the early classes, Rock arrived in just before lunch. He shambled along the corridor lost in thought, head reeling at what he'd been told. He had gone to find out why the rods weren't helping and why, if anything, his leg seemed to be getting progressively worse.

'We're not sure what the problem is,' The doctor with the blue shirt and stethoscope had said, 'but if the pain continues to worsen, we might have to remove the pins. Only thing is, if we do that and there's still no improvement, which is likely, you could lose the leg.'

He looked at but didn't register the soup stain where Orwell had tipped his cup swerving to avoid Hugh who had been endeavouring to beat the bell. What good was a photographer with only one leg? Rock needed his leg, he needed both of them. Photographers didn't have the luxury of taking choreographed shots on squishy sod while being fanned by jungle boys with monstrously big leaves. No, interesting photos tended to hide off the beaten track, and you needed to be able to get down and dirty and into a slew of positions - like a Kama Sutra contortionist getting the perfect shot from the perfect angle - which often meant kissing wet ground or traipsing over ankle-shattering terrain (which certainly wasn't squishy) in horrendous weather fit only for creatures of the deep; unless, of course, you were one of those scruffy porkers who Rock felt gave the vocation - no, the art - a bad name, the ones who turn up wearing ketchup-stained tracksuits and a t-shirt that barely covers their swollen guts. They get a few cushy snaps, wash down some wieners with a glass or two of vinegary wine, and then go home and pull themselves off to a photo of some movie star they'd taken from a distance.

Sometimes photographs were a bitch. They wanted you to toil for them. Rock thought of these as beautiful women. If you wanted to take them home, then you damn well had to work hard for the privilege. How could he be the Master of Disaster with only one leg, for Christ's sake? He'd be the Master of *Crippled Photography*, or *Crippled Disaster*, or some other thing that didn't have the same ring to it. You never saw Long John taking a photo and it wasn't because he didn't have a camera, it was because he only had one leg!

Applause rattled Rock from his saturnine wallowing. He had been so preoccupied that he didn't realise he'd entered the room. He looked around at the cheering, smiling faces, wondering what the hell was going on. Even Sadie was smiling.

'I see we've our very own Hulk Hogan.'

'Yeah, Hulk Hogan!' bawled Leo, delighting in Sadie's comparison of his hero. Of course, Rock couldn't beat Hogan, but he'd probably give one of the lesser wrestlers a hard time.

Rock smiled meekly and continued to his seat. Adoration was the last thing he wanted right now.

'When are you joining the task force, Rocky-boy?' Louis completed a 360º chair spin before touching down with a flourish.

'Here,' Finn said, patting a seat, 'kept it for you.'

The reply of 'thanks' almost needed to be forced when Finn pulled his chair back.

'Not a problem. Just didn't want you beating me up.'

'Very funny.' Rock propped his bag against the table. 'What did Louis mean – task force?'

'Inside joke,' Finn replied. 'Did you see the photo?'

He took his notebook from the main compartment and tried to push away the senseless zing of envy he felt that even the table had all its legs. 'No.'

'You didn't see it?'

'No, why...what photo?'

'Did you come in the back way or something?' Rock sat with his hands firmly set on his knees, thoughts of having to hopscotch it up to the toilet still front and foremost in his mind. 'Come on,' Finn said, when he realised an answer wasn't coming anytime soon, 'you're in for a treat.'

Rock stared at the notice board after catching Finn up. 'Ashley took this?'

'Good, isn't it?'

Trying to come to terms with what he was seeing, it briefly gave him repose from thoughts of how big his other leg would become. 'She had to have been standing at the perfect angle?' he mused.

The photo captured the moment immediately after Rock had caught Loudmouth in the face; or, more accurately, in his loudmouth. Ashley had been standing below them as the cobbled street inclined gently towards a scantily clad mannequin who was watching the whole thing. Taken from a 45-degree angle, with both protagonists off-centre, left of frame, Rock's chin was tucked into his chest, his posture athletic; the type that suggested he may have been in similar situations in the past, and a harpoon of spittle lacerated the air as Loudmouth's face followed in the same direction as Rock's fist. Whether by accident or design, Ashley had deployed the zoom and both men's countenances were knifelike; Rock's a savage concentration, while Loudmouth's betrayed a total disbelief at how events had unfolded and turned against him, his eyes wide and lips like an orangutan.

'She should enter that in a competition.' Finn remarked.

The photo was what Rock had coined 'a pistol of a shot', and he knew it would likely wipe the floor with anything else in the competition. 'It's not too bad.'

Finn was pretty sure Rock would be the first to get a copy; that's if he didn't snatch the one they were currently admiring. 'Hmmm,' he mumbled in response.

Chapter 11

'They've often been spotted wandering through the walls and bookshelves in the library,' Sadie quietly said, explaining the link the college had with the spirit world.

'Have *you* seen them, Sadie?' Leo asked, his booming voice not quite so booming as if afraid he might attract unwanted attention.

Sometime around the turn of the century, and long before it was a place of learning, a couple had been butchered by a young man who the asylum said had 'lost all touch with external reality'. She told them that the door to the roof had to be sealed off as some people had followed the couple up there and fallen off where they'd been either disfigured or killed.

The hair on Finn's neck prickled. He'd seen a ghost before – had even waved to it. He named it Casper and counted his lucky stars that it was a friendly ghost. But even walking past the college at night to buy the jellies he'd become addicted to was unnerving. Coiling shadows from the spinous tree outside would slither across the gothic facade like menacing forms, and when the moon was full and bright, the college stank of malevolence, a veritable breeding ground for irate spirits.

'I haven't, Leo,' she replied solemnly, 'but I know people who have. One of them still has nightmares to this day.'

Leo's spectacles made his eyes look like saucers as the whites spread like an alien fungus. They wouldn't do anything bad to *him*, would they?

To prepare them for the assignment, Sadie sent them to the library to get a 'feel' for the piece. It was her way of edifying them to first do background research, even if the research was based more on feeling and less on fact.

'You want to go together?' Leo said to Simon, swallowing hard.

Simon was just about to let rip at him for being such a wuss when he reconsidered. 'Ok, I'll go with you - jeez,' he scoffed, thinking it might be a good idea to have backup just in case they ran into that old dead couple.

'Hey!' Spikester's low roll seemed to carry forever when she saw Rock (who was among those who didn't believe in ghosts and thought the myth was exactly that, a myth, something beguiling to tell students), Finn and Hugh carrying on up the stairs. 'Where you bitches going?'

'Ssshhh,' Finn whispered back to her, 'we're going to the roof, and we don't want anyone knowing.'

She put her foot onto the third step and used the heel of her hand as a lever to reconnect body and limb. 'Cool. I'm coming too.'

'Where are you going, guys?' Sophia said, as she and Gibby lazily passed by a door where a stick figure wearing a skirt (something few girls in the college wore) indicated that it was the ladies.

'Sssshhhh!' Spikester chastised, turning around, 'we're going up to the roof to look for ghosts.'

'Can we come too?' she asked brightly, and Gibby nodded her purply-speckled head to sway the jury in their favour.

Rock looked back. 'Yeah, come on,' he conceded, 'but keep it down. We don't want the whole college – or Leo –finding out.'

'Guys!' Leo's imperative blazoned up to them just before they'd made it out of range.

'SSSHHHHsshhhh!' the six of them hissed simultaneously.

'What, sorry...are you coming to the library? Just waiting on Simon, he's on the bog.'

'Thanks for telling us that, Leo,' Rock replied blankly. 'Guess the sausage rolls can only come out one way.'

Simon sauntered out of the bathroom. 'Hi guys,' he said, swishing his hands around because the air dryer had been out of order.

'We're coming now,' Finn replied, trying to throw the wrestling twins off their trail, 'lead the way.'

'Now's our chance: Run!' Rock exhorted when Leo and Simon had walked on, and he quickly began taking one step at a time.

Finn took two steps with each leap and passed him with ease. 'Hurry up or we'll be caught!'

'Damn leg!'

Leo ran his library card across the scanner and butted the turnstiles aside. 'Excuse me,' he said to the first people he saw, 'journalist from the journalism class. Have you seen anything unusual since you've been here, maybe in the last few minutes?'

The boy-girl duo who were studying together regarded Leo with interest. 'Like what?' the girl replied.

'We have it on good authorise – that's it, 'authorise', isn't it?' Simon mumbled to Leo, checking that the lingo was correct. When Leo nodded authoritatively, Simon continued. 'Yes, good authorise, that there's been sightings of some funny stuff in the library.'

The boy made eyes with his study partner that conveyed the question of whether these two were really students in the college. 'Don't you mean 'authority'?'

'Hang on, Simon.' Leo said, looking back. Where were the others, they'd been right on their tail.

'What?' Simon replied unheedingly to the boy, rubbing his belly. Those sausage rolls were playing havoc with his stomach.

The girl irritably turned some pages. 'I think you mean you have it on good auth-'

Leo lay a hand flat on the table and smiled intensely at them both. 'Thank you, you've been most cooperative,' he said, then started back the way they came.

When Simon and Leo rounded the corner, the guys had disappeared - like ghosts through a wall. Did ghosts leave behind any residue when they walked through walls? Leo wondered, scanning them. There seemed to be a vague outline of a figure, but he quickly dismissed the idea, it was too crazy.

'What's that noise?'

Leo traced the staircase straight up before it veered off into obscurity. 'I think it's coming from up there.'

'Looks kinda scary, doesn't it?' A barb of fear, along with the effects of undercooked sausage, harried Simon's insides.

When the school didn't want to pay to dump stuff anymore, they swept everything under the rug of this hidden alcove, and old tables and boxes and chairs with bent legs brought Finn to a stop.

'I think we can get over.' Sophia said when she caught up.

'Maybe you can,' Rock replied, leaning against the banister, grateful that Sadie's classes weren't conducted from up here.

'Don't worry, Rock, we'll move the stuff so you can get through.' Sophia picked up an empty chalk box and threw it deeper in.

Finn eyed the door that had been cinched shut with metal wire. It was flaking and contorted and a padlock which had once kept out snoopers was chewed open by time and damp. 'Anyone good with knots?'

'I am.'

Rock arched an eyebrow and accidentally stood on a long obsolete VHS tape. 'Something you're not telling us, Gibbs?'

'I wasn't called a Power Ranger for nothing,' she said, striding purposefully forward and unhooking the yellowed lock.

'Not too sure what that means,' Rock replied, 'but alright.'

Gibby flung the wire over her head and held the finish like an Olympian ribbon twirler. 'Got it!' she cried.

Leo paused at what was midway between the third and fourth floor, swearing he heard something landing on the stairs. 'What was that?'

'Not sure but keep an eye out.' Simon warned, fighting the urge to grab hold of Leo's hand.

'Come on, would you,' Rock urged from a floor above, 'lift it!'

Finn and Sophia had cleared what they could and carefully climbed over the rest.

'Why is it so heavy?' Hugh said, practically having to squat to get Rock's leg over a cracked blackboard that had become lodged between the walls, and which, in faint chalk outline, were the words; *Chloe & Sean 4ever!* 'It's like lifting a goalpost.'

'Oh, quit your bellyaching,' Rock replied, as Hugh made the type of noises you might hear in a gym, 'best workout you've had in years!'

The warped door grinded against the outside as Gibby pushed it open, forcing the six of them to squeeze through; though for Hugh, it was less of a squeeze and more of a comfortable fit without touching the sides.

The city of Bridgewater fanned out from the roof, and you could see as far as the river to the north and the park to the east. Finn went to the edge. Right below him, swigging from a teacup, was Sloppy, the town's most gregarious character. Sloppy never seemed to mind the cold, though that might have had something to do with what he was adding to his tea. 'Hugh, your best friend's down here.'

'Must be Sloppy?' Rock quipped.

Hugh was incredibly intimidated by Sloppy and was convinced that Sloppy knew this. Whenever he spotted him, Sloppy would approach - even going so far as following him across the road when Hugh tried to avoid him.

'At least he can't get me up here.' Hugh said, bringing his shoulder up to his ear and back down again to ease out the tension in his tendons.

'Do you still think he's stalking you?'

'He is, Sophia, I'm telling you!' Hugh looked down onto Sloppy's hairless saucer. 'Last week, alright, on my way to the car, I slid past him when he wasn't looking, then when I turned around a while later, he was right behind me, almost jumped out of my skin...had to give him two Euros.'

Spikester directed an impressive roundhouse kick over the side, setting down into a lunge when her leg made landing. 'Maybe he likes you.'

'Hope not,' Hugh replied, 'can't afford to give him money every time he sees me.'

Leo prowled up without them noticing, while behind him Simon was stuck in the gap, neither fully horizontal nor fully vertical. 'Fancy meeting you dudes here!'

'Oh fuck, it's the ghosts!' Rock exclaimed, recoiling in faux fear.

'Did anyone see you coming up here?' Finn said, concerned that breaching breaking and entering laws might get them in trouble.

Leo tilted his head and stuffed his hands in his pockets, which normally translated into him not knowing the answer. 'Don't think so,' he confirmed.

Sophia snapped some shots of Sloppy from above, and she thought it would have worked well with the word 'lofty' for the earlier project, the one Louis had made disparaging remarks about and had subsequently found himself without a grade. 'We'll just say we were doing research for our stories.'

'And we had to break out to do that,' Spikester joked, laughing.

Finn closed his two main eyes, unlocking his third one. 'I can sense some presence, something decidedly unfriendly.'

'You should join the Ghostbusters,' Rock said.

Simon's steps were measured and deliberate as he walked past them. He had suffered a fear of heights ever since falling off a donkey on what was supposed to be a safe ride on the beach as a wean.

'I'd love that,' Finn broke the connection and aimed a rather large double-barrelled slime shooter at Rock, 'you'd be the first person I shoot with my ghost gun.'

'It's called a proton pack, Finn.'

'And you'd be the second person I'd shoot with my ghost gun,' Finn replied, pulling the trigger, and covering Leo from head to toe in slime.

Leo put his arm around Simon and gave him a playful shake after he'd cleaned off the goo. 'Thought you were afraid of heights?'

Simon suddenly became aware that he was peering down at Sloppy, who seemed to be getting farther away. 'We should go down,' he said, blinking quicker than usual and taking an agitated step out of Leo's embrace. 'It's giving me the willies.'

* * * *

As they penned their stories many were very aware of what they were writing about. Like doing a Ouija board it brought the subject out into the open and made it real, and more than a few took nervous glances over their shoulders.

It was Rock's first time writing fiction, and along with Blanche and Gibby had been selected to read his aloud in front of the class. Gibby's story was about a number of students who managed to get up onto the roof, where two of them had fused hands and walked straight off like they were walking into the Promised Land. Finn and Rock glared at her, hoping that Sadie wouldn't jump to the right conclusion.

Blanche, on the other hand, had a wanton and fertile imagination. Hers was a chilling anecdote about two corrupt spirits who waited till the college was quiet and darkness had encroached on the light. They would then use the most appalling methods to steal the souls of wandering students (she often used characters resembling people she knew) who had stayed late to complete assignments.

Finn felt lightheaded. One of the students sounded just like him. 'I'm doing my work at home from now on,' he said after Blanche sat back down.

'It's ok, Finn, just make sure Rock is with you at all times,' Daisy replied, tweaking her fleecy ears back into equilibrium.

'You heard the lady.'

'Eh, no,' Rock said, standing, impervious to tales of ghouls and goblins. He cleared his throat and began to read.

After hearing the first few sentences, Ashley turned and whispered to the table behind where the boys were sitting. 'Hey, is this a porno?'

'...and Donal, who was with the other women, patted the bed and motioned for Mary to come and join them.'

Hugh was chewing the top of his pen. 'I think it might be.'

'It's definitely ghost porn, lads.' Red confirmed, twisting and pulling his hair-covered golf tee.

'...The women – the nuns – were propped comfortably beside Donal, who had his hand on Sister Margaret's leg–'

'Jesus,' Kennedy murmured, 'he's bringing the nuns into it now.'

Ashley's eyes widened and Leo leaned forward, pressing his chin into his palms. Finn thought if it became any more explicit Leo's hands would have migrated down his pants the next time he looked over.

'...and Mary walked towards the bed. She sat beside her man, and they embraced, kissing passionately.' Rock looked up.

'Yeah? Then what happened?' Billie asked with more gusto than the story deserved.

'That's as far as I got,' he replied.

This was met by an outcry.

'What?' Rock said, somewhat taken aback. 'Did you like it?'

'Of course we did, who doesn't like ghost-porn stories?!' Finn replied to a chorus of laughter.

Rock closed his notebook. 'What are you talking about? It wasn't porn?'

'Even I was a little hot under the collar there.' Sadie said, fanning her cocoa-coloured blouse.

The pitch of Leo's voice rose steadily as he spoke. 'Tell that to Donal on the bed with four different women!'

'Those women were ghosts,' he tried explaining, 'Donal couldn't see them.'

'Maybe he couldn't see them,' Billie cut in gruffly, 'but he could sure sex them up real good!'

Rock was aghast. His first attempt at flash fiction – a story he thought was quite good and which should have evoked at least a little emotion – and people thought it was a porno!

Dot was levitating off her seat and smacking the desk. 'Who fancies going back to the library after lunch to see if Donal, Mary and the nuns are still at it?!'

'That's the last story I ever write.' He pettishly swotted away the notebook so that it came to rest half off the table.

'Ah, don't say that,' Finn replied chuckling, 'we need a randy nun sequel.'

'Yeah, and I want to see if Donal gets any of the ghosts pregnant!' Leo tacked on, adding the final nail to the coffin of Rock's life as a writer.

* * * *

Rock traipsed on ahead of the others, still smarting that everyone thought his story was smut; they just didn't understand the subtle clues he'd left deep within the plot (like when sister Anne had sat on Pat's knee and felt nothing), wasn't his fault they couldn't keep up. He walked into the workshop and was clipped by Lena as she hurried past, armed with a camera and a see-through sack. Wincing, he turned around and followed her out.

'We're going for a nature walk so leave your cameras and take one of these instead,' she told the group when she met them coming across the courtyard. 'Sorry,' She gave Rock's arm a quick rub, 'didn't mean to bruise you up.'

'Wrong arm, but you're ok,' Rock replied.

There were just enough film cameras to go around as quite a few people were absent (this might have had something to do with the flu that was doing the rounds, or more likely it was because the biggest nightclub in town had thrown a student party the night before and all drinks had been cut-price), though Daisy and Leo had to share one.

Lena's colourful Doc Martens cut through the drabness like beacons as she led them behind the buildings and towards the park. 'These shoot only in black and white.' She held a camera up over her head. 'Remember what you learned in class, be on the lookout for contrast, and watch for repeating shapes and patterns because those work best.'

Two large swans moved serenely on the canal beside them, matching their tempo.

'Guys look, swans,' Daisy said, pointing to the first signs of nature. 'They'll make good con–'

'Contrast!' Leo yelled, wresting the camera from Daisy, and dragging her head-first towards the wall.

Swans, of course! Finn was encased by a graphic recollection of inhuman animal cries, fragmented oars, and feathers. If it hadn't been for the paddle-boat operator wading out to challenge the dominion of the swan, a glazed donut mightn't have been the only thing he lost that day in Silver Strand. *No wonder I'd blanked it from my memory.*

The fat of Daisy's cheek was pushed into #her mouth as she was pinned by at least four bodies, while a chest-high barrier kept them from falling in. They leaned forward, trying to capture the contrast of sparkling white swans against the inky waters of the canal. Rock was just about to depress the shutter button when he felt an easing of pressure around his ears.

'No!' He watched his treasured cap plummet six feet to the water below.

'Quick,' Finn called out after he'd shaken away the repressed fear, 'take photos so that we can remember it!'

Rock sighed and watched it drift slowly downstream. 'Had that cap for nearly three years.'

'Don't worry, Rock, I'm sure some bum will give it a good home,' Simon said cheerfully, pleased he wouldn't have to look at that stupid taxi cap any longer.

'Be careful, Simon, or you'll be swimming after it.'

'Enjoy your new hat, Mr. Bum,' he replied, low enough so Rock wouldn't hear.

They passed through rusted steel gates, one of which looked as if it could give way at any moment, and into the park. Despite the dullness of the day, people were cycling and jogging and working out in the park gym – mostly pull-ups and sit-ups; it was a minimalist gym.

'Excuuuuuuse meeeee!'

The fledgling snappers parted to let a woman pass. Her breasts were flawlessly round like they'd been drawn on with a pencil and compass, and they bounced as if they were on trampolines.

'Her back looks like her front.' Finn said, almost in a whisper.

Her buttocks were smooth coconuts that had been chopped in half and turned curved side up, protruding like frisky 3D cartoon characters. Lena shook her head and dragged her scrutiny away as the jogger continued along the path that ringed the park.

'That's what Simon would look like if he ever jogged.'

'Miss your cap yet, Rock?' Simon scowled, but he quickly walked on when Rock's expression turned foul.

The children's play area was deserted, apart from one child who rocked gently back and forth on an animal spring swing. Rock fired off three shots. 'Louis, found your brother over here.'

'Whoa, Village of the Damned.' Louis said, prancing over. 'Don't stare directly into its eyes!'

'Is there a horror movie you *haven't* seen?' Finn asked him, as the fair-haired child stared at them without emotion, spring swing squawking on every downward pulse.

'Don't think so,' he replied, 'even seen the remakes.'

Louis was reciting lines from Hitchcock when they came to the old bandstand, where unclad branches arched over like wilted spines and tapped on the roof like ghastly visitors calling at the front door, and where hardy flowers still vibrant with diluted colour were clinging to a warmer time. But it was a circular bush set apart from the main body of shrubbery that drew the most attention. Red told them about the time he had spent curled up deep within that bush after a night he'll never quite remember. All he could recall was waking up wet and cold from the morning dew, with a spider suspended above his head and a headache that came from the devil's armpit.

'Took about ten minutes to get out, was so fucked I kept getting tangled up,' he said, smiling at the memory, 'good times.'

They took pictures of the Viking horns, two ebony talismans that rose like ruptures from either side of a fountain (residents of Bridgewater believed that if you paid homage to the horns, vitality and virility would be yours), and which graced the majority of postcards that were sent to aunts and grandparents during the summer.

'You coming, Billie?'

Billie barely heard Daisy as she offered up a silent invocation while palpating the engravings that ran in a helix shape around the varnished wood; one etching for every year since the city's founding.

'Careful guys,' Mia called over, as Louis was inspecting the orb-like bush, doubting whether Red could have spent a whole night in it.

'Get out of the bloody way!' yelled the silicone steamroller.

The group watched with amused detachment as Red and Gibby jumped aside, and as Louis was premeditatedly sent into the bush by a trailing arm as she tramped on at an unbroken pace.

'Jasus, lads, life flashed before me eyes.' Red removed himself from the flowerbed and stamped his feet clear of soil. 'Need to head over to the girlfriends'.'

'You're going now?' Rock asked him.

His boots were already ponderously clunking over the jogger's footprints. 'Yeah, just realised there's a couple of things we haven't tried yet…' he trailed off, passing where Louis was spread out like a starfish on the hedge.

****

Rock and Finn arrived at the studio just as night was starting to get the upper hand on the day as both were given the middle slot. Simon wasn't happy with the order of the groupings and made his feelings about it very clear in O'Malley's.

'I'm going to be starving coming out of that studio,' he had moaned, negotiating a pizza slice into his mouth.

Rock watched till only the crust remained. 'Don't worry, Simon, it'll make the walk home easier,' he replied flatly.

Simon felt like asking Rock why he was such a nob, but he was engaged in a chew-off with large hunks of beef, along with the extra slices of pepperoni he'd requested. He sat in O'Malley's in a huff, and a long sliver of cheese was still dangling from his fleshy jowls from when Finn and Rock had departed for the Pod, the college's offsite training facility.

Sadie had divided the class into groups of six and seven and each group had an hour in the studio; long enough to give everyone a feel for what it was like to be on radio – in theory, at least. After explaining the instruments, Sadie went into the adjoining room to mark assignments that a weekend spent entertaining duds from a speed-dating event meant she was late handing back.

'Testing, testing.' The others heard Red through their headsets and nodded in breezy agreement.

'You sound like an angel.'

'Wouldn't say that now, Finn,' Red replied, his accent potent and in keeping with that of a fisherman.

'Could Old Man Grey please report to the hot seat, Old Man Grey to the hot seat?' Rock announced into the mic.

Finn generally kept his hair short, but when it grew out so did the grey, starting in the sideburns and creeping farther outwards with each passing year. 'It's the distinguished look,' he argued.

'Are your pubes grey too?' Rock enquired.

'At least I have them, cue ball.'

By the time Finn had introduced the first song and sent three little birds fluttering soulfully into their ears, he had managed to secure the nickname 'Silver Jingles', which he thought was infinitely better than the alternative.

'Are you going to have a bash, Sophia?' Red said to her, as she swivelled contentedly on the highchair listening to the verbalized sparring.

Her air became grave. 'No, I'm alright.'

'I'm nervous too,' Finn said, trying to reassure her, 'but it's not that scary.' But it was that scary, and Finn questioned if he'd ever be able to let his voice be heard by a hypercritical collective.

'I'll just listen to you guys,' she replied, terrified by the thought of having to hear her gabbling through the headphones.

'Go on, Sophia! Do it!' Leo's voice reverberated around the padded studio walls, startling her and everyone else.

Rock frowned and massaged under his ear lobe. 'Think this studio needs more soundproofing.'

'You sound like old Betsy when she's getting going.' Red said, referring to the trawler he'd once been married to before EU Fisheries came between them.

'I'll tell you what,' Finn said, getting back to Sophia and her gripe with being seen through her vocals, 'how about we have a chat, just you and me without the mics – like we normally would?'

Sophia looked no less like she'd been selected to walk down a Paris runway and answered timidly: 'Ok.'

Finn was just as wracked as Sophia was, but that she was too scared to try managed to cover his own insecurities and made him want to show her that there was nothing to it; anyway, they were in a darkened room cut off from both civilisation and outsiders ready with scathing critiques.

'Alright then,' he started, smiling easily, 'I have it on good authority that you enjoy bringing chocolates into class?'

'Authorise.' Leo whispered to Kevin from the bundle of jackets they had been forced to occupy when the stools were bagged.

Sophia nodded, chomping on her bottom lip.

'Is that because you think we're all great and we deserve chocolate?'

'Yeah.'

Finn kept his voice even and light, and he noticed that it didn't sound as bad as he'd feared. 'Although I understand Hugh won't eat them.'

Sophia shook her head.

'What does he call them?'

'Fake Ferreros,' she replied, almost inaudibly.

'Because they're from the cheap German supermarket, yes that's right. He's a bit silly, isn't he?' Sophia nodded in agreement. 'Is it true that you won a beauty contest last summer?'

She giggled gently. 'Yes.'

'You're lucky Simon didn't enter, or you'd have come second,' Finn said waggishly, trying to chip away at her defences. 'Did you win a prize for coming first?'

'A gift certificate for my hair – oh, and I also won a voucher to buy my camera...a camera.'

Her guard was down. Finn saw his chance. 'That's brilliant.' He glanced quickly at Rock. 'What camera did you buy?'

'I bought a Canon.'

As she was speaking, Rock moved the mic closer to her mouth.

'Ah, Rock's favourite,' Finn ventured, 'I think my Fujifilm is the best, but anywho.'

Before she knew it, Sophia was speaking freely into the mic, the sound of her inside voice matching the one that was coming into her ears. 'I love taking pictures of animals,' she said, her earlier angst easing with every reply, 'dogs especially, but when I was in the wildlife park last year, I got some great photos of the tigers.'

'I hope you were a safe distance away. Or armed with a gun – that was it, wasn't it,' he replied, waggling his finger, and experiencing that same shedding effect that Sophia was feeling, 'you were armed with a very powerful gun?'

She laughed. 'No, they were in an enclosure so they couldn't harm me.'

'Speaking of animals,' Red said, tickling the underside of the mic with his crimped dimple rod, 'do you think you could get a few good shots of Leo?'

'My camera isn't that good.' Sophia felt comfortable enough to quip.

Leo rubbed the raggedy beard that grew in patches on his face like spotty turf. 'Pfft, you'd love to photograph me!' he said, tipping his index finger to his tongue and posing as seductively as he could.

'Oh, don't photograph that,' Rock groaned, lowering Sophia's mic, and rubbing his eyes like they'd been damaged.

Chapter 12

Leo came bouncing into the canteen like a child who found where his parents had stashed the sweeties. 'Look what I bought!'

He took a garment out of a green and white bag. It was from the costume shop uptown. Leo had spent a small fortune on it, and no one had the heart to tell him that if he'd waited until Halloween, it would have been half the price.

'You gotta wear that to class.' Finn said as a radioactive headpiece was the next thing to come out.

Leo was shaking like he had swallowed an entire tin of Uncle Joe's mint balls. 'You think?'

'Yeah,' Finn replied, 'it'd be hilarious.'

'Alright, I'll do it!'

Leo began stripping off at once, blissfully unaware of the quizzical stares he was attracting. One girl's fork stopped mid-transit, not noticing – or caring – that gravy was dripping onto her jeans, and Ashley and Mia had to cover their mouths to disguise their mirth.

'Go for it, Leo!' Ashley managed, before a fit caught hold.

This encouragement, particularly from a member of the fairer sex, spirited Leo on until he stood in the middle of the food court dressed as someone who specialized in containing hazardous bioagents. Ashley began clapping and the class – followed by other students who thought Leo was suffering from some form of mental deficiency – joined in.

'Who are you meant to be?' Simon said when Leo had stopped bowing to dumbstruck rubberneckers.

Leo waved his yellow arms about like someone giving out orders. 'I've been in any number of movies – I'm the guy who comes in and rescues everyone after there's been a deadly outbreak!'

'Oh yeah,' Simon replied, 'I see it now!'

'Sometimes I need to use heavy-handed tactics to force people into quarantine,' he continued matter-of-factly, 'it's for their own good you know.'

'You need to be quarantined.' Sophia said, admiring Kennedy's braids – which had slowly begun to turn into dreads such was the amount of Rasta music she was listening to – and wondering if they'd look good on her.

'What's that, Sophia?' Leo shouted, 'It's a bit hard to hear.'

She mumbled some words that to Leo sounded like a swell of noise under his mask.

'What?!' A build-up on the face guard made it seem like there was a miniature smoke machine hooked up to the inside.

'I said it doesn't matter!'

'Oh,' he replied, giving her two rubber thumbs up.

Leo was shadowing the others as they dodged around Sadie who was setting up the overhead projector. Today they were learning about how social media was distorting the real world and leading to the emergence of something called 'fake news'. Sadie intended to elicit from them ways how this phenomenon could be used as a tool to subvert the freedoms of everyday people if used in a disingenuous way.

'A heap of hippy shite!' Red had answered when Kennedy asked why he wasn't on Facebook. 'People want me they know where I am, down the pub or on the boat.'

'Hi, Sadie.' Leo said, vibrating as he waited for her to look up.

'Oh, hi Leo.' Her reply to the masked man in front of her was indifferent.

Leo hesitated. He wasn't sure if she saw him properly. She mustn't have, she didn't react to his costume.

'Take a seat, Leo,' she said, returning to her slides.

She definitely saw him that time. How did she know it was him, he puzzled.

Rock and Finn chuckled as Leo's visage was that of someone who had the air let out of their balloon. 'Nearly feel sorry for tipping her off,' Rock admitted, as Leo shrank into his seat.

The pages slid across the glass plate as Sadie let go of them. 'I have some bad news.'

'Yeah, you didn't say how cool my costume was,' Leo muttered, still wondering how she knew it was him. Had his accent given him away?

'Barbara was attacked this morning.' This was said with the same chilly undertone as the one when she'd told them about the handsy dictator.

Rock's eyes glazed over as if an iron curtain had been dropped. 'What happened?'

Barbara's attendance had been sporadic since Leo had told everyone that tiredness and not stupidity caused her to fail last year's exams, and she spent as many days with her head on the table as she did taking notes and making amends.

'She was over at the homeless centre interviewing the guy who runs the joint, thought it would be a good addition to her assignment,' Sadie said evenly. 'But she was followed as she left. Only thing was she fought back – gave your man a good gouging by all accounts.'

'Good for her!' Ashley said.

'Yeah, good for her,' Sadie agreed, but lacking Ashley's ardent enthusiasm. 'Because she refused to let the mugger have her camera he gave her a nasty clout and knocked her to the ground. She's in surgery as we speak.'

Rock turned and looked at Finn, who held his gaze. It was a cold, vengeful look. After the class, which had been mostly unproductive and subdued by the news of Barbara, Rock marched over, clobbering two seats out of the way. 'We should go and find him.'

'And do what?'

Rock's fists were crunching stress balls that weren't there. 'Give the bastard a good hiding, that's what!'

'We could, but then *we'd* be in trouble,' Finn replied. 'And let's face it, Hugh isn't exactly cut out for prison life.' They all looked at Hugh, who nodded in devout agreement.

'I hate seeing assholes like that get away with it.'

'The police will find him,' Hugh offered up, 'down-and-outs aren't exactly known for their brains.'

'Those muppets couldn't catch a cold in a hailstorm!' Rock retorted, reducing the stress balls to flattened discs.

'I'm sure he's heard that the Master of Disaster is the classmate of the woman he attacked,' Finn said, 'probably in Belfast waiting on the boat to Scotland by now.'

'He better be,' Rock replied, 'because if I ever catch him he'll wish he'd stayed there.'

* * * *

Halloween was just around the corner and Rock couldn't believe how fast the time was going. All his early fears about college – and whether he'd fit into an academic lifestyle – had been swiftly put to rest.

Not that long ago, his attention span was a troubling source of concern. He couldn't read a book – couldn't even read the pamphlets the *God Boys,* as he had christened them, regularly dropped into his house, urging him to give his body over to Christ – without becoming distracted and having to commit them to the 'unread' portion of the shelf, which itself was threatening a coup and to take over completely.

Rock's mouth caved in with the slug from the blended malt as he kicked out his armchair. 'Needs a drop more water, I think.'

The first assignment the class had been given was to write an 800-word feature piece about a moment in time. Rock chose to write about one spectacular day that he and Suzy had spent in a small – yet exquisitely picturesque – mountain village in Albania. There had been no tourists and nothing to spoil the peace, just salve-for-the-cells tranquillity (a description he used in the piece, and which he thought was quite nifty) and lots of it. It was one of those days that made you think that maybe there was a God and maybe he did love you; he would be in no hurry to admit that to the *Boys*, however.

Rock initially struggled with the structure. Then, when he discovered he had to include a bibliography of every website he visited, he thought that most absurd. But he soon took to college life like a deer that had finally learned to walk on the ice. He noticed a marked improvement in his span of attention – so much so, he was now able to sit down for three hours and, with the aid of only two cups of coffee, power through an assignment like he'd been doing them for years; not to mention that he hadn't bothered to make a shopping list on the last two occasions. It even came to the stage where he looked forward to getting a crisp new brief, that sense of achievement like a shot of endorphins every time.

    He and Finn had forged something of an unspoken alliance; Finn would assist him with writing, while he'd help Finn with his photography, and because of this both rose like frothy cream to the top of the class. Rock couldn't believe it. Being on top of a mountain, possibly, or his girlfriend Suzy, sure, but being on top in college was a different prospect and a heady feeling indeed, like looking down from a Ferris wheel at the top of its arc to the street below. This was a place normally reserved for intellectuals, not former truck drivers who liked a glass of the hard stuff in the evening.

    Maybe he'd been underestimating himself all these years. The race for President was hotting up in America and if Donald Trump could run for office, then maybe he could throw *his* hat into the ring; if it hadn't tragically drowned, that is. Rock doubted if Trump could have matched his grades, they were nothing short of a mind-fuck so far. The only things holding him back were some hair and the little matter of a billion dollars. But the girls in class could help spray on the hair and he'd heard the banks were lending again.

* * * *

It was a grey Tuesday and the day after midterm, but Finn couldn't have been happier. The short break had dragged the way school used to when summer holidays were approaching; so close, yet so maddeningly out of reach. He never thought he could love a course this way, especially after the last time. It had been a four-year torment of rainy, never-ending bus commutes in traffic that barely moved, and Finn dreaded having to do it all again the following day.

He had found something worth getting up for, and that it was cold and dark outside made no difference. When his miniature travel alarm (which went everywhere with him) said it was time to get up, Finn would be out of bed as if he were attached to a bungee cord. He was sleeping less than ever but he wasn't tired like before and his eyes no longer felt like lead weights staring lifelessly into the distance. For now, the wraith of despair was but a dried-in blotch on his memory.

His scholastic comrades could hardly say the same as they looked like the stumbling dead after a week of lazy afternoon lie-ins.

Ashley yawned deeply. 'Why are you so chippy?'

'Your smiling face, of course,' Finn replied, seeing the matted tooth at the back of her mouth where Ashley and her dentist had recently gone four rounds.

'Leave me alone,' she said, rubbing the sleep from her eyes. 'I should still be in bed.'

Sadie came into the room, hair dishevelled, and looking like the leader of the dead. 'Welcome back guys.' She coughed out a frog that had put down roots in her throat. 'Hope you all studied hard over Halloween?'

Daisy giggled under her fingers. 'I did nothing except watch Japanese cartoons.'

'Hey, me too - I mean, I watched wrestling videos, not Japanese cartoons.'

'Sure you did, Leo.' Leo fired Louis the evils. No matter how much he tried he just couldn't like him, couldn't work out who he was.

Kennedy rapped an empty carton of Marlboros against the manual she'd yet to see the inside of. 'My desk is full of assignments,' she said, 'not sure what any of them are though.'

'Mine too!' Blanche replied, and they began nattering about how best to make their assignments disappear.

'You're not the only ones,' Sadie figured she wouldn't need to see the actual Tower of Pisa having a to-scale model in her own home, 'if I get any more assignments to correct I'll be shouting, 'timbeeerrrrrr.''

'Lads-' Dot maaed suddenly like she was in a rush to get it out, '-did anyone go trick or treating?' Dot had gone as someone who likes drugs and did a fairly good job of imitating their quavering movements.

'I went with my little brother. We got loads of stuff!' Leo stopped short of mentioning how they'd gone back three times to the blind homeowner, and how it was Leo's idea and not his brother's.

'Did you bring in any sweets for the rest of us?' Even Sadie couldn't help stealing a look at Leo when Rock raised the question.

He hoisted his glasses back onto the bridge of his nose. 'No, sorry, I ate them all.'

'But Halloween was only two nights' ago?' Sophia didn't like the way Leo always made her sound so brassy.

Leo ignored her and put his head down, hoping to deflect attention away from his newly acquired – and mostly uneaten – bounty of candy. He did feel a little bad for clearing out old man Ernie, but only until he'd eaten the first of his legendary Halloween mallows.

The day shunted along uneventfully. Sadie took it easy on them seeing as it was the first day back and seeing as how Leo was still on something of a sugar high. The only thing of significance she did was to go round the room and give out stapled briefs, the main assignment for the year.

'I want you to get your teeth stuck into this,' she said, placing them neatly in front of everyone, 'I don't care if you pick astrology, as long as you get Mystic Medusa on–'

Hugh came into the room like a one-man cyclone and almost swept Louis off his bucking bronco. 'Sorry I'm late,' he said in a throwaway tone that suggested he wasn't sorry at all. Hugh had somehow mislaid his brush and had to resort to combing his hair with his fingers: It hadn't turned out well.

'Come up here and grab one of these.' Sadie was in no mood to retrace her steps.

Hugh tutted. He knew people were gawking at his hair. Now he'd never live down the Wolfman. 'Will you just drop it down to me, would you?'

It took Hugh the length of Kevin's abrupt inhale to get out of his seat, and just quickly enough to quell Sadie's ire. 'Sorry, sorry,' he said, barrelling up and taking the proffered double leaf.

She tracked his movements intensely as he almost ran back to his seat. 'Where was I before I was rudely interrupted?'

'Mystic Medusa,' answered Daisy.

'That's right, Mystic Medusa,' she said, making sure that Hugh knew how close he came to being strung up by his intestines. 'By all means, pick the mad bint, it's your choice, just get her on tape. If you don't get an interview with someone who backs up your hypothesis, you'll lose a quarter of your marks.'

'What should we do if they don't want to talk to us?'

'Daisy, I find the use of threats to work quite well.' Rock said.

'Run after them, of course.' Leo had made up his mind. If he put the mallows Ernie had been kind enough to gift him in the fridge, he could eat half of one each day until his birthday, when his birthday cake would then take over.

Kevin volunteered that it would be better to leave them alone, 'don't want to make anyone cross,' he said.

'Bit of flirting never hurt anyone?' Finn suggested.

'Use polite aggression,' Sadie finally advised. 'You catch more flies with honey, but don't put away the stick either, you don't want to be fobbed off straightaway. Sometimes you may have to be flattering, like Finn said, or unyielding, as Rock suggested, but always be honest, people appreciate a straight shooter, especially with the amount of shysters who only care about acclaim and bullion.

'So, get out there and enjoy yourselves. Talk to people, wangle your way into their lives and their hearts, the worst thing that happens they say no or tell you to get bent.' She started with Daisy, looking hopefully down at each as they passed along a moving student caravan, finally stopping in front of Hugh. 'Time to see if you have what it takes to be a journalist.'

Chapter 13

It sounded like megalithic dolmens being hefted across the floor as Rock and Simon pushed two giant tables together. Mia advocated trying somewhere different for lunch, somewhere more fit for a monarch (Mia had been voted class president after Sadie had taught them that for bare-bone detail and fact-assimilation, journalism was the gold standard, the Rolls Royce of verity. It was only when this raw data was put through a sausage maker that it came out looking like a ham), and when she confirmed that the Stone Cross had a student menu Rock had paraded single file past their regular eatery and towards the gastropub.

'They *do* care about us poor students,' Finn said browsing the menu, 'there's more than one option.'

'Still think we should have gone to McDonalds.' Ashley was blowing the gum she'd been chewing on ever since Sadie had explained that the extent to which a readership eats out of your hand – intellectually speaking – is directly correlated with how many times you can bombard them with the same message. *Eyeballs are dollar bills, whether the message is true or not*, she said, *and exploit headlines, they're like neon lights to the uninitiated*, she had told them.

'That's right,' Rock replied, 'you have a weird fetish for Mickey D's.'

Ashley liked nothing more than commandeering the biggest table and having what she described as dinner parties with friends.

'They should really give me shares in the company,' she said, after failing to work out how often she'd eaten there in the past month.

'Would you settle for unlimited apple pie?' Louis asked, taking up his can after it had jostled and jived on the table like it was alive.

'No, I want unlimited food.'

'Someone's high maintenance,' Finn quipped, throwing the menu on the table for the others to browse.

Ashley's primary fantasy involved watching dolphins frolic from the deck of a rich lover's yacht while eating chicken nuggets. 'That's why I'm going to marry a doctor – or a sheikh, I don't care.'

Simon couldn't decide on the burger or the wings so he asked the waitress if he could have both with just one portion of chips but pay a reduced price. She said she didn't think he could. 'Fine,' he grunted moodily, sending her away like a lowly servant, 'just bring me them both.'

Ashley leaned over into the middle of the table and sifted through a bowl of condiments. 'Anyone want some?'

'But the food hasn't come yet?' Hugh replied, shifting into the only bit of available space left.

'I mean for now.' She ripped open the sachet and squeezed ketchup into her mouth.

'Ashley!' Mia exclaimed.

Hugh came through Simon and Leo like a joey in a pouch and shrieked in disgust. 'That's worse than Finn and his pineapple!'

Finn's knife and fork were already in hand and at the ready. 'I feel quite normal now,' he said.

'What?' she replied, wiping the vampire signature from the corner of her mouth. 'I'm sure most of you like ketchup?'

'Yeah, but I like it on actual food!' Leo's winter hoard of maple syrup he'd brought back from America was all but gone and watching Ashley peg back the sauce gave him ideas.

'Thirsty now.' Ashley next tore open a sachet of vinegar.

Hugh turned his cheek so that he was facing the lavatories. 'You're all kinds of sick, you know that?'

'Your boyfriend must be one happy dude.'

Ashley downed the vinegar in one. 'What do you mean?' she replied to Rock.

'Nothing,' he said, changing the subject, 'how are you all getting on with your shows?'

Louis crunch-killed his Coke. 'Think we're going to give away our ideas to you?'

'After you told the whole of Cairo that you roll ninety-year-old women in molasses and lick it off, it's probably better you didn't,' Finn said, moving his knife rapidly in between the tines of his fork.

'I wasn't meant to say that.' Louis protested, 'I was nervous!'

As much as he liked ketchup – and why wouldn't he being a proud American – Leo thought he'd start small with just the one sachet. 'Was it really broadcast in Cairo?' he said.

'Ask Sadie if you don't believe us,' Finn replied, enjoying the enduring lifespan of the Cairo joke.

'Just don't insult pyramids or camels and you'll be fine,' Rock added, helping to keep the yarn spun.

'And I didn't say I rolled her in molasses,' Louis was clarifying exactly what he had said during his first attempt at radio, 'I said I *met* her at a molasses convention and then we started dating.'

'Is that why you left our group, the shame of being a granny-banger?' Red said and everyone around the tables laughed.

Louis grabbed his backpack. 'I'm not a granny-banger – God!'

'Does he actually fancy grannies?' Daisy asked, after he'd skulked back to the library to finish some work which he hoped Lena would still accept.

'It's Louis, of course he does,' Rock replied.

Hugh was on his feet and frowning. 'I'm going too. I've finished the work, but I can't look at those sachets anymore, brings back bad memories.'

* * * *

After lunch, they marched grudgingly to Monday's sermon. Orwell was in a great mood, full of beans like he'd just won a storytelling tell-off. 'Can anyone tell me what police vetting means?' he asked, feeling completely self-satisfied.

Mia normally handled the questions. She was one of those people who when a question was asked was biologically programmed to answer it. It was like an itch that had to be scratched, which was why class president was the perfect job for Mia, even if she had so far done more talking about and less implementing of peer-enriching policy.

'It means you can play with kids.' Was she just that much smarter than the rest of them, she wondered, feeling as if they should just hand her the student of the year gong now and be done with it.

Orwell, who was a bit hard of hearing, asked her to repeat her answer, and it was no less funny the second time.

'Eh, doesn't it mean you can play with small baby kids?'

'No...no, it doesn't mean that,' he enunciated slowly.

The laughter hadn't totally died down when Orwell explained that it didn't quite mean what Mia thought it meant.

'Certain professions request that you have a background check done to prove your suitability to work in occupations that deal with vulnerable adults or children.' He was pacing along parallel with the tables at the head of the room, fingering cufflinks that had been passed down generations and which as he explained had been worn by the gentry from as far back as the 1600s – not that his were that old, mind.

'She's kind of right then.' Finn remarked.

Orwell's fine mood had been ruffled, like the feathers of a peacock when it spies the arrival of another even jazzier peacock. This was the one class that always seemed to antagonize him. He wished they could be more like the art class who just accepted everything he said and then went home. 'Let's move on,' he said. 'If you turn to page twenty-six in your workbook, you'll see the section about employees.'

'My workbook is under my table at home.' Hugh whispered in the back row.

'What's it doing there?' Finn said, throwing open the beefy book to page twenty-six, where there was a picture of two officious-looking people shaking hands.

'It makes a great footrest.'

Rock's scalp almost kissed Hugh's lips as he leaned across to engage Finn. 'Think we should tell Orwell his book is under his table?'

'Ah no, don't,' Hugh pleaded, pushing Rock out of his immediate vicinity.

'We won't say anything if you don't annoy us for the next forty minutes,' Finn said, and they chuckled when Hugh turned away and ignored them.

When the flipping of pages had ceased, Orwell spoke again. 'Does anyone know what employers look for in employees?'

Mia homed in on the question like she could see it hovering in the air. This was her chance at redemption. She was just going to say it, she was right anyway: 'For people who are grateful.'

She was confused then when again her classmates, 'lost their shit', as Dot would have said.

'What?' she gasped, once again finding herself the comedic centre of attention. 'What's wrong with that? I'd show gratitude if someone gave *me* a job!'

'How would you do that, Mia?' Finn said, smirking.

'I could think of a few ways,' Louis replied, imagining the type of things an employee could do to pay back a domineering boss.

Orwell was looking for a prompt off Kennedy in the front row. 'What did she say?'

'She said-'

'She said she'd get on her knees and show her boss how grateful she was if he gave her a job.' Spikester said impassively.

'Oh, no, that wouldn't quite be right either,' Orwell replied, showing genuine concern at Mia's replies.

'We're seeing a whole new side to you, Mia.' Rock said.

'But I didn't say that!'

'You.' Orwell pointed at Dot, who looked as if she was seeing swirly unicorns made entirely of liquorice whip romping around the room. 'What do you think employers are looking for when they hire someone?'

Dot had been tuned into a different frequency since the beginning of class and that Orwell was even there came as something of a surprise. 'What?' she said.

Everyone except Orwell could feel Dot's growing agitation.

'What traits should a good employee have?' It wasn't like he was asking her to solve the issue of world poverty. 'Come on, it's an easy one!'

'Huh? I don't know, do I? What, loyalty...'

'I'm sorry, what?' Orwell replied, moving closer.

Dot had purposely camped in the corner, thinking she'd be safe from participating. Her eyes darted to and fro like they were on springs and her tongue flicked at her lips. Orwell stood in front of her, peering down, waiting for an answer.

'What? GO WAY!'

Orwell backtracked a few steps and wore the face of a man who had just been shooed away by a group of mothers after finding out he wasn't police vetted. He looked briefly at the class before quickly abandoning his line of questioning. *What was wrong with this girl*, he thought, *was she possessed?*

Dot smushed her things away, causing chunky upturned bends in her books. 'Lads, bye,' she said with a cracked voice, 'I have to go, lads.'

She tripped on Daisy's plus-sized suitcase, which Daisy used to carry around her plus-sized laptop. The bell chimed – the one Rock called a cowbell and couldn't understand why Daisy had it attached to her bag in the first place – but she somehow managed to stay upright.

'Fuck, shit – gotta go, guys,' Dot sputtered, testing the strength of the door hinges on the way out.

Rock brought his fingers to his mouth, making the universal 'getting stoned' sign. Finn nodded and they grinned. Orwell looked to the class for an explanation and Rock brought his fingers to his mouth again, making the universal 'getting stoned' sign. Orwell smirked and his forehead creased into a frown.

'Let's keep going, shall we?' He tried to get himself back into the teaching groove, but Orwell had been stripped of his earlier zeal. 'For instance,' he proposed weakly, 'what would you look for in a nurse?'

Mia urged herself to have another stab at the answer. Then she thought better of it.

'That she's a woman.' Louis pushed back the strands of hair which had fallen over his left eye.

Orwell blinked a few times. 'But...not all nurses are women?'

Louis had never been to a hospital and every doctor he ever went to see was always assisted by a female nurse. 'Hah?'

More laughter met Louis's lack of worldly wisdom, and Orwell started to feel quite befuddled. 'Men are nurses now, too.'

'Really?' he replied. 'What if they had to examine your junk?'

'Don't worry, Louis,' Billie said, pretending to snap on a latex glove, 'I'll give you the once over.'

Louis winked at her, and Orwell sighed and noticed a trelliswork of striations (some deep, some superficial) on Hugh's desk where a tome of boring case studies and ham-fisted exercises should have been. 'Where's your book?'

'He keeps it under his table at home.' Rock said.

'To use as a footrest.' Finn added.

Hugh glared at each of them. 'No, I don't – I don't!' he quickly retaliated, his hair now so inexplicably bedraggled that it was hard to take him seriously. 'And stop looking at my hair!'

'Make sure you bring it in next time, won't you?' Orwell sighed once more. 'Alright, we'll pick this up again,' he said, as the church bell tolled for the end of class, 'though maybe not exactly from where we left off.'

Orwell felt like he'd been put through an emotional spin cycle and all he wanted to do was get to that new coffee machine in the teacher's room (two years of diligent campaigning had finally put an end to pleas for clemency from the breadline in the canteen), put his feet up and read the *Times* for twenty minutes; and he didn't give a flying fig if he was late for the next class.

* * * *

November was a slog, and as the number of assignments grew, so the initial novelty of college quickly wore off. The darkening days reflected the mood. Barbara's collarbone had been badly damaged in the mugging, and she'd spend the remainder of the year dosed up on opioids for a mangled shoulder that fought like hell against the cold. Even Sloppy's warm-hearted salutations lacked their usual cheeriness.

On one singularly miserable day – when the early rain had made everyone's jeans and leggings heavy with wetness – Mia followed Sadie out to the corridor at her behest. She had come back into the room in tears and urgently packed away her stuff, forgetting that her USB was still in the port, and left without another word.

'Her godfather passed away this morning,' Sadie said when the class had looked to her for an explanation, 'they were very close.'

November became even gloomier.

But when the calendar in the teacher's room (the one above where Orwell would sit drinking his coffee imagining that he was teaching at Harvard) changed to a photo of an Irish landscape beneath a winter sun, things began to improve. People came to terms with the darker side of college life – cold days, long nights, and the dreaded brief, which involved actually having to sit down and work. Christmas was just a few short weeks away and that meant the Christmas holidays were, too.

It was a day just like the picture on the calendar. The sun was low and brilliant, and a light dusting of snow had painted the grounds during the night, making it feel decidedly festive. Under the bare branches of the oak trees, which had lost some of their majestic aura when the leaves had fallen, the journalists were huddled together.

Rock and Sophia sipped from take-out coffee cups and everyone except for Hugh was wearing a woolly hat. Rock had asked the girl in the canteen why it was so expensive, seeing as things like coffee and sausages were meant to be subsidised. The girl said it was cheaper than across the road and he had shot back, 'Yeah, by five cents!'

As they chatted, attention turned to how each of them came to be there, distracting them from the numbing cold. 'Any later and the janitor would have been off mopping the gym,' Finn splayed his digits to get the circulation going, 'and I'd have left Bridgewater and never got to meet you guys.'

'That wouldn't have been good, Finn.' Blanche replied. She and Kennedy were plaited together like Siamese twins and their gaze caused him to look away. Crediting the intervention with his renewal, Finn would stop and play agony aunt to the janitor's woes of not being appreciated (or for having the wrong type of soil for his seeds) whenever he saw him tending the grounds.

Rock casually sipped what he was pretty sure was instant coffee. 'I didn't even apply for the course.'

'What do you mean?' Louis said.

'They made a mistake with my application. I should be hanging out with Harold and co. right now - lucky break, eh?'

'Why didn't you tell them they made a mistake?' Louis continued, making gyrating movements as if he were sitting on a chair.

Rock made a gesture with his free hand. 'I didn't realise. I turn up for the interview and next thing you know I'm being asked to show things that I've written. Thought it was a bit strange until I got the offer and by that time it was too late, the art and photography course was already full. So, I figured, what the hell, I'd give it a try.' Anything was better than staring at those four walls and at least it had an element of photography to it, he had thought.

Finn was stunned: First him, now Rock. 'That's mad,' he said in a tempered voice.

'I applied for it and got it, no dramas.' Simon was chewing a piece of sausage he'd also bought from the canteen, but unlike Rock, he had no problems with the cost.

'They have to take in a certain quota of special people nowadays.'

'And not forgetting old people!' Simon retorted but quickly moved around the other side of Leo when Rock peered at him.

'I applied to another college,' Hugh said, ignoring Simon, 'got accepted and all.'

Sophia tucked a loose lock of hair behind her ear. 'How did you end up here then?'

'Me and my dad were having a beer watching Man United - one of the few games we won last year,' Hugh's thoughts strayed back to that screamer of a goal Rooney had scored, '- and out of nowhere he asks if I'm sure about the course and would I not try it out here for a year first. We weren't even talking about college, which I thought was a bit weird.'

'I only got in because the other guy dropped out.' Fredrik's father had burst through his bedroom door like there was a house fire on receiving the principal's call and commanded that he get up at once.

'I remember you were a week late.' For Daisy, it was plain as day that she'd be attending Bridgewater. The pendulum had told her as much.

'And then you wanted to bugger a goat.' Finn said.

Fredrik chuckled, then, scratching the tip of his nose, confirmed with almost bookish sincerity, 'I was playing with myself when the college rang.'

'Ugghh, Fredrik!' The girls caterwauled in unison.

'Please, nigga,' Ashley was mouthing a tuft of oily hair and pivoting from side to side, 'we don't need to know that!'

'Yeah,' Fredrik lamented, 'it was a real turn-off.'

Looking like he was chewing on a nettle, Simon turned to Red and said, 'Did Ashley just use the n-word?'

'Guess she did, yeah,' he replied. It was an admission he wouldn't broadcast but wanting to prove to his ex-girlfriend that he could do more than just fish in the hopes of a reunification had been the motivating factor for Red applying to be landlocked for a year.

'When I went for my interview, I was asked to show some of the photos I'd taken. So, I show them the ones of my two huskies,' Spikester said deliberately, and less animated than normal. 'The women liked them - you know, the interviewers - said they were beautiful.'

The others nodded, sensing the story might not have a happy ending.

'She shouldn't be saying that.' Simon decried, 'She's white...'

'Anyway, when I got home, they weren't in their usual place. They'd somehow gotten into where we keep the calves.' Spikester took a deep breath before continuing. 'Three of them were dead. The dogs were covered in blood. We had to put them down the next day.'

Spikester shook her head and gathered herself together. She was uncomfortable at being thrust so far out into the spotlight. 'So, when I got the offer a few weeks later it was down to the huskies that I got it. That's what I think at least.'

Mia placed a comforting hand on her shoulder and tried to keep the sorrow she felt from showing. 'I'm sure it was,' she replied softly.

'Don't worry, Spikester, I'll give you one of my dogs,' Rock said, 'you can have any of the ugly ones.'

Spikester laughed hard and told him where he could shove the ugly ones.

'I'm a bit like Rock–'

'You're nothing like me, Yank.'

'Shut up, I'm Irish! Anywaaaayyy,' Leo began again in his American drawl, 'I got refused the course I wanted so I decided to apply for journalism instead – you know, to keep the Man off my back.' He whispered the last part in case any government lackeys happened to be lurking.

'I heard the nursing course filled up quickly.' Finn tapped Hugh on the shoulder and watched as he turned to stare at Fredrik, who became puzzled.

'How did you know that?' Leo didn't think he had told anyone about the nursing course.

Finn chuckled at both Leo and Fredrik's perplexity. 'Lucky guess, I suppose.'

'Anyway, I'm a dude so I'm not allowed to be a nurse – that right, Louis?' He bent over and hooked his fingers between his cheeks. 'Bend over and say 'aaagh!''

There were very few things that grossed Louis out, but the thought of Leo going anywhere near there grossed out even him. 'I'd rather stick a Lego cucumber up there.'

'I came to the open day to doss off school,' Gibby said. 'It was a spur-of-the-moment thing because I didn't want to face Mr. Matthews. He had it in for me and I didn't have the homework done.' She curled her hair around her middle and index fingers. 'He used to call me the Purple Power Ranger because of my hair. My friend came too and when we got here, I followed her into the journalism room. I put my name down for the fun and the rest is history.'

'And you still kept your purple locks,' Louis said.

She extended her hand and let the hair fall and uncurl itself. 'Gotten attached to them now.'

'Can I tell my story,' Mia put in, 'it's kind of similar?'

'Only if it involves being grateful to the class.'

Mia pouted and aimed a hand-on-hip diva pose at Finn. 'Ok, well I applied for a teaching course, and I got accepted but it's five years and I didn't want to sign up for something that long cause I'm still young.' She paused, looking from Rock to Finn and back again.

'Ooohh!' Spikester and Kennedy both jeered as the two eldest looked at each other and frowned.

'Sorry, guys!' Mia apologised. 'So, I applied here instead and I'm really happy I did because I got to meet so many great people – and because I became queen of the class,' she said proudly, and without a hint of debate from the other girls.

A draught ran up Finn's leg like a creepy crawly trying to evade being prey. 'Do you think the universe conspired to bring us all together? Like a deranged group of slightly useful superheroes?'

'The universe brought us here for two reasons; so we could have wedgies on a Friday - god I *loovve* wedgies-'

'Who doesn't?' Simon yelped.

'-and so we could rip on Simon.' Rock said. 'Fact.'

He was being jocund, but Finn knew it was more than just that, he was certain of it - and after hearing everyone's accounts of how they wound up there only served to imbue a belief that some higher power was covertly running things. 'I do like Pizza Friday, but you have to admit the coincidence is something.'

'That's all it is, coincidence.' Rock replied.

'Hmmm, but what if there's something mor-'

'Anyone want to create a new food day?' Simon said, butting in. Whatever silly thing Finn was waffling on about came a distant second to matters of the stomach.

'You know something, that's not a bad idea.'

Simon stared agog at Rock, waiting for a withering punch line.

'How about *Sub-Wednesday*?' Finn was also eager to have another day when he didn't have to bring in a sandwich that would be rancid by lunchtime. 'Café up the road does a sub and coffee special?'

'Done: *Sub-Wednesday* it is,' Rock decreed, and banged his fist on the bench like a judge making a ruling.

Chapter 14

Rock clambered over the gate with care, making sure it didn't rattle. He couldn't afford to risk his headlights being seen or the engine being heard so he left his not so inconspicuous camper five minutes up the road. He came under the cover of darkness and like a spy in a movie was donned out in black. Rock even wore a black beanie in case the moon's light should reflect off his head and give away his position. This was an extreme situation and it called for extreme stealth.

He kept low to the ground, using the grass to disguise his movements, and his leg keened at having to stay in a hunched position for so long. A narrow path with weeds straining to embrace from the margins connected a barn to the main house about eighty yards away. He leaned against the wall and waggled his bad leg to get the blood moving again.

Rock peered around the corner. A cloud of moths was assailing the only working light at the front of the house. He took one last breath and began edging his way along the side of the barn. He had almost made it to the front when a motion-detecting spotlight sprang into action. 'Oh, shite!'

He looked around before darting back behind the barn. Standing statuesque, Rock waited to hear if anyone had come out of the house. Everything was silent. He peeked from his hiding place; no one there, apart from the frantic fury of silent wings. Maybe the sensor was always being triggered by the likes of foxes or rats and the owner had grown used to seeing it flicker on and off, he supposed.

He decided to try and dupe it by going round the other side, where he'd be shielded from view from the two-storey house. If he could just make it to the window he wouldn't need to get to the actual door. All he was looking for was proof they were inside.

The barn was so big it could have housed not just an entire puppy mill, but also the eight reindeer with space for Rudolph in the corner. Sadie's words rang in his ear: 'Don't do anything illegal for these assignments, but if you do don't get caught,' she had told them during a lesson about 'covering your tracks', both literally and figuratively.

'I'm trying my best, Sadie,' Rock whispered.

He moved at a snail's pace, embracing the front wall like a blind man a wall he didn't know, hoping the spotlight wouldn't tattletale. 'Please don't go off, please don't go off.' The spotlight craned its inflexible neck, searching for movement.

Rock thought of another problem while he was involved in the illuminating game of cat and mouse: what if the windows were tainted by grime and he couldn't see through them? If that was the case, he'd need to get to the door. He was only a couple of feet from the first of two windows when a sharp bark made him jump. There were dogs in the barn, the tip-off he'd received was right, and despite his heart thumping he was glad of that.

Cobwebs dotted the corners of the window, but he could see clearly inside; puppies, lots and lots of puppies. From what Rock could make out the whole place was crammed with little balls of dark fur. Seemed the rumours about the conditions were on point too. He didn't come this far to stop now. If the light snitched him out, he'd bail and return with help the next day. It was bordering on one in the morning and too late to take any sort of definitive action.

The spotlight was dozing, and Rock made it to the door undetected. He slid aside the unbolted latch, took one more glance towards the house, and then stole into the barn, pulling the door shut behind him.

The first thing he noticed was the smell. It was a pungent mix of excrement, soaked newspaper, and whatever else came from stuffing so many dogs into so few cages. He patted himself with his sweater. Sneaking around and breaking into barns was a sweaty business, even in near-freezing temperatures. Though he knew it was pointless, he covered his nose with the same sleeve and carefully tread the narrow arteries of dirt. There were maybe thirty cages in all, and all pumped full of puppies who whined as one, producing a noise so thorough that Rock would have been at a loss to hear if anyone had been approaching.

'Sssshhhh, guys, you'll get me in trouble,' he implored them, thinking they must have felt he was going to lay on some food.

Less than a hundred yards from where Rock was trying to get his head around what he was seeing – and feeling like he'd stumbled into one of those Chinese dog warehouses – a figure walked past the upstairs window.

He poked his finger through one of the cages and let three fur balls nibble it. 'How could anyone do this?' He tried his best to remain impartial, but Rock couldn't stop himself from running hot. He was ready to make someone pay and spent longer than he should have imagining ramming whoever was responsible for this into the tinniest cage.

He took out a small camera from his jeans pocket. Rock would get the evidence he needed and bring it to the police. Then, along with animal rights people, they'd all come back and bring this sick puppy to justice. Maybe the cops would let him put the perp in handcuffs; he'd make sure to rotate them just enough so that the ratchet couldn't click anymore, he fantasised, as he fired off a few rounds.

The figure in the house, who was now downstairs, froze for an instant, and then quickly moved from the window. It never occurred to Rock that the flash might be able to be seen from the house and he continued to unwittingly snap away.

'Don't worry little guys, I'm coming back with the Feds to break you out.' *Feds*, ha, should just give *me* my own TV show, Rock thought to himself. Inquisitive faces considered their emancipator with interest and seemed to give an affirmative when he asked if they could hold on one more night. He briefly thought about taking a cage with him but decided it would be better to come back and get them all at once.

As he stepped out of the barn, so, too, a man stepped out the back door of his house. A long, slender barrel lay draped across his forearm and he and Rock caught sight of each other at the same moment. They both hesitated, like they'd each caught the other doing something they shouldn't be. The man shouted and proceeded to raise the black barrel and lodge it against his shoulder.

A frown worried into Rock's forehead. 'Is that a...' he said, and then, horrified, he realised it was a shotgun and that it was pointed right at him. 'Shit!' Rock spun on his heels, knowing that if he could just get around the side of the barn he'd be safe.

Against the express wishes of his leg, something told him to crouch lower as he ran. Somewhere in the recesses of his mind, he knew that when a shotgun was fired the buckshot spread out like a swarm of wasps. Just as he bent, the barn rumbled in his ear like a pissed-off drill sergeant. It wasn't the shed rumbling but the sound of a splaying mass of projectiles implanting themselves in the guttering above his head.

Rock grazed the corner (bringing the bruise Lena had given him screaming back to life) and out of the firing line, arms and legs pumping like pistons in a tank. The thought, *that bastard shot at me*, played over and over again in his head as if bound to a loop.

'That *bastard* shot at me!' Rock exclaimed, as it finally sunk in, and he realised he was still flat out. He must have been well away from that maniac ('who actually shot at me!') by now so Rock slowed his roll. He doubled over beside a leafless tree that had been ravaged by winter. His throat was breached by saliva and bile which he had to spit out numerous times. When there was no sign or sound of anyone coming from behind, Rock calmly - and angrily - trudged back to the deserted lane where he'd stashed his motorhome.

'That guy is going to pay,' he said. Rock put the key in the ignition and turned it. 'I'm going to make him pay.'

* * * *

Some thirty miles from where **Rock** would soon be running for his life, **Finn** was pulling open the door to a building hidden in the crisscross of historic side streets. He had chosen a topic for his assignment that he had first-hand experience with and had an appointment to meet someone from *Gamblers Anonymous.*

Finn had started gambling when he was twenty-two and had quickly fallen under its enchanting spell. He loved the thrill of watching his horse sweep round the outside of the pack, and the dash towards the finish line. He loved the challenge of solving the oft-futile riddle of who was going to win, and maybe unearthing that big-odds winner that would allow him to buy new clothes or get away for the weekend. More often than not, however, when he did solve the riddle, it would be junk food and beer as recompense for his stressful efforts. Then, with illusions of riches and grandeur, he'd dive back in, and that new t-shirt he was in such need of – and which hadn't been subject to disappearing tracts of fabric – would remain on the rack for another day. His bookmaker would merely grin as Finn greased his palms with the money which, he knew, like an obedient boomerang, would always come spinning and swirling back.

When he spoke to Joe over the phone, Finn had been given clear instructions about the interview. He wasn't allowed to reveal Joe's identity and wouldn't be permitted to record the conversation. In fact, Joe's real name wasn't even Joe. Finn felt like he was going to parlay with a member of the **KKK** who was intent on keeping his identity secret, lest the boys discover who was beneath the hood and robe.

He asked for 'Joe' at the front desk and was led into a small communal kitchen. It was warm, which came as a welcome relief after walking twenty minutes through the biting December wind. The kitchen was empty apart from a woman making tea. She sang quietly to herself, and three lumps of sugar made three *plop* sounds as they fell into the cup.

A man came into the room and walked over to Finn like he'd spent more time in the centre than he had his own home. 'Hi,' he said, 'I'm Joe.'

'Nice to meet you, Joe (*if that is your real name*),' Finn replied, taking the man's hand.

After shaking what felt like a frosted paddle, Joe made two cups of steaming-hot coffee and picked a table at the far end of the room where they could talk in private. 'You mentioned on the phone that you're writing a gambling article?'

'Yes.' Finn quickly grabbed the handle of the mug with his other hand such was the heat of the dated ceramic. 'I'm looking to write a balanced piece so I'm interviewing those promoting it and those who have been adversely affected by it.'

'Sounds fair,' he replied, 'just don't use my real name.'

'I don't even *know* your real name, Joe.'

'Perfect, we'll keep it at that.' Joe stroked his beard like he was happy with the arrangement.

Finn smiled and then threw himself diffidently into the role of inquisitor. 'Obviously, you've had problems in the past,' he said, presenting the room around them, 'how did you find yourself in that world?'

Joe explained that he first started gambling when he was at school. He and his friends would go to the bookies every Saturday and put down accumulator bets on the football. It was fun at the beginning, but by the time he left school at eighteen, his bets had become noticeably bigger.

'I had a part-time job in those days, three evenings a week in the local shop - you know, serving people at the register, stacking shelves - that sort of thing. It got to the point where I'd have my wages spent the day I got them.'

'Was it just football?' Finn said.

The woman's low warbling became steadily louder.

'At the start, yeah, but then I discovered horse racing and that was the end of my footballing days. They were so much more exciting; the speed, the tactics - the long-legged finesse, they just reeled me in,' Joe replied, unaware that his whole body was becoming more animated. 'From that first bet on the nags I was hooked. I didn't know it at the time, but I was.'

Finn saw sentimentality married with resentment on Joe's face. Sadie explained the power of body language and what to look for when interviewing someone. 'Everybody lies, whether they mean to or not,' she had told the class that first week. 'It's vital you realise this - even your own family will lie right to your face. Don't take it personally, it's just human nature.'

The more Finn learned about journalism the more he realised there was no such thing as a 'journalist' per se, but rather an individual who was a collection of many things rolled into one; including, but not limited to, a poker player, a shrink, a communication-specialist, a lie-detector machine, and a mind reader - and if you happened to be able to write words in the proper order, then that was good too.

'But what you need to do,' she had continued, 'is to recognise when this is happening, and cut through all the falsities, attention-seeking, and protecting of fables (she explained these as being the filters through which you saw the world; optimistic like Pooh, or pessimistic like Eeyore) until you get to the little nuggets of truth; or at least the *most* truth of any situation, because truth is a funny thing and can differ from person to person.'

'I'll never forget the first time I put a hundred pounds on a horse,' Joe began again unspurred, 'placed it right on the nose. No each way that day. Name was *See Me Dance*, tip from one of the old codgers in there.' He turned a fraction, sensing her rather than seeing her. 'Are you alright, Mildred?'

Mildred had gotten close enough that she could almost read Finn's shorthand. She took a mouthful of sweet tea. 'I'm fine.'

'Awful nosey Nellie, that one.' Joe confided in Finn when Mildred had plodded off to overhear someone else. 'So, this guy was in the bookies every day, open till close – even had his own seat, and heaven help anyone who sat in it.' Joe had ended up with a cauliflower ear the first and only time he made that mistake. 'I'd never been more scared or more excited in my life. I felt if I could just get that one big win that I might have a chance, a springboard to better things...you know what I mean?'

Finn nodded. He knew that feeling well, and he knew what it was like to lose big – rob-from-the-fountain-outside-your-local-STI clinic kind of big – and he found himself hoping that Joe's horse would win.

'I didn't know how I was going to eat if it lost. But if it won, I was planning on marching straight over to the restaurant beside the pub – the one with the fancy curtains – and ordering a filet mignon. I'd have a glass of wine and get some waiter I didn't know to lay a white serviette across my lap like they did in the movies.' He recounted to himself that his life up until that point had been anything but cosmopolitan. 'Since then, of course, I've come to realise that most tips are bluster and typically finish out the back.'

Joe's smile came out his eyes and even the most novice body-reader could tell it was unfeigned. 'But this one wasn't,' he said, 'this one won – at thirty-threes.'

He might have been trying to escape the clutches of a malignant habit, but that memory was one of Joe's favourites and one he'd cherish till he either died or forgot. Finn felt genuine jubilation for him as if they were somehow battling a common enemy. 'I'm glad you won.'

Joe had instructed the waiter to leave the entire bottle of wine, deciding that a glass just wouldn't cut the mustard. '£3,300 was a lot of money back then.'

'It's a lot of money now,' Finn replied. 'Did you get your steak in the end?'

'Paraded into the place like I was the Sultan of Brunei.' He said, grinning. 'The mignon was as nice as I'd imagined – even with all the blood. Bought my first car too that week, of course, I had to sell the damn thing three months later.'

Finn felt like he needed to use kid gloves in case he knocked him off the wagon. 'Do you ever miss it?'

Joe hesitated as if weighing up his answer. The smile crept back onto his face like the stalking of a cat. He nodded his head first, and then the words tumbled out. 'Sometimes,' he replied, almost resigning himself to the unsavoury truth. 'Sometimes I'd like to experience that surge of adrenaline again, even once.'

'Would you not allow yourself a one-off, like when the National comes round?'

'I'm a compulsive gambler and a recovering addict.' Finn felt that these words had been uttered in that order plenty of times up till now. 'If I had one bet, I'd have another and another until I ended up back under the proverbial bus.'

He supposed if Joe was still calling himself a compulsive gambler, then he'd probably sat out the last National or two. Finn readied his pen to add a number. 'How long is it since your last bet?'

He didn't need time to work it out. 'Just shy of twenty-two years.'

'Twenty-two Grand Nationals?' Finn enounced slowly.

'It'll be twenty-two next month,' Joe said, 'the fourteenth to be exact.'

Joe hadn't bet for the same number of years it took Finn to have his first wager, which he remembered had come in paddy last. He was unsure if he should take a slightly firmer line of questioning. 'Have you been coming here *since* then?'

'Even before then,' Joe replied, 'but I wasn't ready to give it up. It was only after my wife walked out and took my daughter–' Though his tear ducts had long run dry, the thought of his little girl whose face he now wouldn't recognise always caused him to well up, '–that I committed to giving up for good.'

Finn knew he was walking on thin ice, but he felt compelled to get to the root of Joe's state of mind. 'Do you not feel that constantly labelling yourself a 'recovering addict' is kind of unfair?'

'What do you mean?'

He shifted in his seat. 'Continually reinforcing the view that you're *recovering* – even though you haven't bet in over twenty years – might actually be keeping you stuck in a false mindset?' Finn hoped

Joe wouldn't grab his jacket and haul ass to the betting shop a few doors down.

He stroked his greying beard again. 'I never really thought about it like that-'

Bugger, I've broken him.

'-maybe, I'm not sure.'

He had pushed things far enough. Finn didn't want his first interview to result in the regression of a man back to his teenage years. That's what hypnosis was for. 'I've one question left if that's okay, and then I'll be out of your hair.'

'Let me have it.' Joe, who, after pushing away the image of his daughter as she was being led away screaming by her mother, seemed to be enjoying the interview, replied.

Finn could see Mildred's shadow lingering in the door frame. 'Do you believe gambling should be banned?'

Joe ran his finger around the periphery of his near-empty china cup. 'I used to think that the government should get involved, that I'd still have my family if they only stopped me.' He looked at Finn. 'Now I'm not so sure. Humans are fallible. We have addictive personalities. We're always going to want to cling to something and if you ban that something then we'll just find some other destructive *something* - if that makes any sense?'

The air, which had turned colder during his chat with Joe, didn't bother him as it had, and Finn sauntered home happy to have found that rare gem journalists search high and low for: the truth.

Chapter 15

'How would you feel if a lion was walking towards you?' Sadie swigged from a bottle of Lucozade. She was engaging the class in another of her lessons where the textbook was purely ornamental.

'Scared.' Daisy replied.

'I'd hope I was wearing my tennis shoes.' Billie held out both feet and gave an under-the-table fashion show, 'can't run for nuts in these.'

'Depends,' Rock said, 'do I have Athena with me?'

Sadie put the cap back on and screwed it tight. 'You'd probably run or try to hide – or release Athena, right?' She replied. 'What about a kitten?'

'I'd pick it up and rub it all over my face.'

Sophia's tone was one that was normally reserved for Leo. 'Why would you do that, Louis?'

Louis strummed the pull ring on his can. 'I don't know, doesn't everyone do that?'

'You'd need five needles in the arm if you did that in Asia.' Finn thought back to the strays that often peered at him with demonic remonstration, and he made it a point not to pet those cats.

'Ok, most of us would steer clear of the lion and hug the kitten. Another one-,' Sadie went on, '-murder. Say you wanted to have someone knocked off, who would you ask, Rock or Kevin?'

Apart from Spikester, who said Kevin and made everybody laugh (apart from Kevin, who insisted he would never murder anyone), everyone said they'd pick Rock if they needed to do away with someone.

'Think I'd pick Rock, too,' Sadie added, chuckling, 'no offence, Kevin.' Kevin shook his head and smiled like it was a perfect compliment. 'Do you think your answers make you prejudiced?'

'Against the lion?'

'Or against Kevin,' Sadie said, responding to Louis.

The pull ring came off at the letter F. 'Don't think the lion would mind?' he replied.

'Might eat you if it found out,' Finn teased, and Louis ran an imaginary claw through the air.

'Or do you think we're just generalising?' she said, slinging in a conceptual curve ball.

'I don't understand,' Billie replied, making figure-of-eights with her legs, 'how can you generalise about something like that?'

Blanche raised her hand. 'Maybe the lion had just eaten someone and wasn't hungry anymore?'

'And maybe Rock found God and didn't want to kill anyone anymore?' As usual, Kennedy's thinking followed along the same lines as her best friend's.

Sadie always loved seeing her students teasing things out for themselves. It was the reason she had stayed in teaching so long. 'Now we're getting somewhere.'

The principal often got on to her about not adhering to the official curriculum – and for 'hardly ever using the prescribed textbook' – and Sadie's riposte was always the same: 'Do you want to help form young people who can think for themselves, or do you want to help form mindless androids?'

'More chance of the lion scenario, I think.' Finn said aloud, knowing whose tail he would rather stand on.

'So, Rock's found God-'

'Yeah, right!' The *God Boys* had been trying that one long enough and they still hadn't relieved him of his soul.

Sadie tossed the half-full bottle from one hand to the other. 'What about Kevin?'

'He's in a bad mood?' Simon suggested.

'Yeah - like a Taz bad mood.' Leo confirmed, and he and Simon high-fived to celebrate tag teaming the problem.

'I know,' Mia was pointing at the ceiling as if she'd thought of just the thing, 'maybe he watched one of Louis' movies and it brought out his wicked side?'

'Or he got his hands on some of Dot's delights.' Red added, without needing to expand on what he meant.

Kevin was now shaking his head vigorously. 'I don't...I'm not like that,' he tried to explain.

'It's alright, Kevin, we know you wouldn't go on a bloodthirsty rampage.' Sadie knocked on the projector and placed a sheet of paper over the light. Two shapes came into being on the screen wall. 'What's this?'

'A bullseye on a dartboard.' Rock said straight off.

Simon covered his eye to see if anything happened to the ball. 'Is it one of those games that when you cover your eye the ball disappears?'

'No, silly boos,' Daisy said, 'that's the Japanese flag; circle on square.'

Leo slapped Simon in the hand and when he took it away from his eye ended up seeing a ball that wouldn't stay still.

'A glory hole?' suggested Fredrik.

'What's a glory hole?' Daisy uncapped her pen, ready to transcribe the answer to her copybook.

'Well,' Fredrik began, always happy to clue in the illiterati, 'a glory hole is when a man takes his phal-'

'I can assure you,' Sadie said, 'it's not a glory hole.'

'Nope.' Billie was rolling her pen across her fingers, first slowly and sedulously, then quickly and grindingly as it traversed the humps of her knuckles, 'definitely not a glory hole.'

Fredrik scanned her with a new-found intrigue. He had never noticed the way the tongue of her shoe stood up like that. It was kind of perky.

'So,' Sadie said, placing the bottle back on the table, 'we've discovered we're a pretty presumptive bunch, and that one situation can look quite differently depending on your perception-'

'Certainly does to Fredrik.' Ashley commented, just as Fredrik had decided that Billie's shoe tongue was more than just perky, it was erotic.

'-What did you all think of that little girl over the weekend?'

'The one killed by the drone?' Mia said, having put her earlier inglorious answering in Orwell's class behind her.

Sadie responded with a deferential nod. Some stories could still hit her in the solar plexus. 'Why do you think the world took notice of her?'

'Because it was a child?' Mia replied. She was still the brightest among them, despite a couple of extremely rare hiccups.

'We hear about children dying by the hundreds in places like Syria that go completely ignored.'

The class was deep in thought as to why this little girl, face charred and caked in dirt, and who had expelled her final breath under cinder, steel, and ash, would attract the attention of Western people.

'Was it her clothes?' Blanche asked.

'What about them?' Sadie replied, pulling at her students' chain of thought.

Blanche paused and Kennedy goaded her to keep going. 'They're the same as what we'd wear?'

Sadie's head and finger nodded thoughtfully together. 'We don't get much news about terrorism in Middle Eastern countries and when we do it's normally shoved to the bottom of page twenty in small font.'

'There was lots of news about the French attacks?'

Light-hearted laughter met with the reply when Rock informed Leo that France was in Europe.

'Why is that?' Louis asked, his normal chair aerobics slowing to a gentle rocking.

'Because sad as it sounds, unless they wear a Western face and remind us of *Us*, then no one cares.'

'That's a bit racist?' In Mia's book of decency, all kids were the same and they all deserved the same level of care, 'a life's a life.'

'Possibly,' Sadie replied, 'but if it's not in the papers or on a television screen then it's a case of out of sight out of mind, and as we've already learned the media can be very discerning typists.'

'At least we're not racist like that,' Ashley said, 'we gave it front page coverage.'

Sadie started into a circuit of the room, a move that often foreshadowed a journey deep into subject matter. 'Are these things discriminatory or racist, I wonder? But, yeah, us Irish are pretty great, aren't we?'

'You betcha we are!' Ashley confirmed, speaking for the room.

'Mm-hmm. And do you think there could be any bias there?'

A roomful of opened mouths, high foreheads and malleable minds waited to be led down the rabbit hole to greater awareness. 'What do you mean?' Ashley was slightly sore that Sadie would even ask such a question.

'Do you think the history books would tell us if we weren't all we were made out to be, or would they tell us what we wanted to hear?'

'They'd tell the truth.' Billie was retying a lace that wasn't undone, 'wouldn't they?'

Red noticed that Fredrik was very interested in how Billie was tying the knot in her shoe.

'One of my dad's favourite sayings is that history is written by those who won the feud,' said Finn.

'They'd probably tell us what we wanted to hear.'

'I think Finn and Blanche are right.' Sadie stopped and looked down. 'No one wants to be reminded of the bad stuff they've done, do they?'

Kevin and Simon shook their heads.

'One of the easiest things to succumb to – and one of the things you will need to look in the mirror and face up to – are predisposed notions instilled in you because of where you were raised. Look at slavery, for instance.'

Rock's arms were folded high on his chest, blocking the logo on his jumper. 'The Yanks you mean.'

'Kunta Kinte.' Louis declared, grinning.

'I thought you'd be a bit young for Kunta Kinte?' Sadie said, throwing the thrusters into reverse.

'Nah,' Louis replied, his inanimate steed now back on barley and oats rather than sugar water, 'I've seen them all.'

Sadie became more ruminative as the smile melted from her face. 'Do you know that when it came to slavery the Irish weren't always the victims?'

'Yeah, but we were sold and shipped across the world by the Brits!' Ashley said, making sure that everyone knew about it.

'Including Bridgewater's favourite son.' Finn had always wondered how it was possible to build a relationship with someone who had left this world, but he felt an unusual pull towards the legend of Bridgewater and there was the baffling feeling that he had also been banished from his homeland some centuries previous.

Ashley shook her head as if a pet had done something unexpected. 'Feckin' English.'

'You're right, guys, Cromwell and his friends do indeed have a lot to answer for. But as truth-seekers, we can't ignore the *fact* that the Irish were slave owners too and that sometimes they could be just as cruel as their British and American counterparts,' Sadie said, explaining about judiciously forgotten Irish history. 'In America, the blacks used to dread being owned or sold to an Irish master.'

Daisy's fingers took it in turn to caress an onyx gemstone. 'Why?'

The class was reticent, smothering their feelings like they were expecting to have to defend themselves.

'Because the Irish had a reputation for not treating them very well,' Sadie replied. 'There was one particular owner from Mayo who ran a tobacco plantation down south. He was a barbaric individual, his name known three states away for its callousness. When one day one of his slaves fell to his knees out of exhaustion - as he'd quite literally slaved since dawn - this Mayo master instructed his son to 'feed the nigger in the sty with the rest of the hogs".

Simon's ears twitched and he quickly scanned the room, while the others fell silent.

'Did the father really say that to his son?' Ashley had no qualms about putting a gun to the head of an English infidel, but she thought doing something like that to someone who was helping to run your estate was downright unnecessary.

'Yes, Ashley. The son was made to mix the slave's food with the slop. He was thirteen at the time.'

'Did she-' Simon clacked, '-did she just say the n-word?'

'Bro,' Leo replied distractedly, taking in what Sadie had just told them.

There came the sound of crinkling aluminium as Louis' fingers tightened gently around his can. 'What happened then?'

Sadie paced from person to person. She had come to realise that this held students' attention more than just preaching from her podium. 'The slave had no choice, he was starving.' She looked along the line of disenchanted faces. 'He got onto his hands and knees, and he ate.'

The class wasn't used to such truths, especially about their ancestors. They were astonished that one of *them* could be so heartless.

'But...she's a teacher?' he spurted, the pen falling from his mouth. 'She-'

'Shut up, Simon.' Rock demanded, 'We're trying to listen.'

'When you are writing a story, you have to leave aside what you *think* you know. You must let go of any bias or preconceived ideas you might have and be prepared to accept the truth, even if you don't like what that is.'

'She should have said the "n-word". Simon shuffled his notebook, let it go, and then shuffled it again. 'I have a good mind to report her to–'

Finn milled across Rock and Leo. 'Do you think the father used the "n-word"?'

'Probably not, but–'

'Exactly,' he replied, 'so *hush* up!'

'Definitely racist,' Simon muttered with a highbrow tilt, making sure to have the last say on the matter.

Sadie believed that to be a truly proficient journalist, you had to look beyond the obvious – and very often the commonly accepted – and drop all prefabricated narratives you had built before even considering picking up a pen. 'If you can't do this,' she went on, 'you'll never be able to write a fair and "uncoloured" article.'

'It's hard not to be biased about certain things.' Louis thought it sounded exactly like something that would happen on a Sunday morning when he would watch *Roots* in the family bed.

'Shouldn't we try and use our voice to change things for the better?' Mia asked, picturing how dreadful, how childhood-marring – because at thirteen he was still a child, no doubt about that – it would have been for the son.

'It is hard, I agree,' Sadie replied to her mentees. There were times – like with the story that had made her a household name ('don't mess with this bitch' were the words she had uttered after seeing her article move like treacle until it eventually got back to the covetous

President) – when she struggled to be a bystander too. 'But what you need to realise is you are not trying to be a moral authority on people's actions. You're there to record and disseminate their actions so that the world becomes the authority.'

'What about all the terrorism that's happening?' After a barrage of images and stories forced him to flick from the news channel to the cartoon channel, Kevin had decided that from now on he was going to rely solely on his strengths in other areas to pass the year.

The can crumpled like the crushing of an old car in a scrapyard. 'I'd bomb the bastards!'

'And I'd help ya!' Billie then reconsidered her offer of military intercession, 'You think I could wear these while we're doing it?'

Louis inspected her shoes. 'Yeah, I think so, they're pretty sporty.'

'That, too,' Sadie said, 'you need to be able to silence your ego – that part of you that knows right from wrong. Your job is to report the facts. If you can't do that, you'll be just another hack journalist who writes to vindicate their own beliefs, instead of what the story deserves.'

'Sporty?' Billie murmured, 'wasn't really what I was going for...'

Although Kevin's digital design skills had taken an impressive turn since he'd struck journalism from the rota, he had no time for those people. 'I don't really like those people,' he insisted.

'Remember,' Sadie said, as the class got gingerly up from their chairs, 'rarely is a story – and by extension, a *history* – ever as clearcut as it seems.'

'I know France is in Europe,' Leo was saying as they formed an alighting cluster bomb, 'everyone knows that.'

Sadie called over the body of the incendiary, 'Finn, can I see you for a minute?'

'I'll meet you in the lobby,' he said to Rock, who was following Ashley out the door, who was muttering about how she'd shoot the fuckers right in the face.

'I've been reading some of your stuff.'

Somewhere in the ocean that was Finn's psyche, a small sailboat named 'Hope' capsized and sank.

'I think you've got the potential to be a very good writer,' Sadie said, grinning ironically as if she could tell exactly what he was thinking.

Finn liked to write, and deep down there was always that desire to write, but he never knew if he was any good. Suddenly, the sailboat righted itself on a passing wave. 'Really?'

'That piece you wrote about those poor kids being abducted in the Philippines so their organs could be harvested was heart-breaking, almost made me want to fly over there and kick some ass myself.'

He smiled reluctantly. For sure his spelling and grammar could do with a spring clean, but that was doable with a little elbow grease.

'Have you submitted it?' Sadie said.

'No...not yet.' Finn's head was still swimming from the praise.

'Well, you should,' she went on, 'I know if I was an editor, I'd print it.'

He nodded absently as his mind tried to grab hold of the tendrils of sense that drifted on Sadie's words. 'I'll do it tonight.'

'Do. And if newspapers aren't your style, you can always try travel writing, certainly if those Tasmanian sunrises are anything to go by.'

Writing was much like the rest of Finn's life, where there were choices to be made he'd become utterly stumped, and what could have more choices than choosing what to write about? Could he write for a newspaper? Or a magazine? Or become the next travel-writing sensation, which sounded ever more interesting?

'Oh, and Finn.'

He caught the word *Believe* under a picture of a craggy mountain peak as he turned around.

'Learn how to use 'whether' correctly, won't you?' she said.

Chapter 16

It was Christmas Day – not the actual Christmas Day, but the college version of Christmas Day. Two sparsely decorated trees had been erected to help spread cheer amongst stressed-out students, one of the synthetics tucked in the corner of the canteen, the other in the lobby of the reception. Gaunt and aged strips of tinsel hugged framed inspirational photos, while scraggly, half-torn garlands hung from the ceilings. It was the thought that counted, Finn supposed.

The normally desolate aroma room was buzzing with students enjoying the free hot chocolate and sugared jellies – no doubt leftover rejects from Halloween. Music ding-donged in the background as teachers in Christmas hats mingled with their proteges. Even Santa Claus had turned up and was handing out selection boxes to whatever little boy or girl he thought deserved one.

'Santa?' Rock rose to his feet when the man in red passed by. 'I'll take one of those.'

Santa peered up at the unwavering face. He couldn't work out if he was a student or a crazed inmate so he acceded and handed Rock the biggest selection box he could.

'Thanks, Santa, appreciate that – happy Christmas.'

'Yeah, hap-happy Christmas to you, too,' came the pruned reply.

Rock grinned and held the box up like a trophy. 'Anyone want a chocolate bar?'

'I'll have the Maltesers,' Mia said, 'if you don't mind?'

'Bags the Crunchie,' Finn called, holding out his hand over Mia's shoulder.

Ashley waltzed over and swiped the Curly Wurly from its rut just as Simon was reaching for it. 'Hey, I wanted that!'

'Should have been quicker,' she replied, pirouetting away like a Russian ballerina.

'Then can I have the Turkish Delight?' Simon asked, slightly perturbed at seeing the dwindling number of chocolate bars.

'Of course, you can.' Rock handed him the flaming pink square of jelly. 'No one likes them anyway.'

Morning classes had been cancelled so students could unwind and enjoy the festivities. Among the diversions taking place was a decoration-making tutorial for those who didn't want to bow to the corporate machine, a talk on nutrition (which, in hindsight, probably wasn't the best time to have it), and an hour-long mindfulness demonstration.

Finn had always wanted to see behind the hype of mindfulness – and if it could really mollify a mind a million – so he encouraged the others to give it a try. Within six minutes, Hugh was immersed in a Manchester United press conference on his phone, Rock was asleep, and Fredrik continually derided the lack of scientific evidence for the so-called 'benefits': He should have known better.

Outside under the oak tree, Leo brought his hand back and forth. His right eye was closed and his glasses were misted from concentration. He held the ball tightly, maybe a little too tightly for the purposes of accuracy. Leo didn't have a good throw – certainly not an all-American throw, and Orwell sneered at him, fully confident that he was as safe as a concrete house in a gale ten metres away.

Marshalling in behind were others who hoped that Leo would make a mess of his two attempts, so they could lay claim to having dunked Orwell themselves. But Leo couldn't have this. He didn't care about the others. He wanted all that lovely infamy for himself. After missing the bullseye by two metres with his first effort, Leo sensed a lull in the watching crowd. He humped the ball out in front of him with a foisting of his hips, pretending to drop it. It staggered a handful of revolutions towards Orwell and the huge vat of water that he was perched over. People looked briefly and Leo was ignored as he picked up the pellet-filled ball and continued forward. Orwell's mouth flapped open and closed – like a fish when it sees a bigger fish swimming towards it with fixings on brunch – as he registered Leo's intentions. He began pointing and for the first time in his life was stuck for words.

'Hey...hey, what the – look at him...' he trailed off hopelessly.

If Leo couldn't hit the target with a ball, he most certainly could with his fist. He was mere feet away when he realised that it might hurt if he punched the serrated tin outpost. He opened his fist; he'd slap the target instead. On reaching it, he then realised his hand would be at the wrong angle and he stalled, momentarily panicking.

'No...you can't do that, it's CHEATING!' Orwell roared.

Leo needed to strike, or he'd lose his chance. He rotated his hand and hit the bullseye with a sideways slap that made him look not dissimilar to a drag queen waving to an adoring mob. The target depressed and triggered a mechanism that snapped the seat back against the wall. This was his crowning moment, the moment that would seal his status as a college superstar, never to be forgotten even after he was long gone and had moved on to bigger and better things.

Orwell's look of horror contrasted delightfully (like white swans on a polluted canal) with Leo's look of anticipatory glory. Orwell slipped legs-first into the vat, flummoxed that he'd gone to the trouble of getting donned out in his best tweed just to be dunked by Leo, of all people. Cheers and laughter rose from the crowd and two girls from the beauty therapy course scampered to drier land and scowled as water dripped from their flat black shoes. Leo turned in slow motion, basking in the limelight and absorbing every bit of adulation he could. This was the greatest day of his life! This must be how it felt to fight in the Colosseum or pitch at Yankee Stadium. He would never forget this day, he thought, and was consumed by a blur of colour and euphoria.

* * * *

The following morning, Rock came into class looking like the bird who had caught the juiciest worm, and Finn eyed him suspiciously. 'What are you up to?' he said.

'What do you mean?'

'I mean you grinning like a hyena on a promise.' Finn replied.

When he should have been detailing the social ramifications of fake news (Sadie said this was a new thing, but in his humble opinion Leo's government had been doing it ever since that Jefferson fella wrote that document) the previous night, Rock was busy instead constructing Leo's legend. Unbeknown to Leo, Rock had noticed his shiftiness and had captured it with his camera. What's more, he had used burst mode. 'All will be revealed my friend,' he said, grinning even more, 'all will be revealed.'

Sadie walked in and placed a folder – which was so swollen with paperwork that it looked pregnant – on the desk, and when she opened it, loose sheets spilled out like they were making a run for it back to the woods. 'I'm going to call you up individually and give you your results,' she said. 'I've also got some very exciting news.' Sadie finished by throwing a mega family bag of assorted sweets on top of the pile.

'Are those for us?'

'They might be, Simon,' she replied, jumbling what was once a baby forest back into one cohesive unit.

'What?' Simon barked when he noticed Rock surveying him.

Rock sighed. 'Never mind.'

'I'll have yours if you don't want them?'

'Not in this lifetime you won't.' Rock replied.

Finn couldn't help smiling at the heated exchange. There was nothing quite like getting a treat when you were in any form of institution. It was somehow more special than buying them yourself and he wondered how prisoners must feel when the warden breaks out the teacakes.

'How'd you do?' Rock asked after Finn came back from his consult with Sadie.

'It's not fair,' Hugh said, when Finn held up a grandiose 'A-', 'I do more than you guys and you still get better results than me!'

'Wouldn't mind but you're always copying ours,' Finn replied, as Hugh's pen rebounded off the keyboard.

Sadie looked over and frowned at the outburst.

Rock caught the pen as it fell off the table and tucked it behind his ear. 'Don't worry, not everyone can be as good as us.'

'Not everyone can be as *old* as you either,' Hugh fired back, his arms tightly crossed on his chest.

Finn took the pen from Rock's ear and made it disappear in Hugh's bird's nest. 'At least you have the best hair, that'll never change.'

'Rock has none and yours is grey – go figure,' he replied, covering the hole the pen had made with his own version of a comb over.

'He has you there, Rock.' Finn said, admiring the grade that he seldom got last time in college.

'You can talk, Silver Pubes.' Rock placed his test sheet into a ring binder and snapped it closed. 'Another one for the highlight reel.'

'Now for the good news.' Sadie interjected before Hugh could go off on a tangent about conspiracies and grades and writing an article on always being singled out.

'And the sweets, right?' Simon said.

'Yes, and the sweets.'

Simon nodded, biting his bottom lip. Rock stared at him. 'Are you sexually attracted to those sweets or something?'

'Oh, yeah, Rock, I want to have sex with the sweets - jeez!' Simon flipped his eyes to heaven. Even the jellies with the hole in the middle he would never consider doing something like that.

'*Like* I was saying,' Sadie tried again, 'some of you decided to enter your short stories into the national flash fiction competition - about nine of you in all, I believe.'

'You should have sent the nuns in. They'd have won for sure.'

Rock leaned across and turned off Finn's desktop. He was still disgruntled by people's critique of his story.

'Haha!' Hugh cried.

Despite Hugh's best efforts to stave it off, Finn pressed his finger to the power button for the required two seconds. 'Don't know what you're laughing at,' he replied.

'Agghh, why'd you do that?' Hugh tutted. 'You know it sounds like a jet plane when it's starting.'

'Better fire up the engines so!'

'Well, I'd like you to put your hands together because, from all the entries around the country,' Sadie paused for dramatic effect, 'the winner is our very own Blanche!'

Like one giant organism, all heads scanned the room, finally locating Blanche tucked away in the corner, her mouth spread into a wide, retiring smile, the kind that appears of its own volition when you're nervous.

'And according to my source, two of the judges had to sleep with the lights on after reading her story.'

'Don't blame them,' Finn quipped, as the fighter jet beside him was being prepped for take-off.

Tentatively clapping at first the class broke out into full rapturous applause. Blanche believed she was nothing more than perfectly average, that any accomplishment was more dumb luck rather than inherent talent.

'It's always the quiet ones,' Rock commented, as Blanche tried finding a way to get into Kennedy's skin by pulling up her top.

'But she doesn't just win your applause,' Sadie broke back in, 'oh no, she also wins a weekend for two in the beautiful county of Sligo!'

Blanche's words came out from behind the honeycomb motif of Kennedy's knitted Aran. 'You're coming with me!' she said.

'Sure, who else would you bring?' Kennedy replied, like the idea of her taking anyone else was preposterous.

And just like that, Finn knew he belonged to a remarkable lot. Sure, from the outside they looked like a bunch of misfits, riddled with flaws like some of the women he'd encountered on his travels. Some were loners, some eccentrics with purple hair, while some were probably on an FBI watch list, but all of them added a unique ingredient, and as a group, Finn believed they could achieve anything. Blanche was a metaphor for the class; unassuming and unthreatening on the surface but do a little excavating and you soon discover the quirky treasure below.

'*They're just so spoiled*', Rock had insisted when the topic of generations had come up during lunch one day at their new bistro, 'little brats the lot of them.'

'Just because you were sent to work in the coal mines when you were in nappies and they weren't,' Finn had replied, laying into a sweet chili and meatball sub.

He also saw the differences between young people now and when he was first starting out. Now they were technophiles, straddling that line between virtual and real like expert jugglers, and because their focus was on two different realities there had been a marked degradation in attention span (a development Rock was secretly pleased with as it levelled the playing field), causing the balls – and the occasional sputtering chainsaw – to hit the deck.

'Maybe,' Rock said, 'but at least I learned about hard work and responsibility.'

'Was that a choice?'

'No,' a jerky motioning sent coffee up and out through the rectangular hole, 'I had to do it!'

Finn casually lapped up the sauce from his fingers. 'Maybe if you had the choice, you mightn't have worked the mines?'

'You do know I didn't work in coal mines, don't you?' Rock replied, shaking off the dribbles of coffee.

'Sure, grandad,' Finn had said, 'I believe you.'

They headed up the pinched stairwell to Orwell's lecture on the third floor – or useless-facts-they'd-never-need-unless-they-were-on-a-game-show lecture, as Finn had once called it – sucking on lollipops and chewing fizzy cola bottles. Blanche had been allowed to pick first and she chose the sour dolphin, which was causing her lips to retreat into her mouth like a gummy pensioner.

Orwell set his hickory suede shoulder bag down, but before he could enlighten them on how the simple bow tie (floppy for the girls) could help to engender feelings of trust among the public as he had planned, Rock made his way around his desk and spoke quietly in his ear. Orwell nodded thoughtfully, straightening his bow tie. Rock crossed to where the computer was kept and slotted in a Jim Beam USB fob. His extracurricular project popped up on the screen with an image of Leo holding a small Hacky Sack ball.

The chime of a bell foretold Daisy's arrival long before she was seen, and as the door glided shut behind her, a bubble of fag smoke obscured Blanche's and Kennedy's features below as they chewed on jellies, with only the dolphin's tail remaining.

'As you guys know,' Rock was now standing in front of the class, 'yesterday Leo sent our beloved teacher, Orwell here, into the dunk tank.' Orwell looked at Leo and pursed his lips tightly together – did Finn sense some genuine displeasure in that look?

'Yes, thank you for that, Leo,' he said, drawing out each word. 'I believe the red pen will be making quite a few appearances for the remainder of the year.'

Rock smiled; *think I've found my rightful place up here*, he thought, before speaking again. 'But as many of you won't know, I was on hand to document the whole thing...you know, for Leo's sake.'

Leo simpered and his head yo-yoed off its axis – fame *was* as glorious as they made out.

'So, without further ado.' Rock hit the space bar and the sequence of photos began playing out like a stuttering black-and-white motion picture. He had even gone to the trouble of adding some background music, which he thought had been no trouble at all.

The spliced-together stills (some of which were a fraction faster or slower for desired effect) showed Leo striving fervidly towards the vat that Orwell was squatted above. Orwell's countenance changed rapidly from suspicion to surprise to anger before finally settling on resignation and, if you were to isolate two, maybe three frames, you would see him mouthing a word that began with 'F'.

As Leo neared the crudely drawn-on smiley face, performing a robot dance that would have been the envy of many, he raised his fist to head height, elbow pulled back like a retracted slingshot. His fist then transformed itself into an open hand with his elbow bent ninety degrees like he was waving at someone. Heads of intrigued onlookers bobbed and changed direction over and over like comical personas on a car dashboard. Leo's hand turned inward, moving in front of his face.

When the classical music struck its crescendo, Leo slap-pushed the target with his leg cocked out like a dog urinating against a lamppost. Orwell, his arms raised above his head, plunged into the water, sending splashes like geysers into the air and over the sides. Two girls standing close by scarpered away and Leo continued to turn until the candy cane on his red and white jumpsuit became visible. His head then flicked back and forth like something from one of Louis' movies as he repeatedly glanced back at the submerged Orwell. Facing the crowd, mouth curled up at the edges like they were being pulled by invisible strings, his face wore the look of a scheming genius whose plans had come to fruition.

Orwell was the first to break and lose his cool, followed by the class which ruptured and exploded into a wave of howling, mocking joy. Leo's smile crumbled and was replaced by the cruel realisation that he wouldn't be remembered for dunking his teacher, but rather for *how* he had dunked his teacher.

'Agghhhh, Leo! You look like a gay cruise ship performer peeing out his vagina - AGGHHHH!' Dot cried, further stoking decibel levels.

Leo was crestfallen. He was a laughingstock, and the only thing he'd be famous for was a prissy push-slap. Any dreams of world fame had been destroyed in the time it took to play a sequence of roughly a hundred photographs. He lowered his head while the others around him struggled to regain their poise.

'Don't be upset, Leo.' Finn slapped him on the back, 'Not many people can say they sent Orwell into a tank of water.'

Maybe Finn had a point, Leo figured. If he couldn't be the world's next hottest property, then at least he could give his new friends a decent laugh.

'Like two sitting ducks it seems we were both taken out by the same reel; hook, line and sinker,' Orwell said to Leo, as the laughter raged on like a bushfire.

****

Finn agreed to walk Hugh as far as the shoe shop at the river end of Main Street – the one that knew Hugh by face and name because he'd already bought three pairs of trainers from them ('you just won't look the part if you don't have the trainers to match,' Hugh had replied when Finn asked if he had a different pair for each outfit) – as he had to go and purchase a bottle of drain unblocker.

Leaning against the gate outside the principal's window, Red took a drag from the stem of his stubby pipe. He was wearing the same denim bootcuts he did every other day, looking nonchalant and cool, a throwback to another era – the sixties, perhaps.

'Alright, Red? Not in a rush to get home?'

'Nah, Finn,' he replied, 'just waiting on someone.'

After purging his body of a questionable post-racing kebab the previous night, Finn had flushed the toilet only to see the contents come straight back up through the plug hole in the shower and paint the acrylic floor with a thin film of aqueous gunk. Finn imagined it being similar to when you swallowed something that went down the wrong tube and had ruled out the idea of a shower until the blockage could be blitzed with a bottle of chemicals. 'Must be a girl?' he said in jest.

'It's a friend...well, the ex,' Red replied, trying his best to explain the intricacies of their relationship, 'I mean, we're not going out or anything – but like, we're riding.'

Hugh started to laugh but he was laughing far harder on the inside. 'It's alright, Red, we get it.'

'And I thought my life was complicated?' Finn quipped as they left Red to meet the girl who wasn't his girlfriend but used to be but were having sex but weren't in a relationship.

Hugh released the laughter he had battled to restrain. 'That was hilarious,' he cackle-scoffed, 'I thought he'd just lie to us!'

They rounded the corner and were besieged by a brume of vinegar coming from the chip shop. 'Do you reckon we'll see your friend?'

'Sloppy?' Hugh replied, 'hope not, I've only got a Euro.'

They passed the used bookshop (the one where Louis had contrived to find work experience, arguing that he would be in direct contact with publishers when Orwell asked how the job related to journalism. So far, the only people Louis had spoken to were the characters from *Misery*, as he bade Annie Wilkes to catch that dirty birdie from between the columns of paperback pylons) and the new ice cream parlour that stayed open late for peckish night owls.

'We should go there after the exams to celebrate,' Hugh said, as they stopped to watch a shop worker drizzle chocolate sauce over a waffle.

'You sure you're going to pass?' Finn replied.

'Going to do more than that,' Hugh did a small jig in his scarlet-red runners, 'going to come top of the class.'

Finn laughed as two dollops of ice cream were lumped on top like plump drumlins. 'There's confidence for you.'

A little way ahead, a street performer was wowing crowds with his ability to remain perfectly still. He was painted all in cement grey to fool people into thinking he was a statue. Hugh thought it perfectly pointless and couldn't understand why anyone would spend their lives pretending to be made of stone.

'Let's walk over to the other side.' Hugh stepped into the road when there was a gap in company cars snaking out from the local business park.

'I didn't think you liked the granite man?' Finn said.

'I don't,' Hugh replied, 'he's stupid.'

Then Finn saw the unmistakable bowlegged gait of Sloppy. He was laughing and saying 'gesundheit' to people, whether they'd sneezed or not. 'Speak of the devil.'

'Why do you think I wanted to cross the street?'

The stone man shifted on his rostrum and slowly reached into a bucket. Finn caught his eye and pointed at Hugh, who was busy tracking Sloppy's movements in case he decided to come over and harass him again.

'Hugh, look.' Finn said.

'Gesundheit!' they heard Sloppy echo in the background.

Hugh glanced petulantly at the living statue, who nodded and held out a lollipop. Hugh shook his head. He had no interest in taking his lollipop. The 'performer' feigned a throw and Hugh bucked attempting to catch nothing, before a raspberry lollipop streamed through the air and Hugh caught it just in time.

'You have to give him money now.'

'But I only have a euro?' Hugh replied.

'Count yourself lucky,' Finn said, chuckling, 'Sloppy would have taken two.'

His last Euro clanged against the side of the small bucket. 'I was going to buy an energy drink with that money,' he whinged, catching Finn up.

'Last time you had one of them you nearly fell off the chair doing those weird moves, you remember?'

Hugh tutted at Finn's ignorance of all things up-to-date. 'Those were young-people dance moves!'

'No wonder I wasn't familiar with them.'

After seeing off an energy-depleted Hugh (and after buying two brands of drain unblocker because he didn't know what each of them did), Finn stopped into the bookshop. Ms. Humphreys was becoming more fretful with people handing up dog-eared pieces of paper that were splattered with all sorts and she demanded that everyone buy a folder or face the repercussions. Finn wasn't sure what these repercussions would be, but he didn't want to find out – especially after the whole 'passing note' saga.

A majestic Christmas tree welcomed him as he stepped into the sprawling five-storey edifice. Finn ran his fingers along the pine branches, conscious not to knock any of the tennis ball-sized baubles onto the ground. 'College could sure learn a thing or two from this place,' he said, leaning in close and taking a deep breath of the scent of Christmas.

The bookstore had always been the jewel in the town's crown, even challenging the horns for most iconic 'thing'. And even when businesses were shutting down around it like they were in a row of dominos – including the store that sold only cactus plants – the bookshop had weathered the economic storm and come out the other side battered but still standing.

A crowd had gathered and stretched out in front of him. He'd never seen it so busy; maybe Ms. Humphreys had ordered *everyone* to buy folders, he jovially thought. Finn tunnelled his way through the bodies as far as the amphitheatre, a space in the middle where patrons could sip a cappuccino while flicking through the pages of a long sought-after book, and which was dwarfed by towering shelves spiralling their way to the upper levels.

'Excuse me, sir?' Finn eyed the girl balancing various flutes of wine on a gold platter. He would tell her he was a journalist covering whatever event was happening if she asked to see his invite. 'Would you like a glass of wine?'

'Why, yes, I would,' he replied, trying to sound important, and taking a glass of white before anyone realised that he was an imposter.

Facing two medium-sized tables, which were overlaid with owl-embossed tablecloths, were curving tiers of chairs that ascended gradually towards the back where you could look down and see what page someone was on. Stacked on one were dozens of copies of the same book, all symmetrically arranged in a pleasing manner. At the other was a man bedecked in chains and a pendant, while sitting next to the mayor a woman waved at members of the audience, looking relaxed yet tense at the same time. She was the author.

Chapter 17

After O'Malley's - and after Hugh had threatened to lodge a complaint with management about always getting his food last - they went back for the final couple of classes before the Christmas break. Blanche and Kennedy stood in their usual positions, taking simultaneous drags of their cigarettes.

'Do you girls ever eat?' Finn said to them.

Kennedy extended her rollie and regarded it with the sort of affection that was missing from the genetic makeup of Ms. Humphreys. 'This *is* our nourishment.'

'Are we passing the note today?' Blanche asked, flashing him a warm smile as he declined Kennedy's offer of a pull.

When Ms. Humphreys had caught Rock and Finn brokering a ruler ransom, Ashley suggested passing a class note; a note so epic, it would go down as the best note in all of note history. The note would be passed from one student to the next, each of them adding five words, until it evolved into an unrepressed and riotous story - like elves adding parts to a zany toy along the conveyor belt in Santa's workshop.

'You better believe it,' Finn replied, smiling back at her.

But Ms. Humphreys was a classroom veteran, a pro at reading body language, so they would need to take the appropriate caution. She would offer no quarter to whoever was caught with the note on their person and the axe of punishment would be brought down upon them with a brisk and detached fury. In the first of two close calls,

Billie had been forced to give Ms. Humphreys the 'come to bed' eyes to throw her off the scent, while Louis had flung himself from his chair when he thought Humphreys had made him. She hadn't.

Finn was nervous. They were taking bigger risks than was prudent and he for one didn't want to get expelled – or worse, spoil the memory of the note. It had somehow made it this far, and if it survived this class, he was going to suggest floating it down the river before Ms. Humphreys cottoned on; and that was only a matter of time.

'Settle down now. There's a class in session.' Ms. Humphreys yawped, placing a box of corrections on the table. She quickly leafed through the comment-laden and alphabetically arranged assignments. 'And don't think I'm letting you off early just because it's the holidays.'

'So much for festive spirit,' Rock murmured.

Finn looked over at Red, who was sitting precisely opposite. He scribbled some words when Ms. Humphreys had gone to the board and then eased the crinkled paper – which was filling nicely – along the line to Fredrik, who did the same. 'I just know it'll come to me and I'll be the one who gets caught.' He whispered.

'Stop worrying,' Rock said, taking down what was being written on the board, 'you're too quick for her.'

A low level of hysteria was building in Finn as he watched Fredrik pass it on to Dot. College had been the best thing to happen to him since his coming of age in San Diego, and now some dirty jottings on a page were going to take it away. 'Take the fall for me?'

'No way, I'm doing great.' Rock replied.

'Please,' He was pleading now, 'she already has it in for me – last week she blamed me for throwing that ball of blue tack at Ashley's head when it was Red.'

Rock squinted, straining to see the words; why did he always pick the farthest away seat? 'Just throw Hugh under the bus like we normally do.'

Finn momentarily forgot about his predicament. 'Remember we volunteered him to give his presentation first and he was up all night preparing for it because we didn't tell him until the day before?'

'That'll teach him for spending all day wearing those ridiculous goggles!' Rock said.

'I still can't believe he spent all that money just to see what his hair would look like in virtual reality.'

They both laughed but stopped instantly when they saw Ms. Humphreys glaring at them, a lower that made Finn's blood freeze over. When she turned to the board again, Dot fired the note at Mia. The president plucked it from the air with such speed that had she been any slower, Ms. Humphreys would have seen her tuck a note under her folder. If Ms. Humphreys sensed anything, it would have been the wave of relief that swept the class. She might also have thought it unusual that most of her students were covering their mouths as if they were being force-fed liver.

'That was close.' Finn said, feeling as if the temperature in the room had been ramped up several degrees.

'Too close, Dot's fuckin' crazy,' Rock replied.

Mia got it as far as the table that linked Blanche's. She smiled mischievously and Finn bowed his head like he was protecting his eyes from a bright light.

Ms. Humphreys had been true to her word and kept them there going on the entire hour. Her job was to prepare them for the coming years, not to extend their weeks-long leisure time, which she was sure they were going to waste anyway. The note made its way all the way around to Rock, who scrawled another five words, before edging it with a grin across to Finn.

...*on a fuckable goat which strangely enough has Hugh's eyes and every Wednesday Ms. Humphreys rubs olive oil on Rock's bald patch and whips out her Clitmaster 5000 turbo which Red had found on the ocean floor while riding seahorses.*

He quickly turned a burst of laughter into a very loud bout of coughing.

Ms. Humphreys snicked the top back onto her marker, satisfied with the amount of material she'd covered. 'Are you alright, Finn?'

'I'm good,' he grunted, coughing again, 'just have a bit of a tickle.'

'Pull it together, dude.' Rock urged.

This is bad, Finn thought. If Ms. Humphreys latched on to what they were doing the whole class would be expelled. He imagined the story being plastered on the front page of the Bridgewater Times: 'ENTIRE JOURNALISM CLASS BANISHED FROM COLLEGE FOR PASSING AROUND DEPRAVED AND HIDEOUSLY UNFUNNY NOTE!' the headline would read in evil red lettering, like that of Ms. Humphrey's revisions. Then, of course, the note would earn global infamy when it was put online and Leo would finally get his wish, maybe even get an invite to Connecticut as a special guest of the WWE.

As Finn's body was convulsing, the note which was on his lap fell to the floor.

'What's that?'

'I'm sorry, what's what?' he replied.

There was a momentary lull in time as Ms. Humphreys pointed to a wrinkled and raised edge poking into her eye-line. 'That paper on the ground.'

Oh, no! I knew this was going to happen! His brain screamed as Finn looked between his legs. Could he blame it on Hugh? Probably not, at least he couldn't work out how with the benumbing slush that was running through his veins. 'What's that?' he parroted, staring down at it. 'That's eh –' he was spluttering now, unable to find the words; 'that's a piece of paper.'

Well, he'd given it the old college try. He had done well just to make it this far, he thought, filling with remorse.

'I know it's a piece of paper, but what's on it?'

As he frenetically tried to come up with an excuse that would keep him out of the *Times* and in college, Simon began choking. Ms. Humphreys, who had already stood up, expecting to quash some monkey business, looked sharply at him. 'What's wrong with you?' she said.

'Urrghhhhh, agghhh...urrgghhhh.' Simon tried to speak but instead sounded like an anteater that had sucked up a porcupine.

Ms. Humphreys softened when she realised something was markedly wrong. 'Oh my God.' She paused and turned to Mia. 'What's his name?'

'Simon.' Mia replied limply, wondering if Simon was going to die.

'Are you okay, Simon...what's wrong?!' Ms. Humphreys was now showing the same level of panic that Finn had shown only seconds before. 'Quick, get the princip–'

Simon forced a clearing hack and the pastille that had become lodged in his throat pitched out and seemed to hunt salaciously for

Ms. Humphreys. Angling her boreal gaze downwards, the frantic concern exhibited by Ms. Humphreys was replaced with utter disdain as the moistness of Simon's saliva glistened on the tip of her polished shoe.

Her eyes popped out more than usual as if trying to 'get' the spluttering specimen. 'Are you alright now, Simon?' she asked.

He raised his thumb, 'yeeess.'

She kicked the chewed pastille away, breaking the bonds of fruity love. 'Good, now *get* over here and clean up this gross thing!' Her blood pressure had risen in tandem with her rage, and she was fit to kill: And she knew exactly who would fit that bill. 'You were saying - Finn?' She said loud enough that she was heard two classrooms away. She knew the immature little yahoo had been up to no good, he normally was. But this time she'd get him.

When Ms. Humphreys looked away from Simon, who was rubbing her shoe with his fingers because he didn't have any tissue, eager to make Finn's Christmas one he'd never forget, she saw only a vacant seat and the flittering of a net curtain. He was no longer there.

* * * *

Finn looked back to make sure Ms. Humphreys wasn't tailing him. He tucked the note into a small pocket at the front of his backpack and ripped out a fresh page from his A4 pad. If she wanted a piece of paper, he'd show her one. He had now crossed the line into paranoia.

When Simon had started to choke (Finn wasn't sure if it was real or a decoy, but he guessed it was real), he had swiped the note from the ground, grabbed his bag and jumped out the window.

'Did you like the bit about the Clitmaster?' Hugh trooped out ahead of everyone else, keen to check into one of his online haunts.

In his haste to escape Ms. Humphreys, Finn had left his jacket behind and his teeth were chattering from the cold. 'The turbo model and all,' he replied.

'Thought of it just like that,' Hugh said, waking his phone up, 'I surprise even *myself* sometimes.'

Her suitcase sounded like a train over the uneven ground. 'Here's your jacket, Finn.'

'Thanks, Daisy,' he said.

'Good to see you're alive, Simon.'

Simon looked up piercingly at Rock. 'I did it on purpose to give Finn a chance to get out, didn't want Ms. Humphreys getting the note!'

'I'm off to bang the girlfriend, lads,' Red announced, 'I mean the ex – see ye all later.'

'You should get it framed, Finn…get it framed!' Dot harped, as Red lolloped away into the near distance behind her.

'Yeah, I'd love it on my wall!' Louis said, thinking that the note would look well between his many horror movie playbills.

Rock jingled the keys of the houseboat. 'And what celebrity would you need to take down to make room for it?'

'Right now?' Louis considered his bedroom wall, where idols and icons were living on all four sides, 'Alan Cumming.'

'I knew you were gay,' Billie slapped her thigh, 'it's all in the footwear, baby!'

Finn wrapped his overcoat around himself like it was a foil blanket. 'Alan *Cumming*?' he mused.

'Au contraire, Billie,' Louis replied, 'I'm actually partially gay.'

'Hey!' Spikester hollered, interlocking her hands beneath Louis' butt and launching him into the air, 'I'm partially gay, too!'

Louis was the same height as Rock as he addressed him. 'You mean you're bi?' Rock said.

'No, I'm fully straight but a bit gay.' Louis reached out and petted Rock's baldness.

'And I told you to bend over?!'

'Think it's always gay if you offer to stick your finger in another guy's ass, Leo.' Finn said, feeling much snugger now that the back of his neck was covered.

'So, you're bi then?' Rock pressed. He could never understand young people and their words these days.

'No, you see I love girls, but there's a part of me that wants to be taken from be-'

'You know what, never mind, I'm glad I'm old.' The keys of his houseboat (Rock's camper had been given the endearing nickname of 'houseboat' when Leo asked if it could go on water after Rock had given them the all-clear to come out of hiding during a routine police check on the way to Silver Strand. Leo was still called an American, only now more so) jangled again in his hand. 'I'm heading off before the traffic gets any worse, you know what that hairpin bend is like this time of day.'

Louis giggled as he was lowered like a dumbwaiter when his weight became too much for Spikester.

'Have a good one, everyone,' Finn said, 'and don't work too hard on those projects – especially you Blanche, we know what you're like for the old hard work.'

She replied softly that she wouldn't, whilst offering Kennedy a cigarette because she was all out.

'Do yourself a favour,' Rock advised, 'skip the Christmas pudding this year?'

'I don't like Christmas pudding.' Finn called after him, fastening the uppermost button that would all but close his throat off to the elements.

'I'd like to believe that!' Rock called back.

The weather closed in around him and he smiled as a blast of icy wind made every hair on his body stand up. Finn hadn't been this happy in years.

Chapter 18

'Jesus, you look terrible.' Rock said, on seeing his complexion.

Finn had returned early to Bridgewater to get away from the never-ending cavalcade of turkey and trimmings - why was eating your weight in turkey and ham and mince pies always celebrated, like it was somehow something to aspire to? He wondered falling into a philosophical exchange with himself. Finn had been too afraid to stand on the scales in the bathroom, holding that if he didn't know the number then it couldn't undo all his good work. 'Thanks, you're full of flattery.'

'Seriously, what's wrong with you - you're transparent?' Rock stabbed him in the stomach with his ruler. 'Too much Christmas pudding, I think.'

Winter had settled in and touched everything with her frosty finger, including his flat. With the students all gone home for Christmas, the landlord had blown the fuse and put the building into lockdown. Finn's covers were so damp that he thought Sloppy and his band of streetwalkers had broken in and pissed sonata on his bed. He was also convinced that the spotty black patch on the wall had become even spottier.

'Told you, don't like pudding...' Finn looked like he was trying the only meditation trick he'd picked up when there had been sufficiently large gaps between Rock's snores at the mindfulness demonstration. '...got pneumonia. Can't walk more than fifty yards without dying.' He replied, tired after saying so many words at once.

'I'll bring my heater in tomorrow.' Rock was primping and preening the clear plastic sleeves that contained his completed assignments, 'can't have you freezing to death. Otherwise, who'd help me with my commas?'

Finn gave him a thumbs-up and swallowed as much oxygen as he could. His chest still felt like it was wound in barbed wire, and he was avoiding anything that looked like a hill wherever possible; so much so, that he decided against going back to the supermarket to buy milk because there had been a slight incline and three steps to get there.

'How was your Christmas everyone?' Sadie announced, striding into class as if Santa had been kind this year, 'Don't tell me, you all ate too much chocolate and lapsed into sugar comas as well?'

Finn's laugh was wheezy and cumbersome; maybe that's why he was so weak when it came to willpower, it was a country-wide thing.

'I went home, I mean back to America. But I had to come home – here, like,' Leo explained, pointing to the ground, 'because there was so much snow.'

Sophia was uttering swear words internally that Leo's visa hadn't been revoked...or worse. 'Did you forget it was winter?' she asked.

'No, it's not normally that bad!' Leo didn't always go home for the holidays and the last time he went – three years ago – the worst they had was a bit of sleet which had cleared up before his breakfast pancakes.

'Right, first things first,' Sadie said after Leo confirmed that the forecasters had predicted only sunshine, 'I'll be taking up your assignments next Friday.'

'Which one?' Ashley was considerably miffed by the amount of briefs they'd been given in the last month, 'we have so many.'

Sadie always had students (more than she'd like to admit) who lost track of what they should be doing. She used to make everyone keep an 'assignment diary' but had abandoned the practice after discovering that aside from the swots nobody used it. 'The one where you've to get an interview with some–'

'That's due next week?' Ashley threw her arms up like she was worshipping an unseen deity. 'I haven't even decided on a topic yet!'

'Better hurry and pick something then.' Sadie replied.

'What about a stripper...' there was a pause as Finn's breath caught up to his words, '...since you'll be working as one soon?'

Ashley stared at him through the muffled laughter, mouth open and agog. She wasn't used to being on the receiving end of insults, she had been the cool girl at school, the one with the acid tongue that could cut a person down with just the casual lobbing of a few words.

'Can you interview a celebrity?'

'You mean a wrestler?' Rock answered, checking the notes he'd made on his brief. He had used the words *acrobatically, plucky* and *conqueror* when it came to describing his confrontation with the farmer and his shooter.

Leo scraped flecks of loose cheek hair with his nails. 'Yeah, I know The Undertaker personally.'

'Really, Leo,' Sophia quizzed, now veering towards the other option (the one with the leg irons) for him not being able to return to the country, 'would he come over to your house?'

'Well, no,' Leo said, beginning to look uncomfortable, 'I'd probably meet him in a hotel uptown.'

Sophia was about to ask him if he spent much time in hotels, but Rock got in ahead of her. 'If you get an interview with The Undertaker, I'll give you a thousand Euros.'

'Okay, but you better bring a briefcase because I want it all in fives.' He made two cash gestures with fingers on either hand but because he didn't bring them together looked like he was milking a cow.

'In answer to your question, Leo; yes, you may interview a celebrity...if you know one.'

Leo sat with his head high, vindicated by Sadie's belief in him. Of course, Leo *didn't* know The Undertaker, had never met him in his life, but no one else needed to know that.

'Second thing on the agenda – and something far more exciting than assignments, I think you'll all agree,' Sadie said, drawing the attention from an irrepressible Leo, 'is the Radio Showdown.'

'What's the Radio Showdown?' Leo said gasping, his spectacles freefalling onto the fat of his nose.

Sadie chuckled, 'The Showdown is a competition we host every year,' she replied, content to remain put in her designated spot as she was still bloated from eggnog and inertia. 'Each group – of which there will be three – will produce a thirty-minute radio programme to be played to the entire college. You can keep with the same people you've been working with or you can ask to be changed; for instance, if you're not gelling well with certain people, or if you feel that some aren't pulling their weight.'

'What? I always come to college!' Ashley groused when the class turned to her. 'Most of the time I do, anyway.'

'I don't think I've ever seen you in the Pod?' Leo said.

First it was Finn calling her a stripper and now this. She should have stayed in bed – was going to and all, she'd watched some really cute animal videos before finally rousing herself; the one with the dog who had barked so loud that his cat sister had leapt on top of the grandfather clock was particularly hilarious. 'Shut up, Leo, you're obviously going blind and need stronger glasses!'

'What's more,' Sadie continued, feeling the usual foaming consternation when she brought this up every January, 'the winning show will be broadcast on Strand FM, which has a daily listenership of seventy-five thousand, give or take a few housewives.'

It was as if Finn's bacteria had grabbed their satchels and headed for greener pastures. 'You're serious?' he said, the words fluid and flowing.

'Yep, one of the teachers here used to DJ for the station back in the day,' Sadie replied.

Rock leaned in close. 'We need to get rid of Simon if we want to win this thing.'

Simon had been in their group since the start, much to Rock's displeasure. 'You think anyone else will take him?' Finn was now wide awake and breathing like he'd been chewing eucalyptus leaves all morning.

Rock's expression faded to resignation. 'Guess not,' he sighed. 'Okay, then if we're taking the special one, we're definitely not taking Billie.'

They looked over at Billie who was alternating between doing straight-leg raises to admire her shoes, and doodling thick, tapering shapes on the back of her copybook.

'Sure, she never turns up–' Finn replied. He was actually going to get his chance to feel like those smiling students in the newspaper advert. Simon hadn't been one of those people, but he was sure it would feel quite nice all the same, '-we'd have minutes of dead air.'

'Not to mention constantly talking about the D she never gets,' Rock added, 'don't get me wrong, it's funny-'

'-but not exactly family-friendly.'

'Precisely!' Rock replied after Finn finished his thought.

Chatter and trepidation filled the air and people were already going about securing friends and allies, not to mention trying to attract those who were seen as radio personalities.

Sadie was smiling widely. 'Guys, there's no need to panic, there'll be plenty of time to sort out groupings and all that type of thing. I just thought I'd give you something to look forward to - and maybe fret over a bit.'

'I'm going to do a wrestling segment with my group!' Leo was almost delirious, 'Maybe get the Hogan on the phone!'

Finn looked at Rock. 'We need to keep him away too.'

'Imagine we had both of them?' Rock thought about the kind of calamity they'd air if Leo and Simon were on the team.

'Nah, we're not that unlucky,' Finn said and they both watched as Leo did finishing moves with his pencils on the desk.

* * * *

The workshop was warm, but what's more, it was dry, and everyone was grateful for that after being caught in a downpour on the way back from O'Malley's. Even O'Malley himself had got in on the act and told Finn to 'take his panties off' after he'd slapped down a pizza with extra pineapple, much to the delight of Hugh who laughed so hard that orange spewed out his nose.

Lena came into the room, camera fastened to her hand like they were sown together. 'Hi guys,' she said cheerily. 'We're going to do a bit of theory on working in a darkroom. Then we're going to go to the *actual* darkroom and develop the black and white photos you took in the park.'

'Were they the ones of the woman with the bouncy bazookas?' Louis enquired.

'Yes,' she replied, stifling a laugh, 'that was the day.'

Louis cupped both hands a considerable distance from his chest. 'Cool,' he said, 'want to see how those turn out.' This time Lena couldn't stop herself chuckling.

'Because it's a little on the tight side up there, I want this side of the room to come with me.' Lena cut the class in two with her arm. 'The rest, I want you to grab a book from the shelf, pick a photo you like, and write about it using the descriptions we went through last week.'

Leo hesitated. 'Should I?' he said, looking around at the others in the dry area of the darkroom.

'It would be pretty funny.' Gibby told him, pulling a long-pronged comb resembling a rake through her hair.

'Ok!' he replied.

Leo had found a Halloween mask when he'd gone rifling through a box in the corner to see if there was anything interesting he could take home. Finn guessed someone had used it as a prop and forgotten to take it with them afterwards. Ashley switched off the lights and they waited. The sound of footsteps coming up the staircase made them all giddy. Lena felt around for the handle and pushed open the door.

'TRICK OR TREEEEEAT!' Leo intoned in a sublimely deep voice. Lena jumped and dropped her camera, only for the strap to snag on her elbow joint when her hand went to her mouth to smother a scream.

'Jesus Christ!' she shrieked, as strands of light from outside revealed *Michael* or *Leatherface* or whoever the hell was standing in front of her. 'You scared the shit out of me, Leo!'

The class wasn't used to hearing Lena curse.

'Did I really scare you?' he said.

'Don't do that ever again – and take that bloody thing off!' Leo handed over the mask and she flung it into a different corner. 'Now if we could get on with learning how to develop photographs that would be great!'

After going over the basics, Lena led them from the enlargers into a separate smaller room – the actual darkroom, the room that got positively no light.

'Guess this is why they call it a darkroom.' Mia commented, after Ashley, who was next to her, had been erased from sight.

Finn brought his hand as close to his face as he could without thwacking his nose, but it made no difference, he couldn't see it. It was the sort of darkness that you wore, heavy and claustrophobic.

'As I showed you outside,' Lena said, hands moving as if the absence of light was of no consequence, 'we need to remove the film from the camera in pitch dark, otherwise it will spoil.'

Daisy's breathing was becoming more laboured, like the times when her head would spasm uncontrollably from one K-pop poster to another.

'How are you doing, Daisy?' Lena always expected at least one student to freak out every year and she was pretty good at guessing who it would be. The drinks were on her again tonight, just as they were last week when Harold had run full force into the door trying to get out.

'I'm just a bit scared of the dark,' she nervously replied. 'I usually sleep with the light on.'

'Don't worry, Daisy, we're all here,' Finn said, 'and so is that poltergeist beside you.'

Mia would have smacked him, but she didn't want to hit Daisy by accident. 'Don't mind him, there's no poltergeist beside you!'

'No, Finn agreed, 'just Leo, who I think might be scarier.' Daisy started to laugh, which took her mind off the blackness.

'Who's touching me?' Ashley asked into the room, 'Someone just touched my neck.'

'No one's touching you,' Lena said, 'it's just your imagination.'

Ashley rubbed her neck rapidly to warm it back up. 'Something definitely touched my neck just there,' she protested.

'Stop it, Ashley, you're going to scare Daisy again.' Mia said.

'Do you think it's one of the nuns from Rock's love story?' As novice as the story was - and Blanche thought it was incredibly novice - she also thought it had the green shoots of a believable entanglement between souls from different astral planes.

'I believe that was a porno.' Red replied from somewhere in the room.

Finn pointed to a long gangly piece of thread hanging from the roof when Lena threw open the door and everything was normal again. 'Were you a little scared there, Ashley?'

'No! I was just trying to scare the rest of you,' she retorted, following them out and giving her skin one last rub. 'Anyway, I'd kick a poltergeist's ass.'

'I don't doubt that.' Finn replied, thinking that the last person a malicious poltergeist would want to see in a darkened room was Ashley.

They had each printed two photos before the other half of the class came streaming through the doors, disrupting the meditative peace of a room bathed in dusk.

'Make way for the serious photographers!' Simon declared.

Rock ditched his jacket on top of the others, looking forward to seeing if his shot of Louis' brother could be added to his 'pistol' collection. 'If you're a serious photographer then I'm changing groups.'

'Too late, buddy.' Finn's photos had come out exactly how he thought they would, out of focus.

'By the way, there's something in the darkroom,' Leo said, blowing on his picture of Simon's torso standing next to the bandstand, 'it was feeling up Ashley.'

'Sure that wasn't you?'

Leo looked embarrassed. 'No, it wasn't me,' he replied to Spikester.

'Then why are you turning red?' Her sweater came off to reveal a skin-tight t-shirt of two knives through a ripe tomato.

'Because it's hot in here!'

Spikester walked towards the darkroom as if naturally inclined to seek out sensory deprivation. 'I'm only yanking your chain,' she said, as the dark robbed her of her corporeal form.

* * * *

Finn was in his kitchen - or his *do-everything-in* room as he'd renamed it - putting the finishing touches to the investigative assignment. The portable heater Rock had lent him was pumping out as much flame as it could, but the room would still take on the qualities of the polar ice caps if he moved more than a couple of feet away.

He had managed to get interviews with people from both sides of the gambling spectrum, but neither had allowed him to record the conversations. He considered sneaking a recorder in his pocket, but as integrity seemed in short supply in the journalism game lately, he decided to start as he meant to go on. He hoped Sadie wouldn't dock him too many marks for his principled stance.

To his surprise, the head of one of the most prominent gambling awareness groups felt there was no point in banning it, that gamblers - like drug addicts - would always find a way back in through a side entrance. 'These are people very susceptible to addiction,' he had said with lamentable surety as if it were somehow catching, 'If the government wades in then these poor wretches will only harm themselves some other way.'

This person, to Finn's not-so-great surprise, also had his finger in the pie of supplying slot machines to those grim arcades where old-age pensioners would stare dispassionately at the flashing lights until their coin buckets were empty. Having experience as he did of helping to cure this 'illness', he knew how hungry the beast was, and that no matter how much you fed it, it would never be satiated. Only, when Finn had spoken to Joe (if that is *still* your real name) on that cold night before Christmas, he had said the very same thing; that people would always find something to 'compulse' over.

His phone oscillated gently on the table. It was Rock. Communication was so fast and easy now it made his head twirl. Last time Finn was in college the options of getting a message to someone were either a simple text message or an email if you wanted to discuss something in more detail. There weren't things like *Snapchat* - which Hugh spent most of his time immersed in - that allowed people like Justin Bieber to share videos of him stroking his cat like they were made just for you.

'They're not losers.' Hugh had rebuked when Rock asked one lunchtime why you'd want to watch a load of losers doing losery stuff. 'You can go backstage with bands like *One Direction* like you're there! You can even go inside their gaffs - how often do you get to go into your hero's house?'

Rock had stared expressionless at him. 'See, this is what I'm talking about, young people!' he had scorned and walked away.

Finn unlocked his phone:

MasterofDisaster: Finished the assignment yet?

Silverballs: Just writing the conclusion

MasterofDisaster: Same. Would you have a read of mine and check the grammar and all that shit is good...

Silverballs: Sure, but if it's better than mine I might have to steal it

MasterofDisaster: Do you ever want to be able to take a decent photograph?

Silverballs: I'd have to rob your camera to do that. You keep saying mine has a crap sensor!

MasterofDisaster: Crop sensor! But yes, your camera is crap

Another message came up before Finn could threaten some interesting 'edits' to Rock's work.

MasterofDisaster: See what happened to that puppy prick?

Silverballs: Last I heard you got the fuzz onto him

MasterofDisaster: Charged him with running an illegal operation, might actually get jail time

An implacable Rock had returned to the farm the following morning when the sun had crawled its way up to the middle of the trees, leading police and animal welfare inspectors past the emaciated tree and through the long grass he had run only hours before, fleeing for his life. When they rounded the corner of the metal structure where the puppies were being held captive, the farmer was piling cages into a Sprinter with more dings in it than a bumper car and a registration plate that was undecipherable.

The man's eyes had gone wide at the sight of intruders on his property, and he thrust another cage into the back of the van, eliciting a sharp, yet timid yelp. 'Where do you think you're going?' Rock had said, moving with more spryness than his leg should have allowed, and grabbing the man as he was reaching for another cage. The farmer effed and blinded and struggled to get free, but Rock was bigger and stronger and herded him like a cowboy a misbehaving calf.

Silverballs: Look at you, all you're missing is a cape!

MasterofDisaster: He deserves what's coming to him - and he shot at me! He'll be lucky to end up in jail because I'd do far worse to him!

Rock snarled that the farmer's last - *and dare I say, main mistake* - was when he'd shot at him, and one of the officers had to dive to catch the man when Rock took him by his dungarees and gave him the bum's rush. 'Cuff him, boys, and make sure they're nice and tight,' Rock said before the same officer told him that they couldn't really be throwing people around like that.

Silverballs: I know, I'm afraid to borrow your *Minions* ruler in case it goes missing

MasterofDisaster: My pride and joy? You'd need to leave the country

There were so many puppies it had taken all day to transport them to the dog shelter. But that wasn't Rock's job, he had played his part by rescuing them, and now all he wanted was to go home and get a good day's sleep. He figured Sadie would understand if he didn't show for class, might even give him some extra hero marks for saving the day.

Silverballs: I'd be across the border and into Mexico before you could say sombrero

MasterofDisaster: Don't like sombreros

Silverballs: You prefer taxi-man caps...

MasterofDisaster: They make me look cool! You need one too, cover all that grey

Silverballs: Throw in some shades and we're the Blues Brothers!

MasterofDisaster: Speaking of brothers, you think we'll get the special bros for the radio thing?

Silverballs: Told you, there's no god up there who hates us that much

MasterofDisaster: Guess you're right. We'll have to come up with some ideas if we want to win

Silverballs: We'll chat about it over meatball subs tomorrow

MasterofDisaster: Sounds good. Just about to have a sneaky one for all my hard work...Master of Disaster, over 'n out.

Rock backed out of the messaging app and couldn't help but give a wry smile. He would have had to send a letter, wait a day for it to arrive, and then wait another day for it to come back with an answer when he was at school. He poured himself a glass of whiskey – the good stuff, Irish – which had been left to age in a basement somewhere since the time that he said, '*I Do*'. He took a sip. It tasted even better than he remembered. Maybe it was the taste of success, he thought, sipping it again.

Since he'd applied for college, Rock had climbed a mountain to get footage of a plane crash no one else had gotten (and been paid handsomely for it by the national broadcaster) and had single-handedly shut down a deplorable puppy farm; that he was getting the best grades in the class was simply the icing on the cake.

'What are you so happy about?' Suzy said when she saw him smirking.

'Just thinking about the past few months, feels like I'm actually achieving things.'

She brought a glass to her lips and took a sophisticated sip that only women seemed to be able to do when drinking wine. 'You are and I'm proud of you. And there's a few little ones out there who would agree with me.' She flashed him a mouthful of stained-red teeth.

The sheer volume of puppies meant they had to be sprinkled far and wide and given to any and all who would agree to babysit until more permanent homes could be found.

'This fella is just so cute.' Rock lifted one of the small white balls of fur to his cheek, 'you think I'm great too, don't you?'

'You'll be running the country soon the way you're going.'

The puffed-up ball let a decidedly drawn-out and unimpressed yawn when Rock replied that he'd do a far better job than 'that gobshite who is in now'.

'Are you handing your work in tomorrow?' Suzy asked him before he went off on one of his colourful rants about the leader of the country.

'Yep, before lunch, then Sadie's finalising the groups. I swear if that pair are in the same group as me and Finn, we might just have to box them up and ship them off to Africa.'

Suzy topped up her glass. 'Oh, Rock, I'm sure they're fine.'

'They are – if you like hearing about wrestling non-stop through a loudspeaker.'

'They might feel the same way about you,' she replied teasingly, and even the spatter of wine on the surface was more genteel and ladylike.

Rock held the puppy out in front of him, 'This silky-smooth voice?' he said, 'The residents of Bridgewater aren't going to know they're born when they hear me coming across the radio waves.'

Chapter 19

Spring was rushing by like it was in a hurry to be somewhere. It had turned cold after a mild enough winter and the rains had come, heavy and miserable. Finn knew this was a ruse, a trick to make him think he had more time than he did. Nature could fool people so easily with a morning frost or a run of stormy days. What would happen when college was finished? Would he find himself back on life's shitlist again – or worse, back in his cell?

    A light layer of moisture settled on his heavy green coat (the one his grandmother had bought him to keep him warm while he was being a 'preppy') and he passed by a little cleaning van that was busy sucking up broken beer bottles and clamshell containers from the night before. The rain was forecast to stop that evening, but that was scant consolation after he stomped in a puddle deep enough to plunder his shoe.

    Finn had two short months left before he would be exiled from the security of the course and tossed back into the so-called 'real world'. *The real world,* he scoffed, pernicious thoughts swirling in his head, *who'd want to live in that?*

    The lights burned red, bringing the early-morning traffic to a standstill. He quickened his stride and walked straight out into the road. He'd been walking this intersection every day for the past seven months and knew well the sequence of the lights. He also knew that when old people or kids with parents were waiting to cross it was generally safe to assume they'd hit the pedestrian button and he wouldn't be squashed by the bus to Silver Strand sailing through a green light.

The real world was selling yourself out by working a job you hated so you could give your earnings to a grubby landlord for some hovel of a flat, he thought, latching on to his previous thread, or shackling yourself to a mortgage that you're finally able to pay off when you're propelling a Zimmer frame into the bathroom before you went potty in your pants. Finn pursed his lips and snorted through his nose as the little man began flashing noisily when he reached the other side. He thought of the word 'mortgage', and how in French it meant *Death Pledge*. The French had it right, even tried to warn us. He swore he'd never fall into this middle-class trap; the one that made you think you were well off, but which was just an illusion. He'd never be a slave to the banking carte-

Finn's cerebral roiling was interrupted by a commotion down the street. Two people were standing next to a large campervan that looked like it'd been rolling around in the mud with its other campervan friends.

'Of course, I can,' said a bald man shouting at a woman half his size, 'who made you queen of the street!?'

A smile quickly formed on Finn's face; it was the bald head of Rock. They had become close over the months, and he found Rock's blunt style like a squeeze of lemon in an often staid and shrinking violet world. He was a vestige of a time when people didn't discuss their feelings over skinny lattes, and when you could call someone *chubby* without being harangued because you'd made an overly sensitive person cry into their brie.

They had quite a bit in common also. Both had life experience and were the oldest in the class, though Finn would point out that he was, in fact, the second oldest in the class. Despite this affiliation, life had caught them with their trousers down, and it was nearly as if experience counted for nothing as they thrashed about in the same pool of ambiguity as the younger ones.

'It's right outside my door,' shouted the woman in the hairnet in return, 'and it's an eyesore!'

'I'll park it here if I want!' He gestured toward her windows. 'Anyway, your house is nothing much to look at, those window ledges could do with a serious scrubbing'.

Rock walked away before the bristling homeowner could counter that she had already tried washing the ledges but that nothing worked, and he waved when he spotted Finn.

'Making friends again I see?'

He shrugged nonchalantly. 'Thinks she has a right to moan just because the houseboat is outside her gaff. It's a public road.'

Louis was at the whiteboard drawing an image of a woman on a slab when they got to class. Rock stalled by the teacher's desk while Finn went over for a closer inspection. 'Who's dead, Louis?' he asked, noticing two coins on the woman's eyes.

'Sadie's sick,' he replied, taking a break to chug some cola, 'she won't be in today.'

'She won't be in today or ever?' Rock suggested.

Finn unhooked his bag from his shoulder and fished inside for a post-breakfast snack. 'Hope that's enough for the boatman,' he said, clipping Simon in the elbow as he was pushing aside his study material.

'Time to catch up on the sports news then.' Simon declared, pulling the keyboard closer.

'That's all you do anyway,' Rock said, looking at the website Simon had brought up on the screen, 'anytime I look over you're watching naked bearded guys rolling around on the floor.'

'They're wrestling, Rock,' Simon replied, glancing behind at the guy who he thought with a bit of training could have been one of those wrestlers who was always jumping from the top turnbuckle.

'That's what I said, rolling around on the floor.'

Simon turned and ignored him. Rock didn't understand the art of wrestling and all the skill and athleticism it took. So what if they sometimes wore very little clothing? They had to, Simon reasoned, otherwise they'd be too restricted and wouldn't be able to perform all those awesome moves.

Louis burped gas bubbles and skipped out of class when he'd finished his depiction of Sadie heading to the underworld. Louis was particularly fond of Coca-Cola, and it was rare that there wasn't a can of it somewhere on his desk. This annoyed the teachers greatly, who continually had to hound him to put it away, and had he not seen the signs asking students to refrain from drinking in the classrooms? He had. And, eventually, the teachers stopped asking.

'Hey, watch this,' Simon said when he noticed the door beginning to open again. It was almost fully ajar when he cupped his hands around his mouth, forming a primitive, yet fully functional sound amplifier. 'NERD!' he roared, as loudly as he could.

That would teach Louis for taking a bite of his cookie last Friday in O'Malley's. Simon hadn't even offered him a bit - he'd never offer someone his cookie, they were just *too* nice - and Louis had grabbed it from his plate and took a bite, just like that. He couldn't believe it, the gall! It wasn't even a small bite, either.

Simon drew a sharp intake of breath through gritted teeth as the school chair materialised in the room. Finn stuffed his head into the crook of his elbow, laughing so hard that his body shook like he was suffering from withdrawal symptoms. Praying the principal – whose expression was caustic – wouldn't demand who had called him a nerd, Simon faced his computer and pretended to read the images.

As the principal was wall-eying the room, mulling over whether to root out the pup who'd shouted at him, Louis entered with a broad-set smile. 'Your teacher is ill and won't be coming in today,' the principal said curtly at last. Most of the class was trying their best not to laugh because it was impossible to judge what side of the room he was looking at. 'But she asked me to tell you about the political debate series the college is hosting.'

'Ohhhh, politics!' moaned Ashley.

He looked at Ashley, or at least it appeared like he was looking at her. 'Yes, well, as you all know we have an important election coming up in a few weeks.'

'Important my arse.' Finn was inherently distrustful of politicians, and he drew giggles from those around him. He believed that they were all out for what they could get, and once their palms had been crossed with silver, then to hell with everybody else.

'Representatives from four of the parties will be there, so you will have ample chance to put forward any legitimate concerns you might have –'

'So they can fob us off with more lies?'

The principal was engorging all before him, including Finn. 'Then it'll be up to you to call them on it, won't it?'

'It sure will.' Finn replied, intending to do just that.

He decided not to quiz the class on who had called him such a degrading term because they would have played dumb anyway. 'Tickets are free and can be picked up from reception.'

'You really love the politicians, don't you?' Rock said, after the principal had scuffled out no happier than when he'd come in.

'About the same as you love millennials.' Finn retorted, the suggestion of him giving any sort of damn about politicians causing a salivation in his mouth that had nothing to do with hunger.

Daisy strolled daintily over, bunny ears pinning her hair neatly in place. 'Hi, guys.' She smiled shyly at Rock.

'Hey, Daisy.' he replied.

'I'm doing my presentation on K-pop and the way they're like, you know,' she explained, 'treated badly and all.'

Finn and Rock eyed each other briefly before Finn spoke. 'Sure, Daisy...we know what you mean.'

'Well, I was wondering if you'd mind watching a few clips and telling me how you feel about how the industry makes them sign slave contracts?'

'Of course, we will,' Rock replied, thinking that a few video clips to break up the block of classes would be just the ticket, 'happy to.'

Daisy's excited reaction sent her bunny ears skew-ways. She quickly adjusted them so they were perfect again. 'Thanks, guys!' she beamed and scampered back to her computer. 'Oh, it'll be after lunch, if that's okay?' she called over the monitors.

'Think you've got an admirer there,' Finn said under his breath, smiling in agreement, 'must be the whole grand-daddy effect.'

'What's K-pop?' Rock scratched his head. 'And what the hell are slave contracts?'

* * * *

'Right, I think we should do a chat segment on wrestling – maybe a discussion on when Hulk Hogan body slammed Andre the Giant – still don't know how he did that, have you seen the size of him?!' Leo said.

Over in the Pod, each group was having its first practice session for the Radio Showdown. Outside of the hour spent every week working on their magazine productions, Sadie also encouraged them to have weekly meetings so that everyone knew what role they were playing. Then, just before the exams in May, the shows would be broadcast over fibre optics (Sadie was offering odds on the winners in a bid to whip up online interest among her contact base) and live to the college.

Rock glared at him. After watching a group of porcelain teenagers dance around a stage like they'd been denied basic nutrition ('that was the worst fifteen minutes of my life – and I've had a motorbike land on my leg', Rock had said when Daisy shut the laptop lid), Leo's voice seemed amplified in the soundproof room.

'Or we could-'

'For the love of Christ, Leo, calm down! I can't hear myself think.'

Much to Rock's vexation he hadn't been able to shift Simon from the group, even resorting to bribery when his threats had failed. Then, when Sophia switched allegiances, leaving them a person short, Leo had somehow wheedled his way in.

'I'll give you a lift home every day,' he had begged Sophia, 'I don't care if it means being late for my dinner – just please stay, two window-lickers are too many.'

'Sorry, Rock. I already prom–'

'Too late, suckers!' Ashley interrupted, making a hand gesture Rock wasn't familiar with, 'She already promised to be in our group.'

'Both the wrestling twins on my team,' he had lamented, 'now Bridgewater will never hear my silky voice...'

'So,' Leo said, his voice now small-room friendly, 'about the wrestling feature?'

'We'll include wrestling in some way,' Finn replied, trying to gauge to ideal distance his mouth should be from the microphone, 'but if we want to win, we'll have to concentrate on slightly different things.'

Rock sighed and moved some songs from the desktop and into a new folder. 'What's the point? We're doomed anyway.'

'I think we can win,' Finn said confidently, moving back from the mic, 'look, we've got Red on our team.'

The five of them turned to look at Red.

'I'm with ye lads,' he said with a twist of his head, 'in it for the long haul, just like me boat Betsy.'

Finn tried galvanising the group. 'There you go! Now, if we can just minimise Simon and Leo's roles, then we can still do this thing.'

'I want a big part!'

'Yeah, me too!' Simon said, echoing Leo's protestations.

'That settles it then,' Finn renounced, hopping off the tall studio chair to let Kevin test his vocals, 'we're screwed.'

A momentary quietness enveloped the room. None of them - apart from Leo - was confident they could win and have their programme buzzed straight into the homes of Bridgewater residents.

Rock pressed some turntable buttons and spun some knobs. 'Okay,' he said, 'might as well start by figuring out what each of us is doing.'

'Lead presenter!' Leo clamoured, raising his hand high into the air.

'I'm choosing the music and doing the news, sport and weather!' Simon said.

Rock turned the volume dial up full tilt and imagined blowing Simon's eardrums to kingdom come. 'Are you going to leave any jobs for the rest of us?'

'You can announce each song if you want?' Simon clasped excitedly at Leo's shoulder. He had the most perfect song in mind, too.

'Think we're going to need a lot of weekly meetings,' Finn said, sighing, and leaning against the wall like an outcast.

It had been a wholly unfruitful hour. The only things that were decided were that Leo wasn't lead presenter, the name of their station was to be called *Houseboat FM*, and Simon wouldn't be doing most of the things he tried claiming.

'I don't want my name associated with that achy-breaky country crap.' Rock had said firmly after Simon presented his playlist choices.

They agreed to meet up the following day to brainstorm ideas and hash out what structure the show was going to take. They would need to find a way of working together if there was any chance of winning the Showdown and having their thirty minutes of Bridgewater fame.

Chapter 20

The turnout in the theatre was meagre, but it came as a welcome relief from the bitter wind outside and no one felt like removing their jackets when they sat down. Despite coming to hear the people he disliked the most, Finn had begun to feel relaxed, content even. Sitting next to Simon and Hugh he felt like he was sinking into the chair. It was quite a pleasant feeling, he thought.

'Nice in here, isn't it?' He asked whoever was listening. Rock glanced over from a few seats away.

Hugh looked at the velour drapes that protected the dignity of those behind them. 'It's not too bad, I suppose.'

'Would you like to be up there now, Hugh?'

Stage lighting was arranged around a semi-circle of empty chairs. 'For what like?' he replied.

Dot leaned in and whispered something in Rock's ear. 'Thought you said it wasn't strong?' he said to her.

'They're not for me,' she replied, and they both laughed.

'Pfft, whatever *you* want, Hugh, you could be anything,' Finn cooed, 'absolutely anything.'

'Okay...thanks, I think.' Hugh sat forward and saw Dot grinning like she'd uncovered three fifties on a scratchie.

Only eleven had taken up the offer of putting themselves through the political ringer, the rest coming up with weak excuses. Simon had been forced to go because he used the excuse that he had no money, forgetting the tickets were free. When organisers conceded that no one else was coming, they closed the doors on both sides of the theatre.

'Hope this isn't going to be too boring.' Rock said, watching as they bolted the doors shut.

Dot laughed heartily. 'Asking for miracles there, Rocky-boy!'

'Good afternoon, everyone. You're all very welcome to the first in a series of political debates leading up to this year's election.'

'More like political *stu-pid-ness*,' Finn hummed, feeling very woolly in his seat.

There was sporadic clapping as the MC took an intentional pause. After introducing the politicians and confirming which party each represented, he then spent the first thirty minutes asking what many in attendance considered inept and flaccid questions. If Mia had turned up like she promised, instead of going for afternoon tea with Ashley and Sophia, she would have said that the MC was being too 'grateful' as he tiptoed around the guests' feelings.

A sense of disquiet met the continued newspeak of the candidates, and one of them was causing much muttering. 'You see, I'm just like you,' chirped the politician who was wearing a rather unflattering dress suit that made her resemble a pear retaining water. 'I care deeply that you – all of you – come out of this election better off and happier with your lot. And if you elect me, I guarantee that none of us will ever go short again!' She said this with such unbridled theatrics you'd swear she thought the eyes of the world were upon her.

If Finn hadn't activated the dopamine receptors with Dot's wacky tobacky and wasn't oblivious to what was going on around him, he would have noticed Rock (who was one of those angrily muttering at what the dumpy politician was advocating) squirming in his seat. She was not only toeing the party line, but toeing the historical political line, the one where you felt sorry for the masses, empathizing with their plight, and promising to fix everything if they just prop you up on the golden throne. Rock thought that if a sniper didn't take her out soon, he might just be put off his feed in O'Malley's.

'After all,' she said, 'you make this country what it is, and you all deserve to share in its spoils!' Despite the other candidates being forced to wait longer than they'd like to get their own points across, they couldn't help but admire their rival's passion and performance.

Rock was unable to humour the vile drivel any longer and he shouted: 'You sound like a tape recorder that's stuck on repeat!'

The muttering dried up like a salted slug and the four politicians gawked at the person who had interrupted the public servant mid-roll.

'Here he goes again,' Simon said to himself, but which was also heard by the row behind.

'Oho, you go, Rock,' Finn mumbled dreamily, 'hate to be that chick...mmm.'

Heads turned briefly to look at Finn before turning back to Rock and there was a blanket hush as if everyone was waiting on a thespian to deliver a notable monologue.

'Sorry, we've decided not to take questions from the crowd today.' Rather than diffuse the situation, the MC only managed to whisk things up even more.

'Everything you say is empty promises,' Rock said, fobbing him off. 'It's jargon and no one here believes a word of it.'

The master of ceremonies was now clearly uncomfortable and stood up like that were going to make a difference.

'I don't believe that's the case,' the politician responded, pressing her green suit with the backs of her fingers like an iron against an unseemly crease.

'Of course, it is,' Rock growled, his glare boring into her, 'you're so predictable it's embarrassing!'

'I'm saying what I think to be true.' The raising of her voice puckered a calm exterior. 'I'm telling the truth.'

Fredrik's pupils dilated like a cat registering the misguided intentions of a wandering mouse. He, too, was squirming in his seat, but unlike Rock, it had nothing to do with being angry. He didn't realise it, but he was smiling fervently, eager for the psychological warfare to continue, only wishing that he was the one engaged with the office-seeking politician.

'What you think, what the party thinks, yeah, whatever – and that *bullshit* about not being able to afford a pair of socks just so you could look like one of the little people is beyond pathetic.'

'I'm telling you, I couldn't!' she replied, as an overweight leg slipped from its crossed position.

'Okay, that's enough.' The MC barked over the cheers and claps from the select crowd. 'We're here for a polite discussion. A slagging match won't get us anywhere.'

'And your lame questions will?'

A girl sitting directly behind Rock, who, like most others in the hall, was just as frustrated by the belly-patting, reaped further cheers from the emblazoned crowd. The youth of today might just have some hope, Rock thought, as they gathered in a show of unity against the crooked status quo.

'You've all had your say, now that's enough.'

'Don't worry,' Rock said, 'I'm not staying to listen to this fruity-flavoured cunt any longer.' The MC wanted to speak but he couldn't find the words. 'You're a fraud, just like the rest of your cronies!'

'Get out of here!' he finally cried but was drowned out by raucous hooting and hollering.

The journalism class rose and marched down the aisle like a squadron of crop dusters. Finn, still feeling the effects of Dot's super weed (*was it always like that?*), was the last to join the exodus and slowly ambled after them. 'Why are we leaving?' he said.

'Rock got us all kicked out.' Simon called back.

They flooded onto the pavement outside, and their flushed cheeks made it feel warmer than before.

'First thing that bitch is going to do is retire!' Dot said, now giggling freely.

The growl in his voice was still present. 'Couldn't afford socks, fuck's sake – who does she think we are, a pack of Simons?'

'I heard that, Rock.' Simon thought her sock story had sounded very plausible. There was a time during the worst of the recession when he and his family had to go without their weekly takeaway, so he knew exactly the hardships people had to endure.

'Well, I didn't whisper it,' Rock replied.

Fredrik sat on the low wall and put one leg over the other. 'She was merely attempting to schmooze the proletariat by using established lexicon to secure the support she needs to further her own egocentric agenda.'

'I'm too angry to work out what you're trying to say, Fredrik.' But despite his charged emotional state, Rock was feeling surprisingly good after his clash with the enemy.

'I was merely inferring–'

'Who wants food?' Rock said before Fredrik could continue. 'I feel like wedgies.'

The door banged Finn's behind on his way out. 'Count me in,' he said, moving as if gravity had been dialled down.

'Of course, you do,' Dot howled, already rolling her next stogie to replace the one Finn had coughed and scalded his throat with, 'you've got the munchies!'

It was true. Finn hadn't felt hunger pangs this intense since the time he lost everything on the 'lucky last'. 'Think I might have nodded off for a bit there, as well.'

'Right, come on,' Rock urged, 'let's get out of here.'

* * * *

Kennedy and Blanche were standing in the rain, huddled around their cigarettes like tramps around a barrel fire.

'Are you girls going to make an appearance in class?' Rock said as he and Finn came within range of the toxic fallout.

'What class is it?' Kennedy replied.

Rock's look was parental in its disapproval. 'Slogans and Stereotypes.'

'Not sure.' Kennedy held his gaze, her eyes impenetrable as she inhaled. 'Maybe?'

'You're not going, are you?'

Blanche and Kennedy exhaled simultaneously and for a second Rock disappeared into a spherule of smoke. 'Probably not, no,' she said.

'If you keep standing in the same spot a sinkhole's going to open up.' Finn pointed at the ground. 'Look, I can already see one forming.'

The girls looked down before realising Finn was full of it and they both flipped him the bird. They didn't fancy him or anything, but he was cool enough for an older guy.

'Why would you bother signing up for a course and not go to the classes?' Rock was old school. He was also older, and for him, the course had been a choice. 'How else are they going to know how stereotypes and slogans are weapons of propaganda?'

Finn meanwhile had been led to believe by a society that valued certification above all else, that were he not able to put some capital letters after his name, he would become an instant washout, undesired by women, companies and the institutions that would help bolster him through a turbulent life. 'Their parents might have pushed them into it,' he said, as the girls faded from view.

'Even still, a qualification is a qualification,' Rock replied.

'We'll just have to keep the class afloat by ourselves.'

They walked through the sliding doors and started up the stairs towards the library and the daily struggle of finding a computer to sit at. The tech department didn't have the same standard of donors as the university, which meant having to defend a vague and structureless territory.

'You know I'm going to beat you and become class emperor, don't you?' Rock said, as assuredly as if the results were already known.

'Maybe if I shave off all my hair and sit your exams you might,' Finn replied, getting hampered twice by the mechanical gates when they refused to budge.

'Want to have a little bet?'

Finn nodded to where two students were getting ready to leave. 'What are we studying for?'

'A decent bottle of whiskey – winner chooses.' Rock said.

What was he doing? He'd never get better results. Assignments were one thing where he had time, not to mention the help of the internet, but his crappy three-second memory wasn't built for memorising minuscule details. His only hope was that Finn didn't know what decent whisky was.

'Haven't had a good whisky in ages.' Finn shook his head. He had barely passed college the last time he was there. 'We're some geeks, aren't we?'

'Yeah, but we're badass geeks,' Rock replied, and they nabbed the seats before a couple of flat-shoe and white-tops could steal in from the flanks.

* * * *

'God that was boring, how does he do it?' Rock groaned as they entered the tunnel that led back to the old part of the college.

Finn was convinced it hadn't been an hour at all, but that he'd been trapped in a mind-razing black hole where time ceased to exist. 'Think you had it bad?' he replied, 'I was stuck up the front on my own!'

'Teach you for coming in last!' Rock had made everyone in the front vacate to the back rows, leaving Finn stranded on the front line and at the mercy of Orwell's intellectual musings. 'That was hilarious when he asked you about income tax, but you didn't know because you never work.'

'Lap it up while you can my friend, revenge will be sweet when I'm supping that fine vintage in front of you.'

'I'll even buy you some red lemonade, amateur like you would appreciate that.' Rock teased in return.

The Houseboat gang congregated by the bike sheds, taking refuge from the cold rain. Since that first day in the Pod, when Simon had sulked because he wasn't allowed to pick the music, they had managed to agree on a few more aspects of the show. It would be a high-octane, high-comedy breakfast production, impregnated with edgy humour, laughs, and, hopefully for Leo, a seat at the victors' table.

'If you would please, Kevin.' Rock said when the plastic straws had been cut and held securely in Kevin's fist.

As there were six of them, straws needed to be drawn to decide who would get to pick one of the available four songs. Kevin obliged and held out a handful of gangly straws of apparent equal height.

'You guys fixed that!' Simon wailed, convinced there was a conspiracy against him when he drew the fourth straw. 'That's the end song, the fade-out song - Bridgewater will only hear twenty seconds of it!'

'Lucky for Bridgewater.' Rock mumbled.

'I'm not picking one, I refuse-'

'I'll pick it.' Red said quickly, claiming the tune that would bring the programme to a close.

Simon glared at him. He hadn't really meant it - he was just trying to see if someone else would offer him theirs. 'Fine, I didn't want to pick one anyway,' he said, and his foot got caught in the spokes when he lashed out at one of the bikes.

'Okay, here's what we have so far,' Rock said as a gust whipped across the tarmac and sent spray into their faces. 'Finn and Leo are co-presenters-'

'Lead!' Leo insisted. 'And I want a cool DJ name, like DJ Sparkles or something.'

'Let me finish, Leo!' Rock gathered his thoughts again. 'So, I'm running the desk, Kevin's got the news, Simon's doing the sport and weather reports when he gets over his wobbly, and Red is the guest musician being interviewed by Kevin.'

'Can I choose the ad since I don't get to pick a song?'

'No.' Rock replied.

'You can pick the ad,' Finn stated, wanting to bring them together as a group rather than having everyone at each other's throats. He was sure that any listening audience would be quick to sense animosity in the team, and that would derail their chances of radio fame.

Simon grinned mischievously. He'd have the last laugh. Rock was staring at him before Simon noticed and his grin promptly disappeared.

'You're not allowed to do a food ad!' Rock said.

'I'll do whatever I want, it's my ad,' he retorted. He'd most certainly have the last laugh, Simon thought.

'What should I do for the news?' Kevin was unsure of what being a newscaster entailed. All he knew was that it wouldn't feature mass explosions, casualties, or fatalities.

'Make it up,' Red said encouragingly, 'put your own spin on things – brainwash the bastards with those headlines Sadie taught us about.'

Kevin's eyes fluttered as if inventing his own headlines would somehow be akin to hoodwinking Bridgewater. 'I wouldn't want to trick people into believing things that weren't true. I think I'll use real news.'

'Cool, you do that man.' Leo's lip then curled up as if his favourite wrestler had been bamboozled from behind with a ladder. 'But maybe use stories that are more interesting than the election.'

Finn suggested that Kevin do the story of how a renegade lone wolf ruined a political debate in Bridgewater.

'And how he streaked across the stage afterwards.' Red added, having already worked out that the instrumental part of his favourite rock song would be a supreme way to top off their show.

'I couldn't do that,' Kevin replied solemnly, 'what if children are listening?'

'Give advance warning,' Rock put in, his straw tumbling around in his mouth like a farmer chewing on a corn stalk, 'something along the lines of how there might be news of an indecent nature.'

'Very indecent, I'd say.'

'Keep that up and you won't be picking any ad,' Rock replied boot-faced to Simon.

Kevin then helpfully suggested that they should do three different segments if they were playing three songs, one between each song.

Leo massaged his chin. 'We could do a phone-in, chat to someone live on air – they could do a quiz?'

'What if the line was bad? We only get one shot at this so if we keep things simple, we'll have a better chance of delivering a good programme.' Finn said.

'What about bringing in a band?' Simon was thinking of something country, a few band members should be enough.

'That's hardly keeping it simple, Simon,' Finn replied, clearing the rain from his face like a sole windscreen wiper on a bus, 'no pun intended.'

'You sure about that?' Rock said.

In his head, Simon told Rock to keep it up, that he'd be sorry.

'How about doing the finale to a station giveaway?' Kevin had drawn the shortest of the straws, but the pressure of matching the tune with the theme would have been hefty so he was alright with that.

'That's good,' Red replied, 'We could do a build-up and then announce the winner.'

'And that winner might just be Sophia,' Finn was tapping his fingers together, 'and maybe she wins something *very* special for bailing on us.'

'Yes,' Rock agreed, nodding thoughtfully about how her exit had allowed the town trombone into the group, 'she'll rue the day she messed with the Houseboat gang.'

'You know something? I think we have a chance of winning this.' Finn said, daring to hope.

'We've got a long way to go yet,' Rock cautioned, which was his way of saying it all depended on certain people not making a hash of things, 'but Bridgewater might just be unlucky enough to have Simon and Leo live and in person in their living rooms.'

* * * *

The slip pooled on the floor with the others. Finn had decided to take shelter from the wind and nipped into the betting shop not far from the old distillery. But he was having a bad case of seconditis – the worst type of sickness in a place like this. He scanned the screen and saw the next race was almost away. '*Prometheus*,' he said, 'name like that it has to win.'

Finn scribbled the race time and the horse's name on a docket and then hurried to where it could be logged into the system so the wigs in head office would know how much to pay out when it won.

'*And they're off...*' He heard the commentator say as he accepted a print-out of his bet from a girl so malnourished that all he wanted to do was pick out the flesh from between his teeth that brushing had missed and give it to her.

Finn was still riding the subsidy the government had been kind enough to give him, so it didn't matter if he lost a few races here and there. It was plenty to keep his head above water and it wasn't like the money was really *his*. He was just having a bit of fun – like when an employee gets access to the company petty cash for non-official use. He paid no attention to the other punters; though he had noticed the musk of body odour and alcohol (a smell common to bookie shops) when he first crossed the threshold. He guessed it was from the two men at the table by the counter, one of who was becoming quite agitated.

'*And it doesn't seem to be a going day for Prometheus today...*'

He just wasn't catching a break. How hard was it to find a winner from eight horses? Prometheus was dropping farther behind, and the jockey looked like he was going up and down on a hobby horse. Finn smooshed the docket in his fist and was just about to bring it down on the table when there came a tremendous whoomph, followed closely by two yelps: one high-pitched, the other deeper.

'I've just lost two hundred quid and you're fuckin' laughing at me?'

The guy and girl behind the counter could only stare at the man with ajar, fly-catching mouths.

'We weren't laughing at you,' the girl, whose jaw was more skeletal than human, replied. (Their exact words had been, 'He's a smelly dart-thrower,' and, 'I wouldn't let him near yours!' all to a background of indelicate sniggering). 'Please,' she pleaded, 'relax.'

The man was now well past the 'relax' stage and he hurled the high stool at the tempered glass again with so much force that he fell back against the table. His acquaintance, who'd come from the pub to watch him lay down some twenties, stood well back from the purview of the stool and into the confetti of losing bets. He wouldn't join in, but he had no problem with his bar buddy smashing the place up; bastards had taken much of his drinking money in the past and were only getting what they deserved.

'Have you got a problem!?' Said the man whose baser inclinations were now at the helm.

He had yanked up the stool, ready to resume battering the glass (which appeared to have a crack in it). Spittle dribbled down his chin like an infected rat and he was ready to tear the world apart, including Finn, who was almost as stunned as the personnel.

Finn's life was good now. There had been no regression to the past and he hadn't been thrown out of college – or contracted AIDS, been electrocuted, or rained down upon by a sheet of airplane waste.

Basically, he was still here, and life hadn't pulled a fast one like he expected. So why was he still behaving like he was in the past? That six-foot ball of drooling rage was him, granted a version of him that looked like it would take a bite out of your rotator cuff, but him, nevertheless. He had also been feeling that same brewing irritation after his latest second (and after Prometheus had failed to live up to what was expected of him as a demigod), and unfortunately for Finn, there were no prizes for 'almost-winners'.

Rightfully his or not, the grant was a bridge between the old and new, and each time Finn passed beneath the heater that spat recycled air down his neck, he was removing another rivet. Was it enough to just scrape through to the next cheque from the ministry? Or did he want to use this chance and make something of it? Finn had seen his future self, and he didn't like who he'd become. He had enough problems with life without adding drool to the mix. He met the man's bulging eyes: 'No problem at all,' he replied, lobbing his ticket onto the shelf with the newspaper cuttings of the day's greyhound action.

Finn thought of Joe, and how he'd gone cold turkey from his harmful habit as a rush of arctic air greeted him when he opened the door. 'Still having a bet on the Grand National,' he said, flippantly, and the two men watched him leave as the crack in the glass got a little wider.

Chapter 21

It was Monday. And the world was pallid and lifeless. And ever since that trip to the coast at the beginning of the year, it seemed that come photography class on a Monday it was always miserable - and normally teeming with rain. At least it wasn't raining today.

'What are we doing in photography?' Rock said to anyone who would answer. He was in a bad mood as one of the dogs he was minding had kept him and Suzy up all night barking at nothing. Sleep deprivation could make you crazy, and if he'd had a submachine gun at that moment, he would have blown the annoying little yapper straight into the next life.

'Portrait shots.' Sophia replied.

'Oh, that's right,' he said, yawning like a mammy bear. 'Who wants to pose for me - Sophia?'

Leo perked up in his chair. 'I'll pose for you.'

'Sophia?' Rock asked again, pretending not to hear Leo.

She cocked her head and was deliberate with her answer. 'Only if you make me look like a movie star.'

'That shouldn't be too hard,' he said.

'Ahhh,' she replied, 'thanks Rock.'

The smell of spices from the lunchtime curry reached their position in the canteen. 'What? I was talking about my awesome photography skills.' Sophia pouted and punched him in the arm. 'Okay, how about your one from the *Fantastic Four* movie?'

'Ooohh, I love her!'

Leo gripped the sides of his bucket chair. 'Who would you make me look like?' he excitedly asked.

'The Thing.' Rock replied dourly.

'Hey, superhero's a superhero!'

Finn sighed and a series of groans were uttered when he told them that it was time for Orwell's wonderful world of useless wisdom. They never learned much under Orwell's tutelage, but paradoxically some of the funniest moments tended to happen during the hour that everyone dreaded.

Just last week, for instance, as Orwell was telling the class about his strange foreign neighbours and how they were always doing strange things, Mia had unexpectedly launched a Scud missile of a one-liner by suggesting that perhaps he was the strange one. Louis had found it so uproariously funny that he'd fallen off his chair and made Daisy's suitcase tinkle fiercely in objection. The jury was still out if this had been retribution for making Mia sound like a neophyte (a word they'd learned from Orwell) some months previous after Orwell had brought her up for giving the type of answers they'd come to expect from Dot or Simon.

Rock grabbed the handle of Finn's backpack and halted him in his tracks. 'I'm not in the mood for this useless wisdom class,' he said, 'you want to bunk off and go to the old bridge instead?'

'I had to leave twenty minutes early last time because my brain was so overwhelmed with useless information that I almost stroked out. So yes,' Finn replied, nodding at Gibby as she passed, 'yes I do.'

Rock nodded. 'His class will do that to you, alright. Let's go before anyone else realises and wants to tag along.'

*

Overhanging branches made it sound like rogue kids were pelting rocks at the houseboat. To get to the railway you needed to negotiate some very narrow lanes which nature seemed intent on reclaiming. They came to a low bridge and had to stop and get out to make sure they could proceed without paring the roof off. They could, but the houseboat aerial would be interred in weeds forever after.

'Isn't exactly much room to park around here,' Rock mused, looking at the brambles that dared put themselves in harm's way.

'There's a verge up ahead.' Finn replied.

'It's on a corner?' Rock said, 'But then again it's not as if we'll get a parking ticket or anything.'

It was meant as banter, but when he said the worst thing that happens is a roving gang robs it and they have to walk back, Finn resolved to bring his battered-fish-and-beer crisps – the latest in a long line of 'taste mauling' flavours – just in case.

A dilapidated shell with specks of green on the back door was still defying Father Time as they pulled themselves up a steep bank using the thin wire fencing behind the cottage. 'Wonder when someone was up here last.' Rock said, pushing aside the overgrowth, 'like trying to get through the Amazon.'

Finn kicked out his feet to remove the heavy clods of mud. 'Not sure, but runners are not the best thing for the Amazon.'

They emerged through the tangle and came upon an old railway bridge that had once spanned the watery expanse and which connected **Bridgewater** to distant lands where goods arrived on boats from countries people had never heard of.

'Looks like it's been sealed off.' Finn said, noting a corroded paling that was cordoning off the bridge.

'We could climb it?'

'Don't really fancy impaling myself on *those*.' He nodded at the fence's spear-like ends which looked sharp enough to carve through your thigh, or worse.

'Well, we've come this far,' Rock said, and if there was a citation that could sum up how Rock went about his life, this would be it. 'Hold these.'

Finn put Rock's camera around his neck for safe keeping (life wouldn't be worth living if he damaged it - might as well jump into the river and let it carry him to a faraway place) and plonked the bag containing his graded papers on the ground.

'Watch my camera.' Rock told him.

He nodded again at the spear tops. 'Watch your groin.'

'I'll try.' Rock stepped onto the railing and then up onto the higher one where he used the thick beam of the bridge to support himself. 'Not sure Suzy would hang around if anything happened.'

'Kind of surprised she's stayed this long,' Finn replied.

'She knows how lucky she-'

Rock's foot slipped as he went to take the last rail and his arms came away from the vertical post as a yowl escaped from somewhere deep within. Finn could only look on as Rock grasped desperately for something - anything - to grab hold of. His right hand found the bottom chord and he gripped it tighter than he thought was possible. Using what little momentum he had, he swung his left hand up; both hands were now cemented to the wrought-iron chord like someone had pranked him with 'no-slip' glue.

Finn leapt across the deformed sleepers and leaned over the side railing, making sure to sheath the camera as he did so. 'Are you alright?!'

'I'm alright.' He watched the empty wrapper Finn kicked on his way over disappear under his feet, 'unless this thing snaps!'

There was a nervous laugh. 'I'm going to pull you up.'

'Wait! Wait!' Rock cried when he started to feel his jacket become like a scarf around his neck.

Finn thought it was a splinter or rusty outcrop. 'What's wrong?!'

'Have you taken a photo?'

The pause was like an eternity to Rock, who could feel his grip slackening. 'But you might fal-'

'Hurry up before I lose my grip!' he demanded, 'not getting any lighter here.'

Finn unlatched his fingers, which had threatened to go into spasm such was the force of their grasp, and he pawed at the camera.

'Settings should be fine,' Rock instructed like he was advising how to photograph a meadow, 'just point and shoot.'

'Yes, Your Majesty,' Finn replied, sweating.

'Hurry up, hands are getting sore!' Rock said after hearing a couple of clicks, and after testing the robustness of his scapular muscles.

Finn carefully placed the camera on the worn-down deck, conscious that there was no point in both of them dying. 'Ready?' he said, grabbing Rock by the scruff of his jacket.

'As I'll ever be.'

Pulling with all his might - and Rock doing the same using the bar - he cursed as it repeatedly slid through his fingers. 'Why did you have to wear such a puffy jacket?!'

'Oh, I'm sorry.' Rock's words were a mixture of growls and grunts and sounded like someone getting to the limit of a push-up routine. 'I didn't wake up this morning with a plan of falling to my death!'

Finn fell backwards like a deep-sea fisherman who'd landed a prize marlin. Their pulses beat wildly and neither spoke for a while. 'You were inches from impaling yourself,' he eventually said, when he could talk without his voice hitching.

'Thought I had, all the women I've ever slept with flashed before my eyes,' Rock joked, feeling the coarseness of the wood beneath him.

'Eh, Rock?'

Rock was examining the damage to his jacket. *Finn and his clumsy fingers.* 'What?'

'Did you know there was a gap in the paling?'

'What?' Rock looked up to see a gap just wide enough for a normal-sized person to fit through if they turned sideways and held their breath. 'Shite!'

When they'd finished laughing, they took it in turns to squeeze through the gap that had been there all along. They traversed the sleepers and stepped over the ones that had rotted and were no longer there. The bridge ended abruptly halfway across the swollen river; the other half washed away one night during the worst storm in a century. They sat on the edge and let their legs dangle over the chasm.

'You think we can win this radio yoke?' Rock said, watching the river flow through the mist and towards the sea which was out of sight.

Finn measured the distance with his eye and wondered if it would have been broken bones or a trip across the Styx had Rock not held on. 'Look at Hugh's group, Ashley will get held up in the queue in McDonald's and Barbara's still MIA'.

'She'll be back for it apparently.'

'That rumour's been going around for weeks,' Finn replied, trying in vain to make out the ocean after deciding that it would have been a boat trip rather than a reset and cast for Rock. 'As for Hugh, he'll burst in when the credits are rolling. Sophia, on the other hand-'

'You created a monster there,' Rock said, cutting him short.

After helping her gain her 'radio legs', Sophia had commandeered the mic from Finn, rolled Rock away from the screens like he was in a child's stroller, and took them all on a trip down the *Highway to Hell* as ACDC set the little cabin ablaze. 'If I'd have known she'd become all wonder DJ and put the Houseboat effort in jeopardy, I would have let her continue to swing in her chair.'

As much as Rock was relieved not to have fallen, he was angry that he'd have to replace his jacket. 'Let's just hope she has an off day,' he said, stuffing polyfill back into its original place.

Finn concluded that without the aid of moisture-piercing binoculars, he couldn't see the ocean. 'The other group is the real danger.'

'The all-girl group?'

'All-girl group *plus* Fredrik,' Finn replied.

'That's right,' Rock said, 'Fredrik's in that group. We won't need to worry about them so.'

'He's surprisingly good, no fear at all - and teamed up with Mia behind the mic?'

Rock dismissed the threat. 'He'll start rambling on about feminism or neo...liberal, Nazi...whatever the hell he waffles on about.'

'Think they're doing a phone-in feature,' Finn said, 'heard them talking about getting someone in the news to ring in and give an exclusive update.'

'What, they going to get that fat little fucker – what's his name – Kimmy Jong to call in from Korea-land?'

'Fredrik probably has him on speed dial.' Finn watched as Rock looked distastefully at the fatal gash. 'Or else Daisy will ring in from Japan where she's bringing down the music moguls for forcing their prodigies to sign those contracts.' Whatever about withholding their pay, or not allowing them to regularly date, only allowing them to eat a thimble-full of rice at dinner was barbarous, Finn thought.

Most of the innards fell back out when Rock turned the jacket right side up. 'And she'll be wearing a kimono.'

'When in Japan, and all.'

The gliding of wings swooshed by in front of them, blending with the greyness, and becoming almost invisible. Rock snapped the bird in mid-air before Finn could choose the appropriate setting. 'How do you do that?' Finn said.

'Inherent talent,' Rock replied, taking a couple more as the heron shrank in size.

'Probably come out blurry anyway.' He sighed and lowered his camera. 'I'm going to miss this.'

'Herons?' Rock asked.

Finn laughed out loud. 'No, not herons – college, friends...having a life, I guess.'

'You'll find something. Probably just around the corner for all you know.'

'Hmmm.' He wasn't quite ready to share that he thought he might already have found that something. 'Have you started studying?'

Rock grimaced and his reply was one of dejection. 'What's the point? I won't be able to remember anything.'

The sun was sending ray bars along the parcel of land where vegetation had engulfed the once venerated track like they were hitching rides. 'That's where you're going wrong,' Finn replied, sizing up his next snap.

'What do you mean?' Rock said.

'Look.' He pointed with his lens to what the sun was doing. 'Well take photography, did you have to memorise how to take a good photo?'

'No, I just know it.'

Finn took the shot just before the bars evaporated. 'Ha, got one. Don't kill yourself trying to *memorise* things,' he said, 'try to *know* them instead.'

'But don't we have to answer the way they want, like word for word?'

One of the things that had turned Rock against formal education – and which had driven him out at such an early age – was one, Bradley. Bradley (Rock had stopped calling him 'Sir' in his last year of schooling) was an outspoken proponent of corporal punishment and often took out verbatim failures on his students. Along with being painful, Bradley had ensured that Rock's ingress into puberty would be a turning point in his young life.

'Nah, your own words are fine.' And then Finn smirked. 'All you have to do now is *understand* the material.'

'You shouldn't have said anything,' Rock shifted his weight into a more comfortable position. 'That bottle of whiskey is mine now.'

'Had to give you a chance,' he replied, 'bad enough beating a cripple.'

Rock laughed aloud. 'Think I'll make it a 21-year-old.'

Finn peeled wood shavings from a sleeper and dropped them over the edge. 'Hope you're talking about whiskey because I'm not sure we've much chance if you mean women.'

'Speak for yourself.' Rock picked up a pebble and tried to displace the shavings on their descent. 'Did I tell you I got an interview?'

'No?' Finn gave him a searching glance.

'Regional newspaper saw my work and got in touch. Their main photographer is retiring in September, and they want to talk to me about replacing him.'

'Master of Disaster,' Finn said, 'probably heard about your fondness for catastrophe and plan on sending you into terrorist country.'

Until he signed on the dotted line, Rock wasn't going to fall into that silky dream of being able to fund his life by using what he thought of as being his gift. 'Pay me enough and I'll go anywhere, sandbox or no sandbox.'

'Like Bond with a camera.'

'Rock Bond?' Rock replied, 'Like the sound of that...'

Finn let it out slowly, like a fragile skeleton being removed from its sarcophagus. 'Think I might have found something too.'

Rock was still repeating his new alias in his mind. 'You've finally decided to join those bums outside the clothes shop?'

Finn had been struck by the idea as suddenly and obviously as if he'd been hit by a brick a few weeks ago. He spat out the jelly he'd been sucking on and ran home to write it down in case his train of thought decided to pull out from the station early. After blagging his way to another glass of wine (journalistic credentials not required),

Finn had stayed to listen to the author speak in the bookshop. She was as nervous as he would have been addressing a multitude who'd come especially for her and he had felt inspired by the whole thing; the three-year slog to bring what was in her head into being, and the prestige and kudos heaped upon her by a buoyant crowd, made buoyant because they knew they were part of something bigger just by being there.

'I'm writing a book.' He listened out for the sound of a nuke dropping somewhere in the vicinity, but to Finn's immense relief, he heard nothing but the humming of insects in the reeds below.

'That's great! You should have told me.'

Since catching the literary bug, he'd been going full tilt at the Grand Hotel – the one VIPs and dignitaries would use because it was the only decent hotel in the town – every day after college, continuing to use it as his writing sanctum after the manager, who harboured her own creative aspirations, had told him that *we blue-sky people need to stick together*, before clanking down a second unordered coffee.

'With my history of dead-ends, I wanted to be sure it was going somewhere before I told anyone.' Finn replied.

Rock was suddenly feeling the warmth of a possible future for them both. 'What's it about?'

'Some friends who go on a road trip in a beat-up camper – driven by a belligerent old man, of course.'

'Sounds like a bestseller!' he replied.

Finn stood and brushed the shavings from his trousers. 'Would you look at us,' he said, laughing, 'you a famous photographer and me a famous writer.'

'Only if you actually *finish* it,' Rock teased, and a crescent moon of white viscera encircled him as he swung his coat up and over his shoulders. 'By the way, whose portrait are you taking?'

Finn took a deep breath of unpolluted air. For once in a long time, he felt excited for the future and not cowed by it. 'Fredrik's.'

Rock began to laugh. 'I'm shooting Sophia.'

'You want to swap?'

'No.'

'I'll go easy on you in the exams?'

Rock was headed back towards the fence, fully intent on taking the safe route this time. 'Ehh...nope.'

'Last time I save you from certain death.' Finn said, but not even that could obfuscate the promise of the lights ahead.

* * * *

Finn yanked off the headphones and the stool squealed harshly as he leaned back in it.

'You're trying too hard!' Rock berated him, resetting everything for the umpteenth time since they'd taken over the room from the 'Smoking Babies', a name undoubtedly the wit of Blanche or Kennedy.

'I know I am!'

This was the group's last practice before the exam – not just that, but the last practice before it was streamed to the entire Tech and possibly the entire city of Bridgewater – and Finn couldn't introduce the show without sounding like a scratchy 12-inch.

'Give me that.' Rock grabbed the sheet of paper that Finn was clutching like it was a buoy keeping him from going under.

'Why'd you do that?' Finn said, watching as the detailed script he'd written in case of 'stage fright' whizzed past Simon to the far end of the studio.

'You don't need it. It's distracting you.'

Distracting him? If anything, it was going to be the thing that saved him – and the whole group. 'I won't know what to say without it!' he argued.

'It'll come to you.'

'Yeah, but–'

'Do you remember what Sadie told us?' Rock said with the type of austereness that any high-school preceptor would have been proud of.

'I don't exactly have much experience presenting a live show, do I?' Finn replied.

Rock continued to bat away his excuses. 'What did she tell us?'

Public speaking had never been Finn's strong suit. As much as he tried, he could never stop his voice from tremoring, or stop the forgetful fog from coasting in, and because he was always so afraid to look stupid, he always wound up looking stupid. 'About the fisherman,' he said impertinently.

'Exactly, the fisherman, who's out on the boat all on his own and yours is the only voice he hears.'

'And mine!' Leo butted in.

Rock's tone softened and the tough love evolved into a parable. 'You're not talking to anyone else except that one fisherman – in fact, let's call him Red – you're a fisherman, right Red?'

'Sure am,' he said, tinkering with protrusions that may have either blazed a music track or sent Leo through the roof.

'And it's your job to keep Red company, keep him from getting lonely.'

'You wouldn't want me getting lonely, Finn, would you?' He pushed a button that would have crashed the whole system had they been live.

Finn smiled reluctantly, letting the headset swing by his side. 'No, Red, I wouldn't.'

'It's not a show you're putting on,' Rock explained, 'you're having a cup of tea with Red out on the ocean, that's all.'

'Is there rum in that there tea?' All the old salts brought lucky trinkets when they left for the high seas. Some had charms given to them by grandkids, some had photos of loved ones (one of the younger seafarers even brought a computerised tablet that had lots of photos on it, much to the contempt of the sea dogs), others still had compasses that told them the direction of home, but the one time that Red forgot to bring rum they had run into a squall and were nearly all guests at Neptune's table. 'Never leave port without a good bottle of grog.'

'You're having a cup of *rum* tea with Red out on the ocean,' Rock said.

Simon tapped Leo on the shoulder to alert him that it was his time in the hot seat. 'But it's not just Red,' Simon argued, as he mounted the chair, 'there's loads of people.'

'Can you see those people?'

'Obviously not,' Simon replied.

'Well then, you don't know they're there, do you?' Rock looked back at Finn. 'Can you see Red?'

Red brought an imaginary mug to his lips and pretended to drink from it.

'Suppose I can.' He brought the mug down and rubbed his belly. 'Ok,' Finn said, acknowledging what Rock was saying, 'let's do it again.'

'That's what I want to hear!' Rock replied, readjusting dials and resetting volume levels that Red's tampering had thrown off.

Finn placed the headphones back on his ears. His confidence had grown steadily over the past months, and he wasn't going to let something as trivial as speaking in front of some invisible people get the better of him. Everything that he'd achieved and all the blessings bestowed upon him had always been against an undercurrent of doubt. Like the final boss in a computer game, he needed to face the buttressed 'voice' one more time.

'You ready?' Rock's fingers hovered just above the sliders.

Finn returned a look that said he was ready to walk across hot coals. 'Yep.'

'Just chatting to Red,' Rock repeated, and then gave the signal which meant he was free to try again.

If it was possible to clear your throat in a confident manner, then that's what Finn did.

'*And welcome to the Morning Show here on Houseboat FM, your haven from the billows and breakers of life. I'm Silver, your host, and I hope you're all wearing your woolies because it's draughtier than a group of feminists at a knickerbocker convention today. But on a brighter note, we have a special guest joining us in the studio. You wouldn't exactly call him a feminist, but he does enjoy the company of a nice woman every now and then...*'

As Finn opened the show - or rather, chatted to Red - with ease, Rock looked to the others and they smiled at one another, and it was at that moment when they felt the outcome of the competition was firmly within their grasp.

* * * *

Kevin's head bobbed past the window of O'Malley's. He strode with purpose and looked like a man on a mission.

'Why does Kevin never eat with us?' Daisy was doing her usual brief of watching the others gorging themselves while she abstained.

'He has the hots for the waitress up the road,' Louis replied.

Fridays were Dot's 'delivery' days, and she was particularly jumpy this Friday because she was yet to receive confirmation of the meeting place. 'Wait – what, really?'

'He's been going there while we've been coming here to get Finn his pineapple.' Rock said.

'Don't mention pineapple when I'm having my pizza.'

Finn held up a chicken burger so Hugh could see what he was eating. 'Does this look like a pineapple to you?'

'Probably asked O'Malley to mash it into the patty,' Rock joked.

Finn changed the subject before he was asked to prove there was nothing between the smoothed-down baps. 'Anyone know if he's asked her out yet?'

'Nah,' Leo confirmed, 'don't think so.'

'We'll have to do it for him if he won't.' Rock popped two wedges on the fat of a pizza slice and consumed it all.

'Yeah,' Dot agreed, checking her messages again, 'she could be his one true love.'

'Imagine dating someone who could give you free coffee and bagels whenever you wanted – definitely my idea of true love.' Finn said.

Leo had sauce spatter all around the hair on his chin. 'I'd prefer free pizza myself.'

'You'd prefer to date O'Malley?' Sophia prodded, always willing to call Leo up on the stupid things he said.

'What? No!'

'O'Malley?' Rock said as he approached the table, 'you've got an admirer here.'

'I'm sorry, Sophia,' he replied, taken aback by the number of empty sachets on the table, 'you're a lovely girl and all, but I'm happily married.'

Sophia giggled and a straw fell from her mouth. 'It's not me, it's Leo.'

'I don't fancy you,' he protested sharply, 'they're lying!'

O'Malley looked him up and down. 'Sorry Leo, you're not my type.' He started nipping up the packets of ketchup and vinegar from the table. 'When's the big showdown?'

Dot's phone lit up like moon dust and she charged from the table. 'Gone, lads!'

Rock saved the last wedge before O'Malley could take his tray, and just as Dot was crashing through the door. 'Monday,' he replied.

'Ohhh, not long now,' O'Malley chimed, 'did you get your segments all worked out?'

Leo and Simon had become the epitome of being '*spanners in the works*' and had staged a protest when they felt their reasonable demand for more airtime wasn't being given adequate consideration. 'Took a bit of squabbling,' Finn said, 'but we think so.'

'We're hoping Simon gets struck down with Ebola over the weekend.'

'Rock – that's terrible!' O'Malley couldn't stop himself from snickering. 'I'm sure Simon's a valuable member of the team.'

Rock still hadn't forgiven Simon for initiating the whole sit-in debacle, which had resulted in the loss of a week's effort. 'The special team, maybe,' he replied.

'My money's on Ashley's group.' *Kids of today really did enjoy their condiments*, he thought. 'Will just take this back and restock it.'

'Agghh, thanks, O'Malley,' she replied, flashing him a warm smile as he went for the condiment-less bowl.

Ashley reminded O'Malley of a girlfriend he once had, and when the summer – and the romance – ended, he had been crushed. O'Malley could feel himself burning at the neckline of his collared t-shirt and started to walk away. He stopped momentarily as Finn was biting into his burger. 'How's that pineapple working out for you?'

Finn froze and glanced around at the faces. Hugh looked as if he was ready to be sick.

'You're some bastard, O'Malley,' he said, mouth awash with chicken and shredded pineapple.

Chapter 22

The sun rose like a helium-filled balloon above the hill behind the station, bathing Bridgewater in resplendent sunshine. Rock sped past as a train was pulling out on its way to the capital, and Finn's woolly hat was left on the nob of his chair as he snatched up his notes; no need for that today. Ashley and Mia spotted him from the newsstand a little way back and Ashley told her to hold on while she ran over to buy some powder tubes; the stuff that so resembled cocaine that had she brought it through the airport, she would have been led into a small and windowless room. Kevin stepped off the bus, news articles clutched tightly to his bosom. Red kissed his girl – his ex-girl – and marched past where Blanche and Kennedy were further hollowing out the pavement by the edge of the railing.

'Hey, Silver.' Blanche flicked ash onto the ground without taking her eyes from his.

That was the first time he'd been called Silver outside the recording studio, and he quite liked the ring of it. 'Must be something important to drag you girls from your beds at such an hour?'

'We wanted to see you, Finn,' Kennedy said.

'Knew it had to be something like that,' he replied grinning. Though Blanche lived life adamantly downplaying any qualities she had, her smile would always brighten his day.

Blanche tilted her head and watched as Finn followed Red into the college. 'I would.'

'I know you would.' Her best friend replied, sending ash tumbling down the path in the same direction.

Rock vaulted across the road, seeming full of new-found sureness, and was followed closely by Leo and Simon who he could hear but not see. Hugh looked at his phone, he was late again. His group had been first out of the hat (the younger students had found this a very archaic way of determining order), and he stamped the accelerator of his Micra to the ground, while Sloppy dawdled outside a shop not far from the college as if he was waiting on something; or someone.

**

The auditorium was already chock-full of restless students keen to hear the best Bridgewater Tech could offer. Every class had been excused from the first two lectures and it was as much this reason for the electricity in the air.

'Jesus,' Rock said, peeking in at those who would ultimately be responsible for deciding which group snagged a spot on the radio, 'it's packed.'

'Let me see.' Finn stuck his head in below Rock's. 'Whoa, it's packed.'

'That's what I said.'

The auditorium was by far the biggest space in the college and enlivened students continued to fill every seat in the hope of hearing some crash and burn radio – and tears and tantrums all the better.

'Look at the amount of people!' Simon exclaimed, bursting through the door where they were spying from.

Finn was now questioning the logic of having such a big breakfast. 'Tell us about it.'

'Is Hugh's group over in the Pod?' Rock closed the door back over so they wouldn't lose face if Finn barfed.

'The rest of his group are anyway.' Red replied, as only a few eagle eyes in the back row noticed their discomfort.

'He'll be late,' Rock affirmed, 'guarantee it.'

The rambunctious throng was making Finn feel like he was abseiling down the Grand Canyon. 'Sophia will have his testicles on a stick,' he replied absently.

'Nah, he'll be early today.' Simon said.

'Well,' Rock replied, checking the fitness band which told him how many steps he'd already put his knackered leg through, 'he's got about ten minutes before they go live.'

**

'I'm never going to make it!' Hugh bemoaned, looking at his phone again as the speedometer registered ninety. He pushed the pedal as hard as he could, but the car wouldn't go any faster. He cursed himself for spending so much time sledging the Manchester City starting eleven on Twitter (some of the things he said were not strictly in keeping with Sadie's lesson on defamation), but it would all be worth it if he could put them off their game for this weekend's decider; a summer of having to wear a City jersey depended on it.

**

Sadie looked around at those who had gathered in the studio. They seemed short in number. 'Are you guys all set?'

Sophia jammed her thumb in her mouth, a move that always told her parents when she was anxious. 'Hugh's not here yet.'

'Neither is Billie!' Louis added, turning around in loose, slipshod circles like he was trying to untangle himself from fish netting.

'Can we wait for them?' Ashley said, tossing a hair band from one hand to the other, unbothered either way.

'Sorry, folks, your audience awaits in four minutes,' Sadie replied.

'Fuck.' Louis barked, still tangled up.

The words were barely understandable as they fought their way around Sophia's bony impediment. 'Will you be co-presenter?'

'You know I'm not good at presenting,' Louis stopped on a dime and looked beseechingly at Sophia. 'Remember I said that every time was a new time for my 98-year-old girlfriend because she couldn't remember the last time?'

'You'll be fine,' she said, 'just follow my lead.'

'Okay,' he replied, 'but I hope I don't start talking about sucking molasses syrup off her fingers again.'

'We're ready, Sadie.' Sophia confirmed.

**

'Do you think it's good we're going second?' Finn's voice rumpled like a slept-in bedsheet.

'I think so.' Rock answered.

'We can learn from their mistakes,' Kevin said, though the sentiment was lacking in oomph.

Leo tried to boost everyone's morale by causing their ear canals to tighten. 'We'll be grand guys!'

'Attention everybody,' bayed the principal, his walleyes ingurgitating the entire room, 'if you could now take your seats, the shows are about to begin.'

'Neerrrd.' Simon growled from the back of the auditorium like he had a hidden vendetta against him.

Finn's heart began to beat faster. They were next in line.

* *

'And-' Sadie started, '-five, four, three, two,' and when her hand came down like a martial artist chopping through a rick of blocks, the light glowed red, and they went live.

* *

Finn had chewed off almost half the nail on his middle finger. 'I'm nervous for them.'

'I'm more nervous for us,' Rock replied, hoping that Simon and Leo wouldn't bugger things up and ruin all their hard work.

'Once Finn doesn't blow the intro, we should be fine.'

His finger was already beginning to feel that early rawness that would eventually lead to future throbbing. 'Gee, Simon, that doesn't freak me out at all!' Finn replied as Simon smirked back at his co-star like he'd one-upped him.

The speakers in the corners of the room crackled to life and the crowd quietened as a short piece of music came on.

'Kinda sounds like a cheesy TV show.' Red said when he heard the catchy intro jingle.'

'Is that-' Rock began.

'-it's the theme tune from *Dallas!*' Finn said, laughing in stutters.

'What's *Dallas?*'

'Don't worry about it, Leo,' Rock replied, 'you were still swimming around your daddy's tighty-whities when that was on.'

'*Hi guys.... you're welcome to - along to - the show today...*' an apprehensive-sounding Sophia announced.

They looked at each other.

'Told you he'd be late.' Rock declared.

'Sophia wasn't expecting to open the show,' Kevin reminded them, remembering that Hugh had planned to start it off with a short skit.

'*Yes, it's going to be a smashing show, and I'm the other host, Louis the Leprechaun.*'

Some of the crowd giggled.

'Why did he say that?' Red asked, boffing his fuzzy conical - which had been given a trim and now looked like it could pick locks or break ice - with the pads of his fingers.

'You know what Louis's like, says crazy shit when he's on the radio,' Finn replied.

'*We'll be talking about all things celebrity with our resident Snapchat guy,*' Sophia took a pause, '*when he arrives in. We also have our 'Animal Spot', where we tell you about the best advice for looking after your pets.*'

'*Yes, pets,*' Louis agreed, '*everyone's favourite animals - just don't feed them molasses, probably wouldn't be good for them, too thick, probably too sweet too... really only meant for romantic relationships.*'

'*Thanks for that, Louis,*' Sophia said glaring at him. '*Before that, we'll play our first song, which is-*'

Ashley shrugged and brought her hands together like she wanted to wrap them around something soft and squeeze for all her worth. '*Hugh has the music!*'

The door of the studio burst open after Hugh zig-zagged around Sadie and he let his bag slip to the floor by the entrance. '*It's alright guys! I made it.*'

'*Shut up, we're live!*' Ashley scolded him in the background.

'*Oops, sorry...*' Hugh whispered, and the crowd, unsure if this was staged or not, saw the funny side.

Rock gasped, 'That jammy git is actually helping them.'

'It's the hair,' Finn opined, bringing his hand to his mouth, and starting in on another fingernail, 'he's like Samson.'

'I think we should go now.' For Kevin, the thought of being tardy for something was worse than the something itself, 'it's a nine-minute walk to the studio.'

'We'll listen for just a bit longer. We're not lucky enough to do a Hugh anyway,' Rock replied.

* *

'How'd you get on?' Finn knew the answer, but the question had to be asked.

Hugh pressed his teeth together and sucked air through them as he led the group of condemned from the building.

'We would have done alright if Hugh hadn't turned up late - again!' Sophia said with venom, 'And if he remembered to bring the right music!'

He bowed his head like a puppy who'd been caught peeing on the floor. 'I was in such a rush I grabbed the wrong stick.'

"Doing it like they do on'-' Sophia waved her hand in the air trying to think of the words, '-on some Discovery Channel or whatever doesn't work so well when you've just talked about neutering your cat!'

Sophia was so angry her words were fighting each other to get out first. 'Or if Louis hadn't talked about picking up his girlfriend - *OAP* girlfriend, sorry - from the old folks' home and then, then, having to get her back before it was time for her sponge bath - which he'd be giving her!'

'I got nervous.' Louis' grin was chuckle-inducing.

If there was upset at all this dishing of blame, then at least Ashley was being spared a few pies for a change. She thought her performance had been flawless, and she'd definitely kept her best for last.

'And Billie...she didn't even come in or tell us where the recordings were, or Gibby-'

'Sophia?'

Sophia's dramatics came to a halt before she could lay into Ashley for completely missing the introduction of their main topic: '*Boys, are they worth it?*', because she'd been texting her boyfriend about whether they should sleep in his or hers at the time.

'You should have stayed with the winning team.' Rock said.

'Ok, guys,' Sadie tapped the face of her watch, saving Rock from a re-engagement of hostilities, 'you have five minutes to get set up.'

'Just don't mention sticky substances and you'll be alright,' Louis warned them as if it was an existential threat that everyone faced at some point.

The studio looked the same as it always did; low lighting, the gentle hum of computers, and a sense of repose that should have brought nothing but feelings of quietude, but instead only served to heighten expectations.

A pair of flat panel monitors surrounded Rock as he jostled into position, each with a different thing on the screen. It was his responsibility to run the desk, as it was called in the radio world, and to ensure the smooth transition from chat to songs to ads and everything in between. 'I see your car's been clamped, Sadie,' he said.

Sadie paused from updating the digital community on the progress of the Showdown, and how the second favourites would shortly be taking to the air. 'I don't believe you?' she replied.

Rock brought up their hamper of songs on the right-hand screen. 'Yeah, you parked in the handicapped spot.'

'Well, bollocks–' she retorted, her big Sunday plans of lunch in the local followed by a few vodkas now up in smoke because of a usurious release fee, '–there goes my weekend!'

He lowered his seat a couple of rungs. 'I'm kidding, just thought I'd get you back for making me walk an extra twelve yards.'

'You do remember who's correcting our exams, don't you?' Finn whispered after Sadie had called him a rascal for making her think she wouldn't be able to watch the boys in green hammer the boys in white.

Rock turned the monitors, so they were all directly in his eye-line. 'Ah, she's cool,' he said.

Leo hopped up onto one of the stools which broached two floating microphones and it rolled back and bumped into Rock, squealing all the while. It was then decided that Finn would sit on this stool. Leo found it hard to keep still at the best of times and couldn't be trusted to remain composed should topics such as wrestling arise.

'Theme and background music, check; folders open, check; playlist minus Simon's song, check.'

Unknown to the others, Simon had wound his song around his ad like masking tape around the mouth of a hostage. 'That's what you think,' he replied quietly.

'Two minutes guys...'

'Mics up and we'll do a sound check.' Finn said.

'Both up.' Rock confirmed.

Leo's low purr droned through their headsets. 'One, two, one, two.'

'They can hear you in Bangladesh, sit a bit further back.' Rock told him. 'Go for it, Finn.'

'Is this being broadcast in Cairo again?' Leo said.

'Sure is.' Finn replied. 'One Mississippi, two Mississippi - is that anywhere near your house, Leo?'

The laughter helped to ease the tension.

'Remember, after the first segment let in Kevin and Simon so they can be ready with the news and weather.'

'Got it, Rocky-boppy,' Leo confirmed, taking his new high stool for a joy ride, and content with its sleek handling.

'Thirty seconds...' Sadie advised from the far corner of the room where Finn's pulverized script had once lived.

Finn peered at his compatriots, all of them looking like whack-a-moles ready to stick their heads up and brave the mallet. 'I fancy being on Strand FM. Let's win this thing.'

'Me too,' Leo twisted to make sure it was safe to twist during the show, 'I want to be famous!'

'You're going to be one of those people who gets famous and then dies a horrible death.' Rock looked at Finn from his instrument pit, finger hovering over the slider that would send his voice from the cosy room where they were and out into the outside world. 'The fisherman,' he said.

Finn felt a wave of calm come over him as if a fuse had suddenly been tripped and the pressure had been switched off. 'The fisherman.'

'And five, four, three...'

* *

'*So, I'm asleep yesterday morning and my cock starts going berserk-*,'

Leo went red, trying not to burst. '*You mean your 'clock'?*'

Finn was so in the moment he could barely remember what he'd said. It was like the less he tried to direct things the better directed they became. '*What did I say?*'

'*I can't repeat it,*' Leo replied, laughing feverishly.

* *

'*Have you got a receding hairline, or maybe you're completely bald? Then this might just be the thing you've been looking for!*'

The riff of a well-known and amicable country tune that had once two-stepped up the charts danced in line with an ad that sought to give back the boon of a 'macho 'fro'.

'Little fuckin' pup-'

Finn brought his finger to his lips, urging Rock to reign it in. If looks could kill then Simon would have been pinned to the studio door, held up by a plethora of poisonous spears.

* *

'*And that's all your sport on-*'

Simon went dead as if he'd run into a vocal wall. He held out his arms and silently but urgently entreated for help. '*On...*'

The crowd heard only a dull thud, but Kevin felt it through his whole thigh. Simon's fist had come down onto the nearest thing as he racked his brain trying to think of the station's name. Red turned an imaginary wheel, while Leo tried to convey a boat on the open sea by patting his hand rapidly which looked more like he was dribbling a basketball.

'*On Boathouse FM!*' Simon proudly exclaimed.

**

'*Can you share with the listeners why you wanted to become a musician?*' Kevin asked with the pronounced and measured elocution of a dyed-in-the-wool broadcaster.

'*Sex, drugs and roll n roll, baby.*' Red replied in the way he would were his musical talents ever discovered by a scout who happened to be responsible for sourcing talent on a ship.

Kevin wilted back from the mic. He wasn't sure if you could say such things on the radio. '*Was it not for the love of music?*'

'*At the start it was, yeah,*' Red admitted. '*But then came the other side of music – the love of the blow and bitches side.*'

**

'That was amazing!' bleated Leo when they'd made it out to the car park, leaving the studio free for the last group. When Mia had threatened that the Smoking Babies were going to blow them out of the water, Finn told her it wasn't polite to be making lude references all the time.

Red tapped some tobacco onto his wrist. 'Went well, lads.'

'Can't believe how well it went,' Rock said, 'even with you saying how your cock woke you up this morning!'

Finn was beaming. The newspaper advert had been right all along; those smiling faces weren't just put on for the camera. 'Was going for alarm *clock* on that one.'

'It would have been perfect, too,' Rock added, 'if Simon hadn't put on that shite and dubbed it with that other shite.'

'And I introduced it!' Leo bawled, fearing that a country tune would lower his stock as a serious disk jockey.

Simon grinned smugly. He didn't care. He had been determined to bring back *Achy Breaky Heart* and now if they won all of Bridgewater would hear his favourite song – maybe even give it a new lease of life. 'You guys wouldn't let me play it.'

Rock fixed Simon with his trademark stare, the one that bent people to his will. 'If we lose, it's because the whole place tuned out when they heard that song!'

'And Red, what a voice – you really do sound like an angel.'

'Thanks, Finn.' Red secured the pipe in the corner of his mouth, 'sang a few sea shanties in my time.'

'And when you said the best thing about being a rock star was doing shots off the bellies of sexy ladies,' Rock added, laughing.

Finn chuckled as well. 'I can hear it now: "Mommy, what does doing shots off bellies mean?"'

'Creativity, lads,' he replied, striking a match, and repeatedly sucking on the lip to get the tobacco going.

Kevin was still reeling from Red's seamless diffusion into character. 'I wasn't expecting that answer,' he said sheepishly.

'I think *I* did very well.'

'Right up until you forgot the name of the radio station, you numpty,' Rock said.

'Yeah, well,' Simon replied, 'I was concentrating so much on the sports that I...kind of forgot.'

Red chortled loudly, the pipe waggling up and down in tune with his laughter. 'And Leo with his 'old minty' - classic.'

'When I looked at his head from the side, he just reminded me of one of those after-dinner mints!'

Rock allowed himself a smile. 'That was a good one, Leo, I'll give you that.' He turned to Finn. 'You know Sophia's going to kill you?'

'For what?' he replied, 'winning a date to the liquorice wrestling expo with Leo - Houseboat FM's most eligible bachelor - for the competition she texted in twelve hundred times for? Sure, she loves liquorice.'

'I didn't know you were going to say Sophia!'

'Does someone have a thing for our Sophia?' Rock teased Leo, grinning and clouting him in the arm.

Leo readjusted his glasses after they'd scuttered down his nose. 'No, I mean she's a nice person and all, and I think she might fancy me, but she's not my type.'

'If she's not your type, then you really shouldn't pursue he-'

'And you didn't botch up the intro this time.' Simon said, talking over Kevin like he was confirming a lunch order.

Finn was delighting in having figured out how to keep a leash on the butterflies. Once you got into it and forgot you were being listened to by an entire fraternity, he thought it came almost naturally. 'The fisherman and I had a heart-to-heart.'

'When did you record that vox pop?' Leo said, 'It was pretty spunky!'

Rock caught Finn's eye and they shared a private joke. After the emergency of the night before - when Rock discovered that their expose about the necessity of politicians had disappeared ('Simon's either deleted it because it isn't men in spandex or he's eaten it', Rock had lambasted) - he assumed artistic license and tracked down a clip of a helicopter in mid-flight. Making sure his voice took on a distorted quality, he pretended to be hundreds of feet in the air reporting on traffic. 'Last minute addition, Leo - got creative like Red.'

'It was interesting how you said that the Taoiseach's car had overturned and was responsible for a fourteen-mile tailback.' Kevin was slightly put out that they'd broadcast a fake news story; what if it caused motorists to avoid that road and their whole day was ruined because of it?

'And seeing him crawl out of the car and then run down the road with his wig on fire,' Finn added.

Red looked like the conductor of a locomotive who had just thrown a fresh log into the wood burner. 'And how you emptied your bladder over the side to put out the flames.'

'And then how he got - what was it,' Finn asked, 'smushed'?'

'Squished,' Rock replied.

'Squished, that's right,' Finn continued, 'by an oncoming truck when he fell over the median wall.'

Rock replied with a smirk. He never failed to become impassioned when talking about his current oppressor. 'Yeah, I was particularly proud of that.'

'The others looked quite confident, didn't they?' Simon said, 'And did you see the way Blanche stared at Finn as she walked past?'

Finn had noticed the look too. 'They're just trying to intimidate us,' he replied.

'When do we find out who won?' Rock was fidgeting like he'd gone with Dot to her weekly meet.

'Sadie said it'll be announced after the last ex-' Kevin tried saying.

'And then played on the radio the following Monday when listenership is at its highest!' Leo cried as if they'd already won.

Rock's eyes lit up. 'Kind of exciting, isn't it?' he said, and the eyes of the rest of the team lit up too.

* * * *

'What will I say?' Kevin said, standing where patio furniture would soon accommodate those wanting a tan with their mocha.

Apart from Rock, who could see over them all, they craned to get a peek of Kevin's abiding - and relatively secret - love interest through the narrow slice of window.

'Just ask her if she wants a pint, and then afterwards you can take her home and show her your thunder stick.' Red said, taking out a zippo with a mermaid waving off a pirate ship on it.

His amore was overrun with steam as some type of coffee drink fizzed and gurgled into existence. 'I don't think I could do that?' Kevin replied sincerely.

'I think what Red means,' Finn said, stepping in, 'is ask her out for a drink, maybe to that wine bar up the street.'

'What about a coffee?'

'She works in a café, Leo,' Sophia linked arms with Ashley, 'that's the last place she'd want to go!'

'I'd want a guy to take me for a lobster dinner,' Ashley said dreamily, 'with candles and a bottle of French plonk, and then McDonald's for dessert afterwards.'

'So romantic,' Sophia gushed, and they swooned over the thought of a handsome stranger throwing down a five and demanding two soft serve cones.'

Kevin nervously rustled around in his pockets. 'Not sure I could afford that.'

'Only one person canoodles in the houseboat!' Rock retorted after Finn suggested that if all went well a night of rocking in the granddad mobile might be on the cards.'

'I hope you mean two people?' Sophia enquired.

When he saw her adorable grin, Hugh had to hold himself back from taking Sophia in his arms and kissing her. 'Oh, burn! She gotcha good there, Rock.'

'Shut up, Wolfman,' Rock replied, going for a clip around the ear only for Hugh to pivot out of the way.

Ashley watched as Kevin's girl placed a fruit scone onto a plate. 'She looks nice.'

'Graceful, too.' Sophia said, noticing the refined way in which she plopped the cream next to the scone without touching it.

Kevin didn't need to see through the window to know the languorous lines of her body and the lithe dexterity of her fingers. 'What if she has a boyfriend?'

'Only one way to find out, Kevin-boy,' Red replied, relighting his pipe that the walk there had extinguished.

'Right, either you go in and ask her, or we will.' Rock said stoically. 'All those times you blew us off just so you could be with your fancy piece, time to make it count.'

Kevin's jaw started to clatter like he was standing in a blizzard wearing nothing more than a string onesie. 'What if I come back during the summer?' he asked.

'She'll have forgotten about you by then.' Finn replied, suddenly feeling peckish.

'He's right,' Spikester confirmed, 'at least if she turns you down now you can stalk someone new next year.'

'Stalk?' Kevin said.

'Do you want us to come with you?'

Kevin heard Leo's question, but he couldn't focus properly on the words coming out of his mouth. 'No...I can, best if I do it.' What if that happened when he asked her out for a drink? Or was it a coffee he was meant to be asking her out for?

'You're Bridgewater's premier newsreader,' Finn said encouragingly, 'just pretend you're telling her the news.'

'Good luck, Kevin.'

'Oh, thanks Ashley,' he replied to Sophia, and without having made the decision to go in, his hands were pushing the door open, and his legs were carrying him ever closer to the counter.

Mia covered her eyes but peeked through the gap in her fingers. 'I can't look.'

'He's just tripped over his foot!' Simon started to laugh, 'even I wouldn't do that.'

Ashley planted her face in Mia's back. 'I can't look either!'

'He's coming!' Leo called, his voice rebounding off the breath-stained window.

The world was a fast-moving blur, and Kevin looked vacuously at the others. 'I forgot what I had to say.'

'Did you at least order something?' Rock said.

Worms could have been crawling out of Rock's nose and Kevin wouldn't have registered them. 'No. She asked me what I wanted and I walked out.'

Finn pressed a supportive hand to his shoulder and Rock did the same on the other side. 'That's fine, gives us something to work with.'

'What – what are you doing?' he said.

'We're getting you a coffee,' Finn replied as Kevin's feet rose an inch off the ground, ensuring he at least wouldn't trip over them again, 'and a girlfriend.'

'But-' Kevin tried struggling but his muscles went limp as the checkout came closer.

'Hi,' Rock said stoutly, 'my friend here has a crush on you.'

Kevin couldn't make anything out clearly, and the large-lettered writing on the mug had arranged itself into a black barcode. 'Eh-'

'Rock,' the woman with the wart above her lip stared back with stony indifference, 'wrong one!' Finn prompted him.

'Which one is it?' he whispered back.

A girl delivering a vanilla latte with a chocolate-chip fudge brownie to a man sitting by a window (and whose bulk was touching a grossed-out teenager, who was getting ready to leave with her partly eaten bagel) stopped when she heard Rock's brusque tenor. She thought it was unusual as no one had ever come close to admitting they liked Agnes - not that she wasn't a lovely woman when you got to know her.

'That's her.' Kevin said faintly, attempting to smile, but looking more like someone in need of a suppository.

When she turned around, she saw that one of her regulars was wedged between two bigger guys, like bouncers throwing him out of a black-tie event for being improperly attired. She had come to know him over the months because of how frequently he came in, and how he was the only person to ask for paprika on his bagel.

'Hi,' Rock began again, 'our friend here, who I'm sure you know-'

'Hey, shy cute guy.' She had nicknamed him this because she didn't know his actual name and it kind of just slipped out.

'*Shy cute guy?*' Rock mouthed across to Finn who shrugged.

'Eh,' Kevin stammered, about to ask a girl on a date for the first time (though he often imagined delivering a confident and full-blooded 'Hi!' when he lay awake at night thinking about how to win her heart), 'would you, eh, like to come in with us for a glass of coffee – I mean, a cup of wine?'

'What my lovely friend is trying to say is would you like to accompany him for either a glass of wine or a cup of coffee?' Finn said, helping to translate the language of love, something he was once a dab hand at before self-image demoted him to sleazy motel rooms.

She blushed under the heavy curiosity of both the lunch-hungry and the romantics who had formed a small but fascinated coterie. 'Yes, mmm-hmm.'

Rock let go of Kevin's shoulder. 'Our work here is done,' he declared.

'You guys stay and work out where you're going for your coffee wine.' Finn looked on as Agnes took the order from her doughy-eyed colleague, 'That cake looks delicious.'

'Forget about the cake fat boy,' Rock had already held the door open for two ill-mannered schoolchildren who neglected to thank him, 'come on.'

'Maybe next time.' Finn said, and Agnes, with courtship no longer on her wish list, recommenced delivery to the large man by the window, who was just as frequent a customer as Kevin, and who sat up taller in his chair when he saw Agnes approaching.

Chapter 23

The soon-to-be journalists rambled into the exam hall like they were attending a summer fete and all that remained were seats in the front rows.

'Nice of you lot to finally join us,' said a stern woman with bone-straight hair, 'hurry up and sit down.'

Finn recognised her from his interview all that time ago and her hair still looked like petrified wood. 'We're not even late,' he murmured.

'Hey,' Louis said inquisitively when he saw what Rock was wearing, 'where'd the cap come from?'

'A gift from Finn,' Rock replied, thinking he recognised the woman from somewhere, 'but if Simon asks it floated back to me, okay?'

'Take a seat, please,' she instructed, laying out exam papers on the tables. 'And don't open these until you're told.'

Finn's chair looked as if it had been on the circuit since Orwell's first day at the job and it whined and buckled when he sat in it, and the discoloured legs bent like they'd spent too long in the desert. 'Jesus!' He grabbed hold of Mia's table and just about stayed off the floor, 'chair's trying to kill me!'

'Would ya lay off the puddin'?' Rock's voice implored him.

Louis was told in no uncertain terms to close the booklet when she saw him peeping between the covers.

'Why, just going to fail anyway?' he replied. Louis brushed away a sheet and it glided carefree to the ground, landing text-side up.

'Pick that up, the questions are on show!'

'Oops.'

'Armrests and all,' Finn commented from a few rows ahead as he was given an arbiter's chair, and the rickety one retired to the scrapheap, 'nice.'

Kevin's hand went up into the air. 'Eh, I saw one of the questions when I looked at Louis' exam sheet?'

'It doesn't matter.' The interviewer-cum-autocrat glanced over her shoulder and saw the fast hand strike twelve. 'You may begin,' she dourly announced.

Hugh caused echoes to bounce off the nude walls when he came into the hall. 'Sorry I'm late, I, eh - ah, whatever,' he said, waving his hand and taking a seat across from Rock.

'You're some fella.' Rock said before being hushed.

'Thanks.' Hugh eyed the leather cap as he waited to be given his first paper.

Finn had seen the reincarnation of Rock's hat at a flea market stall down by the wharf and he couldn't resist buying it to see Simon's reaction at how it had returned to its master. 'It floated back to me,' he said to Hugh.

'Ssshhh!' came an even louder admonishment.

Twenty minutes into the exam, Fredrik's nostrils began to flare; he was feeling the onset of a sneeze. In the past, Fredrik had tried different techniques to try and control it (like the time he kept his mouth closed and had nearly blown out his lungs) or, if possible, try and reduce the volume when one did manage to infiltrate his defences. Because he hadn't been very successful, he decided instead to embrace his sneeze the way a supervillain might embrace an unusual, yet socially uncelebrated superpower.

This is going to be funny, he sardonically thought, and, without warning, unleashed a sneeze of such proportions that everyone in the hall leapt in their seats as if electrical charges had been sent up each of their anal cavities.

'What was that?!' asked a foreign voice besmirched with alarm.

'Not sure,' Finn said, having once been on the receiving end of a Fredrik special when the Pod had spontaneously turned into a heavy metal mosh pit after they both requested extra practice time, 'but I think the Russians are here!'

The woman was gaping at Fredrik, seeming in a state of semi-shock.

'Sorry.' He wiped the splatter from his workbook. 'It's an involuntary response not under my conscious control.'

'Ok...well,' she replied, watching as Fredrik mopped the goo with the body of his T-shirt, 'if you could all just get back to your exams, please.'

****

Rock put down his pen after four days of examinations and shook his misused hand back and forth. He hadn't written that much ever, and he wondered what people did in the days before computers. Must have been downright torture, he thought, massaging his palm with his thumb.

Finn was peeling a banana in front of him. Rock looked at the lady who seemed to have missed her calling as a Gestapo commander – where *did* he know her from? – because he was fully sure she wouldn't be impressed with his eating in the hall. He watched as Finn brought the banana to his mouth, but before he had a chance to close it, Spikester noticed and broke into peals of unexpected guffawing before being severely shushed.

'No eating in the exam hall.'

He tutted. 'But I'm hungry?' Rock smiled; he was going to miss college life. Whether or not he passed (though, of course, that was a formality after Finn's advice on the bridge), he'd had a glimpse at another way of life. He'd proven that he could turn his hand to something completely outside of his wheelhouse and had passed the test of that experience, if not the actual tests.

'*Attention journalism class of 2016, this is your rather cool teacher here, and I have a most important announcement to make.*' Sadie's voice came loud and clear across the PA system.

'It's the radio result!' Leo pushed his booklet away with such ferocity that he had to slam his hand down to stop everything from falling.

'She's going to tell us who won!' Simon added and they all tensed in much the same way that Fredrik had done before he had detonated.

The examiner had no choice but to accept the chattering. How many times had she asked Sadie to wait until the exam was *finished* before she made her announcements? She swore she did it just to wind her up.

Finn chuckled, 'We know it's not going to be Hugh's group anyway,' he said.

'How do you know?' Hugh shot back before he remembered Sophia's fixation on ending his life prematurely. 'No, you're right, we don't have a chance.'

'*I know you're all dying to know this year's Showdown champions, so without further ado-*' The woman rolled her eyes so high that they were almost absorbed into her brain. '*Drumroll, please...*'

'Oh, Christ.' Finn heard her mutter.

'*In third place, with ten percent of the vote - Nastybiebs 92.2!*'

'You named your station after Justin Bieber?'

'Told you we shouldn't have called it that,' Sophia said tamely, while Hugh grinned back at Rock.

'*I would say it had something to do with the name, but I won't kick you while you're down, guys,*' Sadie cracked as if she were listening to what they were saying.

'Wasn't the name, it was Sophia's fault for picking me as chief DJ.' Hugh's grin morphed into a smirk as he dodged an eraser.

'Please!' Sophia was told, but which came out more like someone scrabbling to retain control of a lost cause.

'*In second place – and in what was a truly gargantuan tussle and the closest it's been in all the years we've been running the course here in Bridgewater Tech – with forty-four percent of the public vote...*'

The examiner was more than irritated now, and she lumped her hands through her hair. Finn noticed that it hardly moved like the hair had been injected with Botox.

'*...Smoking Babies 98.2! Which means the winning team with forty-six percent is Houseboat FM! A gallant effort, Smoking Babies. Houseboat FM, your show will be aired on the radio this coming Monday at 7.30 am. Have a fantastic summer and I'll see you all at the grad. Congratulations again!*' With that, the intercom hissed and went dead.

Rock rose from his seat and declared joyously: 'This deserves ice cream.'

She pointed a long index finger at the clock four feet above Fredrik's head, and her voice took on an almost begging hue. 'But the exam isn't finished yet.'

'Mine is,' Finn said, placing his workbook on the table.

Fredrik threw his workbook on top of Finn's. 'Yep, so is mine.'

'You can't just leave!' she gasped.

'Watch us.' Louis added another book to the pile, concealing where Fredrik's mucus had suffused over the cover page.

The examiner replied with icy chagrin when Billie told her she needed to get herself 'some of that D'.

'Word.' Ashley said, brandishing her small and index fingers in full agreement.

'Yeah,' Simon blasted, gormlessly gawping into two spherical pits of fiery damnation, 'word, nigga!'

Dropping their bags at the bench, Finn and Rock were followed out by a stream of students keen to be free of exam-hall confines. 'They weren't as bad as I thought,' Rock chirped, relieved that his fears of forgetting everything and leaving a completely blank book hadn't come true.

'You're smarter than you look,' Finn teased, while at the same time trying to think of an ice cream that would go well with pineapple.

Ashley threw her bag in the air and made no effort to catch it. 'I can't believe it's over!' she cried, and the revulsion she felt at someone so uncool as Simon pirating her word ebbed away with every emancipated moment.

'You think you passed?'

'It's summer, Rock, I don't care!' she replied.

Everyone concurred that ice cream sounded like a swell idea and Simon (whatever about Ashley saying it, Simon had to admit it sounded quite natural when he used the n-word – maybe he was part homie, he reasoned, his skin *was* sallow after all) decreed that he was going to get the super-duper sundae to celebrate. As Ashley was retrieving the used serviettes and burger wrappers which had wriggled free from the bag's side netting, Ms. Humphreys approached looking like she was intent on spoiling the convivial mood.

'Guys, incoming,' Finn warned, telling of the impending arrival of his nemesis.

'Hi everyone.' Ms. Humphreys said.

Daisy gave her a smile and a dinky wave like they were forever friends.

'As you all know, Barbara wasn't able to be here for the group project – because of her...accident,' she said awkwardly, 'but seeing as how she's been such a trooper,' Ms. Humphreys continued, attempting to sound as if she was on their level, 'I thought we'd do it now if you wouldn't mind volunteering?'

There was a brief and regretful silence before the group assented to going back to college despite it being officially over.

'Good, and don't look so glum. I'm sure you'll all make up for it tonight.'

'We'll be making up for it straight after this,' Hugh muttered, stubbing his toe repeatedly against the curb that protected the lawn.

'Hell yeah!' Dot yelled. Ms. Humphreys gave her a long look that after a full year still was unsure if Dot was playacting or if that was her real nature.

'I'm all better now, guys,' said Barbara feebly, feeling a smidge guilty that everyone was being lured back into class just so she could get a passing grade, 'I promise!'

Ms. Humphreys guided the nine people who hadn't snuck away (Dot carried herself off, desperate for one of her mind-ticklers after the stress of the exam, while Louis said he'd rather rub honey on his nether regions and let loose an army of hungry ants. Ashley insisted school was over, and that she would never set foot on a college campus again, while Red ignored everyone and strode out to where his ex was waiting) back through the automatic double doors.

'Never thought I'd walk through these again.' Rock could tell Finn didn't think that was so terrible, and if there was such a thing as 'summer school' he had a feeling Finn's name would be top of that list.

'This collaborative enterprise will examine how well you work as a team.' Ms. Humphreys said, gliding round the rim of tables in a room that smelled like make-up and being surprisingly light-hearted.

'This is boring,' Hugh sighed, ignoring whatever it was she had put down. If he could just beat the rest of them to O'Malley's, he might get his food first for the only time all year.

'A ship carrying nineteen people is about to sink...'

Hugh raised his head from his folded arms.

'...each person has specific talents and possessions, and you must pick the ones that will help you to survive. You need to decide – as a group – which eight of these people you will save, and in the process, save yourselves.'

'Cooool,' Hugh uttered.

'If we make people walk the plank, can we take their possessions?' Finn asked.

He noticed that her reply was a little less honed than usual. 'Possessions must stay with their owners.'

'We should probably get rid of the DJ first.' Rock said, scanning the list of possible lifers.

'No way!' Hugh retorted, the idea of a silent raft almost as bad as being left to go down with the ship, 'The rave never dies!'

'Sorry, Hugh, he's shark meat.' Finn had found someone of interest two-thirds of the way down, 'but we should definitely keep the cook, he's vital for survival.'

'But it says here he might have been responsible for two separate outbreaks of E. coli in his previous job?' Daisy was concerned what a dose of poisoning would do for morale on the raft.

'Weak constitutions,' Finn replied, patting his stomach. In all his travels across third-world countries, it was the one thing that never failed him, 'not the chef's fault.'

'And two people actually *died*?' Daisy said.

Finn clicked his tongue and shook his head. 'Weak-willed, too.'

'Should we keep the captain?' Barbara asked, 'Says here he's an alcoholic.' The thought of any person under the influence of a 'toxic' substance and in control was now abhorrent to Barbara. 'What if he gets drunk and becomes violent with the others?'

'He could be a happy drunk?' Rock replied, thinking that it might be nice to have a jokester around to lighten the mood.

Mia read further on, 'says he recently converted to Christianity and tries to convert people when he's had a few.'

'He's out.' Fredrik said, bringing his finger to his nose before everyone's folios could be covered in snot.

'Just because of his religion?' Barbara probed.

Fredrik was of the strong opinion that anyone who believed that an all-powerful man with a beard and a dress was controlling things from the sky was clinically deranged, and therefore, in this situation, undeserving of a spot in the raft whatever item or skill they happened to possess. 'Yes,' he confirmed.

'There's a priest?' she said hopefully.

Barbara carried on after putting lines through two names on the page, a little peeved by Fredrik's staunch dismissal of anyone of a pious ilk. Her vicar had been a rock of support after she was mugged and, if anything, she now felt closer to her saviour. 'The doctor is next, we'll need her.'

'She's married to the captain,' Rock said, winking and grinning at the same time, 'if we save her, we'll have to save that lovable old rogue too.'

'Could we not just take her and leave the captain?' Sophia suggested.

'She's not a puppy, Hugh,' Mia said, after Hugh questioned if she'd be alright without her husband, 'she'll be fine.'

'I'm not so sure,' Finn argued, reading the fine print, 'they've been married a long time. Would she really want him to go down like the Titanic?'

Mia thought back at how upset Rose had been (and how upset she had been watching it) when she disengaged Jack from that piece of door frame. 'No, I guess not.'

'Leave them both and take the DJ instead. He doesn't cause problems and he'll help everyone to stay upbeat with his tuneage.'

'Look,' Daisy pointed out, 'there's a musician, too?'

Hugh read the paragraph and expectantly scanned the faces around the table. 'She has water purification tablets! And a knife!'

'Ok,' Barbara announced, 'hands up those who feel the musician should be saved.'

Hugh grabbed two handfuls of his hair and pulled. 'Come on, guys, I'll never forgive you if you don't give her a spot.'

Leo raised his hand. 'Look at that face, how could I refuse?'

'Look at that hair,' Finn said following suit, 'how could I refuse?'

'Ahaha, yes! Musician's saved!' Hugh screeched as if listening to the rendering of current pop songs would make the perilous journey to the nearest landmass acceptable, even a joy.

'I have something to say before you leave.' Ms. Humphreys said when Hugh eased back into his chair after performing a dance similar to the one while on energy drinks when it was agreed that the chef and musician would both claim berths and avoid certain death.

'Here we go,' Finn muttered. Could he still be expelled even at this late stage? Maybe they'd hold his diploma back?

'Despite being an unruly lot, all the teachers agree that you're the best class in the college – the best we've had for a while actually.'

It was as if someone had pressed the pause button on time itself, and Finn was almost afraid to speak. 'Do you feel the same way, Ms. Humphreys?'

Her features softened and an unrecognisable smile emerged through the poker face. 'I do, yes.'

The unexpected tenderness assailed him like a shock and awe war tactic.

'You've just made his year.' Rock said, negotiating his pen into his pencil case for the final time.

'Kinda feel like crying,' Finn said and was about to ask Ms. Humphreys if she'd like to come for ice cream before she spoke again.

'Please don't do that,' she replied, the smile still present and in place. 'Now enough of the paly palies, get out of here, you've earned your holiday.'

* * * *

'*Best Buds Forever, Athena.*' was inscribed on Rock's hip flask as he wagged it in the air. 'Anyone fancy a little celebratory tipple with their lunch?' he said.

'Oh, yes, daddy-o.'

'We'll see who the daddy is when you're handing over that 21-year-old,' he replied, tipping some of the tinted liquid into Finn's coke.

'He's talking about whiskey.' Finn said when Daisy looked queerly at them.

O'Malley was doing his best not to make a return trip and was only short of stuffing Louis' can in the only available orifice left. 'I see you're having the old college-is-finished tipple-o-rama?' he said, scooting and shuffling his body to keep everything from falling.

Ashley flashed him the smile he loved so much. 'You don't mind, O'Malley, do you?'

'You go right ahead,' he replied, letting the serviettes fall from under his arm and dropping the pizzas down without so much as a disturbed wedge, 'I'm sure you worked very hard for it.'

They all stifled snickers and Louis quipped; 'She did alright.'

'Don't mind them, O'Malley,' Ashley said frowning, 'and thank you.'

O'Malley smiled shyly, feeling like he was beginning to redden. Why did she always have this effect on him – and why did he have to be married? 'You're welcome, Ashley. Enjoy your lunches, everyone.'

'He's going to be heartbroken when you're not here next year.' Rock snatched the tray from Hugh, who rubbed his hair in frustration.

'If you steal him away from his wife you can inherit the family business,' Louis said, then quaffed most of his can.

Ashley considered this for a moment. 'If he was Mr. McDonald I might.'

'Can I have a celebratory tipple please?'

Rock regarded Simon with aversion. He wasn't exactly the type of person he was keen to share his beloved whiskey with. 'See that cookie you've got there?'

Simon glanced down. He knew what was coming next.

'Half that and you can have a tipple.'

Simon swallowed hard. He had never shared an O'Malley's cookie with anyone (apart from when Louis had taken a bite without his permission, which he still hadn't forgiven him for). 'Ok,' he agreed, comforted that there'd been two wafers the size of dinner plates in his sundae.

'Guys!' Dot exclaimed, snatching a chip from Hugh, 'restaurant is booked for seven!'

'We're not going to some hippy soup kitchen, are we?' Finn combined a wing with cola to make soaked alcoholic chicken.

'No, it's this new Turkish place, all decorated with cushions and shit, you'd think you were actually there...in Turkey, like.'

'Isn't that where they smoke those pipes?' Daisy said this quietly in case someone got the wrong impression.

Dot's head was flickering off a true line like it was being attracted by two opposing magnets. 'Shisha pipes – they have them too!'

'Hippy soup kitchen knew it.'

Daisy was still wary of being overheard. 'Will the pipes make us funny?'

'No funnier than you already are, Daisy,' Dot replied, her mouth tugging itself into a smile before fading again.

'I wanted to go to McDonald's.' Ashley held up a chip and sighed because it wasn't skinnier. 'They just released a new burger.'

'All's forgiven, Dot,' Finn was gnawing the remaining meat from the bone, 'rather be fed in that pigsty.'

Rock threw the crust of his last slice of pizza onto Hugh's tray. 'Right, I'm going up to the lookout to get some kip, no point driving all the way home and back again.'

'Did the exams take it out of your old man brains?' Louis asked smirking.

'Bet I get better results than you,' he replied, tightening the lid, and settling his hip flask back into the chamber of his bag.

'Everyone will get better results than me, Rock, I spent most of the time drawing pictures of dicks.'

He slotted the cloned cap onto his head, 'Jesus, Louis,' Rock groaned, 'keep that type of thing to yourself.'

'I have to go and change my bunny ears,' Daisy broke in, 'I got a new pair for tonight.' She wondered if Rock would like them. He liked hats after all, and bunny ears were kind of like hats.

Mia grabbed hold of Ashley's hand. 'We're going home to make ourselves beautiful.'

'Guess we better do that too,' Finn said to Hugh, who was watching as Sophia coupled with the other two like train carriages clicking together. 'Might sneak in a little rum while we're at it.'

Hugh nodded unheedingly: *You're already beautiful*, he told Sophia in his mind.

'Night, Rock.' Daisy called as he marched off towards the houseboat, the camper that still hadn't seen a soapy sponge since skidding into the disabled spot, and still the only day he'd been late all year.

'Night!' he called back, startling an old woman who was dragging a tiny Shih Tzu behind her. 'Meet you at seven at the hippy kitchen.'

'Can I come with you guys?' Louis had already read every sleep-inhibiting novel in the second-hand bookstore so there was little point in him hiding out there.

Finn pushed away a receptacle of chicken carcass, 'Only if you keep your trousers on this time, don't want a repeat of what happened at Christmas.'

'It was raining, Finn,' Louis protested, as everyone exited the restaurant and diverged in different directions, 'my pants were so wet it was like I'd been in a three-way, and I'd been all the ways!'

Chapter 24

It felt like the end of something as Finn watched people leave in dribs and drabs, not knowing when he'd see them again. Hugh was still playing a game that resulted in significant pain because he didn't want to be the one who detracted from Sophia's happiness. 'Been quite a year, eh?' Finn said, already reminiscing like it had happened years ago. He knew intentions were honest, but people always fell by the wayside, fell into a mental photobook of the past.

'I'll admit it, I'm happy I signed up.'

Finn placed his glass between two rowers in the tabletop longboat, a further extolling of the Viking blood that connected Bridgewater and Valhalla. 'Grouchy grandad is happy? That's headline news right there.'

'I'll remember you said that.' Rock replied.

'That's right, you have a...what is it now, *three-day* memory?'

Rock made a peace sign to the barmaid. 'Yeah, but that's almost three days longer than it was before,' he spiritedly said.

Finn gestured to where Kevin, the human sundial, and his lips were working in silent unison with each other.

'Is he still trying to memorize that?'

Finn ran his finger around the rim of the glass. The effect was a whistling that was steady yet pensive. 'Keeps getting the last two numbers mixed up.'

'Kevin!' The overhead bulb caused a bead of sweat to careen down Rock's foliage-free brainpan as he bayed across the countertop. 'Have you not learned her number yet?'

'Think I have, Rock!' he replied, having finally recited his date-to-be's digits for the first time since the class had come down upon the bar like an unholy plague.

'Love to be a fly on the wall for that encounter.' Finn remarked.

'Voice in his head more like.' Rock palpated a hidden device in his ear canal.

Finn followed suit and brought his wrist up to his lips. 'Kevin, we're going to need you to listen very carefully.'

'And do exactly as we say.' Rock said, sounding like an uncompromising agent of jurisprudence. 'First, you're going to lean across and put your finger in her sticky toffee pudding.'

'No, Kevin,' Finn beefed into the imaginary microphone, 'you gotta talk to her first, work up a sense of trust – then gently nibble on her strawberry.'

'Forget about the strawberry, Kevin, he's an amateur. Go straight for the pudding!'

'But guys–' Finn mimicked Kevin's interior turmoil with bent arms and exaggerated joggling, '–she ordered a custard slice?'

They were still laughing when Red came into view dragging the remains of a body.

'Next superpower under his *steeeelly* guidance?' Fredrik's tone was shrill and reproving, and the heels of his shoes were the only part in contact with the ground. 'Ahhh, that's what you think!'

Fredrik hung from Red's arms like a freshly harvested bag of spuds. 'Think he might have finished that third drink,' Red said with a grunt, pausing momentarily, 'he was arguing with some guy in the jacks about the coup in Turkey.'

'Erdogan will be the end of them, the *end* of them I say!'

Finn smiled as Fredrik was hauled to a destiny with the backseat of a taxi. 'And we proved that we're down with the kids.'

'Still think they're spoon-fed little–'

'Yes, yes,' Finn replied, 'because they didn't work in the mines when they were toddlers, I know.'

'Suppose they're not *all* bad,' Rock conceded, falling into that same snare of wistful recollection. As far-fetched as it would have sounded a year ago, he had come to understand that today's cohort was just a different version of him (albeit a poncier, less-manly version) and that as much as he hated to admit it, they had their good points. 'I'll actually miss some of them.'

Finn took the refilled tumbler from the barmaid, while she set the other one down in front of Rock. 'Even the wrestling bros?' he asked.

Right at that moment, Leo's incensed rebuttal came around the bar and through a decorative wall of liquor bottles. 'He's not! I'm telling you: Hogan is!'

'Stone Cold would own his ass.' Simon countered loudly, casting off Leo's assertion that Hulk Hogan was the greatest of all time. 'He's nothing compared to him!'

'Maybe not now, but in his prime Stone Cold would be stone-cold dead!'

The shake of Rock's head was warm like his smile. 'It's the Ultimate Warrior,' he quipped to Finn.

They both wheeled around just in time to catch Billie grabbing Louis by his shirt and banging her teeth off his in her haste for a kiss.

'Go for it, Billie!' Ashley whooped, as Louis' tongue burrowed into Billie's mouth like a gopher looking for a new home.

Mia wanted to look away but was too entranced by the awkwardness. 'That's only a tiny bit disturbing,' she commented.

'What did they call us?' Rock said, laughing at Billie finally getting what she'd waited so long to get, 'me Homer and you Bart?'

'That's only because you both have the same number of hairs,' Finn replied.

He did often think he bore key similarities to the great man. 'Don't you know bald is sexy?'

Gibby was teetering like she'd been blindfolded and spun around too many times, while the shots had caused Daisy's smile, head, and ears to all tilt in the same direction. 'Rock,' she said, 'Daisy wants to know if you like her new bunny ears.'

'I think they're lovely.'

Daisy whisper-giggled in Gibby's ear; 'he thinks they're lovely!' Then they fled for the safety of the snug where Daisy could tell Gibby all about her and Rock's Japanese-themed wedding.

'Did you notice that they were new?' Rock continued to study them until the girls had weaved into the segregated portion of the pub, 'look the same to me.'

Finn was staring idly at the golden liquid. 'Bunny-ear fashion was never really my thing.'

Rock held out the last of his dregs. 'Here's to taking over the world.'

'I'd settle for taking over Bridgewater – being accepted by Bridgewater would also be good,' Finn replied, wondering if he'd still be in Bridgewater come this time next year.

*

When the sweetened whiskey had been drained, it was their turn to follow in the other's footsteps.

'You like my ears,' Daisy effused but was pushed on by Gibby as Finn stood aside, paving the way for Rock to leave next. 'Age before beauty,' he said.

The song – or more precisely, the lyrics of the song – clawed at Finn's attention and made him look back into the mostly empty bar. It was the Eagles. And they were singing directly to him. They told him to take it easy and not to let the sound of his own wheels drive him crazy. They were right, he knew that, but was it possible? Finn had never been good at slowing the indefatigable wheel-rodent that was his mind and he feared it regaining its former velocity now that college was over.

He got to the door just before it clicked shut. Ashley and Sophia were giggling about how Hugh had told Sophia that she was his 'everything'. It sounded romantic in Hugh's head, but the words had come out slurred and he'd needed to repeat them.

Finn heard it before he felt it, a fullness inside his head, then the roughness of the pavement. Daisy's cries and the sound of breaking glass caused everyone to jolt around. Expecting another blow, Finn instinctively covered his head. When the only thing that came was the sensation of viscous liquid pooling in the crease of his ear, he chanced looking up. Sophia was standing three feet away from Loudmouth's friend (he'd recognise that ashen mien anywhere), who was pressing the back of his hand to his nose.

'You hit me?' The cadence of his voice rose sharply as he registered the metallic taste on his tongue. 'You're going to pay for that.'

Loudmouth was incandescent. He had implicitly told his knuckleheaded pal to wait until *after* he'd plugged the limo guy in the kidney. 'Embarrass me, will ya?' he said aloud.

Bleary, mortifying memories came flooding back to Loudmouth as his knife sheared through Rock's hand like it was warm bread after he'd intuitively raised it in self-protection. Word had spread like a venereal disease about Loudmouth's 'performance' in the city square (that *fucking photograph* hadn't helped either), and people who normally would have set their gaze to the ground when he passed, were now suddenly being all huckabuck and standing up to him. It had given him no pleasure to have had to bonk some heads together to win back the respect he had always commanded, but he knew that until he evened the score there would always be some unworthy pretender looking to knock him off the pyramid.

Finn felt like he was watching all this unfold from under water; voices coming to him from afar the way his old swimming teachers' had when he demanded that Finn come back from the deep end right this minute; movements slow and shimmery like a mirage on a hot day.

Sophia's lush lashes (which had started to clump at the sides) weren't having the same pertinent effect they did when Hugh had to forfeit the slaps game, and Loudmouth's friend easily broke through the frenetic clawing and waving and scrabbing. His smirk revealed teeth that through a rotting osmosis were no longer up to the task of hard foods. 'No one makes me bleed,' he spat.

Her fake nails found their way through the man's shirt, but before Sophia could sink them in, strands of her hair were pulled out by the roots as she was forced into an uncomfortable bow. 'Let go of me!' She screamed hysterically.

The glass bit into Finn's fingers like a shoal of hungry piranha as he set himself. But the pain brought a cogency to his thinking and his leg sprang out like a downed karate master. The connection was so true that Loudmouth's friend didn't realise he was off the ground until he saw the hair in his hand was no longer connected to a person.

Rock clasped his hand over the wound. Blood oozed between the gaps like a stream finding its way through an obstruction. Loudmouth had planned on full-out gutting him, but his stupid friend attacking first had taken away the element of surprise and with it his chance of achieving that high that came from straight insertion. Rock moved forward to meet the challenge of this pipsqueak, to finish him once and for all, but as he did so his leg gave out and he felt a cool and terrible haw as Etna reached desirously for his throat. He fell backwards towards the road and the blare of a passing car.

The brooding anger Finn felt at the cheapness of the shot was quickly brushed aside when he saw Rock sagging against one of the stubby bollards that were spaced out every few yards. He may have brought his heel down onto the man's chest if he knew that the pockmark below his eye was not because of pubescent ache, but from an altercation with Barbara, his luckless classmate. 'Simon!'

Simon was locked between them, and he looked frantically from Finn to Loudmouth (who was changing Etna's position so that she would have access to a larger 'body' of work) and back again.

Loudmouth lifted Rock's cap from the ground. His grin was a jeer, and he thought the feeling was almost as good as a needle in his arm. 'What do you think, Baldy? Look good?'

Rock's only retribution was a slur. 'My cap doesn't look good on winkies,' he replied.

It felt like it did at Christmas when he was young – aside from the arousal – and Loudmouth savoured the small action of raising the stained knife into the air. 'This is what you get for being a cheeky cunt.'

'You're a wrestler,' Finn shouted, 'help him!'

Though his flailing leg had inadvertently kept his jugular intact, Rock knew it had also betrayed him for the final time. Why couldn't Athena have been there? She'd have gone through him and his knife. He thought of Greece – his home – and why hadn't he just gone for it? He could easily have bought a few olive trees and hired a few locals to pick the olives if he'd wanted. And then, for a reason he couldn't work out, he thought of Janey, Suzy's only decent friend, but instead of him 'inheriting' her, it was Suzy. Rock put up his arms, a painful deflection the best he could hope for.

As Etna started her downward journey to send Rock on his way, Simon, like a jacked-up American footballer tackling an opponent of far slighter dimensions and keening like a tightly bunched group of widows at a wake, barged into Loudmouth with such force that it sent him scudding over both Rock and the waist-high bollard that Rock was propped against.

Prowling up the rise in the road a motorcyclist lifted his visor and pinned his eyes to a girl – a very pretty one – who seemed to be chasing somebody up Main Street. After the squelchy feeling of punching somebody in the nose (and the fact that she'd now need hair extensions if she wanted to defend her pageant title), Sophia had caught blood lust and rared off after Loudmouth's friend with a brush taken from her handbag. She made solid contact with his back and shoulder three times before he veered off down an alleyway and lust transmuted into common sense.

Loudmouth's fingers coiled around the worn grip as an orange moon coursed by overhead. She was still there. Etna would never abandon him the way so many others had done. Bending at the waist, he sat up like an Egyptian mummy with unfinished business. He glanced over and saw a big slab of meat standing next to the bald guy – he must have run into him, who fights like that? No matter, he always fought better when there was more than one person on his shit list (it was like his brain shut off and his knife arm slashed and gored of its own accord), and now there were two on which Etna could feast.

'You're going to fuckin' die.' Loudmouth said, hitching his knees up so as to propel himself back onto his feet, 'because I'm going to kill you.'

As he was readying to give Etna the stiff one she always craved, the biker, whose attention had now turned to Ashley and her alluring form (where were all these girls coming from? he thought), almost lost control when he thwacked over what he thought was a speedbump doing the best part of forty.

'My groin!' came a heinous shriek that slid under doorframes and through letterboxes of surrounding homes and businesses. Angling out like a flagpole that had been planted by a mountaineer with altitude sickness, the blade was pressed into Loudmouth's uppermost thigh right to the hilt.

When the motorcyclist regained control of the steering, he pulled up outside an underwear store with an advertisement for the new 'sultry summer' range in the window. Finn thought he heard the word 'groin', but he couldn't be sure. Spiralling blue lights from a patrolling police car – which seemed to be coming from all directions – made it feel like someone was shining a survival torch in his eyes. Blanche dabbed at the red streaks that had wormed their way under his Tahitian shirt with a scented wet wipe. Her lips were moving but her voice was a blur. 'Silver, are you alright?' she was saying. He pointed to his ear and shrugged.

Hugh pressed against the bodies in front of him. 'What happened?' he asked, almost casually, wondering why Rock was on the ground.

'Where were you?' Ashley said, having chosen to eye-bang the biker rather than make it an angry-girl twosome.

Before he could respond that he'd left his phone on the table and had to go back for it, Simon screamed; 'You missed it, I saved Rock!'

Rock was stuffing his fist with the tissues Daisy had given him. 'Thank you, Simon,' he shook his head, 'that hurts more than my hand.'

'Shoulder block off the ropes.' Simon, who had turned and used the wall as if it were rigid rope for added impetus, walloped his shoulder with a cupped hand, 'always loved that move.'

'My fucking dick,' Loudmouth was whimpering over and over, feathering his beloved knife, but not daring to pull her out. Without any knowledge of Schrödinger or his cat, his inclination was to leave well enough alone and not test the resolution of the gods who may yet have a hand in sparing his manhood.

Ashley bent down and swiped the cap from his head. 'You have a tiny one now, don't ya?'

'You bitch!' he replied, as his tears caused a small wet patch to blot the road.

A blue jersey (which looked so good on him that Hugh was beginning to think it wasn't so bad that Manchester United had been pipped by their old adversaries) and two chartreuse feet settled either side of his head. 'And stay down.' Hugh said firmly but quickly moved away when Loudmouth swung for his ankle.

****

A loud clonk at the window made Hugh wince. He'd been so drunk that he'd fallen asleep on Finn's kitchen table, forgetting that there was a folding bed in the same room. 'What do you want?' he asked, pulling back the insulating boards that did their best to snuff out the noise of a student town.

'Morning, Hugh,' said a cheery Rock. 'You look like you've seen better ones?'

'Hmmm,' he groaned, massaging a crick-neck.

Finn breezed into the kitchen like last night had been just another thing to add to his 'experience' list. 'Knew I heard trouble.'

'Not you, too...am I the only one who feels like they want to die?'

Finn went to the window and opened it outwards. 'Please, sir, won't you step into my humble abode?'

Rock grabbed Finn's hand with his own good hand and stepped carefully onto the windowsill, and even more carefully into the kitchen. 'Hope your landlord doesn't see or you'll get another telling-off.'

'Doesn't matter, some other poor schmuck will have to deal with him soon.' Finn's landlord – while explaining in detail the difference between a door and a window – had told him he needed to move out as the place had to be overhauled for next year's 'wannabes', so he pushed the thought to the part of his mind that ignored certainties. 'How's the leg?'

'This old thing?' Rock pointed to his leg, 'saved my life don't you know.'

For the first time since his accident, Rock was glad of the weakness in his leg and glad not to have been on the receiving end of Etna's whetted wrath. He wasn't ready for the long sleep just yet, and if this year had taught him anything, it was that he could pretty much accomplish whatever he put his mind to. 'What's wrong with your face,' he said, turning to Hugh, 'looks worse than my hand?'

Finn touched the knobbly line of stitches that ran parallel to his ear. 'And worse than my head.'

'I slept on the table.'

'Why'd you do that?' Rock replied.

'He didn't see the fold-away,' Finn said, and the three of them looked at the unslept-in bed.

'I was snapping Sophia when you guys were at the hospital—' Hugh's voice faltered before he could finish the sentence.

'What happened?' Rock said, impatiently pressing him for an answer.

Hugh stared at the smudge on the floor that had been there since Christmas when Billie had drizzled chocolate over buttered popcorn and Gibby had fudged the catch after suggesting they play *toss and catch*. 'I might have told her she was the girl of my dreams.'

'And what did she say to that?' Finn asked, already having a fair idea of what they'd hear.

'Thank you,' he replied.

'Ouch, you got friend-zoned – and on Snapchat,' Rock bawled, '– your favourite of all chats!'

'Leave me alone,' Hugh said, 'heart is broken.'

Finn placed a sympathetic hand on his shoulder. 'There'll be a million Sophias in college next year.'

'Not like this one there won't.' He replied, as forlorn as any art gallery painting.

'You know what,' Rock declared, feeling a hunger cramp taking hold, 'you need cheering up and I need breakfast. Half the night in A&E after that spalpeen prick (Etna had tacked Loudmouth's penis to his leg, resulting in the severance of the top part and a forever-after explanation to future consorts about his 'stump') has given me an appetite.'

Finn was already taking out a bag of cashew nuts from the press. 'Is the houseboat nearby?'

'Yep, right around the corner.'

'Isn't that a taxi rank?' Finn said.

Rock confirmed that it was.

'Where are we going?' Hugh asked this as if a big black cloud was dumping rain on only him.

Finn couldn't help but smile at them. Why did life have to be so surgical? These two wounded warriors had come to mean a lot to him and now time was taking them away. 'Let's drive out to Silver Strand.' Finn thought a fry-up breakfast overlooking the bay and watching kite surfers face-plant the sand sounded like the perfect way to delay the inescapable ingress of the future. 'It's a beautiful day after all.'

Chapter 25

The rain came down as a mist and he could feel his jumper beginning to get heavier. The cascade of water was still the same torrent he remembered; even the boulder was unmoved and unbroken by time and the crashing of water.

Finn leaned over the railing to get a better view. They really were explosive. He figured there wouldn't have been much left of his head had he been braver this time last year. His stomach twisted as his writer's imagination went into overdrive. He looked away, thoughts of jumping conspicuously missing during his time in Bridgewater. *Was it all down to having something to get out of bed for - was it really that simple?* Finn asked into the abyss of empty space.

'Also changed location,' he added as if having the last word on an ongoing two-year tit-for-tat with a professional know-it-all.

The rustling was playing a downcast melody through the branches and leaves. '**LIFE ENDS**' was still tattooed in paint on the wall but when the wind swished gently again the branches moved just enough that Finn could see there was more writing after a heart that was turning to ash.

Much as he tried, he couldn't make out what the other words were, so he pushed himself off the railing and followed the bridge around to where the L-shaped wall was camouflaging stuff that once splurged across Finn's shower floor. From his vantage point at the corner of the wall came the rest of the sentence: '*WHEN IT'S NOT LIVED*'.

When he eventually got up off his haunches, a million revelations zooming through his head, he realised that the graffiti hadn't wanted him to jump, it had wanted him to live; he just couldn't see it at the time. The wind was the full stop, not the heart. It didn't blow that day because he wasn't ready for it. He had to figure it out on his own. If you needed to be told to live, were you really making that choice for yourself? Whatever happened now, Finn knew he would never come back to this waterfall again. When you have found the answer, you needn't ask the question any longer. He had seen the light of the wind's inflection and Finn was grateful for that.

'*To bright times ahead.*' he spoke, an incantation rather than a wish. '*And always something to live for.*'

* * * *

'Would you hurry up, Suzy!' Rock grumbled. 'I want to rub my medal in Finn's face.'

'Alright, hold your horses,' She was preening in the mirror as if the world depended on her having evenly applied lipstick and bangs with no splitting. 'I'm nearly done.'

Rock checked his watch again in case the hands had decided against all odds to go backwards. 'Traffic is going to be manic.'

'Okay, okay, I'm ready,' Suzy said, waltzing into the hall.

'Praise be the *God Boys*.' he replied, catching his bunch of keys by the small titanium anchor, a representation of something larger that had become just as much an integral part of the squad as any of the founding fathers, 'now let's go.'

'Oh wait.' She stalled. 'I forgot my cardigan.'

Rock tutted loudly while thumping lightly on the door frame. 'This isn't helping my temper, Suzy.'

'Well then,' she said, winding past him like a summer breeze, 'what are you waiting for?'

'Not sure why I bother sometimes?' He gripped the brass knocker and pulled the door shut behind them.

When she'd hooshed herself up into the houseboat and strapped herself in she replied, 'Because you think I'm the greatest thing since sliced batch, that's why.'

'Hmmm, wholemeal batch maybe.' Rock requisitioned the rear-view mirror and turned it so that it faced the rear again.

Suzy was still preening sans mirror, 'I'm really proud of you, you know that?'

'Thanks, baby,' Rock said, warming up the engine with a few pumps of the gas pedal. 'What's next I wonder?'

'That's up to you my hunky intellectual,' she replied, 'but whatever you decide I'm with you all the way.'

'Kinda like Bonnie and Clyde–' for all her faffing about she was beautiful, he had to admit, '–only Rock and Suzy.'

'I think you'll find my name goes first,' she said, flicking the brush at her eyelash one last time.

Rock laughed and shoved the stick into first. 'Suzy and Rock, it is,' he agreed.

* * * *

Leo came barrelling through the candlelit bar and tripped on the second step he didn't realise was there. 'Guys!' he blurted. Everyone at the table glanced amusedly at each other as he got back to his feet. 'Guys...did you see the email from the station?'

Since their winning show was aired after the exams, the group had become somewhat of a cult hit in Bridgewater, and there had been an outpouring for them to be given a regular slot on Strand FM.

'Nope, been here toasting my success.' Rock flashed his student of the year medal like a cop flashing his badge. 'What do you think, Finn, pretty isn't it?'

'If I have to see that once more-'

'Admit it, I'm just smarter than you are.' Rock said.

'So much for being a good sport,' Suzy remarked to Finn's grandmother, who had insisted on coming to watch his 'coronation'.

'There's a pair of them in it,' she replied, 'Finn kept saying how he was looking forward to tasting a whisky he'd never tried before.'

He tried snatching the medal from Rock. 'Anyway, you only won because I was too busy writing about an angry man in a white houseship.'

'Make sure you put in that I won best student.' Rock showed the medal to everyone again before snapping the velveteen case closed in front of Finn. 'And it's houseboat, not houseship.'

'Absolutely,' he replied, 'you'll be the best gay student in the school.'

'Oh Finn,' his grandmother said, smirking guiltily at Suzy.

Rock already had plans to construct a medal holder, like the one he had made for his beer all those years ago. 'Don't you even dare,' he threatened.

'Guys, never mind all that!' Leo was still getting his breath back. 'I've far more important news than a bronze medal.'

'Gold actually.' Rock said, raising his eyebrows Finn's way.

Finn ignored Rock and his precious medal. 'Spit it out so, Leo.' He was also casting him as gay no matter what happened.

'The radio station-'

'So you've said,' The uncooked pink colour of Spikester's gums could be seen as she pulled at her lip ring, 'really wish you'd say something else.'

Leo scratched the beard which had come on over the summer so that now almost all the hairs joined. 'Yeah, well, the radio station-,'

'The radio station what?!' the table in the corner of the pub erupted.

'-want us to go on an adventure!'

Finn's attention was piqued, and Rock's future character foibles were forgotten about. 'What do you mean they want us to go on an adventure?'

'An adventure! Like, a real adventure!'

The case was still in Rock's grasp, and he was in a sort of daydream as he ran his thumb along the smooth lid. Not that he'd admit it to the rest of the gang - especially not to Finn - but he hadn't believed it when the principal announced 'Brock' as top student, and when his fellow classmates had chanted the name of his alter ego his legs had seemed to lose their ability to operate. 'Leo, you're not making any sense,' he said.

'The boss man...he said that due to our popularity, the radio is sending us away for an adventure along with a houseboat - I mean, motorhome - and a fridge stocked with goodies!'

'Who's us?' Finn said, 'the whole group?'

'The whole group, Finn!' Leo boomed in reply. 'They want us to document the whole thing by taking photos and doing live interviews and and-'

'Take a break, Leo child.'

'Thanks, Finn's granny.' Leo pulled up a seat and took a swig of the nearest drink, which happened to be Louis' Crème de Menthe. 'God, what is that?!'

Louis pushed the glass away from him. 'It's not mine anymore. Take your germs with you,' he said sourly.

'I don't have germs. Anyway,' Leo began, taking another quick gulp, 'actually, that's not bad.'

'LEO!'

'Right, and it's all-expenses too!'

'They want us to pay for everything?' Simon quizzed, the beer mat becoming unstuck from the bottom of his glass and rolling off the table, 'they can stuff it.'

'Simon, all-expenses means-' Rock thought for a second, '- never mind.' Suzy gave him a sly nudge with her elbow.

Finn looked as if he'd been presented with a thousand-piece puzzle and told he had an hour to assemble it. 'How didn't I hear about this?'

'You don't have social media.' Hugh was lazily swiping and snapping and whatever else he did.

'I do - just never check it,' Finn confessed.

He made one last tap on the screen before giving it a rest from his grip. 'I took it as a challenge. Wanted to see how much I could raise from you guys' popularity.'

'So, it's your fault it's all-expenses then?' Simon said accusingly.

Again, Finn had no idea what Hugh was talking about. 'Where are we supposed to go?'

There was a stripe of dust down the centre of Leo's plaid white shirt from when he'd bobsledded across the floor. 'That's the thing – it hasn't been chosen yet!'

Rock slipped the gilded case into the inside pocket of his dinner jacket. He briefly thought of having it framed, but then thought he wouldn't be able to caress its jagged ridges if he did. 'Probably sending us to Mayo or Meath or some other hellhole.'

'No, it's foreign. They want us to go abroad.' Leo said, barely able to keep the excitement from his voice.

Reality and fiction blended into one at that moment. 'Abroad?' Finn spoke as if in a trance, 'it's just like my novel.'

'Okay, snap out of it there, Bilbo.' Rock said, suddenly missing the ragged feel of the precious metal. 'When are they telling us where we're going?'

Hugh flexed his fingers till he heard popping. He had outdone himself this time. It didn't matter that he hadn't won something as trifling as student of the year, because, through technological savvy and mastery of the social zeitgeist, he had managed not only to create an online following that any up-and-coming band would have been proud of, but also leverage the group's marketability to fundraise a worldwide expedition that wouldn't so much involve them having to spend a penny of their own money. 'I've arranged for a location reveal during the show on–'

'Saturday!' Leo screamed like he was being beset upon by tier-two wrestlers, 'they're telling us about the destination on Saturday!'

Printed in Great Britain
by Amazon